Praise for
Waiting to Surface

"Heartbreaking . . . In muted prose, Listfield movingly takes us through Sarah's day-to-day grief, coupled with her hardheaded determination to figure out what happened to Todd. She juggles her sense of loss, her job and raising a daughter who blames her for her missing dad with the antics of her younger colleagues and her own investigation into her husband's fate."

—*USA Today*

"A well-thought-out story about wife-husband relationships, mother-daughter relationships . . . and perhaps most of all—living with uncertainty."

—*St. Petersburg Times*

"Listfield deftly balances multiple plots."

—*Booklist*

"*Waiting to Surface* is gripping, eloquent, honest, and wise. Fans of Elizabeth Berg and Jodi Picoult will appreciate Listfield's pitch-perfect account of marital trouble turned missing persons mystery, which is enhanced by the author's intimate knowledge of Manhattan's fashion and art scene."

—Alisa Kwitney, author of *The Dominant Blonde* and *Flirting in Cars*

"With her unrelenting tale of a husband who vanishes in what may be an accident, a suicide, or a scheme to flee his wife and his life, Emily Listfield leads us by the hand into the dark waters of an unresolved marriage. *Waiting to Surface* forces us to grapple with doubts that swirl beneath the assumptions that comprise our lives: If we do not know the one we love, do we truly know ourselves? The answer will leave you breathless."

—Jacquelyn Mitchard, author of *The Deep End of the Ocean* and *Still Summer*

"In this compulsively readable novel, Listfield creates a compelling portrait of grief and resilience. This is a story that will stay with you."

—Lisa Tucker, author of *Once Upon a Day* and *The Song Reader*

"Emily Listfield has written a suspenseful and poignant novel that beautifully captures the complexity of a marriage and the troubling uncertainties of life. *Waiting to Surface* haunted me long after I read its last page."

—Leslie Schnur, author of *Late Night Talking* and *The Dog Walker*

Praise for Emily Listfield

Acts of Love

"A chilling meditation on the so-called acts of love."

—*The New York Times*

"A beautiful, compelling novel . . . It's impossible not to instantly care for these flawed people. They are us."

—*Los Angeles Times*

"What a ride! Dialogue like a burning house, revelations like shotgun blasts and descriptions that zip you straight in your chair, spine quivering like a tuning fork."

—*The Kansas City Star*

"Listfield's prose is clear and fluid as she tells this grim, edgy tale in which homicide is not always the worst crime committed in the name of love."

—*Publishers Weekly*

"Tightly written and suspenseful."

—*Library Journal*

The Last Good Night

"A taut and disturbing inquiry into the many layers of identity that lie beneath the glossy surface of a television newswoman."

—*The New York Times*

"More than a thriller, *The Last Good Night* is a modern cautionary tale. The touch of Calvinism in Listfield's tone energizes a conventional story and makes for a gripping novel—and a bit more."

—*San Francisco Chronicle*

"A solidly crafted, increasingly suspenseful narrative . . . ratchets up the tension and fully involves the reader in her heroine's harrowing ordeal."

—*Publishers Weekly*

"A suspenseful and interesting look at the lives of TV's elite."

—*Library Journal*

"It's not hard to become absorbed in the nail-biting, knuckle-whitening suspense that Listfield expertly creates and develops."

—*Booklist*

ALSO BY EMILY LISTFIELD

It Was Gonna Be Like Paris
Variations in the Night
Slightly Like Strangers
Acts of Love
The Last Good Night

WAITING TO SURFACE

A Novel

Emily Listfield

WASHINGTON SQUARE PRESS

New York London Toronto Sydney

W

Washington Square Press
A Division of Simon & Schuster, Inc.
1230 Avenue of the Americas
New York, NY 10020

First Washington Square Press trade paperbck edition August 2008

WASHINGTON SQUARE PRESS and colophon are registered trademarks of Simon & Schuster, Inc.

For information about special discounts for bulk purchases, please contact Simon & Schuster Special Sales at 1-800-456-6798 or business@simonandschuster.com.

Designed by Jaime Putorti

Manufactured in the United States of America

10 9 8 7 6 5 4 3 2 1

The Library of Congress has cataloged the hardcover edition as follows:

Listfield, Emily.
  Waiting to surface : a novel / Emily Listfield.
    p. cm.
  1. Disappeared persons—Fiction. 2. Periodical editors—Fiction.
  3. Mothers—Fiction. I. Title.
PS3562.I7822 W35 2007
813'.54—dc22 2007000198

ISBN-13: 978-1-4165-3783-0
ISBN-10: 1-4165-3783-X
ISBN-13: 978-1-4165-3785-4 (pbk)
ISBN-10: 1-4165-3785-6 (pbk)

For Sasha

In Memory

George Wolfgang Dudding

WAITING TO SURFACE

One

It is possible, after all, for someone to vanish off the face of the earth.

Sarah Larkin took the hand of her six-year-old daughter, Eliza, as they waited for the traffic light to change on the corner of Fourteenth Street and First Avenue. At 8:00 a.m., the air was already thick and tufted with smog, the streets littered with the detritus of a summer that boasted record levels of heat and rain. Eliza's hand was cool and dry, her long fingers not quite closing around her mother's, primed to slither free as soon as possible. Sarah noticed that she had removed the Band-Aid from her right forefinger where a splinter had grown infected. She had a habit of denying illness, cuts, anxious to erase any evidence of vulnerability. All summer, Sarah had watched her closely, subtly poking for soft spots or internal bleeding. It had been three months since she and Todd had separated, three months since they had sat Eliza down at the dining room table early one afternoon, her blond head tilted to the floor as they spoke slowly, carefully, words they had meant to rehearse but couldn't quite bring themselves to. The weight of knowing that they were about to change their daughter's life, and their helplessness to stop it, caused them both to pause, look at each other, look away, start again. "Daddy and I have something to tell you," Sarah finally said. "You know that we both love you very much." Eliza arched, instantly suspicious. All through the spring she had listened to the yelling, the door-slamming, hiding in her room while she hummed softly to herself as if the repetitive nursery tunes could drum out the sounds of disintegration. "Daddy is going to move into his studio," Sarah continued. Before she could go any further, Eliza ducked to the floor and covered her head with her hands, protecting herself from incoming news. "We are still a family, we will always be a family," Sarah said.

Todd and Sarah sat in silence while Eliza crouched at their feet. They hadn't planned this conversation, they hadn't planned any of it. They had been pushing and pulling, picking over their ten-year marriage for months when, after a particularly bitter argument, Todd stormed off to his studio twelve blocks away—and never quite managed to return. The first day apart stretched into a second and then a third until what had started out as a spontaneous act came to seem inevitable. Neither had truly wanted to end it, but they had been at an impasse for so long that their tolerance of each other was worn away; everything had become an irritant. Nevertheless, beneath it all—the fights about his drinking and lack of financial responsibility, her excessive expectations and constant nagging—each still hoped that the other would give way, give in, that they would somehow find a way back to each other. They were still tied by the sticky net of habit and remorse. They had not figured out how to do this yet.

Eventually they coaxed Eliza up off the floor, and the three of them played a game of Parcheesi, clinging to the vestiges of familiarity, though it was as if they were suspended in space, with no ground beneath them. Sarah left Todd and Eliza alone as they were setting up another game, giving them time to knit back together in whatever way they might find, while she wandered the fifth floor of Bergdorf's aimlessly, wondering when she could go home, what home would be now. That night Sarah placed a photograph in Eliza's room of Todd holding her in the hospital a few hours after she was born, his head bent to hers, their eyes closed, a smile, beatific and peaceful, curling his lips. It looked, even now, like the simplest kind of joy. She wondered, as she dusted it and placed it carefully amid the origami Todd used to make with Eliza every morning as they ate breakfast, how it happens, how you go from that instant to this, unable to alter course even as you saw it unfold before you unwanted, the small incremental steps of marital crime and then the larger ones, the zigzag rents of a failing union when physical attraction outlasts common sense.

Eliza let go of her mother's hand on the northeast corner of Fourteenth Street and stepped around a broken beer bottle, her toes with their chipped pink glittery nail polish hanging over her blue jelly sandals.

"Daddy said he'd send me seashells," she said, her voice tinged with accusation and neediness, one of the new sounds of the summer. She did not look her mother in the eye.

"They'll come," Sarah said. She wondered if Eliza could sense the doubt lurking beneath the reassurance. Todd had gone to Florida eleven days earlier to help an old college friend in the final stages of remodeling his house. He had only told Sarah of the trip two nights before he left, and though her first response was resentment—at his freedom, at his willingness to leave his daughter at such a crucial juncture—she had twisted the information around until she saw its potential. Perhaps the absence, the tangible miles between them, would make him appreciate all that he was in danger of losing: his family, the very life they had until recently taken for granted. Perhaps, she thought, it would make him decide, finally, to change. She still couldn't believe that love, at least for a child, wouldn't win out in the end. "He'll be back on Monday," she told Eliza. "That's just three days away."

Sarah pulled open the heavy door of the Y where Eliza was attending day camp. They waited for the elevator and stood crammed in with other parents and children as it lurched unsteadily to the third floor, where the halls were lined with the garish primary colors of rainy-day art projects. As soon as the doors opened, Eliza ran out, her long legs, knobby and thin, splaying like broken wings. She had Todd's body, all lankiness and limbs. Sarah watched her enter room 303 without looking back. She had never been a clinging child. Like her father, she was stoic, independent, stubborn. Eliza would wander out of playgrounds, out of sight; she would follow any stranger, certain she could fend for herself. They had to watch her carefully. Today, she was crackling with anticipation for the outing to Coney Island. Todd had taken her there last summer, and she still savored the memory of the crammed and swirling kiddie park, its dragon roller coaster and teacup whirligig. He had also taken her on a ride called Dante's Inferno, which had given her nightmares for a month, though she now flatly denied any such thing.

Eliza scanned the room and spotted her best friend, Jane. The two huddled in the corner, whispering the multitude of secrets that had accumulated overnight, their eyes wide with complicity and delight.

"Comparing notes on lingerie, no doubt." Sarah turned to see Lucy, Jane's mother and one of Sarah's oldest friends, leaning against the wall. "I did, by the way, tell Jane that the new rule is panties have to stay on during play dates."

Sarah rolled her eyes. "Don't set the bar too high."

For months, the girls had been sneaking into any available bathroom to show each other their underwear. Last week, Sarah had heard them in Eliza's bedroom. "Move your leg, I can't see," Jane had said.

"Do you have time to go out for coffee?" Lucy asked.

"I can't. I have a story meeting at nine." Sarah looked over at Lucy in her day-off outfit of Sevens jeans, Juicy T-shirt, and Pumas. "I want your deal," she said, thinking of the three-day workweek she had negotiated at the PR firm she had helped found five years ago, but more than that, her marriage, stable, predictable, without sparks but without melodrama, her general contract to have an easier, if less vaunted life.

Lucy smiled, ignoring the wistful edge in her friend's voice. The two made tentative plans to take the kids swimming the following day and headed out. Sarah hailed a taxi and sat back as it crawled slowly uptown in spurts and pauses past tenements to the midtown crush of people wading into office buildings, Starbucks in hand.

Even at this hour, the city seemed covered in mildew. She played with the ashtray on the car door, flipping it up and down. Whenever Eliza went on day trips at school or camp, Sarah pulsed with a low-level maternal anxiety until she knew her daughter had returned, safe, unharmed. She pictured the rickety rides, the clusters of aimless restless teenagers looking for amusement, for action, for anything to distract them from the bleakness of their lives, the beach littered with glass, the ocean that Eliza did not know how to navigate and yet had absolutely no fear of. She imagined Eliza separated from the group, lost, vulnerable.

The cab inched through Times Square, its lights blinking like an all-night club after the guests had gone, and pulled up in front of the gray steel canopy of the new Compton Media Holdings building. Sarah walked through the heavy glass doors and stepped carefully down the sloped marble entrance, a design that had quickly become hated by editors who, on rainy days, had to navigate its treacherously slick surface in spindly heels. She swiped her ID card through the turnstile and waited by the bank of elevators in a cluster of long-legged women. At five feet five, curvy but slim (at least by normal standards), Sarah—despite her Prada mules, white Chaiken skirt, and wavy shoulder-length hair carefully streaked to the exact blond as Eliza's—still felt as if she were trying a little too hard to pass as one of them. When she had first started at Compton Media one year ago, the unabashed way the other women scanned her up and down, then promptly dismissed her, had been terrifying. Years of working at home as a freelance journalist had left her with a closet stocked almost entirely from the Gap save for a few rather low-cut dresses—cleavage was one of her better assets—to wear to openings. She had rushed out that first weekend and bought an entire wardrobe, trying to accomplish in forty-eight hours what other women had spent years accumulating but without the bone-deep knowledge of how to put it together that came readily to just a few—all, it seemed, located in this building.

At thirty-six, Sarah found herself in a breathless game of catch-up. It hadn't always been this way. In a city mad for money, she had never particularly cared about it. It wasn't a consideration weighed and then discarded—the dangers of marrying an artist, of pursuing her own freelance career, of doing what they thought mattered regardless of remuneration. It simply never occurred to her that there was a decision to be made. From the moment she first stepped into Todd's studio, she was seduced by his passion, his commitment, most of all by the art itself, surprisingly delicate abstract wall sculptures, evidence of a searching tenderness belied by his six-foot-four-inch frame. At a time when bombast was rampant in the art world—"art by the pound," he called it—Todd's work spoke of a world of emotion finely honed by intellect. She had never met anyone who cared so deeply about what he did or found the process itself so exciting. There was, too, his shaggy preppy-meets-artist handsome looks, the dizzying lurch just seeing him brought to her heart, her gut. Even now, after everything, she sat up straighter when he walked into the room.

When they met, Todd's ambition and talent were just beginning to cut laserlike through a small but crucial segment of the art world. His career flourished—there were solo shows in important SoHo galleries, sales to museums and top collectors, favorable write-ups in *The New York Times,* and photos in top fashion magazines—there had been every promise made. In recent years, though, the art market had taken a downturn. That, combined with benign mismanagement by his gallery dealer and an almost predictable midcareer floundering, sent Todd's once smooth and enviable ride into a decided lull. Only one piece from his last solo show had sold. The rest were returned to his studio in an embarrassing truckload on a rainy Friday afternoon ten months after Eliza was born.

At first, Sarah presumed Todd would lick his wounds—after a flurry of early success, it was his first real disappointment—and then go back to his studio with a vengeance. But he became immobilized, unable to finish a single sculpture. It set off nascent doubts that had been kept in check by sales and good reviews. A year passed, two, and still he could not make a move, commit to a new direction. The essential confidence that had bordered on bravado when they first met was gone. He crumpled up drawings, began pieces only to abandon them, convinced that they were mediocre or worse. Sarah wrote down the names of career counselors, therapists, art consultants, and sometimes he called to set up an appointment, but he never went. The lists sat abandoned, collecting dust, until Sarah, knots in her stomach, gave up and threw them out.

It was Todd's energy, his commitment that had so attracted her, and she felt tricked, not by the failure, but by his response to it, the way he was stubbornly, senselessly procrastinating himself out of a career. They had a daughter to think of now. When money from the last of his art sales ran out, he went back to doing the high-end carpentry he had supported himself with during his early years in New York. He built a recording studio for a major record label, an intricate library bookcase for a socialite with too much money at too young an age, and the reception area of a French cosmetics firm. Fiercely proud, this kind of work dented him more than he could say. Exhausted and depressed by the physical labor, he still went to his studio almost every evening and on weekends, waiting for inspiration that seemed forever just out of reach.

And while he waited, he drank.

Alone in his studio, playing an ever-changing selection of music at top volume, sitting at his desk, charcoal in hand, he drank until, by the time he came home, he was cut off from Sarah, from the world itself by the scrim of alcohol.

The drinking itself wasn't new, but the frequency, the amount, the very nature of it had changed. During their early years together, when every moment in the studio was filled with a sense of exhilaration, Todd would sometimes drink beer all afternoon while he worked, forgetting to eat, forgetting everything but his sculptures. When he came home, Sarah could tell in an instant by the slightly cockeyed look in his eye and the surfeit of loopy affection he showered on her, but it seemed celebratory, due to an excess of exuberance rather than a need to dull the senses. She was not worried about it yet, she would not let herself be. Success made it easy to excuse so much. If Todd, never at ease in big groups, occasionally drank too much at openings and stood in a corner, his conversation benevolent but increasingly obtuse, everyone else was indulgent as well. He was so intriguing, so talented, it was all just part of the package.

But as he brooded about the show that didn't sell and his own inability to make art, Todd's drinking began to escalate until it was an unavoidable presence in their lives. There were still nights when, inebriated, he came through the front door filled with good intentions, with love, for Eliza, for Sarah, but his timing would be off and he would miss the natural rhythm of discourse, taking him further and further away from them. Reading the disappointment in Sarah's eyes, his temperament would change and he would blame her for souring the general mood. They would avoid each other then, taking turns playing with Eliza until she went to bed, lessening the need to talk.

Gradually, the silence gave way to arguments.

Sarah never doubted Todd's talent even when he remained paralyzed by this unexpected change in fortune—sometimes she thought she believed in it more than he did, which only added to her frustration. But she lay awake suddenly obsessed by what they didn't have, not the designer clothes or weekends in St. Barts, but any semblance of security, and she looked back in awe at her former oblivious self. Todd refused to plan more than one week ahead or feel any responsibility toward a future he could not imagine. "You do enough worrying for both of us," he said, irritated. Sarah, fixated on their lack of a safety net, was further irked by his ease at falling asleep.

It wasn't simply financial concerns that had made her give up her freelance career. At some point she reluctantly accepted that she would never win a Pulitzer prize for her journalism, never get the really juicy assignments. She had started out with the ambition of being a cultural reporter, but because she had little interest in celebrities, that became an ever more porous goal as stardom increasingly trumped artistic achievement as a salable topic. As magazines slashed their budgets and a greater number of stories were written in-house, she was forced to stray further from her initial intent. She began to take any and every story she could get.

Occasionally, she had an assignment that, though far from her intended purview, seemed to matter—the week spent with ICU nurses in a brain unit at NYU, the almost accidental reporting on the shady background of one of the city's most socially prominent Episcopalian ministers—but those pieces were bought with hours, weeks, months spent writing about various iterations of obsessive love, the scientific breakthrough behind the latest mascara, or women who donated their eggs only to want them back. She had grown tired of the endless proposals she had to write and her inability to turn down any assignment, no matter how insipid, because she feared another would not come. When it became clear, at least to her, that one of them would have to get a regular job with health insurance, paid vacations, a 401(k), she was the natural choice. Todd, after all, was perfectly willing to continue the financial high-wire act that left her obsessively looking down, estimating the fall.

It took Sarah five months of pestering the only simpatico person she knew in the human resources department at Compton Media, but eventually she got a six-week job filling in for a senior editor on maternity leave at *Flair.* When the other woman decided not to come back, Sarah was given the title of articles editor, a salary higher than she could have hoped for, and an office at least near the corner. She quickly found that she liked thinking about an entire issue of a magazine rather than just her particular segment of it and enjoyed the editing itself, matching ideas and writers, moving copy about like puzzle pieces until its structure was seamless. After years of working alone in a room, she found the brainstorming meetings that others vociferously complained about a welcome relief. The perks, too, were still novel enough—the expense account lunches, the movie screenings, the ability to get virtually anyone on the phone when you mentioned Compton Media, the overflowing baskets of free beauty products—to delight her, though she learned to hide her childish pleasure. There were times when she read a particularly good profile or essay somewhere and was struck by a longing to write again. She missed the satisfaction she got on the few occasions when, alone at her computer, she thought she had nailed it. But for the first time in years she did not have to worry about money, and that relief outweighed all else. Overall, she was having more fun, at least on most days, than it was acceptable to admit in the jaded halls of Compton Media.

All the years of being on the outskirts of the magazine world had served her well; she knew more than most about how an article was constructed and worried less about conventional constrictions. She found herself energized by the realization that she was actually good at this. It didn't hurt that the founder and chairman of the company, Leon Compton, a short, hunched-over man with a penchant for faded sports shirts buttoned to the neck, a stutter that some suspected was activated at will to confound his listeners, and $2.4 billion, had bought a few key pieces of Todd's work in years past. Sarah, who found her ambition kicking in like a muscle she hadn't known existed, had judiciously dropped this bit of information in a single conversation during her first week, knowing it would spread like a virus.

She got off on the fourth floor and headed through the heavy glass doors, past the main receptionist engrossed in a guide to landing a husband after thirty-five. She walked down the long hallway, past executive editor Pat Nolan's office. The lights were on, but the door was closed, a combination that always inspired paranoia in the ranks.

She unlocked her office door, glanced to see if her message light was on (though really, she reminded herself, what could have happened between the time she dropped Eliza off and now; they hadn't even gotten on the bus yet). Sarah willed the image of drunken drivers, overturned yellow buses out of her mind and turned her computer on. While it booted up, she went into the kitchen to get a cup of coffee. The shelves above the sink were lined with glass vases in every imaginable shape, rectangular, fluted, round, hexagonal. All day, flowers arrived from cosmetics companies, from designers, from hopeful beaus and recalcitrant husbands. It was a world of women being courted and apologized to, professionally, personally.

She took the coffee back to her office and scrolled through her e-mails to see if Rena Berman, the insomniac editor in chief, had fired off any of her four a.m. missives. Sometimes they were composed of a single word (last week, it was "resilience") and sometimes of long rambling ideas for stories that Sarah spent hours trying to parse, only to discover Rena had forgotten she had even sent the e-mail. She was just reading a company-wide release about the promotion of a publisher to vice president when Paige Daniels walked in and plopped down on the gray tweed chair opposite Sarah's desk.

At thirty-two, Paige was four years younger than Sarah but had worked at Compton Media since graduating from Brown, moving up from her first job as the assistant to a legendary editor who used watercolors to paint the exact shade of lipstick she wanted for a photo shoot and would then have Paige search through every product line available—often one hundred, two hundred tubes—to find one that matched, to her current position as beauty director. (In a world where mastheads were studied with the fine-eyed appreciation of cryptologists, "director" was a coveted title, though there was little discernible difference from "editor" in actual responsibility.) With her impossibly long legs, shapely body, and scrupulously ironed shoulder-length white blond hair, Paige had a confidence in her own voluptuousness that was rare in a building of women who had starved the softness from their bones. Sarah, who had lived in Manhattan her entire life save for a four-year exodus to college in Boston, was always slightly envious of women like Paige, who had come from a small town in Pennsylvania and was free to completely reinvent herself here. The most expensive creams, powders, perfumes, and lotions in the world spilled from her drawers, leaned up against her computer, sat in heaps on her floor. More arrived hourly from manufacturers hoping for an editorial mention, the glossy shopping bags intricately tied with satin ribbons, often containing Frette robes, Prada makeup cases, Hermès scarves. Her office was much visited by her colleagues, covetous of the free products as much as of her window, the only one on the floor that actually opened, where they could stick their heads out and smoke in relative peace.

Paige groaned and took a sip of her latte. She was rarely in at this hour, but the monthly story meeting in Rena's office was a command performance. This morning she had on skintight jeans, emerald green Manolos, and a top that, to the untrained eye, looked suspiciously like lingerie.

"How'd it go last night?" Sarah asked. Since being dumped by Ethan, a Waspy divorcé she had been seeing for the past nine months, Paige had been dating with a vengeance, finding partners online, through friends, in clubs, even dog-walking, though she did not in fact have a dog. Last night was, by her count, her fifth blind date in two weeks.

"He was wearing a Winnie the Pooh tie."

"I always wondered who bought those."

"With Tigger. And he had Tourette's."

"Excuse me?"

"He twitched nonstop. I kept thinking he was going to start barking in the restaurant. Which, by the way, was such a dive no one would have noticed."

"Look at it this way, any date that doesn't involve cartoon characters can now be considered a success."

Paige leaned forward, her perfectly glossed lips parted. "Do you think I should call Ethan?"

"No."

"I could tell him I didn't mean it when I said his ex-wife was a sexless prude."

Sarah frowned. There had been some variation of this call, don't call conversation every day since the breakup. "No."

Paige sighed and took a delicate sip of her latte. "When are you going to start dating?" she asked.

Sarah looked away nervously, unwilling to admit out loud what she barely acknowledged to herself, that she hoped her marriage could somehow be resurrected. "It's funny," she said. "When you're married, dating looks good. You know, going out to dinner with someone who's actually interested in what you have to say."

"Clearly you haven't been out there." Paige shifted in her seat and brushed a tiny speck of lint off of her jeans. "Did I tell you about the guy from JP Morgan I went out with last week? Before I could finish my first glass of wine he told me his previous girlfriend was an ex-lesbian single mother he was interested in converting but she could only come using 'mechanical devices.' Since when did that become acceptable date conversation?" She rolled her eyes, stopped. "Every time I come home from one of these nights, it makes me hate Ethan more for leaving me in this position." She looked up. "Maybe I could just e-mail him."

Sarah ignored this. "Let's go. It's time for the meeting."

"Are you going to talk to Rena about *Splash*?" Paige asked as the two women rose. *Splash* had started as an idea they'd had over drinks at the local Howard Johnson's, a bar in favor for its sense of irony for two or three weeks last spring. Like all ambitious editors, they believed that the most fulfillment would come from creating their own magazine. After throwing around various possible target groups, from working women in their thirties to suburban moms looking for their own shopping magazine, they kept coming back to young women in their early twenties. They were both drawn to those wide-open few years just after college when there is still time to define yourself, your future, when so much is an open-ended question. Sarah often wondered, had she been just a little savvier, a little more confident, if she would have made different choices. An only child, she had longed for an older sister to take her by the hand, to whisper insider know-how more useful than sappy maternal aphorisms on men, on clothes, on attitude.

Splash was to be a guidebook to life (with hefty sprinklings of stars, style, shopping, and sex), for that time when every decision from how to throw a dinner party to whether to switch jobs seems laden with possibility, before parenthood, mortgages, marriages gone awry took their toll. Just thinking about it evinced a certain lightness. On closer study, they were pleased to discover that no one was truly addressing this audience. In an admittedly overcrowded marketplace, there actually seemed to be an opening. They had thrown together a few rough ideas and had been looking for an opportunity to mention it to Rena.

"I tried the other day," Sarah said. "She didn't seem to want to hear it. Let's see how the temperature is today."

On their way out, Sarah turned to her assistant, Maude, who had silently arrived to take her place. "I'll be in Rena's office." Maude, who knew exactly where Sarah would be, nodded patiently. It was a maternal tic, this need to be placed, to be reachable at every moment. Sarah wondered if every mother felt it and just did a better job of concealment or if she was simply more nervous than others.

They walked down the hall toward Rena's enormous corner office, passing the impeccably neat desk of her assistant, an unflappable Englishwoman in her midsixties with gray hair and a penchant for dirndl skirts who had outlasted three regimes.

Rena's office was lined on two sides with floor-to-ceiling windows overlooking Sixth Avenue. Behind her desk was a discreet door that led to a private bathroom—all editors in chief had them, part of a corporate policy of maintaining their mystique. In an industry that was increasingly bottom-line oriented, Compton Media still prided itself on its outsized personalities and outsized perks. There was much speculation that when the next generation took over, this would vanish in a flurry of P&Ls, but there was no evidence of that yet. The plush sage velvet couches and chairs, more suited to a certain type of Park Avenue living room, were already occupied by editors clutching green tea, skim milk lattes, and large bottles of Fiji water. The women of Compton Media were nothing if not well-hydrated. On the far wall, there was a huge white board for mini color photocopies of the issue in progress as well as the alluring if increasingly mysterious clippings that Rena exhumed from her battered handbag each morning. The women were making self-conscious chitchat about last night's movies, this month's magazines, new trainers, crash diets, and a coveted hairstylist who commuted in from LA on a schedule that matched no one's needs but his own—lately they had all been getting haircuts when they didn't need them and mournfully forgoing them when they did. While they spoke, they stole surreptitious glances at Rena, who was finishing up a phone call at her desk, trying to gauge her mood.

Beneath the sotto voce chatter, the room was permeated by a sense of anxiety and false cheer. *Flair* was in trouble. Newsstand sales, the barometer of a magazine's popularity, though not necessarily its profitability, were slipping. There was desperation in the air, a blend of edgy hope and futility, as they tried anything to stanch the flow of readers to other titles—bigger promises on the cover, fewer clothes on the models. Every theory on what made a cover sell was considered: Speak directly to readers, avoid the color green, half-smiles on models are better than full smiles, add more cover lines, have fewer cover lines but make them bigger. Much money was pouring out to researchers who tested story ideas, images, fonts. And nothing seemed to be working. Rumors swirled: Compton was going to close *Flair,* they were going to sell it to a French conglomerate, Rena was about to be fired, Rena was going to fire someone else to offer up a body, she was working on a secret redesign with a freelance staff in a different building, Compton was working on a secret redesign that Rena knew nothing about. People in the building had begun to avoid the fourth floor, as if the downward slide might be contagious. Sarah took a seat next to the empty chair at the far end of the room and caught Rena's eye. Rena flashed her a brief but unmistakable smile. In her midfifties, she looked more like a housewife from Greenwich than an editor in chief. With her fluctuating, though never quite thin, weight, her long hair only occasionally blown out, she was one of the few women, if not the only one, in the building to wear flat shoes and makeup only for television appearances and public speeches. A Bronx girl who was the first in her family to go to college, she had lasted for twenty years in this most image-conscious of companies through the force of her will. She had, along with intelligence and an abundance of drive—which she tried, not always successfully, to keep hidden—the natural charms of a born saleswoman. While others of similar background quickly picked up the mannerisms of more thoroughbred women, Rena made her immigrant, Orthodox childhood an anecdote, part of her lore. Only sometimes did it border on shtick. Rena, with her glittery excitable eyes and poker face, was above all convincing. It was her great talent, this ability to inspire, and paired with a survivor's willingness to turn on a dime, it had gotten her far.

Rena had been given the top job at *Flair* two years ago as a consolation prize when she didn't get the position she truly wanted, and campaigned just a little too hard and too publicly for (visible signs of effort were considered gauche except perhaps on the sales side), editorial director of all the company's magazines. That amorphous job (the previous holder had been a painter who spent most of his days ripping up images and generally terrorizing editors in a thick German accent) had gone to William Rowling, an enigmatic, foppish Englishman with good hair and better suits, a perfectly dressed Buddhist much in demand at dinner parties. He also happened to be twenty years younger than Rena and possessed an uncanny ability to know which book, artist, rap group was going to hit big before anyone else did, a talent Rena had once possessed, and later could fake, but was most recently slipping through her fingers no matter how much MTV she forced herself to watch. She had tried once, a year ago, to make a benefit of her experience, as she referred to it. She had convinced the company to do a onetime issue of a magazine geared to women over forty. But they put no money into it, printed it on the cheapest paper, and unceremoniously let it die. "The problem," Rena told Sarah, "was that the men who run this company don't want to fuck that woman. She reminds them of their wives." She was disappointed, but by 5:00 a.m. the next day, she had moved on, a woman with a plan, always a plan.

Rena's flaw was that for all her intelligence, she was too easily led astray by her own impulses. In Sarah's first week, she had asked her to edit a five-part package on death. Even Sarah, newly minted, knew that this was not a good idea for a magazine dedicated to self-improvement, thinner thighs in ten minutes a day, less stress in your work life, and the eccentric eating habits of celebrities.

Rena hung up the phone and, smiling like a den mother, settled in the large empty armchair. "How is everybody?" she asked. She was warm, welcoming, Jewish. It was only the editors who didn't need mothers, the editors who felt like grown-ups, who were able to maintain a healthy distance. Sarah was particularly susceptible to her.

After the murmur of polite replies died down, Rena leaned forward and paused. "The body," she said finally, her eyes lit from behind, taken with herself, with her latest conviction.

Everyone nodded silently, waiting.

"The woman's body," Rena added, smiling as if she had discovered DNA. "An entire issue devoted solely to the body."

The editors remained quiet. The purpose of the magazine every month was the betterment of the body, but surely Rena meant something different, something more.

"I want a life-sized poster of an anatomically correct body to fold out of the well," she said, referring to the ad-free center of the book. "I don't mean *Maxim*, silicone, airbrushed. I mean a *real* woman's body."

At the words *real woman* the editors cringed.

"What kind of bikini wax are we talking?" Caitlin, the style director, asked. "Brazilian? Landing strip? Au naturel? Oh, please, not that," she said, kidding and yet not.

Real women, or RWs, were the necessary bane of editors' existence. The magazine had a policy of making all RWs being considered for stories (How Exercise Saved My Life; I Discovered I Had Breast Cancer on My Honeymoon: One Doctor's Story) send in Polaroids of themselves—their looks as important a component in deciding who to use as their experience. Caitlin, who'd gone to Chapin and Princeton and considered having three dermatologists—one for complexion, one for injectables, one for mole checks—every woman's basic necessity, had a particularly rough time with RWs. Then again, the real women in her life were decidedly different from the women Rena was referring to. Caitlin was a rising star in the inner circle of young socialites who had recently usurped their mothers as the most photographed at parties. Many of them had taken jobs at PR firms, or launched their own lines of resort clothes, handbags, or insanely overpriced children's wear. Caitlin was one of the rare members of her tribe who had started out as an intern (her father played poker with Leon Compton) but had stuck it out and risen in record time. She had an enviable wardrobe, glossy chestnut hair, perfectly arched eyebrows that she had shaped by a Ukrainian woman every ten days, and impeccable manners that made her overriding ambition more palatable. Sarah, who had gone to Manhattan private schools as well, but second-tier ones, and had been at the lower end of the economic spectrum even there—while comfortable, her family most decidedly did not winter in Palm Beach—had been written off by Caitlin within her first week.

"Think of the service we would be doing for women," Rena continued, "to see a naked woman who actually looks like them. What is the national average, five-four, a hundred fifty-three pounds? Imagine it, life-size."

"Do we have to?" Caitlin muttered beneath her breath.

The editors glanced surreptitiously at Pat Nolan, the executive editor. Few of them liked or trusted her, but they hoped she at least would offer up a word of caution. Pat, dressed in a trademark razor-sharp Dolce suit, was a woman in her midthirties (some said forties, but no one truly knew) married to a much older man who had made a killing in drugstore cosmetics. She had the impeccable manner that only childless women can truly achieve and a vaguely sour look on her angular, suspiciously unlined face that she tried to hide whenever anyone was looking. Her eyes cased the room, a cipher's smile on her slightly parted lips, and remained silent.

"But what would the service be?" Lila, the news editor, asked. At thirty-eight, she was a natural beauty just beginning to look tired even when she wasn't. Compton Media was divided into two types of women: those like Lila who were supporting artistic husbands and those with oversize diamonds given to them by their investment banking fiancés. The former never looked as good as the latter. Perhaps it was because they couldn't afford the regular blowouts and the Botox, but Sarah suspected it was something else, something deeper, the weariness that comes from worrying about doctors' fees, braces, college bills, an innate lack of confidence in the future that the others had no reason to share. Lila's husband, a Cuban painter of vivid voluptuous women in various states of undress, had never had a single show. When Sarah first started at *Flair,* she wanted to distinguish herself from Lila and the others like her. Todd's work, after all, had been written about in every major art publication, bought by the Metropolitan Museum. She still clung to that thought, as if it made all that she had gone through with him—love but other things too—worthwhile, justifiable.

"What better service is there than an honest exploration of the female body?" Rena countered.

Lila nodded. "We could give facts for each part, the best foods to preserve sight, stuff like that."

"Did you know that women who apply lipstick more than once a day have a considerably lower risk of oral cancer?" Paige remarked.

"Who did that study, Revlon?" Janine, the research director, asked in her wry, nasal voice.

"We could follow with stories on health, nutrition, psychology," Sarah suggested, "keying them in to the poster."

"I am going on record in favor of airbrushing, full-body makeup, and serious self-tanning cream," Paige said. "Make a note."

Rena laughed indulgently, Paige was the frilly girl she'd never been.

The meeting continued, gaining momentum, as the editors gradually lost touch with their own reservations and ideas snowballed. Within the bubble of Rena's office anything seemed possible—she was still able to cast a spell.

Forty-five minutes later the women filed out, armed with assignments on how to make this work.

Rena motioned to Sarah to stay and the others took note, wondering what it might mean to the ever-changing balance of power and prestige. Pat stood in the doorway for a moment, glancing back suspiciously. She had been foisted on Rena five months ago by William Rowling in an attempt to steady her, and the two women maintained a barely hidden disdain for each other, Pat, with her by-the-numbers approach to editing, who, it was rumored, focus-grouped where to have lunch, and Rena, with her tenacious belief that a good editor went strictly on impulse. The degree of their dislike was unusual even in this building, where editors planted disparaging stories about each other in the press and then air-kissed over lunch. Sarah shifted her feet uncomfortably until Pat reluctantly turned her back and left.

"So," Rena asked, focusing her attention on Sarah. "How are you? Are you sleeping?"

The two women shared the same form of insomnia, falling asleep easily but rising frequently in the middle of the night, their blood, their brains crackling. Somehow Rena had fallen under the assumption that Sarah worked as hard as she did during these black holes of restlessness and Sarah did nothing to belie it. She did not tell Rena that at three a.m. she was obsessing about the quagmire of her marriage or about the fact that her jeans were harder to zip than they were two months ago, not next month's cover lines.

"How is Eliza?" Rena asked. The mother of two children, both in high school, she had been following Sarah's marital dilemmas closely. She had married young the first time, better the second time, to a man not quite as ambitious as she, a man who hadn't grown up in the Bronx and wasn't as hungry. She had, she told Sarah, spent tens of thousands of dollars in therapy to learn that nice men weren't necessarily as ambitious, and not to fault him, never to fault him.

"She's fine," Sarah answered. She fidgeted uncomfortably. If the general unreliability of men was taken as a given in women's magazines, the reasons behind the shredding of her own marriage remained something Sarah could just barely admit to herself, and never in public. There was a long silence. Sarah didn't know quite what she was doing here but sensed that Rena was looking for a sign—whose side are you on, Pat's or mine?

"I was thinking," Sarah began nervously. "I know you tried that other launch last year. But Paige and I have been studying the newsstand and we both believe there truly is a hole. Since *Mademoiselle* closed, no one has really captured that early-twenties reader."

"She's reading celebrity or shopping magazines now."

"Yes. But what if you combined those elements with service geared just to her life stage," Sarah said, using a term that she had heard bandied about since she started at Compton.

Rena listened intently, giving away nothing, sniffing, considering what she could use.

Finally, she replied, "It's an interesting idea. But now is not the time."

Sarah suspected Compton would never give Rena money to explore anything at all, much less a new launch, until *Flair*'s newsstand figures went up.

Ten minutes later she was back at her desk, the door ajar, trying to concentrate on a story about the multitude of errors in the federal government's food pyramid. She looked at her watch. The bus would have reached Coney Island by now, the children would be lining up for rides or playing helter-skelter on the beach. Restless, Sarah turned to her in-box where Paige had left a jar of $450 face cream made from marine life harvested once every two years off the Mediterranean coast. "Try it out for me," her note said. "I'm not vouching for it; it's made in Spain, a country not exactly noted for its skin care products." Sarah opened it and dipped her forefinger into the silky white cream. She was just rubbing it into her forearm when the phone rang.

It was 11:18. Sarah got the last bit of cream off of her fingers and picked up on the second ring.

"This is Detective Ronald Brook with the Loudon Beach Police Department." The man spoke with a professional calm tinged with a small-town southern accent. There was, in the way he paused, a certain tentativeness. It was too soon to tell whether it was natural or studied, born of a natural desire to delay the imparting of bad news or condescension.

Loudon Beach, Sarah knew, was in Florida.

Before more words could come out of his mouth, she became aware of a keening sound sputtering from her chest. Whatever this man needed to say, she knew that she didn't want to hear it; her hands were pressed against time, against a future she did not want to enter.

Once, years before, the New York City police called to tell her that Todd was in the Beth Israel emergency room. He had been hit by a car while riding his bicycle on St. Marks Place. He was tall, muscular, strong. He had broken his fall with his face, leaving behind a gaping wound beneath his right eye and a mosaic of gravel in his chin. His blood alcohol was three times the legal limit.

After that, he wore a helmet.

After that, they had Eliza.

After that, Sarah waited.

"When was the last time you spoke with your husband?" the detective asked.

"He called from Florida on Sunday. Five days ago."

She had been standing in the kitchen when the phone rang just after 6:00 p.m. She leaned over the counter, her hands cupped around the receiver so that Eliza, sitting a few feet away, would not hear her words.

In the silence that festered between the detective and Sarah, she saw the gray-pebbled Formica that she had always hated, saw herself playing with crumbs left over from Eliza's lunch, pushing them around with her fingernail.

"I'm terrible at this," Todd had said. "I don't blame her for being mad at me. I'd be mad at me, too."

"This" was the separation, fatherhood, this was the marsh they found themselves in, a man a thousand miles away, a child sulking at the dining room table, a husband and wife who could not be together and could not be apart. "She's six years old," Sarah replied. "You have to keep plugging away at it."

"I'm terrible at this," he repeated, beyond hearing.

There was, for a moment, only the damage they had done.

Sarah had tried calling him back in the following days but had only gotten his voice mail. Todd had a habit of forgetting to bring his cell phone charger when he went away and hadn't left a number where he could be reached. Mildly annoyed, she also knew that Todd had a tendency to go underground when faced with potential conflict. He always resurfaced.

Detective Brook cleared his throat.

Memory is an odd, stubborn thing, burning the inconsequential into the brain, refusing to record the stark, hard moments that change the very atoms of your being. Only the effect, the aftermath, is recalled.

Later, Sarah could not remember the precise words Detective Brook used, only his voice as he laid the few facts he had before her.

Your husband has not been seen since close to midnight on Sunday.

He was staying with a woman, Linda Granger.

They had a fight and he told her he was going to the beach.

He was very upset about your separation.

He was drinking.

He had stopped sleeping.

He left behind his keys, wallet, money, ID, cell phone, his return airline ticket, a cigarette lighter.

And two drawings: One said *Lonely Head, Dead.* The other said *Drowned.*

There were, too, pieces of a large copper sculpture he was working on titled *Lightning Rod to Take to the Beach During a Thunderstorm.*

We believe he may have committed suicide.

But, he paused, there is no trace. Of him. Of his body. There is nothing. He could, in fact, be anywhere, anywhere at all. "Do you have his passport?" the detective asked.

"He was going to build a house for a friend," Sarah protested. Surely he had this wrong, had everything wrong.

The detective waited. How many disbelieving wives had he come across in his twenty years on the force? "Do you know Linda Granger?" he asked finally.

She vaguely recalled the woman's name. Linda was an old college girlfriend Todd talked to now and then. Sarah thought he mentioned visiting her in Florida just before he and Sarah started dating. She had a shapeless sense-memory of her as a troubled woman, something about being married to a cop who hit her. “They haven’t seen each other in years,” she replied, but there was a question in her voice. It was not just the present or the future that was changing as she sat in her office talking to a stranger in Florida, but the past, the firmament she thought she had been standing on.

Fragments of questions poked like shards through her consciousness. “You said Todd disappeared on Sunday night. I don’t understand. Why would you wait until Friday to call me?”

Detective Brook’s voice grew defensive. “Miss Granger didn’t call us until Thursday afternoon. It appears she and Todd had an argument and she asked him to leave. She thought he was off drinking someplace, brooding. She assumed he’d come back. His plane ticket is for this coming Monday. Of course, there is still a chance he’ll return to pick it up.”

“But you said he left his wallet with all of his money. She waited four days?” Sarah asked again in disbelief.

“We responded as soon as she called. Two detectives went to her house and examined the garage where he had set up a studio.”

“He had set up a studio?”

“All of your husband’s tools and belongings were neatly lined up. That type of organization is often a sign of suicide.”

Sarah pictured Todd’s studio in New York. His tools were always neatly lined up, cleaned, just so. Though he moved from Dortmund to the United States at eight years old when his mother married an American, he remained German in many ways. There were things she knew that this detective, that Linda, would never know. She knew that this was not a clue, that it was meaningless. If the police could be so mistaken about this, they could be mistaken about everything.

“I don’t understand. Wouldn’t a body wash up? I mean, how far out could he have swum?”

“It is very unusual,” the detective admitted.

Sarah’s mind spiraled as he continued to speak, his sentences circling back on each other, piling up theories and then piercing them with holes. The facts ended suddenly, a road disappearing without warning.

Not one person had spotted Todd after he left Linda's property.

There were no shoes found on the beach.

All the night before, the coast guard had scoured the shore by helicopter and seen nothing.

He could be holed up in one of a thousand cheap motels that line that strip of the Atlantic Ocean. He could be wandering in the nearby state park, lost in the encompassing illogic of a breakdown. He could have staged the whole thing and taken off for California, or Europe. He could be using a false name, a false identity, starting over someplace new. "Sometimes men do that. Especially at times like this. Miss Granger said he was very smart, certainly capable of it," Detective Brook said matter-of-factly.

A foggy ether invaded Sarah's head as she tried to absorb what he was saying. We are taught to believe that facts exist, that if we do not find an answer, it is because of an error on our part, a flaw in our reasoning, in our search. We are not taught that there are times when answers simply vanish.

A staccato sob broke from Sarah's gut.

Outside her open door, Maude sat quietly, pretending to be busy with expense reports. As Sarah raced out through the mazelike floor, there was a silence, an embarrassed pause as someone else's life spilled messy and chaotic into the air, changing the very ions.

Two

The cab crawled back through the midtown traffic that Sarah had made her way through less than three hours ago. But it was a different city now, rendered distant and inconsequential, and she knew that she had irrevocably separated from it. Her own hand, as she watched it reach for her cell phone, seemed ghostly and pale, cut off from her body. She could not tell if she was moving slowly or rapidly, she could not feel herself, her outlines at all. She fumbled with the phone, dropped it amid the crumpled gum wrappers and nubby carpet of grime on the floor, picked it up, misdialed Lucy's number twice before reaching her.

"I think Todd is dead." Her voice was high-pitched, childlike, almost giddy. She was still hovering on the lip of tragedy, when disbelief outweighs evidence. One night last year, Todd had been working late in his studio when he called at 10:00 p.m. to say that he was leaving. It usually took him eight minutes to bike-ride up First Avenue to their apartment. But an hour went by, two, and there were no keys in the door. Remembering the accident a few years ago, she had dialed the studio and his cell phone again and again, leaving repeated messages, "Where are you? Are you there?" There was no answer, no sign of him. At 2:00 a.m., she called the hospitals, the local precinct. This time, there were no bike accidents, no events that seemed to match the contours of her story. The police agreed, nevertheless, to have a cruise car drive by. Todd was just coming out the door with his bike when it pulled up. "I fell asleep," he scolded Sarah later. He had decided to stay and have another beer, maybe two, what was the big deal? "I can't believe you called the police. Are you nuts?" he exclaimed in disbelief. Her relief gave to way to fury at the invidious way alcohol rendered him oblivious to time, to obligation, and they turned away from each other in frustration.

Now, too, there was the chance of an explanation, the possibility that he was misplaced but not lost, that this was all some horrendous overreaction.

"What?" Lucy asked. A shrillness Sarah had never heard before in her even-keeled midwestern voice poked through.

"I don't know. I think Todd may be dead."

"What do you mean, you think?"

"The police believe he may have—" She stopped, stuttered. Her words, her body, time itself, were weightless. There was nothing to latch on to, grasp, offer up. "They think he may have committed suicide. But they can't find his body. I don't know, Lucy. I just don't know."

"Oh, God. Are you still at work?"

"No, I'm on my way home." Lucy agreed to meet Sarah at her apartment in fifteen minutes and hung up.

The cab inched around three red cones blocking off men working on an underground pipe, the gnarled innards of the city street obscenely visible through the surgical incision. Sarah clutched her cell phone, checked to make sure it was on, checked again. She had entered the world of waiting.

Ten minutes later, she turned the key and slowly opened her apartment door, half-expecting to see Todd there. Every fiber in her body was alert, cocked like an animal when it sniffs danger, unsure what precise form it is to take but sensing its presence, waiting for it to make itself known before calibrating a reaction. But there was only stillness, silence, the noontime light pouring in through the sooty windows that Sarah kept meaning to have cleaned and yet never quite did. She stood in the center of the living room, not knowing what to do. She dug her fingernails into the palms of her hands so hard that deep red half-moons formed. There was something comforting about the tangible pain, it grounded her, made her feel that she was still attached to the earth.

When Lucy arrived, the two women embraced. She remained silent while Sarah twitched restlessly, anxious to pull away. She looked into Lucy's eyes; she did not want comfort, she wanted a translator, someone who could parse the tidbits of information, of clues, and rearrange them into something she understood.

"Start from the beginning," Lucy prompted as they sat down side by side on the couch, their knees touching.

But there was no beginning, none that Sarah could locate anyway, chronology circled back on itself, dissipated. "They think he drowned. He said he was going to the beach." She paused. "But he hated the ocean. When I used to try to get him to go swimming with me in Florida he called it 'joining the food chain.'"

Sarah felt as if she were tumbling backward, falling and falling through space. She saw the ocean at night, the sky and the water meeting far out in the distance, indistinguishable from each other, black on black. When they were first married they used to spend four months a year in a strip-mall town on the southeast coast of Florida staying in a house his mother and stepfather had bought as an investment property. She remembered afternoons when she coaxed him in and they swam out past the breakers, had sex in broad daylight, clutching each other's waists to stay afloat as the ocean lapped against their necks, their bodies joined beneath the surface. But that was long ago.

"He called me from Florida," she said. "Sunday. He called me Sunday." Sarah pulled at a strand of her hair. "He was blaming himself."

"For what?"

Sarah stared at Lucy, trying to find words to explain the bog of a sinking marriage to someone who had never experienced it. "I don't know. Everything. He was convinced he was abandoning Eliza the way his father had abandoned him." Todd's natural father, a baker in Dortmund, impregnated an eighteen-year-old girl—his mother. There was no talk of marriage or duty, there was no talk of paternal responsibility. Todd had seen him only once in his life. Inga Larkin raised her son alone as best she could for eight years until she met an American visiting on holiday and married him nine months later. The courteousness Todd's stepfather had displayed during his brief visits in Germany evaporated when they settled in the small Minnesota town where his family was in the real estate business. A man with reservoirs of anger that he was happy to unleash on anyone weaker, he had found a perfect subject, a skinny, friendless boy who, at first, did not speak a word of English. "Do you know what a bastard is?" he asked Todd. "It's what you are. Do you know whose cereal you're eating, whose milk you're drinking? Mine." Inga did not interfere in the war taking place in her kitchen, did not even acknowledge it. She had what she wanted most, a family; she could not risk jeopardizing it. Todd carried with him an antipathy toward all fathers until the day Eliza was born, when holding her for the first time rendered him vertiginous.

"But his voice was clear," Sarah told Lucy. "Not clear, that's not what I mean exactly. Sober. He seemed better, he seemed okay," she said. "I thought he was okay."

Dizzy, a cold sweat pooling across her hairline, her bowels churning, she stood up, paced, leaned against the wall, and sank down until she was crouched in a tight upright ball. "They found two drawings. The police had a hard time figuring them out, but one seems to say *Lonely Head, Dead* and the other, *Drowned.*" She pictured Todd walking into the ocean, the water rising slowly, inexorably to his ankles, knees, shoulders. At what point did he know that it would be impossible to return—ten yards, twenty, thirty? Did he change his mind, try to swim back, fail, sink as his strong, perfectly muscled arms flailed against the surface, or had he kept going and going, blindly, stubbornly, drunkenly until the land was just a rumor?

"Sarah, do you think he was suicidal?" Lucy asked cautiously.

Sarah looked at her and then down, playing with the fringe of a pillow. She remembered a phone call six, seven weeks ago, Todd in his studio, Sarah sitting on the edge of her bed, as they rummaged through their marriage, the harm they had done each other. They were beyond accusations, they were beyond thinking there was any way back, any hope of a cure. "If you loved me enough you would have made this one change for me," Sarah said as they sat on their beds in separate rooms, separate homes. Even then, she refrained from the word *alcoholism.* "I started drinking at sixteen to quiet the voices in my head," he admittedly quietly. But his voice changed, became adamant. "I refuse to be defined by one characteristic."

"It's more than a characteristic," she replied.

He said nothing. For a long while, they listened to each other's breathing over the telephone lines. "I don't think I'm capable of love," he said quietly. "The only person I've ever truly loved is Eliza." They were both crying. They had reached the point where revelations no longer helped; they were interesting, but they no longer changed anything.

He said, "I'm going to blow my brains out."

Sarah thought this was the kind of thing men said when their world was falling apart.

It was close to midnight when they hung up, gently, sadly, at precisely the same moment.

Still, Sarah had hoped that he would realize what his drinking was costing him, costing them both, and, with the distance of Florida, decide, finally, to stop, to return to her. Hope, it seems, is the hardest habit of all to break, harder than love itself, the last twitch of a body whose heart has already stopped.

"I don't know," she said. "There's something else. Besides the drawings. The police said they found a sculpture he was working on called *Lightning Rod to Take to the Beach During a Thunderstorm.*

Sarah saw Lucy flinch. They had known each other for fourteen years, before husbands, children, jobs, when they had shared a loft in the East Village and both believed in art and style and love that lasts, that's how young they were. Now Sarah could not look her best friend in the eyes. "He was staying with a woman," she added quietly. "Linda Granger. He lied to me. He told me he was going to help an old friend finish remodeling his house." Along with her confusion and her fear there was this: embarrassment, shame. The narrative she had thought was true—that despite their differences, she and Todd were playing by the same set of rules—had proven false in the most public of ways.

"Do you know her?"

Sarah shook her head. "She was a college girlfriend. I thought he just talked to her once or twice a year. Todd stayed in touch with all his old girlfriends. Obviously I was wrong. She waited four days. Four days to call the police. What kind of woman does that?"

"What did she tell them?"

"That he was drunk and she thought he would come back." A jagged fury stormed through her, every anxiety and fear funneled into this one point of anger. "Even if that's the case, you don't wait four fucking days. Anything could have happened." She dug the phone number Brook had given her out of her bag.

"Who are you calling?"

"Linda Granger."

Linda picked up on the first ring as if she had been sitting by the phone, waiting for Sarah to call, to come to her.

"Hello?" She had a voice made husky from too many cigarettes and a delivery flattened by a life where men disappearing in the night was seemingly not without precedent. Sarah remembered Todd telling her years ago that she'd had a tough time of it; there were vague allusions to a disastrous childhood, an absent father, a bad marriage. There was empathy in his tone when he mentioned her—Todd always had a soft spot for wounded birds. But she couldn't recall more than that; she hadn't been alarmed.

Linda did not seem surprised to hear Sarah's voice, nor did she sound particularly defensive or grief-stricken. "The police called you?"

"Yes."

Sarah was holding the phone so tightly that her knuckles had turned chalky white. There was a pause as she tried to figure out where to begin in a stream of questions that had no end, that went back twenty-four hours, and twenty years.

"How could you have waited four days to call the police?" She would start there, work backward.

"It never occurred to me he wouldn't come back. We'd had a fight. I figured he went to stay at a motel."

"With all of his credit cards and money still in your house?"

"I didn't realize that until Thursday, when I noticed five hundred and twenty dollars in cash in his suitcase. I didn't look. I'm not the type to go through someone's things."

"When someone disappears for four days, you call the damn police," Sarah spit out angrily.

Linda remained silent, clearly unconvinced that she had done anything wrong. Their very definitions of normal, of acceptable, were incomprehensible to each other, the distance unbridgeable. But it was evident, too, that they were tied to each other, twisted around each other, and total avoidance was not an option. While Sarah resented this deeply, Linda seemed to get a certain satisfaction from it.

She began to recount Todd's stay from the time he'd arrived the previous Tuesday until he disappeared on Sunday night. Sarah listened intently, her heart pounding, looking for clues, not just to that night, but to all that had gone on before, to Todd, to the narrative of her own life that was being altered with every word uttered by a woman she had never met.

"We were both upset about the breakup of relationships," Linda began. "We comforted each other." Sarah wanted details, specifics—how long had they been back in touch? how long had this been going on?—wanted them and dreaded them. It was like picking at a sore, irresistible and bloody and destined to lead to scarring.

"There were years when we rarely spoke," Linda continued. "He called me the morning after your daughter was born, things like that. But then this past year, when we were both alone again, we reconnected. He began calling every day, twice a day, we talked for hours," she told Sarah. "We'd both been knocked around a lot as kids. No one gave either of us a goddamned thing. That's not something that goes away, being on your own so young. You can't explain what it does to someone who hasn't been through it. We understood each other. But he was different when he came down here. It was okay for the first couple of days, but then he started to become manic. He talked nonstop. He stopped sleeping. I'd find him at all hours in the studio I set up for him in my garage. He was drinking so much. He couldn't sit still. He kept washing dishes, cleaning. He started muttering in German."

"What?" This was a far worse sign to Sarah than the drawings, the sculpture of the lightning rod. Todd hadn't spoken a word of German since he moved from Dortmund to Minnesota. His mother, anxious to embrace all things American, had forbidden it. In all of their years together, the only thing he had ever said to Sarah in German was "Ich liebe Dich"—I love you. For the first time she began to believe that there might have been a fissure in his brain, his soul, far deeper than she had imagined. Lucy, noting the change in tone, moved closer and rested her hand on Sarah's shoulder.

"Didn't that make you realize something was wrong?" Sarah demanded.

"How should I know he didn't do that all the time?" Linda asked flatly.

Sarah's voice was slow, deadened. Everything was different now. "What happened that night?"

They had spent the day with Linda's nephew at a nearby state park. "Todd was in a terrible mood. He spent most of the time in the car, drinking beer. When we got back he called you."

The kitchen counter, the crumbs, his voice.

"He was very upset about being separated from Eliza, missing her," Linda said.

Sarah couldn't stand her daughter's name coming out of this woman's mouth; it seemed the most presumptuous kind of intimacy. And yet she said nothing. She needed Linda, needed the very information that was breaking her heart.

"Then he went to the garage. At around ten, I heard him screaming and I went in. He was just standing there, howling. 'You found me naked,' he answered when I asked what was going on. I told him he couldn't do this. I live in a nice neighborhood. I told him he had to leave the next day instead of staying until the following week. He was so drunk he could hardly stand up. He wanted my car keys, but I wouldn't give them to him. He wanted my bicycle. He stormed out, saying he was going to the beach. 'First Sarah, now you,' he said. 'Fuck you.'" She took a drag of her cigarette. "That's the last I saw of him."

"How could you not have called the police?" Sarah demanded, her voice rising, no longer willing or able to hide the fury, coming back and back and back to this one crucial, incomprehensible fact. She looked over at Lucy, who shook her head in shared outrage. "Didn't those drawings or the sculpture make you realize something was wrong?"

"I didn't see the drawings until Thursday. The police found them. And the title of a single sculpture is meaningless. Artists are allowed poetic license. It was a little melodramatic, but that's not a crime. I thought he was off sulking. I still think that's what this is about."

On Wednesday night, when Todd still had not returned, Linda called Todd's best friend, Victor, in Tampa to see if he had heard from him. The three had gone to college together, art majors at the University of South Florida, each finding in the studios and late-night parties a sense of belonging that for various reasons had previously been denied them. For Todd, it was, once discovered, the very reason for existence. For Linda, it was a milieu that she hoped she could pass in, fit into, in a way she couldn't in the "straight" world—there had already been too many transgressions for that. Victor had been in some ways the most romantic of the three and was now the most pragmatic, running the museum at the very same university they had all attended twenty years ago. It was Victor who insisted that Linda call the police.

"What difference would it have made if I called the police right away?" Linda asked Sarah impatiently. "If he had drowned, it would already have happened. Besides, he hated swimming. I don't believe he did that." There was, in her tone, an implied superiority—I know him, I understand him better than you do—that felt like needles pressing into Sarah's skin. "He's just off pouting."

"I can't believe you waited four days," Sarah hissed once more and slammed down the phone.

Without looking up, verifying the conversation with Lucy, Sarah got Victor's number from her BlackBerry and dialed it. She and Todd had visited Victor and his wife numerous times in Tampa; he was the first person Todd told about their engagement and there remained between Victor and Sarah an essential goodwill that went deeper than any differences in temperament.

Sarah remembered the first time she had met Victor, when she and Todd had just begun dating. It was the night of Todd's first solo show in a small SoHo gallery and Victor had flown up for it, a magical night when every sculpture had sold by eight o'clock, red dots lining the walls like a highway to success, and anything seemed possible. They were hungry for the future, giddily running toward it with open, confident arms. Afterward, Todd and Sarah leaned against a car on Greene Street, kissing. She could still feel his chest, his lips touching hers. Twelve years later the sensation remained imprinted on her like the leaf pattern engraved into a stone, it felt so much like home. That night, Daniel Biscardi, the twenty-eight-year-old flaxen-haired gallery owner, took fifteen people to Odeon for dinner. Victor, with his dense black beard and his dislike of small talk, sat next to Sarah. While they waited for their drinks, he asked, "Have you ever thought of killing yourself?" She supposed he mistook that kind of conversation for intimacy.

"Sarah." Victor's already deep voice was lowered with sadness and dread. "They called you?"

"Yes." Sarah began to cry. "How can this be happening?"

"I don't know. I don't know what is happening."

"When was the last time you talked to Todd?"

"He called a lot in the weeks before he came down. He was going to drive over to Tampa, but he never made it." Victor paused. "He and Linda were never any good together. Even in college, when everyone was wild, they seemed to set something off in each other. It was physical, but there was something else. They were both used to being on their own, making up their own rules. In some weird way I think she gave him permission to act out. Anyway, I told him the answer wasn't in the past, but Todd had no idea how to be alone."

"I can't believe she didn't call the police."

"Linda was always trouble. Her own father ran out once and didn't come back for a year. This is her idea of normal. Listen," he said. "Todd called all his old girlfriends after you separated. It was as if he was retracing his life, seeing if he had left anything behind worth reclaiming. Deep down, he didn't think anyone new would take him. Linda was his last resort."

Sarah remembered Todd standing in the hallway a few months before they separated, turning to her. "When I look at you, I can see in your eyes that you've lost faith in me," he said. He turned his back to her, continued what he was doing, hanging up a shirt. She wanted to say no, that's not true, but he was right. Maybe he thought an old girlfriend would remember him when he still had promise. Maybe she wouldn't notice—the way Sarah did—that it was gone. Maybe with someone else it wouldn't be.

"Do you think he's dead?" she asked.

"I don't know. It takes a lot of effort to swim out that far, to keep swimming. It's not a quick decision like jumping or something." He paused and when he continued it was in a lower octave. "He called me a couple of months ago late at night, just after you separated," Victor continued. "He was drunk. He told me he had just gotten off the roof of his studio. He had tried to jump, but he couldn't do it. Maybe the same thing happened, maybe he did go swimming but tried to turn back and didn't make it," Victor said. "I don't know if he truly wanted to die or not."

Sarah pictured Todd on the roof of the four-story building on Rivington Street, the Lower East Side spread before him, a jigsaw puzzle of gentrification and squalor, nouveau restaurants run by posh uptown boys with vaguely English accents and ratty bodegas redolent of fried bananas and smoke; she pictured him rise shakily, lean over, change his mind.

She remembered his words to her: "I'm going to blow my brains out." If only she and Victor had been comparing notes.

"There was something different about him in the last few weeks," Victor continued. "Almost hyper."

Sarah realized that he was right. The night before Todd left for Florida, he'd come over with twenty new drawings to show her and Eliza. He hadn't finished a single piece of work in five years, since his last solo show when only one had sold. Lines of copper lay about his studio like amputated limbs, the walls were hung with half-finished pieces, promises forgotten, the intent incomprehensible to the viewer, to Todd. Now suddenly he was drawing at breakneck speed. That night his face shone with pride and exhilaration—see what I have done—as he displayed the multitude of brilliantly colored sketches, childlike and scrappy and bursting with energy, so different from the methodical charcoals in gradations of gray and black he usually did as preludes to sculptures. "That one's a zinger," Eliza exclaimed as Sarah videotaped them sitting cross-legged on the floor.

The optimism in Todd's manner, in the drawings themselves, the resurrected joy of discovery was contagious. They seemed so happy and so free, with their bright yellows and blues, their loose lines, as if he had willfully pushed past the constrictions of his previous work. Perhaps this was the breakthrough he had been waiting for all these recent fallow years. Sarah was deeply relieved, thankful that he was creating again, and that he wanted to share them with her. Everything would change now, go back to how it had once been when the future seemed so open to them.

She had thought the glow in his eyes, his fervent manner were good signs.

People offer up fragments of themselves to friends, spouses, lovers, leaving each person to create the remaining whole according to what they have in hand, forensic scientists all. But no two pieces are precisely alike, some barely have any resemblance at all. Love, it seems, and understanding, are largely acts of inference.

She saw now, in one crashing brutal thud, how mistaken she had been. The brilliantly hued oil pastels with their multiple versions of the same scrawls, the ferocity of the output after years of frustration that she had hoped were harbingers of an artistic rebirth could just as easily have been the first signs of mania, disintegration. She wondered what the drawings the police found looked like, which direction they pointed to, if she would be able to see clues in them that they could not, or if she would miss those, too.

Everything she had believed, it seemed, was wrong, a misinterpretation.

When Todd rose to leave that night, Eliza touched her parents' hands. "Family hug," she said. Sarah and Todd looked over her head at each other, a universe of longing and disappointment in their eyes. They smiled sadly and looked away.

"He loved Eliza so much. Who knows, maybe he just needed some time to think," Victor said. "Or maybe he had some kind of breakdown. He could be anywhere."

When Todd was thirteen, his parents had begun to make long road trips crisscrossing Florida, trying to gain a toehold in the southern real estate market. Minnesota was not working out, the family business was floundering. They finally got lucky when they bought five acres of swampland dirt cheap eight months before a developer decided to build a mall there. They took their profits and immediately reinvested in more land.

Todd was fifteen when they moved to Fort Pierce for good and he immediately loved the thick, slow tempest of the air, the swoosh of palmettos swaying before a storm, the ancient dripping roots of the banyan trees. He was drawn, too, to the rootlessness, the cheap motels that lined the coast, the pockets of Old Florida inland that had somehow been left behind, forgotten. It was a state filled with people with no past, people who had drifted down to escape trouble, to start over, and who could just as easily drift away, no questions asked. It was the simplest place on earth to disappear.

As his family life grew worse, he would vanish for hours, wandering, exploring, the only freedom he knew. The arguments with his stepfather were increasingly laced with the threat of physicality, but Inga, ripe with the first flush of real American success, did little to defuse the situation. Instead, she snuck into the kitchen at all hours and ate until all that remained was a bloated outline of who she used to be. Within two years, she had gained over one hundred pounds.

More than ever, she was at her husband's mercy. The Larkins gave in to their hoarding instincts, surrounding themselves with reams of old newspapers, dirty laundry, masses of staples bought in bulk, piles of soiled dishes. They ate at irregular hours, rarely picked up their mail, had few friends, and trusted no one, convinced that everyone was trying to put something over on them. All they cared about was land, looking at land, buying land, selling it. Todd spent as much time as he could at friends' houses, in the library, away from them, away from home.

One night, after a particularly brutal argument with his stepfather that culminated in punches thrown, he left for good. He went to sleep in a friend's garage and never went back, putting himself through college in Tampa, grad school at Berkeley, working a multitude of odd jobs, getting his degree summa cum laude, taking care of himself and just himself. It was the only way he could get out, the only way he could survive. He spoke with his mother every few months, but she had made a choice to stand by her husband, and Todd could not forgive her for failing to protect him. He missed her deeply, but he was not ready to go back; he wasn't sure he ever would be.

It was seven years before he finally felt secure enough in the life he had created to return and make up with Inga, seeing through his now-adult eyes how much her choices had cost her. Guilty about the pain his long absence had caused, worried about Inga's tenuous health—her legs were covered with sores from diabetes, her weight made mobility increasingly difficult—he visited as frequently as he could in the following years, affecting a wary détente with his stepfather, and helped out at the motel they had bought. He still remembered when it had been just the two of them, in Germany.

"They'll find him," Victor said, "they have to find him."

Sarah did not know if he meant Todd or his body.

A cold, clammy film covered her skin as she hung up, leaving her shivering.

"I can't believe this is happening," she repeated, turning to Lucy. There was a wonderment in her voice, as if viewing something horrific in a medical museum that defied credulity. Shock operates at times like codeine—it does not take away the pain, but it makes you disconnected from it. You know it is there, but you can't quite feel it.

"He may go back to pick up the airline ticket. The flight is Monday," Sarah said. There was hope, hope again.

"Yes." Lucy nodded, but she was a woman who bet the odds. Beneath her highly polished New York surface, there remained a clear-eyed midwestern lack of sentimentality. Sarah could see in her expression that she believed Todd was dead.

The phone rang before she could protest. She jumped when she saw the Florida number on her caller ID. "Yes?"

Detective Brook's slow, soft voice answered. "Sarah?"

"Did you find him?" she rushed out.

He paused. "No. There is nothing further to report. Did you locate his passport?"

Sarah had forgotten to look, though she did not want to admit that to the detective, as if any slacking off on her part would excuse the same in him. She had no idea if Todd had taken it when he moved out or not. It seemed careless now, but even under the best of circumstances she never quite knew where those things were, passports, tickets, the deeds and titles to life. When she and Todd had been dating for four months, they planned a vacation to the Gulf Coast of Florida together. She was responsible for holding on to the tickets but, in a fury of cleaning that came over her at times, she had accidentally thrown them out. She waited days before telling Todd, fearful of his reaction. But he had only replied matter-of-factly, "Well, get new ones." Twelve years later she still could not predict his reaction to anything or anyone.

"Hold on," she said. She walked with the phone to her desk drawer. Todd's passport was there, attached to hers with a worn purple hair scrunchie. "I have it."

"I see."

Sarah was not sure if Detective Brook saw this as a good sign or a bad one. There was a long silence.

"All right. I'll call you tomorrow," he said. "Unless of course we learn anything sooner. Will you be at this number?"

"Yes."

Emptiness gaped before Sarah as she hung up the phone. She had not truly understood the possibility until that moment that there would be no further information today, tonight, that this was all she would be left with.

For the next couple of hours, Sarah and Lucy sat in her living room, alternately crying, reasoning, turning the periscope, turning it once more. They picked over the possibilities, the clues, again and again in halting half-sentences: his love of Eliza, his depression, his sexual obsession with Linda (for Victor reluctantly admitted that, too), and his heartache at the breakup of his marriage, his fear of the sea and his lasting attraction to the hidden areas of Florida, all seemed to cancel each other out, leading them nowhere. The only thing real was the void itself, the only thing tangible was what was missing.

A sob racked Sarah's chest. "What do I tell Eliza?" She looked over at Lucy. Panic stripped her voice of all modulation, of any last pretense of control. Her eyes darted frantically, looking for an escape—surely there must be a way out of this, a way to stop this from unfolding, if only she could find it. Sarah remembered how, just three months ago, they had told Eliza that despite the separation they were still a family, would always be a family, *always.* She saw her daughter under the dining room table, her forearms covering her bent head, protecting herself from the storm her parents had so carelessly, so selfishly unleashed. How do you tell a child that her father has vanished off the face of the earth, that you simply do not know what happened, a child who still believes that parents have answers?

These are things you lose when someone vanishes: words like *always,* even *death.* And you lose, too, the most basic trust that things are what they appear to be, that we do in fact live in a rational world of substance and matter, that there are certain immutable universal rules. Suddenly those very things that you have based your life on, the structure that you have taken as unquestionable, prove illusory, and everything that they had been holding up crumbles—faith, trust, logic. How can you plunge a child into a world of infinite uncertainty and think there can be any way back?

"I don't think you should say anything until you know more," Lucy advised. "He's not due to come back for a few more days, so you have some time. You're just going to have to pretend nothing's happened."

Sarah nodded, unsure of how precisely to do that but agreeing that it was the best approach. She called her babysitter, Dora, a Jamaican woman of fifty-three with the compact body and sensible shoes of someone who had made a career of chasing after toddlers, and told her that she could have the day off. She would pick up Eliza at day camp herself that afternoon. "I'll tell Eliza I finished work early," she said to Lucy. "I doubt she'll question it for more than a second, especially if she sees you and me together."

It was getting later: 3:40, 3:45.

There were no more calls, no more information.

It was time for them to go.

"I don't know how to do this," Sarah said plaintively as they rose.

"You just have to act as if everything is normal," Lucy said. There was a sternness in her voice, a ballast.

The two headed out the door and into the humid gray summer afternoon. Sarah had gotten good at pretending this year until, worn out by the effort it took to make sure her face wasn't slipping, literally slipping off of her body, leaving her seething emotions exposed, she had suddenly stopped. It was an October afternoon when she had taken Eliza to her school's fair. The street was lined with makeshift booths where parents took turns painting moons and stars in sticky, glossy paint on the soft downy cheeks of children, and old toys, trucks dented and outgrown, unworn frilly clothes sent by well-meaning but clueless grandparents, books with drool dried on them in rippled splotches, were sold for fifty cents to possession-hungry children and parents who knew they would resell them the following year. Sarah and Eliza were at the apple-bobbing booth when Todd strode up and put his arm around Sarah, kissing her just above her ear. Her body tensed. All that morning, he had been refusing to come, pleading work, though what he did in those unfruitful hours in the studio was anyone's guess, it was simply his need to get away from them, from domesticity, an escape hatch in the guise of making art that she did not have access to, a place to brood and drink undisturbed. But here he was, smiling, handsome, seemingly so happy and so loving as he took Eliza in his arms. The other parents smiled back at them; they were such an attractive couple, such an appealing family. They remembered how he'd had the entire kindergarten class to his studio in the fall, painting a Welcome sign and hanging it out on the street, giving them each an origami bird he had painstakingly made and which they proceeded to race about dive-bombing instead of listening to his rather verbose explication on the meaning of abstraction. He had believed so in the gift of art that he was opening up to them. But that afternoon at the fair, she was standing close enough to smell the alcohol on his breath. Suddenly the other parents' approving, almost envious smiles made her blood curdle. She slithered out of his embrace. "I'm not going to pretend we're some happy American family," she hissed.

He stared at her, betrayed, shocked. "Fuck you."

Lucy and Sarah walked in silence down Fourteenth Street, past the fire station, the florist, the supermarket. Sarah kept her head bent, her body tilted forward, weaving slightly. She felt nothing, saw nothing.

They reached the day camp at exactly 4:00 p.m. and rode up the rickety elevator without looking at each other. The children would be seated at their desks now, waiting to be picked up, packed off, one by one, hurriedly throwing away their juice boxes with sticky apple-scented fingers. As they walked down the hallway, Sarah stopped, her feet unsteady, unwilling, and sank against the wall, a single sob escaping. "I can't do this."

"You have to," Lucy said.

Sarah took a deep breath, rearranged her face into a smile, a mother's smile, and entered the room to claim her daughter.

Three

Sarah lay in bed watching the sky lighten gradually from black to slate to a pale dove gray. A single ambulance screeched up First Avenue and she waited to see if it would be followed by others, the way all New Yorkers did since September 11, one ear cocked, poised to calibrate their reaction according to the quantity of sirens, but it was solitary, a harbinger of ordinary terror, nothing more.

The sheets were bunched and damp with night sweat, the remnants of her agitation. She had slept restlessly, skimming the surface of unconsciousness but never quite entering it, dipping in and out of troubled dreams whose plots she could not quite remember. Each time she awoke in the darkest night, in the dim predawn, it was with a different conviction: he was alive, he was not alive, they would find him, they would not. She saw him walking into the ocean, the black water rising against his legs higher and higher; she saw him wandering about, dazed, confused; she saw him slyly plotting a course away from her.

She lay still, watching the red numerals of her clock radio flip slowly over, filled with a mixture of urgency and dread. At 6:00 a.m., she rose and made a pot of coffee. She'd had no solid food for almost twenty-four hours and she was light-headed as she watched it drip its deep brown liquid into the pot.

They had to find him, they had to look harder.

The alternative was inconceivable.

She paced back and forth, her bare feet padding quietly against the hardwood floor. It seemed impossible that it was just yesterday that Detective Brook had called; time had expanded since then, each hour stretching out until it had eviscerated all that had gone before; there was no past, no previous life, there was only this.

She peered through the crack in Eliza's door. Her daughter's face was turned upward, even in sleep she appeared curious, questing. She was snoring lightly, her mouth slightly open, her blond hair a delicate nest. Sarah tiptoed in and leaned down, pressing her lips to her temple, so tender and unsuspecting. Eliza fluttered and rearranged her worn stuffed cat, Snowball, in her arms, settling back into sleep.

Sarah sat down at the dining room table, clutching the scrap of paper she had scribbled Detective Brook's numbers on, a jagged anticipation racing through her.

She put down the cold coffee and dialed his cell phone, reaching him in his car. "Mrs. Larkin." His voice was polite, its studied mildness laced with a subtle but undeniable note of authority.

Sarah muttered a quick good morning. There was no time for pleasantries.

"Did you find anything out?" she asked.

She knew better than to think they had found Todd in the night, wandering about, or his body, washed up, and had simply been waiting for a decent hour to call her, of course she knew better, and yet . . .

"I spoke further to Miss Granger last night," Brook said, matter-of-factly. He was adept at parceling out information as he saw fit.

His slow southern voice, so cool and expressionless, irritated Sarah. Something had changed, though she could not tell precisely what.

"And?"

"She said that Todd was finally making art again after a long period of inaction."

Sarah could hear in the way he pronounced the word *art*, just as he had previously used *artist* that it put everything Todd did into quotations, as if by the very dint of being an artist he had forfeited his right to standard rules and procedures. His behavior was suspect by default. Sarah said nothing, waiting for the point, the follow-up. She wasn't sure where this conversation was going; only that it felt intrusive. Privacy was one more thing she had lost that night, her life, her marriage, her misplaced faith and her naïveté suddenly spread out for strangers to pick over, pass judgment on.

"Is that true?" Brook asked.

Sarah remembered the last night she had seen Todd before he left for Florida, the twenty drawings, the reawakened excitement in his eyes, the optimism for the future it had given her.

"Yes," she admitted.

Detective Brook continued. "Miss Granger believes he would do anything to protect that. She claims that your husband was very upset about your demands for child support. He believed having to earn that kind of money would interfere with his ability to make art full-time."

"What? We never discussed child support," Sarah replied indignantly. "We never even got lawyers. We didn't do anything." She needed to make this man understand that she and Todd had no idea how to separate, that he still came over to cook Eliza's favorite meals—homemade banana waffles, turkey meatballs—and store them in neatly labeled bags in the freezer, that he brought his drill to hang new curtain rods two nights before he left and nagged Sarah about not cleaning the kitchen knives properly, fearful that they would grow dull. Whatever steps they had taken away from each other were still wet, malleable, they hadn't set at all. "Linda doesn't know what she's talking about."

There was silence on the other end of the line. Sarah knew that Brook did not believe her, the spurned wife.

"I thought you said the report led you to believe it was suicide," she continued. "What about the drawings you found, the ones that said 'Drowned' and 'Dead,' and the sculpture?" It wasn't an explanation she was ready to believe, but neither was the idea that she was so horrific Todd would do anything to escape her, that he had made a cold-eyed mathematical equation and chosen art over her and Eliza. There were no good options here.

"I didn't go to Miss Granger's house that night," Brook replied, backing up, backing away, covering his tracks. "Two of my men did. Those drawings could have been done anytime. We have no proof they were made that night. The fact is, a body would have washed up by now," he stated simply. "I've been on the force for over twenty years. Bodies don't just disappear. The tides would have brought it back." He paused. "I spoke to Todd's brother, Peter, and his stepfather. I have to tell you, neither sounded particularly alarmed. They didn't seem to think it was unusual for Todd to disappear."

Sarah rubbed her finger over a spot of dried orange juice on the table, its stickiness covered with a thin film of lint. Todd had run away numerous times before leaving for good at sixteen, convinced that if he didn't escape he risked being swallowed whole.

During their last year together, Sarah and Todd went to a marriage counselor. Todd sat on the couch in Ben Neuberg's softly lit office filled with leather-bound books and African masks, staring at his feet. He did not want to be there, did not believe in therapy, had only come because Sarah had threatened to leave him if he didn't. "We married for life," he told her. She nodded. They both still thought that loving each should be enough, though that was getting harder and harder to support.

Neuberg had leaned back, listening to Todd describe his trajectory, Germany to Minnesota to Florida to California to New York. There was much to respect, the intelligence and resolve, the ambition and the discipline it had taken to get out. It was what Sarah had loved about him, that self-determination, and even then, sitting on separate sides of the couch with only land mines between them, she admired it still. "You needed those survival techniques when you were younger," Neuberg said to Todd. "You had to think of yourself first and foremost. But I want you to consider this: Maybe the very techniques that helped you to survive are hurting you in this relationship."

Perhaps this was what Todd was doing now, moving away from trouble, from hindrances, not allowing anyone or anything to alter his course once he was making art again.

After Neuberg had dissected their backgrounds, he began to delve into their financial predicament, their bifurcated reactions to it. Todd didn't know what Sarah wanted from him. To be someone else. Someone he had never been, never would be, a midlevel manager with a steady paycheck he handed over to her every other Friday.

"This is who I am," he lashed out. "You knew that when you married me."

"Things change," Sarah said. "We have a child." His very insistence that he was the same, that he hadn't changed, infuriated her. She was not asking him to forgo being an artist, but she did not believe it negated financial responsibility. They had no savings, no college fund, no plan. "We should at least have a joint checking account."

"Then I'd have to earn twice as much just to give half to you," Todd said.

"That's ridiculous. It's not about earning more, it's about how we deal with money. Don't turn me into the little woman waiting at home for the paycheck."

"I'd have to earn twice as much," Todd repeated.

Sarah, exasperated, stared at Neuberg, glad to have a witness. Todd turned into a broken record when they argued, repeating the same phrases until she did not know how to break through, get him to hear her. Bad enough when he was sober, it was impossible when he was drunk. Lately she had begun to smash dishes just to stop the cycle. They went round and round like this for the next thirty minutes until Neuberg told them their time was up. They each paid one-half of the one hundred fifty dollars and left.

On the train that night, Todd turned to her. "Do you want stir-fry for dinner?"

"All right."

So there was this: the thin blanket of domesticity, what do you want for dinner, I'll go to the store while you go home and let the babysitter go. There was Todd walking in the door, Eliza overjoyed to see him, reminding Sarah of how when she was younger she would rub her forehead against his neck in happiness when he came home, the rituals of ten years of marriage, five years of parenthood, Eliza, reading a picture book in bed, Todd in the kitchen, cooking Chinese food and drinking too much beer, Sarah's resentment growing with every sip he took. By the time they sat down to eat in front of the television, they were barely speaking, polite, wary, but not speaking. She had no idea how to weigh all that, weigh and measure the ever-tipping scales of unhappiness and comfort, regularity and regret.

It wasn't until their third visit that the issue of Todd's drinking came up. Everything else had been preliminary. Though it was increasing exponentially—there were mornings when Sarah found beer instead of coffee in Todd's mug—he insisted on seeing it as an isolated, private vice. He certainly would not agree that it was affecting every aspect of their relationship. She had only begun to see it, face it, herself. When she brought up various forms of treatment, he did not deny there was a problem but insisted, "I can control this on my own." There were periods when he would cut way back and Sarah would believe, honestly believe, each time, that things would get better. He had conquered so much, surely he could conquer this. But it never lasted.

"AA is filled with divorced men," Neuberg told Todd, after hearing Sarah out.

"How dare you?" Todd, furious, stormed out midsession, leaving Sarah alone with the therapist.

Neuberg smiled nervously. "He'll come back."

But she knew that he wouldn't.

Sarah thought suddenly now of the spare beach house Todd's parents owned in Fort Pierce where, in the early years of her marriage, she and Todd used to spend four months a year. They had been happiest there, in that yellow stucco house from the 1920s a block from the beach, with the herb garden Todd had planted, the hibiscus, the luxury of time. Todd had built a studio in the sunroom and, flush with the first wave of success, he would make art till all hours, the oblong room stuffed with ideas, copper pieces, drawings, finished works waiting only for titles. Often he would call out to her four, five times a day, wanting to share each new curve, each fresh discovery and solution, his pleasure in his own inventions irrepressible, infectious, delighting her, too. How was she to know that his enthusiasm would prove finite, that in just a few years he would be plunged into uncertainty and there would be no more excited calls as he pulled creations into being? He painted a sign on one of the walls, MORE ART FASTER, and at the end of each stay, his gallery would send a truck to bring it all back to New York, selling his work as quickly as he could make it. The city, glittering, attainable, could be reentered, reconquered at will.

She took a sip of her coffee and it dribbled down her lip and chin as if she'd had a shot of novocaine. They hadn't been back to that house in seven years. One March night while Todd and Sarah were at a dinner party in TriBeCa, his mother had dropped dead at the age of fifty-three from morbid obesity while sitting at the check-in desk of the motel they owned a few blocks away. They went back for the funeral, but after that Todd had no desire to return. Sarah was pregnant by fall and life had entered a new stage. He hadn't spoken to his stepfather in years. But they had left things behind there, pieces of their lives they thought they would be returning to, a set of turquoise Fiestaware, giant spools of copper, anvils, acetylene tanks for patinating, a few seminal pieces Todd had not yet figured out how to complete, his great reams of brown paper for drawings, her neat box of white paper for printing out the freelance stories she was able to report from there, an elaborate wicker picnic basket with gingham napkins, heavy dishes, and cutlery that they had bought as if for someone else's life and never used, photographs of themselves on a pontoon boat, beneath the banyan tree at night, her back to the camera as he held her, a smile curling his lips, his eyes half shut.

The house had sat unused for years as far as Sarah knew. All these years, Todd had kept the keys to it on his ring, along with those for his studio on Rivington Street and home—a talisman, a promise. Perhaps he had gone back there, to where they had been at their best and he could not make art fast enough to keep pace with the visions in his head.

"There's a place you might look," she said to Brook, aware that she was admitting his version might have some truth.

Brook agreed to call the police in Fort Pierce and have them check it out.

Sarah, filled with a new sense of hope, looked up to see Eliza standing in the doorway, clutching Snowball by one patchy paw, still slightly stunned with sleep. She climbed silently into Sarah's arms and nestled deep into her chest, her growing independence nowhere in evidence. Sarah enveloped her, inhaled her, formed a cocoon around her. There is such a small window of time that we can be made to feel truly and completely safe by another human being, and knowing that for this moment she could provide that for Eliza made the breath catch in her lungs. They stayed there, enwrapped, one feeling the deep atavistic safety of home, the other knowing how ephemeral and illusory safety is, until Sarah's leg fell asleep.

For the rest of the morning, Sarah let Eliza watch as much television as she wanted. She took the phone into Eliza's bedroom and sat cross-legged on the twin bed with its puffy pale blue quilt. The floor was covered in a thick forest-green carpet, the walls painted a sky blue. Todd had wanted to give his daughter a sense of space, of the outdoors, of freedom. The gifts he had made for her leaned against the dresser, sat casually on the bookshelves: a lacquered wooden fishing pole that caught hand-painted magnetic fish, a waist-high marble run that every child who came over was fascinated by, wooden sailboats for the bathtub. This is what he did in the studio now, and if they were not works of art, surely they had been works of love.

When he was first courting Sarah, Todd brought her flowers he'd made out of copper when he came to pick her up for dates. She thought of him, preparing all afternoon to see her, and then so shy and so proud as he gave them to her. How could she not say yes, yes to everything? One was still hanging on the wall, a long graceful stem with a single petal on the top. Eight years later, Eliza stood before it and asked, "Why is there only one petal?"

"I don't know, " Sarah replied.

Todd stared at her in disbelief. "She loves me, she loves me not?" he prompted.

All these years he had assumed she understood the symbolism, that it meant something to her, this piece of his once hopeful heart, and he was shocked that she had been so unaware, his narrative of their romance so different from hers.

She wondered how many other instances there had there been, how many other misinterpretations, and if they were the minor interludes of subjective reality that all marriages are prone to or something deeper than that.

Later, when Sarah started at Compton Media, she wore bracelets that Todd made for her to celebrate birthdays and holidays, large intricate threads of welded copper. The most discriminating fashion director in the building spied them on Sarah in the elevator and begged to feature them in her magazine. But Todd refused, no matter how many examples of famous artists who designed jewelry and furniture Sarah pointed out, thinking of the money they would make, the salve it would provide. "I'm a sculptor, not a craftsman," he protested. "These are just for you."

There were things Detective Brook, Linda, would never know.

Sarah picked at a thread in the quilt, twisting it until it snapped. She looked over to make sure the door was closed and then dialed Linda's number.

Linda's voice was hoarse, clouded with sleep. Sarah stood up and began pacing, furious that Linda could rest, find relief, however fitful. She should be out searching the streets, the beach, the state park, everywhere, every moment.

"What the hell did you tell the police about child support?" Sarah demanded.

Linda lit a cigarette and inhaled deeply before replying. "What do you mean?"

"You told them Todd wanted to run away from me so he wouldn't have to pay child support?"

Like a politician, or a woman who'd had to rely on her wits from an early age, Linda did not answer the question that was asked, but instead, answered as she wished. "He was a genius," she said. "The art he had begun to make down here was incredible." She coughed briefly. "Nothing would ever matter to him the way that did. He wasn't about to let anything stand in the way of it."

Sarah squirmed uncomfortably, recognizing bits and pieces of her husband in her words, but knowing there was more, a whole universe she and Todd had shared that Linda knew nothing of. She remembered watching Todd hold Eliza the night they brought her home from the hospital, sitting in the rocking chair by the bedroom window, the lights from First Avenue falling across them in diffuse pale yellow strips. "I never thought I'd have this," he said softly. "Thank you."

"My father ran off when I was ten," Linda continued. "You think it's a cliché that men go out for a carton of milk and don't come back? It happens all the time." She paused. "My father came back. It took a year, but he came back." Her tone was fatalistic, tempered, this is how life is, how men are, how could you expect otherwise? "Our fucked-up childhoods were a bond between us," she added.

Todd would never say to Linda, as he had to Sarah, "Teach me what a family is." Maybe he had gotten tired of the effort it took to hold himself in, hold himself together. Maybe the very thing he felt a need to tame with Sarah he found an echo of in Linda, and her allure was a cessation of the struggle. With her, he would not have to pretend he was "normal."

"You're better off without him," Linda said. "He was never going to stop drinking. Men don't change. You'd have a lifetime of him going in and out of rehab. My ex-boyfriend, Bill, has seen so many therapists. He's addicted to Internet porn. Sometimes he would masturbate for so long in front of the computer that he'd have sores on his penis." There was no embarrassment or shame in her voice. In fact, her tone was conspiratorial—we have something in common, you and I, the difficulty of loving men who are elusive in their attentions, destructive in their habits—as if this presumed commonality would unite them.

Sarah sank onto Eliza's bed, momentarily rendered speechless by this woman. If she had thought there would be an apology from Linda, for not calling the police, for being with her husband, if she had thought there would be any acknowledgment or even comprehension of wrongdoing or at least bad judgment, she saw that was not to be.

"Todd didn't love me," Linda said. "He always came to me in between relationships. He didn't really love anyone except Eliza. The first thing he did was put pictures of her all over the garage where I had set up a work space for him. I told him to go home and work on his marriage," she said, her voice raspy, falsely intimate. "I have to go," she said abruptly. "I promised a friend I'd meet her at the mall."

"You're going shopping?" Sarah asked in disbelief,

"I've been waiting for him for six days," Linda said. "He'll come back when he's ready."

Sarah hung up without replying.

Eliza was standing in the doorway eyeing her mother curiously, an anxious spy of domestic disturbances. For the first month after Todd moved out, she would wake in the night, calling for Sarah as she hadn't since she was a baby, Are you still here? That had stopped, but Eliza remained watchful.

Sarah poured some Honey Nut Cheerios into a bowl for her and put them in front of the television on a blanket of unread newspapers. She took the phone into the coat closet and shut the door, the only place she was safe from her daughter's eyes and ears. She took the sleeve of Todd's favorite tweed blazer and inhaled deeply, the fabric tickling her nose, drugged by it, lost in it. She reluctantly let it go and dialed his studio, listening to the phone ring two, three times, the tone so familiar that every memory of him seemed to reverberate within it. Her nerve endings twitched in anticipation. There was always the chance that he would pick up, that somehow he would be there. That this would all just simply stop. Hope and expectation are irrational by their very nature. In a world that has been revealed to be lawless, they make as much sense as anything. But when Todd's voice answered it was the recorded version, a fragment from another time. She listened until the final beep of the phone machine clicked to silence.

She twisted her foot around a box of Christmas tree ornaments, resettling it as she dialed Todd's half brother, Peter, in Gainesville, where he had graduated from college four years earlier. Eleven years younger than Todd, he had grown up after the Larkins had become flush with cash. Inga showered gifts on her youngest child, buying him a house to live in near campus, paying for the phones, the DVD players, the car, slipping wads of cash into his pockets whenever he came to visit. Peter, cosseted, protected, somehow remained unspoiled but learned nothing about taking care of himself. After his mother's death, his father cut off all funds within a week. He had never treated Peter, his natural son, any better than he had Todd. The brothers, despite their difference in age and to a large degree upbringing, were united by this, though their temperaments were so different. Peter, lacking Todd's survival skills or the deliverance he had found in art, floated through a series of odd jobs, living alone in the large four-bedroom Gainesville house. He was a sweet, easygoing surfer boy with vague ambitions that changed weekly. At the moment he was giving some thought to starting his own T-shirt business.

Peter was in a deep sleep when he finally picked up on the sixth ring. At first, Sarah ascribed his lack of emotion to that, but she soon realized that he truly wasn't alarmed by his conversation with Detective Brook. All the trips his parents had taken during his childhood searching for new investments had inoculated him to sudden departures, postponed returns. Peter believed Todd would come back, people usually did.

"But it's not like him," Sarah insisted, trying to make him understand the gravity, the urgency of the circumstances. This was what she wanted to say but did not know how: Todd had broken away from your family, he had painstakingly reinvented himself. We did not have the kind of existence where these things happened.

Except, clearly, they did.

When Todd and Sarah stayed at the beach house, they would occasionally help out at his parents' motel while they went to look at potential properties, stock up at Sam's Club, or simply drive away from their mind-numbing duties. Often, they would say that they would be back by sunset and not return till midnight. Sarah, who had been driven crazy by the Larkins' fluid sense of time and obligation, now saw it as something to pin her hopes on. Perhaps it had infected Todd, too, lying dormant all these years until now.

"When was the last time you went to the beach house?" Sarah asked.

"No one's used it for years. My father moved to the Keys."

"But he still owns it?"

"He holds on to everything. You think Todd went there?"

"I don't know."

"Makes sense, I guess."

"One last thing." Sarah paused. "Did Todd ever mention suicide to you?" She remembered one summer years earlier when Peter was going through a bad breakup and came up to New York, where Todd paid him to help assemble pieces and patinate for a few weeks. At dusk, the two brothers would sit on the stoop on Rivington Street, drinking beers and lamenting the fickleness of love. A year later, Todd made a stunning sculpture with two shattered arms of copper emerging from a single arc and called it *Peter's Dilemma.* It had sold within weeks to the Walker Art Center in Minneapolis.

"No," Peter replied after a long silence. "Never."

When they got off the phone, Sarah called Todd's stepfather and left a message asking that if he heard from Todd to please let her know, though the premise was ridiculous.

She burrowed deeper into the closet. There was one call that she had been putting off for the past twenty-four hours, hoping that before she talked to her mother she would have a conclusion, no matter how horrific, to give her. Fourteen months ago, Sarah's father, Gabe, had died of cardiac arrest while on vacation in London. Sarah had flown over to meet her mother at the hospital where he lay in a deep coma. For five days, the two women sat at his bedside while innumerable tests were performed and her mother relived their romance, including details of their apparently still active sex life that Sarah would have preferred not to know. A week later, they flew back with his ashes.

Lani Sherman, after thirty-eight years of a marriage in which she rarely did a single thing alone, remained distraught, each day a trial of perseverance. Energetic and nervous by nature, she dove into the activities of Santa Fe, where the Shermans had moved from the Upper West Side of Manhattan. Virtually every waking moment was filled with galleries, chamber music, the summer opera season, but she lamented that her world was made up almost entirely of women now, and still slept with her husband's picture on her pillow, still wept through the night.

In the months immediately following her father's death, Sarah began to grow more restive in her own marriage. Seeing the closeness of her parents' union, the stark reminder of mortality, made her less forgiving of Todd's drinking, of his artistic stagnation, of their increasing inability to comfort each other. But when Sarah had called her mother to tell her that Todd was moving out, Lani—who wanted only to have her own husband back—insisted she was making a big mistake.

"I've never seen Todd drunk," she said, as if that settled the matter.

Sarah, who had protected Todd, never spoken ill of him in the past ten years, was forced to rewrite all that her mother knew. Still, Lani could not bring herself to say the word *alcoholic* and referred to it as "A" just as people had once had "the big C."

"This will be tragic for Eliza," her mother argued. Liberal when it came to politics and art, she had an innate conservatism about men and women. She did not understand the plethora of divorces and believed self-centeredness was almost always the cause. Now, more than ever, she could not understand how a woman could choose to be alone.

"I hope we can work it out," Sarah admitted. "But right now we need a break."

"Are you in love with Todd or not?"

"It's not that simple."

"In my day it was."

Todd, a German Catholic artist, was not what Lani would have chosen for her daughter. Though not religious (Sarah had never set foot inside a synagogue), her parents remained strongly Jewish culturally. But Lani quickly grew to adore him. They shared a love of cooking, of classical music, of bargain hunting in used book stores, of Eliza. When they still lived in New York, the Shermans had taken such pride in bringing their friends to his openings, their son-in-law who had work in museums, so charming, so talented.

Every time Sarah called Santa Fe now, Lani hoped it was to tell her they had worked their problems out.

Sarah listened to the phone ring in her mother's condo, three, four times before she picked up.

"Mom." Tears that Sarah had been holding in all morning came flooding out, surprising both of them.

"Sarah? What is it? Are you okay? Is Eliza okay?"

"Eliza's fine." She held the phone away from her mouth and swallowed audibly before speaking again. When the words finally came out they were a breathy jumble. "I think Todd may be dead. I don't know, he's disappeared."

Her mother gasped. "What do you mean, disappeared?"

Sarah laid out the details once and then again. Under the best of circumstances, her mother had a tendency to jumble facts, chronologies. Faced now with such confusing information, she had a hard time concentrating—all she saw was loss, another loss.

"I can fly out tonight," she offered.

But Sarah, worried that she would end up having to take care of her mother, tend to her, comfort her, said it might be better to wait. She would call as soon as there was more news.

She hung up and rested the phone back on the floor, hollowed out, suddenly missing her father more than she had since the day he died. She longed for the protection his stability and calm rationality had always provided. He was a quiet man with a dry wit and a strong sense of morals, and she had always known she could go home to him. He would know what to do.

She was, truly, on her own now.

Two hours later, a cold front was moving in as Sarah and Eliza walked west through Madison Square Park toward Lucy's house. Disparate weather patterns hung over Manhattan in striations of slate gray and blue. To the north, the deserted office buildings of midtown glistened in the cloudless air, masculine, arrogant, untouchable. To the south, gray tufts hung low, and the first drops of rain strafed the brownstones and the tenements. They walked quickly, trying to outrun skies that were about to open up, toward Lucy's 2,000-square-foot loft in the Flatiron district.

Lucy, who had logged three years at Ralph Lauren, had managed that slippery feat of creating a home that was at once deliciously comfortable and impossibly chic. Deep brown plush velvet sofas faced each other in the airy living room, its wall of windows overlooking the verdant canopy of the park. Looking north, the jeweled peaks of the Chrysler building ornamented the skyline. It was, particularly in winter when the snow fell in fat diffuse flakes, one of the most romantic views in the city.

The two girls huddled in Jane's room while Lucy and Sarah drank green tea and Sarah recounted the morning's conversations, hoping if she repeated them enough some crucial kernel she had previously overlooked would be laid bare before them. As a journalist she had been trained to ask questions, go back, ask again, to reread notes until a pattern became evident, to come at it from every angle imaginable. The truth was always there, buried perhaps, expertly camouflaged, but attainable if only you were smart enough to find it.

Lucy's husband, Mark, sat across from them, perched on the edge of the couch, ready to spring into action, waiting direction. He rubbed his broad hands up and down his khaki pants, sympathetic, uncomfortable. His short, sandy hair curling in the humidity, his kind face alert, empathetic, he listened, nodded, and said little until he rose, looking relieved, to slink off to the gym.

Lucy checked on the girls every few minutes, doling out granola bars and juice boxes while Sarah worked the phones. When she finally reached Brook he told her he had not heard back from the Fort Pierce PD. Peter hadn't heard anything more, either. She called her home machine repeatedly, though everyone had her cell number.

When Mark returned, freshly showered but still pleasantly rumpled in the boyish way ex-college athletes never quite lose, as if the New England playing fields of their youth were forever a few yards away, he kissed Lucy quickly on the forehead, reticent to make a show of their togetherness, and opened a bottle of Sancerre. Sarah had only had half a glass when she stood up, her feet numb beneath her. "I'm going to go check on the girls." She swayed unsteadily, other people, other voices, all suddenly too much for her, swirling, straining, everything she had held in threatening to erupt. She had to get away before it all spilled out in public.

Lucy found Sarah ten minutes later, curled in a fetal position on her bed, sobbing so hard her body shook in great violent waves but hardly making a sound, a pillow clutched to her face, fearful of alarming the girls. She stroked Sarah's head, her hair moist and tangled, and then curled around her, her chest against Sarah's back, which quivered as she tried to recover her breath.

"What do you think happened?" Sarah whispered, her eyes tightly shut.

Lucy stroked her temples gently. "I think he died that night."

A vision of the future Sarah had been holding at bay for the past twenty-four hours rose before her: telling Eliza, life as a single parent, aloneness with no end, no chance to go back, try again, fix the mistakes, to talk just once more, that was all she wanted, just one more conversation, one more chance, to touch him, to stop him, to plead with him, just that.

It was dark when she and Eliza left Lucy's house, the musty smell of the pavement after a summer rain filling their nostrils. The air was cool, cleansed, as they stood on the edges of the park, trying to get a cab. Sarah glanced back at her daughter, standing on the curb, so small still, her arms wrapped around her thin chest to keep warm, her eyes off in the middle distance. The two sank into the backseat of the cab in silence, both spent, though for completely different reasons.

That night Sarah dreamed of Todd, of pummeling him, punching him in the face again and again, her anger infinite, insurmountable, and he never said a word, never made a sound. On Sunday morning, Sarah made Eliza her favorite chocolate chip pancakes for breakfast, then set up the large professional wooden easel Todd had gotten her at Pearl Paint two years ago—a chore she usually did anything possible to avoid. She ran the jars of primary paints under hot water until she could open them—it had been so long that the tops had become stuck on—dug paintbrushes out from under the kitchen sink, and found an enormous pad of brown paper. Eliza refused to wear her plastic smock, but Sarah didn't make an issue of it—the painting would keep her occupied for at least an hour, hopefully two.

As soon as the dripping wet brush hit the first piece of paper, Sarah went into her room and sat down with a list and began to call Todd's friends: his grad school roommate from Berkeley, a fellow artist from the gallery, an ex-girlfriend, hoping against hope that one of them had heard from him. Each time, she had to explain why she was calling, the embarrassment and the strangeness of it all fresh with each retelling: I have lost my husband, the word *lost* subject to a myriad of interpretations, but the essence always the same: he is gone, one way or another he is gone. And each time she asked the same thing: When was the last time you heard from him, how was he, what was he like, did he say anything?

She was looking for hard facts or amorphous nuggets, looking for anything at all. Some spoke reluctantly of Todd's references to Linda. Some painted a picture in halting sentences of his increasingly troubled psyche, of midnight phone calls, of a rambling mind and heart. He had not mentioned suicide, but no one seemed surprised about its specter. Everyone mentioned his depression over his stalled career. But others said this: He loved Eliza more than anything in the world. He would never purposefully hurt her.

Not one of them had heard from him.

At four o'clock, Detective Brook called. There had been no sign of Todd at the house in Fort Pierce.

"Did they look in the studio there?" Sarah asked, knowing that the first thing he did each time they returned to the beach house was take the canvas drop cloths off his machines, his copper, and run his fingers over the smooth surfaces; home was where his art was.

"They assured me there were no signs that anyone had been there."

"But did they go inside?"

"Without evidence of a crime, they have no right to enter. Every hospital in the state has been contacted," Brook continued. "There has been no activity on his credit cards. Linda said your husband told her he left ten thousand dollars in cash in his studio. Do you know anything about that?"

Sarah had to admit that she didn't.

She called Dora to come over to babysit. As soon as she arrived, Sarah grabbed the extra set of keys she kept in the kitchen drawer and took a cab down Avenue A to Todd's studio. Her heart sank when she saw the emerald green front door covered with great black and silver scrawls of graffiti. Todd repainted it every week, convinced that if people saw the pride of ownership, they would be more apt to leave it alone. Fastidious, he did not believe in letting down your guard—decay invites destruction.

She walked up the three flights of dusty stairs, holding on to the rickety wooden railing. On the third-floor landing, Todd's spider-thin Italian bike leaned up against the wall. Attached to the canvas satchel on the front handlebar was a picture of Eliza sticking her tongue out, her thumbs in her ears, grinning at the camera. Todd changed the picture every few weeks, preferring goofy ones that made him smile when he glanced down as he rode through the city streets, joy renewed.

She turned the three locks and opened the heavy metal door slowly, peering in, a spy, a thief. She had rarely been in the studio without him. The air was dank, hot. Early-evening light filtered through the skylight and onto the enormous worktable in the center of the open space, the band saw covered in canvas. There were half-finished pieces of art on all of the walls, incomplete thoughts, shunted pieces of copper. Three floor-to-ceiling drawings on brown paper hung in the corner, carefully thought-out charcoal delineations, meticulous, contained, so different from the cacophonous drawings he had shown her before he left.

On his desk, there was the Cycladic replica she had given him on their first Christmas together, on the corkboard above were snippets of drawings, museum postcards of Elie Nadelman, Joseph Beuys, Yves Klein, there were pieces of poems and pictures of Eliza, Eliza with her chubby red infant cheeks, Eliza in a car seat, eating a pickle, Eliza with her blond curls pulled into pigtails on her first day of kindergarten. The walls were lined with thousands of records and CDs. Todd had a historic collection, ranging from some of the first 78s ever made to the latest techno-pop from Iceland, that he had painstakingly built over the years. She had almost as hard a time imagining him abandoning them as leaving her. When he was a teenager he had wandered into the public library and discovered existential literature, the Greek poets, John Cage, and it convinced him that there was a way out, from small towns, from a stepfather who abused him and a mother who loved him but was too overwhelmed by her own life to protect him. Music saved me, he said. To step inside his studio was to view the world through the portal of his taste, his experience, his intellect; it was to step inside his soul. She had been hopelessly seduced by its very air from the moment she first entered.

It was here that they danced barefoot on the uneven wooden floor after a party they gave a decade ago, it was here that she first made love with him, on the single mattress in the tiny side room, and here that she woke in the predawn, reading the entire set of Ned Rorem's diaries all that first fall together while he slept. It was here, leaning up against the worktable, neatly lined with anvils, that she told him she was pregnant, he leaning back too, the protective goggles he wore pushed up on his head, looking at her quizzically, taking it in; it was here, in the first early flush of parenthood when they agreed to share responsibilities equally, that he would bring Eliza every morning thinking he could work with her sleeping in the corner, though he gave up after just a few days when he realized he could not in fact use his power tools around her. And it was here that he sought refuge from her.

The phone machine light was blinking and she pushed "play," but there was only her voice on the tape, calling for him, asking for him, begging him to answer.

She went into the kitchen with its cheerful yellow walls and its rows of cookbooks. Todd loved food and every aspect of its preparation. Cooking was a contact sport for him, flames shooting, pots hissing; often he would cook while he worked and bring home the results for dinner: there was a French stage, a Japanese stage. She remembered how he had called her office her first day at *Flair* and said, "This is your menu for tonight; shrimp on a bed of spinach with feta cheese," his way of showing love, congratulating her. She thought of all the dinner parties they used to have before Eliza was born, the five-course meals they would plan and shop for for days, fish heads for bouillabaisse, rare herbs from Provence; and how all of that went by the wayside once everyone started having children and they were too tired to cook.

On the shelf above the sink there was a glass jar overflowing with pennies, the only money she would find that night.

In the far corner, she found his wedding ring nailed to the wall.

On the refrigerator, there was a photograph of Linda on which she had scrawled, "Eat your heart out." Sarah leaned over, studied it. Linda was a thin woman with dark brown, shoulder-length hair, a bit straggly, in shorts and a polo shirt, sunglasses tucked into the neckline, a perfectly pleasant if ordinary-looking woman, with no great powers of seduction clearly visible. Sarah put the photograph back on the door.

Next to it, there was a note Todd had written in black Magic Marker taped to the refrigerator door that said, "Get mobile."

Four

All that night as she tried to sleep, Sarah saw Todd on the unlit beach, walking toward the ocean. He never got farther than the first scalloped edge of waves before the loop started again, Todd walking closer, just about to enter. Perhaps if she imagined it enough she could stop him. She grew obsessed with whether he had taken off his shoes or not, of what had become of them. It was still pitch-black outside when she woke on Monday morning. She looked over at the clock. Five a.m. Eight hours and ten minutes before Continental flight 1027 was scheduled to leave Daytona for New York.

She pictured Todd waking up in a cheap motel by the beach, the walls permanently water-stained, the small pool filmy with suntan oil, sitting up and running his hands through his shaggy auburn hair, how many times had she seen him do that? She imagined him deciding that he'd had enough. He could return now, pick his things up from Linda's house, go home.

This could all still be over.

There was that chance.

She curled into a ball on the left side of the mattress. She had tried once in the weeks after Todd moved out to shift her legs horizontally, encroaching on what had always been his side, but it felt as if she were hanging off a cliff, naked and vulnerable. Her body had a muscle memory too deep to override, and she quickly withdrew to safety.

Five-thirty.

She envisioned him driving to the airport, handing over his ticket, going through the metal detector. He would board the plane, stash his suitcase overhead, turn on his iPod, and wait for the rev of engines.

For a moment, this scenario felt inevitable: Todd on the airplane, mildly pissed off when he found out about all the commotion his need for breathing room had caused, this past week soon an anecdote, messy and fraught, but an anecdote nonetheless in the spiral of their past year together and apart.

She forced herself to stay in bed for another thirty minutes. The day stretched before her, hours and hours of waiting until 1:10.

At seven, she went into Eliza's room, thick with the scent of a child's sleep, and woke her by kissing the warm hollow of her neck. Sarah knew that if Todd was not on the plane, she would have to tell Eliza something tonight, though she had no idea what that might be. More than anything, she willed him to be on the flight to escape that conversation.

Eliza coiled wordlessly into her mother's lap, an incremental transition to wakefulness that could still be smoothed by a touch. Gradually, Sarah eased her up, laid out her freshly laundered shorts and T-shirt, and left her alone to dress.

Eliza sat at the dining room table, picking at her cereal, maddeningly eating one Cheerio at a time. Last year, her teacher had remarked that Eliza was surely the slowest eater to come along in the school's fifty-year history. Sarah sat beside her, trying not to lose patience. She found herself holding her breath while Eliza raised the spoon, exhaling only when a Cheerio had been successfully swallowed. Todd was always better at this than she was, more patient; it was the upside of his less stringent attention to time. He had an ability to lose himself in the moment with Eliza, and if it meant he was incapable of getting her to bed at the appointed hour, it was not due to procrastination or a lack of discipline but because the two were entranced by a discovery, a project, a conversation, in a way that Sarah could never quite accomplish. They would spend hours drinking hot chocolate and looking at a catalog of Frank Stella paintings, reading *The Big Book of Tell Me Why,* staring at images of Venice, Paris, Rome through an old View-Master Todd had found in a thrift shop. Eliza expanded with Todd.

Sarah got up, went into the kitchen, and packed a lunch box with a peanut butter and apricot jam sandwich, a coffee yogurt, and a bottle of water. Years after they married, Todd admitted that he had set his watch fifteen minutes ahead when they were courting so that he would never be late. "You got me under false pretenses," she replied, touched by his desire to please her, frustrated with its cessation. She scribbled a love note on a Post-it and stuck it in the vinyl lunch box, a habit she had started years ago and continued out of superstition, as if something terrible would happen if she forgot just once.

It had been Eliza she had been worried about all this time, Eliza all of her secret rituals had been devised to protect. She saw now how easy it is to misplace our fears, what conceit our rituals betray, these well-meaning if feeble attempts to sway fate, to get by unscathed.

Sarah and Eliza left the house at exactly 8:15, just as they always did.

Routine, and the boundaries it created, had helped her through the three months since the separation: Eliza, dressed, fed, lunch box in hand, on time every morning, no matter how little sleep Sarah had gotten the night before, her eyes swollen from tears. It was the last refuge, the grid created and adhered to keep chaos at bay.

Sarah clung even more tightly to it now, believing it would be best for her daughter; children needed regularity, repetitiveness, predictability, particularly when faced with evidence of how little control they actually have.

But it was more than that. There was, despite her efficient façade, a deep-seated fear that if she gave up for even an instant, if she let herself go, the flood would be so torrential that she would never be able to find her way back, never be able to piece herself together again. Sarah peered over that ledge, tempted, terrified, and took a resolute step back.

She didn't know if Eliza remembered this was the day Todd was due to return home or not. They walked in silence for a block or two, though gradually she realized it hadn't been silence at all, Eliza had been chattering away the entire time, though the sounds were dim as if from the far end of a tunnel. She shook her head and tried to catch the train of her daughter's conversation, something about a girl named Hallie in her group who had a babysitter who had a boyfriend who had his nose pierced. Twice.

"That must have hurt," Sarah remarked.

Eliza looked at her mother strangely and Sarah wondered if she had gotten the story all wrong, missed the point somehow. She leaned down and kissed Eliza's head guiltily. She longed to be alone, to be free to indulge in her own obsessive thoughts—and she wanted to hold Eliza so tightly their skin melded. Eliza shrugged her mother away, and Sarah watched as she sped a few steps ahead of her. She cursed Todd beneath her breath for doing this to her, to them, cursed him for the chance that she would not be able to spare Eliza if he was not on that plane.

At the door of room 303, she kissed Eliza good-bye and then pulled her gently back, kissing her again with eyes tightly shut, breathing her in.

Sarah kept her head down on the way out of the building, avoiding eye contact with the other parents. She had no energy for maternal small talk, the morning chitchat that provided comfort and commonality. She was separated from other people now with their predictable lives and their minor melodramas, and she did not have the strength to pretend otherwise.

She got a cab and tried not to lose her patience when the driver, nattering into his headset in a foreign language, drove slower than necessary uptown. It was just three days ago that she had taken this exact route, thinking then of the upcoming story meeting, of a pair of Louboutin sling-backs she had seen in Bergdorf's, of nothing at all. She jiggled her foot nervously, disturbed that the buildings, the people, the pace outside the mottled window remained unchanged.

She swiped her card through the turnstiles of the CMH building and stood on the outskirts of a cluster of perfectly groomed women waiting for the elevator. Sarah suddenly hated them, hated them for their oblivious good fortune, for their smooth young faces and seamless lives.

She pushed open the heavy glass doors on the fourth floor and walked briskly toward her office. She knew that everyone at *Flair* must have heard an explanation from Maude about why she'd raced out Friday morning, and she could feel their curiosity and discomfort, sense them looking a little too intently at their computers as she passed, glancing up after her, unsure of whether they should say something or not. A few offered awkward half-smiles meant to show empathy and quickly returned to their work.

Inside Sarah's office, Paige was waiting for her with two large coffees. They had spoken twice over the weekend, but despite Paige's offer to come over, to babysit, to do anything at all, they had not seen each other since Friday. The two women hugged and Paige closed the door behind them with one flick of her manicured forefinger.

"How are you?" she asked.

Sarah shrugged. "All right." She looked quickly away, played with the plastic Starbucks lid.

The coffee tasted bitter in her mouth.

"I can't believe you came in today," Paige said.

"I couldn't just sit by the phone alone, waiting."

"I would have come over."

"I know. It's just that—" She stopped, rummaging for words. "I just need this morning to pass. I need to fill it somehow. I don't know if this will help or not. But I knew I couldn't sit still."

There was something else, too, something that Sarah could not quite express: Responsibility, conscientiousness, were so deeply ingrained in her that even now she could not act otherwise. You came to work, that's what you did. Perhaps it was a failure of nerve that she could not, even now, stray. She was the inveterate good girl, always on time, her homework always done, not, as some like her, driven by a need to be liked, but by a bone-deep anxiety of being thought lazy, incompetent, or worse, selfish.

"What can I do to help?" Paige asked.

"Nothing. I don't know."

They drank their coffee in silence for a moment.

"How was your date Saturday?" Sarah asked. Her voice, even to her own ears, was dull, leveled.

Paige looked up, uncertainty written across her face. "Oh, c'mon, you don't want to hear about that."

"I need distraction," Sarah insisted.

Paige relented, starting slowly but gathering steam. "I don't know how it was, actually. He was good-looking, high cheekbones, close-cropped blond hair, went to Andover and Yale."

"What is it with you and these preppie guys?"

"There's something sexy about them. I used to get turned on just watching Ethan ice-skate. It took two hundred years of breeding to get that crossover leg thing to look so effortless." Paige sighed. "I think he may be gay."

"Ethan?"

"No, he's too repressed to be gay." Paige smiled. "Tom. The date? He's certainly more delicate than I'll ever be. I don't know, he does a lot of Ashtanga and only shops at a food co-op in Brooklyn. Maybe he's just that yoga guy in the back of the class, you know, the thin, aesthetic one that no one can figure out?"

"Are you going to see him again?"

"He asked me out for lunch. Kind of a weird second date, don't you think, lunch? He's probably gay. He was wearing a gay sweater." She looked up. Sarah had wandered off, she was missing the beat, the rhythm, she was lost. "Oh God, Sarah, I'm so sorry."

Sarah glanced up wanly. "That he's gay?" She tried to smile, to show that she was still present. She needed people to talk to her about their lives, needed the distraction it brought, though there were moments when their words seemed foreign, hopelessly superficial. "Go on."

"All right. Speaking of Ethan," Paige said.

"I wasn't aware that's what we were doing."

Paige ignored this. "He listed his profile on Match.com. It's bad enough to be dumped. But he didn't even break up with me for another woman. He is choosing to be alone rather than be with me."

"Well, if he's on Match, he's not really choosing to be alone."

"Thanks," Paige retorted.

"Sorry."

"It's just so weird. Under 'favorite things,' he listed restaurants that we never went to. You kind of want to think people stop existing after you break up. It's annoying that they go on to have all these experiences you can track."

"Trust me, it's not so great when you can't track them," Sarah remarked ruefully. "Why don't you stop looking at his profile?"

"I've tried, I don't have the willpower. I can tell when he's online, I can even picture where he's sitting in his living room."

"Okay, that's dangerously close to cyber-stalking."

Paige sighed. "I need to meet someone new."

While Paige plotted ways to accomplish that, Sarah glanced surreptitiously at the clock on the upper right-hand corner of her computer. 9:48. But it was always slow. She did the calculations in her head. It was really 9:54. Three hours and sixteen minutes left.

She looked over at Paige and nodded at what she hoped were appropriate moments, but her mind was elsewhere, in the Florida heat. Linda had gone to her job teaching art at the community college fifteen miles away and left the back door open for Todd. A police car would be stationed on the corner. What time would Todd have to be at Linda's house to pick up his things if he planned on being on the flight back to New York, what time would he get to the airport? Detective Brook had alerted the airline and they agreed to call him immediately if a Todd Larkin checked in. Sarah had figured out the times once, twice, gone over all the possible permutations throughout the night and yet she could not keep the figures in her head. She blinked, willed herself to return to Paige who, it seemed, had left the topic of men behind and had moved on to work.

"Pat called a mini-meeting for this morning to go over the Body Issue," she told Sarah. "*Issue* being the right word, if you ask me. Anyway, I'm supposed to be getting stats about how often American women wash their hair, how long they go between dental appointments, how much they spend on moisturizers a year."

Sarah had forgotten all about the Body Issue, it was a language learned long ago that she had to pick up again. "What do you make of this whole thing?" she asked.

"I honestly don't know. It's either going to be amazing or disastrous. Turns out the average American woman is actually five-four, and a hundred sixty-four pounds. So that's what Rena is looking for. She's on a 'truth will set you free' kick. But no one really wants to see the naked truth, even if they think they do, especially on the newsstand. Women want aspiration."

"It will get a lot of press."

"But will it get sales? If Rena doesn't rack up some good newsstand numbers, she's in deep doo-doo. Frankly, there's a good chance this Body Issue will make CMH set her free."

Sarah snuck a look at the phone, but the message light remained stubbornly dark.

"Do you think we should talk to Rena about *Splash* again?" Paige continued.

Sarah shrugged. "I guess."

"I wish we could get it to William somehow."

"If you did that without going through Rena, she'd fire you."

"I know," Paige agreed. "Any ideas?"

Sarah shook her head. It suddenly took too much energy to continue to feign interest, it was all being sucked up into the vortex of waiting.

10:06, 10:07.

Paige rose to leave.

"I'm here if you need anything," she said.

"I know." Sarah tried to meet her eyes but couldn't, fearful that if she made any real connection, she would crumble into pieces on her office floor.

When Paige had gone, Sarah rested her head in her hands, shut her eyes, and tried to breathe, but it was as if her body had forgotten how: her lungs refused to fill with air. She coughed, panicking that she could not get enough oxygen.

She saw Todd sitting on the plane with his forehead pressed against the thick glass window, watching the palm trees that lined the shore recede as the plane rose at a sharp angle, banking left over the ocean as it headed north. She remembered the first time they had flown back from Florida. They'd been dating for four months and had just spent two weeks in a rented convertible driving along the Gulf Coast, stopping whenever they felt like it for a night or two in semi-empty beach motels thankful for customers in the off-season. In the evenings, they drank fresh-squeezed grapefruit juice with vodka as they watched the sunset, a ritual they would try to repeat years later in the city, attempting to resurrect that early spell of discovery and delight. On their last night, they'd had too much to drink and found themselves in a conversation that grew more heated as the hours progressed and the vodka bottle emptied. Sarah couldn't recall what started it, but they were talking about how well you can ever really know another human being. Even then, when they were still so new, on the brink of falling in love, she felt a gap between them that was hard to pinpoint, some emotional ground zero that remained forever out of reach.

"You'll never reach that place inside me, that's where my art comes from," Todd said, stubborn, adamant, his voice underscored with warning. She had hoped that love, trust, marriage, that time itself might bridge that gap. She was aware of the distance, though, sometimes as thin as a spider's thread, sometimes a continent, every day of their twelve years together. It took her too long to realize that the gap was in large part created and protected by alcohol, which kept anything from getting too close, feeling too real to him.

But so few of us heed the warnings, spoken or unspoken, when we are on the edge of love.

To see someone come so close to having it together and be incapable of helping himself was inconceivable right up until the night three months ago when Todd had stormed out of their apartment. She couldn't believe he wouldn't come through in the end. His survival skills had kicked in so many times before. Surely they would again.

It was 10:30.

She just had to breathe.

There was nothing else she could do.

Sarah opened her eyes, shook her arms until the feeling began to return. Looking around for something that would not require too much focus, she turned to her in-box, wading through invitations to PR events for the city of Quebec, a perfume launch being fronted by an aging bleached blond HBO sex symbol, and a weekend in Palo Alto being sponsored by the Almond Board of America. She threw them all in the trash save for the nut junket, which the nutrition editor might be interested in. It was an unwritten rule that as long as no specific story was promised and it did not occur during shipping, editors could take full advantage of the numerous offers from resorts, spas, and various product launches that came their way. Within the past few months, Paige had gone to a toothpaste launch in Iceland (white country, white teeth), Caitlin had attended a hair conditioner introduction in Provence (the herbal ingredients were designed to be reminiscent of French fields), and Lila had gone on a cruise in Russia that no one quite knew the point of.

10:45.

Sarah's skin tingled with exhaustion as she moved on to try to top edit a story on a woman with celiac disease—a trendy ailment at the moment, in part because it combined food allergies, exhaustion, and weight gain—but her brain was laced with holes.

An hour later, she left her office clutching her cell phone and took her place on the black canvas couch in Pat's office for the follow-up story meeting. If Rena's walls were ornamented with news clips, mementoes, paparazzi shots that captured a mood she hoped to re-create, Pat preferred a more spartan decor. Her office had a temporary feel, as if she had been too busy in the four months she'd been here to properly settle in. It was devoid of distractions, of quirks, of anything that might betray the inner life of its inhabitant. Sarah perched on the edge of the couch, squirming under the gaze of the other editors already assembled there. She could sense their eagerness for an explanation she did not possess, though whether it was out of genuine empathy or a desire to be in the know, she wasn't sure. Regardless, she felt naked, the soiled mess of her life splayed at their feet.

Pat straightened the cuffs of her perfectly starched white shirt, looked down, and rolled her eyes in a theatrical grimace. "Good lord, how did these pants get so tight?" She often complained about her weight in the company of other women, as if she had studied their habits and was imitating their behavior in an attempt to bond, but she was far too disciplined to give in to gastronomic temptation and the attempt fell flat. Pat weighed herself every morning and had never allowed herself to go above 114 pounds. Other conversational gambits—making fun of her supposed clumsiness, bemoaning how long it had taken her husband to propose—met with as little success. She got out the tan ostrich notebook that she carried everywhere and flipped to the appropriate page. "So," she began, "have we located a subject yet?"

"Average women may be everywhere," Lila began, "but they are impossible to find. I've put out feelers for women who meet the exact height and weight requirement on Web sites, with a university research center, I've called all my friends."

"Did you call your relatives?" Pat asked.

Lila, unsure how to take this, simply nodded and made a note.

Story ideas were thrown out into the room: What if a New York (clearly non-average) woman traded places with an "average" woman from the Midwest, ate what she ate, did what she did, and the "average" woman didn't eat what the New Yorker didn't eat, didn't do what she didn't do? Would their looks begin to come closer to some middle ground? Could they find a New Yorker willing to do that? Was it too close to last year's reality shows? Had *Marie Claire* already done it? Did they care? It was an article of faith in women's magazines that although originality was best whenever possible, copying (or rather, being inspired by) what another title had previously done was perfectly acceptable as long as enough time had passed, they used a different model, and it had succeeded the first time.

Pat said little as she chewed her lower lip and took notes. Caitlin watched her for an indication of her opinion before saying anything. Finally, she volunteered, "I think this is a makeover moment. Go from average to awesome: exclusive three-week total-body makeover."

"But the whole point is that this is the anti-makeover issue," Sarah piped up. The room silenced as everyone looked over at her, assessing the visual damage, undoubtedly jealous of the weight she had obviously lost over the weekend, though of course they would never admit it. (The flu was another story. Last month, when a particularly virulent twenty-four-hour stomach bug swept through the office, everyone called each other to see how many pounds they had lost. Caitlin, who had weighed herself every time she threw up all night long, won with six pounds eviscerated.) Sarah reflexively pushed a loose strand of hair into the ponytail that she had hastily fastened with one of Eliza's rubber bands.

"If we give the woman a makeover, we're saying there's something wrong with her. I think Rena's goal is to help women accept themselves as they truly are."

Even Paige cringed a little. Every editor in the room was secretly terrified that lurking just inside of her was an average woman waiting to come out. Sometimes they fantasized aloud about what it would be like to give up the battle, to eat whatever you want, stop the electrolysis, the blowouts, the elliptical trainer, the Botox, the microdermabrasion, but it remained just that, a fantasy at once alluring and horrifying.

Besides, self-acceptance did not sell magazines.

"Sarah, you seem to have a good handle on this. Why don't you come up with the flat plan?" Pat said. The other editors glanced again at Sarah. A flat plan was the blueprint for an upcoming issue. Pat, who had an ability to think three-dimensionally combined with an enviable instinct for successful cover lines, was particularly good at them. Unlike Rena, who started with content, writers, Pat first came up with seven to eight great-selling cover lines that guaranteed weight loss, explanations of men's sexual desires, instant glamour made easy. The rest of the issue was filler. Sometimes Pat came up with cover lines that had no stories and would demand one written to match.

"All right," Sarah said. She wasn't quite sure if this was an act of faith on Pat's part or an attempt to distance herself from the issue. Either way, it was more responsibility than she had been entrusted with in the past.

Pat glanced at her Cartier tank watch, an unspoken signal that the meeting was over. As the others filed out, she motioned for Sarah to stay.

"Are you all right?" she asked. "If there's anything I can do, if you need time off, just tell me."

"I'm okay." Sarah had a hard time admitting vulnerability under any circumstances, particularly around Pat, so crisp and so certain.

"I hope the flat plan isn't too much. I've always found work to be an effective coping mechanism during difficult periods. I thought it might be good for you to have something to occupy yourself with."

Sarah nodded.

Pat studied her for a beat too long. "All right, good," she said finally.

It was nearly noon when Sarah returned to her desk. She drank a Diet Coke and picked at the corners of a chocolate PowerBar, the only solid food she was able to swallow. The red message light on her phone remained resolutely unlit. She picked up the receiver and began to dial Brook's number, then hung up.

12:15.

Paige stopped by on her way to a lunch at Michael's with a marketing executive from Estée Lauder and asked if she could pick up anything for Sarah on her way back, but Sarah shook her head, there was nothing.

It was quiet outside her office door; the other editors were all at lunches or the gym, having manicures or speed-shopping at Barneys.

A few ate take-out salads at their desks while they scrolled the Internet, checking on their bids for Balenciaga bags on eBay or e-mailing lovers.

Sarah gave up all pretense of functioning. She did not open the mail or riffle through the fresh pile of CMH magazines that had been delivered while she was in Pat's office, she did not read e-mails. She gnawed at a hangnail, ripping it with her teeth until her finger bled.

As 1:00 p.m. approached, her stomach contracted in spasms.

If Todd had gone to Linda's house to pick up the ticket, no one had seen him, no one had called.

1:10.

1:20.

In the distance, she heard the microwave in the kitchen ping, someone's Lean Cuisine.

It was 1:32 when Detective Brook called Sarah and informed her that the flight had taken off. "There was no sign of your husband," he said matter-of-factly.

Sarah felt herself falling backward, dizzy, numb.

"Okay," Sarah whispered. "Okay." She tried desperately to think despite the vertigo, to figure out what to do next, grasping for anything to break her fall. "What do we do now?"

"Do you have a recent video of Todd?" Detective Brook asked.

Sarah remembered the one they had taken the night before he left for Florida, Todd and Eliza on the living room floor, looking at his drawings. "Yes."

"Well, if you send me a copy, we can put it on Crime Stoppers. Are you willing to offer a reward?"

"Of course," Sarah said, hopeful once more. Here, at least, was a strategy.

A long pause ensued.

"It would be helpful if you could also get me his dental records," Brook said.

Sarah's heart fell. He was planning for all contingencies, alive, dead, missing. "Okay."

"I must tell you, though," Brook added, "that it is my firm belief that your husband does not wish to be found. In all likelihood he left the state. It's been a week. A body would have washed up by now."

Sarah hung up and sat completely still. A few people walked by on their way back from lunch and peered in, but she did not acknowledge them.

Later that afternoon, she called Todd's dentist and asked the receptionist to send his dental records to the police in Florida. She said he was missing, maybe drowned, and got off the phone before there could be any emotion on either side. She was a story now, a story with the words *dental records* in it.

Sarah walked the thirty blocks home that night, oblivious to the crowded streets, to people racing for buses or jumping out recklessly into moving traffic as they tried to hail taxis. She looked up once and saw that she had gone seven blocks without knowing it. On Thirty-third Street, a woman bumped into her and then stopped, touched her arm. "Are you okay?" Puzzled, Sarah nodded. She hadn't realized that tears were streaming down her cheeks. She could not feel her own skin. There was only Eliza now, what to tell Eliza.

As she slid her key in the door, an exhaustion unlike any she had ever known washed through her. The very marrow of her bones ached.

Dora was in the living room cleaning up Eliza's toys, despite the number of times Sarah had said that Eliza was to do it herself. They exchanged muted hellos before Sarah called out to Eliza, "Hi, sweetie."

Eliza, busy in her room, said hello without coming out to greet her mother.

In the last six months, Eliza had begun making lists, lists of her stuffed animals' names, lists of her friends, lists of her books, lists of the places she had been to on the Saturday afternoon outings with Todd—to Roosevelt Island, Staten Island, Coney Island—Todd searching atavistically for water, an edge, a horizon, the two of them eating buttered rolls wherever they went. "It's a tradition," Eliza said solemnly. For a long time Sarah had told herself that her fights with

Todd went undetected; they took place after Eliza was in bed, on the phone during the day, they were the cold war in the night. But as she watched Eliza catalog her world, seeking in her own six-year-old way to instill an order that she sensed was slipping away, Sarah was no longer so sure.

After Dora left, Sarah went into the kitchen and made Eliza's favorite dinner, macaroni and cheese, mixing in extra butter, comfort food for what was to come. She ate little herself as they sat at the table, barely able to concentrate on Eliza's monologue about her day, something to do with a play in which she was to be the bear, she didn't want to be the bear, no one wanted to be the bear, why did she have to be the bear?

"Mommy, you're not listening." Eliza stopped midsentence, indignant.

Sarah, caught out, apologized.

"Sweetpea, I have something to tell you."

Eliza put down her fork, instantly alert, on guard. Nothing good could follow that opening.

"Something happened to Daddy," Sarah began.

Eliza crawled onto her mother's lap and buried her head in the hollow of her neck. Whatever was to come next, she knew she would need a refuge.

"What happened?" she asked meekly.

"He might not be coming back," Sarah said.

"Did he decide to live in Florida?" Eliza asked, her voice breaking, breaking already.

"No, honey. Daddy loved you more than anything in the universe. He would never do that. I think there might have been an accident."

"Can't he call me?"

"You were the most important person in the world to him. He would call if he could."

"What happened to him?" Panic shot through Eliza's voice.

"I don't know yet. I'm sorry. I'm doing everything I can to find out. You have to believe that."

Eliza curled tighter into her mother's arms and began to cry.

"What kind of accident?"

"I don't know, sweetie." Sarah rocked her back and forth, back and forth, her lips resting on the crown of her daughter's blond head. "I just don't know."

Five

People living within the maelstrom of tragedy often have a brief respite on waking, a sliver of forgetfulness and freedom from pain before consciousness of the new, unwanted reality descends, but for Sarah there was no such relief. She slept with the cordless phone resting on the pillow beside her and checked it throughout the night. Waiting defined every moment, asleep or awake; there was no relief from it.

Eliza was quieter than usual the next morning and insisted on wearing an old overwashed cotton T-shirt she had long since outgrown, unearthed from the bottom of a drawer, its shape and scent wrapping her in familiarity. She did not mention Todd or bring up anything that had been said the night before; mother and daughter were careful with each other as they walked in near silence to camp. At the door of room 303 Eliza pushed Sarah away with stubborn vehemence. There was a heartbreaking bravery in her determination to prove her independence. And there was, too, the first inklings of a blind anger, at Sarah, at Todd, at a world in which a parent can simply disappear. She would not let Sarah kiss her good-bye, furiously wiping off the tiny area where her mother's lips had managed to land. Sarah took a few steps down the hallway, then doubled back, standing on tiptoes and peering in through the glass window on top of the door. She had called the counselor the night before to tell her what had happened, unsure what the day would bring. She spied Eliza standing alone in the corner, the front of her shirt bunched tightly in her fist, and she realized then that its waffle fabric was exactly the same as the security blanket she had clung to when she was younger.

As she sat in the bus on the way to work, Sarah started to write a list in her notebook:

1. born to an unwed teenage mother in postwar Germany
2. abandoned by father
3. moves to America, doesn't speak English
4. has evil stepfather who calls him a bastard
5. mother is crazy

Perhaps if she listed it, it would take on shape, a logic suddenly revealed in its math, X plus Y equals Z, and she would understand Todd's course, how he, how they, had ended up here, perhaps it would explain where "here" was. She read it through, crumpled it up, started again.

When she got to work there was a message from Brook telling her that he had placed an item about Todd in the local paper hoping someone would see it and come forward with information. She logged on to her computer and found the *Loudon Beach News-Journal*'s Web site. On the opening page, there was a brief story under the heading "Authorities Looking for Missing Man." A cold sweat formed along Sarah's hairline, speckled the back of her neck. There was something about seeing it in print—"missing man"—that gave her situation a new and undeniable reality. At the same time, it felt completely detached, surreal, as if the story were not really hers. Her breath shortened as she read.

> *Police are searching for an artist who was visiting from New York before he disappeared a week ago. Todd Larkin, thirty-eight, was staying with a friend on Oleander Drive, police said. Last Monday around 11:00 p.m., he told his friend he was*

going for a walk and has not been seen or heard from since. Police say he consumed alcoholic beverages prior to his departure. His friend said Larkin suffered bouts of depression and is known to disappear for two or three days at a time, but he has never gone this long without contacting someone. He is six feet, four inches tall, weighs 200 pounds, and was last seen wearing gray jogging shorts and a white T-shirt. He did not have a vehicle and left his belongings, including identification and money, at his friend's house. Anyone with information is asked to contact Detective Ronald Brook at 386-385-7839, or the Loudon Beach Police Department.

A clammy film seeped down her back as she moved the cursor up and read the entire article again, looking for herself, for Todd, in the computer's fonts, in the stark newspaper verbiage: a life summed up and yet not, an artist visiting from New York who disappeared.

Sarah remembered a party they had gone to years ago at the height of junk bond mania. One of the lawyers involved in a famously brutal takeover of a fast-food company was celebrating his success. He and his wife collected Todd's work along with that of numerous other young artists thought to be up-and-comers. It was a week before Christmas when they invited these emissaries from downtown and their dealers, so much more amusing than the usual assortment of investment bankers and their flawlessly groomed wives, to their home. The artists came in droves, tourists to the Upper East Side, curious, less jaded than one might expect, anxious for the approbation as much as for the free champagne and blinis with caviar—the party had become a rung on the ladder and it was better to be there than not. The husband stood at the front door in his pressed jeans and greeted guests to their narrow five-story town house. Todd and Sarah got drinks and headed up the stairs, where the couple's most recent acquisition of Todd's work was hung—upside down. Sarah glanced over at Todd, certain he would make a scene, insult his hosts and their ignorance, but he did not seem to be upset. He smiled, shrugged, and then asked for a step stool from a maid, took the piece off the wall, and rehung it properly. He was a visitor here, and he had no expectations, though it could have gone the other way.

A year ago, that couple divorced and the husband was killed under mysterious circumstances in their new house in Southampton, the very house Todd's dealer had been so excited to learn they had purchased, dreaming of all the art they would need to furnish it.

Sarah turned her attention back to the article, read it a third time. The dislocation she had been feeling was gradually replaced with a deep resentment: The words seemed to have been spoon-fed by Linda, as if she alone had the right and the knowledge to describe Todd, to define him, Linda who had been with him for just a splinter of time, who had no context. Sarah began to grow angry, disputing the words in her head. She closed the page and dug out of her bag the videocassette she had made before Todd left for Florida. Only last night, watching it again, did Sarah see shadows beneath his eyes, deep circles of gray sinking into his cheeks as he showed his drawings to Eliza. They seemed so obvious now.

She tried to remember why she had made the video that night, rooting about for a premonition she hadn't had. She had made the video because she was buoyed that Todd was energized by art again, because the three of them were together, because that is what families do, because if she preserved that moment, it would make it real.

Sarah dialed the precinct house in Loudon Beach and got a hold of Brook on her first try. "Todd never disappeared for two or three days." The words rushed out, falling over each other. "I don't know where Linda got that from. Not once. Not once, and I've known him for twelve years." It did not occur to her that Brook might be working on any case other than hers, that he wouldn't be thinking of it every second.

"I can only work with the information we have," Brook replied calmly.

"Well, Linda is not your only source of information." Sarah was aware that she sounded like a jealous, bitter wife and knew that would not help her, but she could not stop herself.

"Did you make a copy of the videocassette for me?" Brook asked.

"Yes."

"All right. Well, we'll get it on the air as soon as possible." This was as conciliatory as he was willing to get.

"Can you send me the drawings you found?" Sarah asked.

"Linda has them. She has all of his personal effects. I'll tell her you'd like to see them."

There was nothing else to report, no news.

After Todd's failure to show up at the airport yesterday, the police had settled into a relatively passive waiting mode. They could not justify spending too much more of their limited resources on this particular case.

Sarah labeled the video, put it in a manila envelope, asked Maude to overnight it to the Loudon Beach Police Department, and called Peter.

"Any word from Todd?" he asked.

"I would have called you," she replied, trying not to show her frustration with his casual demeanor. "Listen, can you drive down to the house in Fort Pierce and look around? The police didn't see anything, but I'm not sure they'd know what to look for. They didn't even go inside."

"I don't think I have the key," Peter protested.

"All right," Sarah snapped, "but if we don't do something the police are just going to give up. Can't you go over to Loudon Beach and look for him?" she implored. "Check the bars, the used book stores, he loved used book stores. I'll e-mail you a recent photo of Todd. Print out posters, okay? Put them everywhere." Sarah described the blue shorts, the Nikes that the police said he was last seen in, his height and approximate weight, all the information necessary to paper the town with.

She recalled the days after the World Trade Center when every storefront and bus stop, every lamppost in her neighborhood was covered with hurriedly made posters, images of smiling men and women, caught in movement, caught in their lives, their names, their stats, their eyes everywhere. It was a city wallpapered with satellites of hope and grief. She remembered, too, how tattered and gray the sheets became in the weeks that followed, and how few of the men and women would be found.

Peter wrote down everything she said and reluctantly agreed to drive the three hours down the coast later that day.

Eventually, Sarah forced herself to pick up her notes for the Body Issue flat plan and begin writing possible stories on Post-its, arranging them on the map, moving each one numerous times, trying to get the pacing of the book just right. There was the diary of a midwestern woman's secret sex life, the best and worst take-out options from McDonald's, four real women confessing their most embarrassing health woes from vulvodynia to herpes. She added one workout story, "Walk Yourself Super Slim." Walking in any variation remained a golden cover line not just for *Flair* but for most women's magazines, as it offered the promise of weight loss without sweat or dieting. *Flair* ran it four or five times a year and lived in fear of the moment it would stop working—a negative tipping point that even the best editor had trouble predicting.

"She's setting you up."

Sarah, startled, looked up to see Paige, resplendent in a cranberry silk camisole and indigo James jeans, standing in her doorway. "Excuse me?"

"Pat. She's setting you up," Paige repeated, coming in and moving aside a stack of magazines. She glanced down at the latest *W* before dropping it on the floor, where it landed with a dull thud. "Have you ever known her not to do a flat plan herself? She's giving herself deniability."

Sarah had considered this, but despite her months at CMH, she still had a hard time believing the worst in people. "She told me she thought it would be a good learning experience. In a weird way, she was trying to help me."

Paige frowned. "Pat Nolan has never cared about anyone but herself. Rumor has it she had breakfast with William Rowling at Heartbeat today."

"I didn't know either of them ate."

"They both had oolong tea and muesli."

"You know what they ordered?"

"Of course. Listen, you need to be careful."

"I know," Sarah admitted, though there remained a part of her that didn't quite believe Pat was as manipulative as Paige made her out to be.

"There is rebellion in the ranks," Paige continued.

"Against Pat or against Rena?"

"I'd say it's split fifty-fifty, but sentiment is moving toward Pat. No one actually likes her, but the Body thing is driving everyone insane. It's not a ship people want to go down on."

"Don't you think there's a chance it could actually work?"

"Women want to look at a gorgeous model and be told that in six easy steps they can look exactly like her. The whole point is to avoid reality."

"That's incredibly depressing," Sarah remarked.

"I like to think of it as hopeful," Paige replied. "There's something so American about the belief in our own perfectibility. So. You know who else William was seen with?"

"What are you, his personal tracking committee?"

"Yeah, me and half of Manhattan." Paige paused. "Helena Armstrong."

Helena Armstrong was the youngest of three sisters known for their immense shipping inheritance, their parents' homes in New York, Paris, Parrot Cay, and Gstaad, and their penchant for dating the most eligible men, usually with titles, though William Rowling's job was passport enough. Helena was one of the new breed of heiresses who had been put on the masthead of CMH's most prestigious fashion magazine as "contributing editor." Though the title was often merely an honorific bestowed on various socialites in the hope that editors would be invited to their swanky parties, Helena took it seriously. She offered frequent, and surprisingly good story ideas, and sent lengthy e-mail updates from her various travels on trends in dress, food, and gardening. Known for her long, streaked blond hair and her impossibly thin arched eyebrows, she was gorgeous, connected, and talented.

"Rumor has it William asked her for ideas on *Flair*," Paige said.

"Are you serious?"

"Of course, he could just be sleeping with her."

Sarah smiled. William Rowling's sexuality was subject to much debate in New York. He was asexual, ambisexual, gay, or unbelievably discreet, depending on who was talking and how late in the evening it was. Regardless, no one knew anyone who had actually slept with him.

"Do you think it's true?" Sarah asked.

"Don't know. This week's newsstand figures suck, though. Our worst-selling issue in ten months."

"August is always bad."

"Not this bad." Paige shifted her legs. "We're talking *Titanic*. The only way out for us is *Splash.*"

"Paige, even if they got rid of Rena, Pat needs both of us. At least in the short run."

"That's debatable. Besides, is working for Pat Nolan really what you want to do?"

There was a long pause. "I don't want to do any of this," Sarah said, her voice flat.

Paige cringed. "I'm sorry, Sarah. Forget the whole thing. I shouldn't bother you with any of this."

"It's okay. I need this job more than ever." Seeping in and out of Sarah's mind all week was the realization that she might now be the sole support of her child.

"I don't know how you do this."

"I have no choice."

Paige nodded. "Just do me a favor," she said, rising to go. "Don't route the flat plan through Pat. Give it directly to Rena."

"All right."

Paige hovered in the doorway. "So, in the interest of leaving them laughing, do you want to hear about my latest dating disaster?"

"Absolutely." Sarah leaned forward, and if not precisely rallying, at least trying to do a convincing job of faking it.

"I went out last night with Jacob Eisenberg—you know, his company makes a lot of the premiums we send out, like those cheesy slippers with our logo we sent to advertisers last month?"

"And?"

"He brought me a cheap umbrella with his company's name on it and a novelty ice cube that was supposed to light up in a drink and didn't." Paige shook her head in wonderment. "He gave them to me after our first glass of wine. I mean, what was he going to do if he didn't like me, keep them under the table?"

Sarah laughed for the first time in a week.

"Do you have any idea how fucking depressing it is to come home from a bad date with a malfunctioning ice cube?"

"So I take it there will be no second date?"

Paige rolled her eyes. "You remember my rule about that. I do not believe in agreeing to a second date if there's little chance you're going to want a third."

"Don't you think that's a little harsh? Not everyone is at their best the first time out."

"The last time I broke that rule was with that guy from HBO. On our first date he ordered a cosmopolitan, on our second date, he had white zinfandel. On our third, we went out for coffee after dinner and he ordered a white chocolate. I realized I was dating a girl. No, thank you."

Paige left to prepare for a merch (short for merchandise) meeting, where she would present an assortment of pink-hued jars, candles, combs, and lotions for an upcoming "Everything's Coming Up Roses" product page. Representatives of the art, photo, and edit departments would descend on the display table outside of her office to choose the twelve items to be photographed. (It was always between nine and twelve for financial rather than aesthetic reasons; still-life photographers had uniformly decided this was the number of items they could shoot in one session. Ask for thirteen and you had to pay for an extra day.) Even this simple act was laden with politics; the art and photo departments chose the products strictly by appearance, the edit department by newsiness and efficacy, and

Paige tried to balance it all with the need to make sure key advertisers were represented.

For the rest of the morning, Sarah remained at her computer, working on the flat plan and reading only manuscripts that had "Rush" written on them. Every time the e-mail pinged she jumped and glanced quickly at the name of the sender. She knew any important news would come by telephone, but her nerves twitched nonetheless.

Paige's warnings bubbled close to the surface, adding to her overall anxiety. After lunch, Sarah closed her door and opened the file that held her original ideas for *Splash*. Sarah remembered being sixteen and standing at a newsstand, trying to decide whether to buy *Seventeen* or *Rolling Stone*. She had the money for both, but it seemed to her that her very identity was at stake. *Rolling Stone* was cool, it was what she *should* want, but *Seventeen* promised to divulge the secrets to being pretty, popular, confident. It did not occur to her that she could buy both, that she could *be* both. She bought *Seventeen*. She would never again believe that her identity could be defined by a single purchase but the memory remained vivid; it was that feeling she and Paige wanted to resurrect for young women.

She scanned the notes and tried to concentrate, but despite herself the obsessive tape loop, the list returned, coiling around her brain—born to an unwed teenage mother in postwar Germany, abandoned by father, moves to America, doesn't speak English—playing over and over, a repetitive pattern of pieces that refused to form a shape, to offer a clue.

When the phone rang, she instinctively buried the notes on *Splash* beneath a pile of manuscripts before answering it. It was Lucy.

"Listen," she said. "Do you remember Ned Harrison?"

"Who?"

"I did the PR for his club in Miami, Firefly? Anyway, I spoke with him last night. He's friends with one of the smartest detectives on the Miami-Dade force. I have his number. I think you should talk to him."

It was just like Lucy to know the best person to talk to in any given circumstance. Her Rolodex was the envy of a bevy of PR girls coming up, all the Pilates-toned, blond-haired junior socialites who saw giving parties as a most appealing career choice. Lucy, who was not born on Park Avenue, had built her web without the initial ties of school and parental friends to aid her. Her success stemmed from a clear-eyed outsider's view combined with a surprising lack of personal desire for climbing and an uncanny ability for matchmaking. In a city where scions and the self-made alike were insecure enough to need constant assurance that they were in the right room at the right time, it was a most useful talent.

"You think Todd is in Miami?" Sarah asked, confused.

"No. But I think you need to talk to someone besides that small-town detective. The guy's name is Jack Ellison. He's been on the force for fifteen years. He's a straight shooter, very respected. And he has no motive for believing one theory or another."

Sarah played with edges of a manuscript. "Maybe Todd and Linda plotted this whole thing to get away from me," she said quietly. "Maybe she's going to run off to meet him." The note "Get Mobile" was seared into her mind.

"I don't think he would do that to you. Or Eliza. He loved her too much for that. Todd was a lot of things, but he was never cruel. If that's what he wanted, he would have told you. Call Ellison, okay? He's expecting you."

"All right."

It took Sarah another hour to summon the energy to dial Jack Ellison's number. She was surprised when he answered the phone himself and instantly recognized her name. Sarah suspected Lucy had done more prep work than she had admitted.

"You realize I have no jurisdiction in that county?" Ellison said at the outset. "I'm happy to offer some perspective if I can, but that's as far as I can go."

"I'd appreciate anything," Sarah replied.

"Okay. Start from the beginning."

Sarah recounted everything she could remember: Linda, the

missing days before she called the police, the drawings and sculpture the police had found, Brook's initial assumption of suicide and his current unshakable conviction that Todd had planned his own disappearance.

Ellison asked few questions, letting Sarah finish before he spoke.

"I obviously haven't spoken to the people involved and I do not believe in second-guessing my colleagues," he began, "but it does sound as if Brook is taking the easy way out. No one likes a missing body on their record. It's simpler to say he left the state. I know someone who used to be on the Loudon Beach force, Karl Medford. He left about six months ago to go out as a private investigator. He's a good man. Thorough. A little hungry. He knows Brook and he has excellent contacts in the county. He can help you more than I can. Would you like his number?"

"Yes."

Sarah scribbled it down and thanked Ellison.

"I'm sorry I can't be of more help," he said. "But I will tell you this. Brook is wrong about at least one thing."

"What?"

"Bodies disappear in the ocean all the time."

Six

The next morning, Sarah stared at herself in the mirror. Her face was becoming unrecognizable, sunken. Exhaustion wrote new lines about her mouth, left deep blue half-moons beneath her eyes. She diligently applied a thick concealer designed to camouflage scars and postsurgical healing, but the shadows remained stubbornly visible beneath the veil of makeup.

When she got to work, she found an e-mail that Rena had sent at 5:45 a.m. In the subject line she had written "Plan for Happiness." The body of the e-mail itself consisted of just three words: "Think about it." There was nothing else, no direction. Sarah wondered whether Rena meant this as personal advice for her alone or if she was supposed to come up with an actual plan, a concrete five-step program that would guarantee readers a lifetime of joy. Rena was convinced that happiness, like depression, spirituality, and irony before it, was the next big trend. It not only peppered her middle-of-the-night e-mails, but she began art meetings with it as a general edict for all photos, even those that were meant to illustrate stories on a parent dying or how to stop regret from ruining your life. "Happy smiling girl," Rena insisted. "I want to see a happy smiling girl."

Sarah forwarded the e-mail to Paige with a question mark and, though she had left two messages for him the night before, dialed Karl Medford's number again. This time, he answered. She introduced herself and explained that she had gotten his name from Jack Ellison.

"How is Jack doing?" Medford asked.

"Fine," Sarah said, though she had no idea, he was a stranger after all.

"He's a great guy. Well, how can I help you?"

The idea that there was even the potential for help was the first encouraging thing Sarah had heard in days, and she felt the weight within if not lift at least shift a little, making room for a sliver of optimism.

She began to lay out the events of the past week, speaking as matter-of-factly as she could, reticent to appear too emotional, as if that would deter him from believing her narrative.

"Tell me about your husband," Medford prompted gently.

Sarah spoke of Todd's essential goodness, his love of his child, his overriding belief in the transformative power of art, veering from Eliza's birth and his early success to his last fruitless solo show in New York and the recent drawings.

Like a doctor used to viewing the messiest of human functions without a change of expression, Medford listened patiently. "What is this Linda like?" he asked when she was done.

Sarah made a guttural sound laced with distaste and frustration. "Doesn't the fact that she waited four days to call the police tell you something?"

"Yes," he agreed. "But I don't know precisely what yet. You say she has the drawings and the rest of your husband's things?" he asked.

"Yes."

"Well, I'll need to see everything. Your husband's address book, his wallet. Whatever he left behind."

"I'll leave a message for her." Sarah stopped. "Does this mean you'll work on this?"

"If you'd like."

"Yes, absolutely," she answered, relieved.

Medford outlined his fee structure and Sarah quickly agreed, promising to overnight him a check for the $1,000 retainer.

She gave him Linda's number, Victor's number, Peter's number.

"I'll start with them," Medford told her. "In the meantime, I'll call Brook and swing by there to get a copy of the initial police report and see what I can learn about their progress."

Perhaps it was because she would be paying him, but Sarah immediately felt that Medford was on her side—for there were sides now, hers, Brook's, Linda's. At the very least she did not believe that he would automatically trust the authenticity of Linda's word over hers.

"Will Brook cooperate?" she asked.

"Up to a point. He may not like it, but there is still some professional courtesy down here. Sarah, there's one thing I need to know before we begin, though."

"Yes?"

"What is it precisely you expect to find out?"

There was a long pause. Sarah no longer knew what to hope for. "I just want to know what happened that night," she said simply.

"All right."

They agreed that he would call her the following afternoon with an update. Unless, of course, there was a reason to call sooner.

Sarah hung up, thankful to finally have an ally, a professional emissary who would know what to do, where to look, whom to talk to—someone with a strategy, as if that in itself could somehow keep Todd alive.

She forced her attention to the flat plan she had been working on the night before, making carefully annotated lists of possible stories for each section. She could no longer trust even the most immediate thought not to dissipate before it took hold; she was never wholly involved in what she was doing, never truly present. She had begun to devise ways to compensate for her lack of focus, for the black holes in her concentration and thinking process, as one in the very early stages of Alzheimer's must do. She made lists for everything: wash hair, brush teeth, buy milk, design magazine, it all seemed to carry equal weight. Still, things were fraying around the edges—she had to dump the laundry out on the hallway floor this morning to find an outfit for

Eliza, there was nothing for her lunch box but a Luna bar and some barbecue potato chips, she hadn't opened the mail in days.

By midafternoon, Sarah was ready to put her final draft in Rena's ornately carved in-box. Knowing that the proper procedure would have been to route it through the executive editor, she waited until she saw Pat head out for a meeting, ostrich notebook in hand, before walking it down the hallway. If caught, her only recourse would have been to feign ignorance, in which case she would look like a liar or a fool. Not tempered as Paige was by years in CMH's offices, where voices were rarely raised but words just as rarely meant what they appeared to, Sarah was not fully convinced that Pat was as devious as Paige believed, but she wasn't willing to take that chance. Though she still took most exchanges at face value, she was beginning to wonder if her own naïveté was not just a liability but a blind spot in her intellect.

It took Rena less than an hour to call her into her office.

Sarah entered with some trepidation. The late-afternoon light created a harsh glare, landing on walls covered with a vast new collage of glossy pictures: bikini-clad girls happily eating ice cream on the beach, jumping happily into the air on impossibly verdant lawns in Palm Beach, Bali, Greece, happily running arm in arm, the muscles of their endless legs perfectly defined, all forever young and tanned, the scent of the sun, the salt air tangible in their seductively mussed hair.

Rena walked around to the front of her desk, leaned against it, and paused. Like all good poker players, she was a master of timing. Her long hair was pulled up indiscriminately and strands, escaping from an approximation of a bun, fell down her pink oxford shirt like dried-up streams. Her face looked slightly puffy, but when she smiled, it creased pleasantly and her pale lips turned up. There remained something overwhelmingly welcoming about Rena, and if it seemed at times contrived, it worked nonetheless. It would have taken great willpower to resist her when she took you in as hers. Sarah fidgeted nervously, anxious for Rena's approval.

"How are you?" Rena asked, and for a moment she was not quite

Sarah's boss, not quite her mother, not quite her friend, but an amalgam of all three. "Are you okay?'

"I'm hanging in there," Sarah assured her.

"Any news?"

"No. Not really."

"Do you need some time off?" There was something beyond mere concern in her voice, something probing.

"I'm all right."

Rena studied her, appraising, then nodded. "Well, you did a good job with the flat plan," she said. "I liked the cover lines, I liked the pacing. I'm a little confused, though. Where are Pat's notes on it?"

Sarah answered a beat too quickly. "She said you needed it right away. She had a meeting and didn't want to slow things down. She'll go over it later."

Rena absorbed this without expression. "I had requested two versions, one with the front of the book keyed to the Body theme and another where it was standard issue news and items."

"I'm sorry. Pat didn't tell me that."

"Really? She assured me you were working on two. I'm sure you're distracted," Rena said.

"I'll redo it," Sarah offered.

Rena nodded. "I've been thinking," she continued, her tone a blend of intimacy and intent, "about that idea—what was it called, *Splash*?—that you and Paige were working on? Maybe you could do up a few pages. You know, a mission statement, a table of contents."

Something in Sarah kick-started into motion, not quite excitement—she no longer had the reserves for that—but an undeniable interest. It came closer to pulling her into the present, away from the waiting, imagining, dreading, than anything had so far. "Sure. Absolutely."

Rena smiled, her goal accomplished.

Sarah called Paige as soon as she got back to her office. "She wants us to work on *Splash.*"

"You're kidding me. Does that mean the Body Issue is off?"

"No. And I need to redo the flat plan. Pat conveniently forgot to tell me Rena wanted two versions."

"Talk about killing two birds with one stone. She managed to make you look bad and take no responsibility for the issue at the same time."

"Thanks. You don't have to sound so impressed by her, though."

"I'm not impressed. I'm fucking terrified. If only she would use her powers for good, not evil."

"I'm beginning to think you're right."

"Listen, Sarah, don't count on anything with either of them. They could decide at any moment that their best chance is to stick together. Enemies can turn into partners in the span of an elevator ride in this building. Let's be sure to keep everything about *Splash* just between us, okay? Don't leave it lying about. Make sure to lock your office at night."

"Don't you think that's a little paranoid?"

"Actually, no." Rumors about Pat had followed her from the past company she had worked at, whispered stories about how she had read a rival's appointment diary and used it against her. Or had she gotten an editor's e-mail password and forwarded damaging missives to her higher-ups?

Sarah agreed to keep *Splash* under wraps.

She spent the rest of the day redoing the flat plan. There was no time to think about a mission statement for a new magazine, and when Paige asked if she would be willing to stay late to work on it, Sarah said no. Like a cat, Eliza could sense when Sarah was due to return home and, her ears cocked, her body tensed, she relaxed only when she heard the key in the door. There were no guarantees, after all. Aware of this, Sarah was scrupulous about being on time, attempting to provide an illusion of normalcy, a safety net they both knew did not in truth exist.

"All right," Paige said. "I'll do what I can, then show it to you."

"I'll try to work on it after Eliza goes to sleep."

They agreed to come in early the next morning and compare notes.

Sarah was just shutting off her computer for the night when Karl Medford called.

"Sarah? I'm glad I got you."

Her blood quickened; he had news already.

"I called the coast guard," he said. "Frank Dupree, the chief officer, told me that if Todd had gone into the water at midnight, as the timeline of events would suggest, he would only have had to swim out one hundred yards for the tides to carry him to sea. Even if he had wanted to, it would have been hard for him to turn around if he was as inebriated as it appears he might have been."

"Did you tell Brook?"

"Yes, but he refuses to believe it."

"That Todd went to the ocean or that there wouldn't necessarily be a body if he had?"

"Both. But just because Brook's never seen it happen doesn't mean it can't. The coast guard is unequivocal on this. Look, Sarah, I know Brook. He's not a bad man, but he's like a scientist who begins his exploration with a thesis already decided upon and ignores all lab results that don't support it. He's playing the odds, making assumptions based on past experience, and that," Medford continued, "is a dangerous mistake when it comes to human behavior. I got a copy of the police report and though it's obviously inconclusive, Brook can't deny the initial impression of his own men." He took a deep breath. "Linda has agreed to meet with me tomorrow. In the meantime, I can fax you a copy of the tidal charts if you'd like."

Sarah hung up and went to stand guard by the fax machine, her eyes focused on its display panel. People passing by on their way out for the night glanced over at her with poorly concealed curiosity. Surely something must be happening if she was at the fax machine herself, a task best left for assistants.

When the single page arrived, Sarah grabbed it and hurried back to her office. The graph of the ocean's hourly ebbs and flows looked surprisingly like an echocardiogram. She traced the inky hills and valleys with her fingertip, imagining the waves, the undertow, the water so meticulously charted and yet so inscrutable. She wondered at which dip or rise Todd had entered, which was the one that had swallowed him up; she wondered if he had tried to turn back, if he felt fear, panic, regret, wondered if, in the last moments, there was consciousness.

She wondered, incessantly, what his last thoughts were.

At home, Sarah went through the motions of making dinner, watching Eliza methodically push her corn kernels away from the pasta, rescuing them from contamination by tomato sauce. Afterward, she ran a bath and watched her poke holes through the white glossy bubbles. She sat on the closed toilet, her chin resting in the palms of her hands, at once hypervigilant of her daughter, searching for any bruises that might have appeared like stigmata on her tender flesh, and absent. She glanced at her watch repeatedly, waiting for the moment she could turn out the lights in her daughter's room and be free to indulge in her own ruminations.

At eight-thirty, she climbed into bed beside Eliza and lay on the soft powder-blue quilt, a slice of their skin touching. It was in this pocket of time, the lights out, a thread of heat connecting their bodies, that Eliza said things that she would not at any other point in the day, opening herself up to her mother in the dark. Now, though, Eliza's legs flailed like the blades of a helicopter that had become detached, carving concentric circles into the air as she asked for news of her father.

"I'm doing everything I can," Sarah assured her. "I hired somebody to help find out what happened to Daddy. His name is Karl."

"Will he talk to the children? Children see things grown-ups don't."

"Yes," Sarah said. "He'll talk to the children."

"And check Linda's house?"

Sarah squirmed uncomfortably. She had told Eliza only that Todd had been staying at a friend's named Linda. "Yes, sweetie, he's going to Linda's house tomorrow."

"Daddy could have gone back there." Eliza's legs shook as if her body could not contain the thoughts it was being asked to absorb. "Tell him to look in the closets."

Sarah rested her arms on Eliza's legs and gently brought them down to earth. "I will."

They lay in silence for a few minutes.

"My mind thinks crazy things about what might have happened," Eliza said quietly.

"What kind of things?"

But Eliza would not go into details. She hoarded certain thoughts, keeping them private with her memories and her growing list of grievances. "Do you think it was a land accident or a water accident?" she asked. "Yesterday I thought it was water, but today I think land."

"I don't know, honey. Probably water."

"Why would Daddy go swimming at night?"

"He didn't realize how dangerous it was. I think it was a red flag day, but the flags were down for the night."

Eliza listened closely.

"When I was at camp today my mind was normal," she said. "I think I need activity to control my mind."

Sarah stared down at her daughter, surprised by her insight. But just as quickly Eliza receded into childhood, pulling Snowball to her chest, the white fur matted from years of being clutched tight.

Todd had bought the stuffed animal for Eliza when Sarah was seven months pregnant. They were in Macy's choosing a baby gift for friends when he spotted the toy and remarked on how cute it was. Sarah nodded absentmindedly and they got on the escalator to leave when suddenly Todd turned around and climbed up the descending steps. He was grinning almost shyly when he returned with it, the first gift he bought his daughter. For the next six years, he continued to bring home overpriced plush animals and handmade European toys, museum pop-up books and professional watercolor sets. His goal was not to spoil her or assuage a guilt he did not feel; his gifts were born of a deep and pure delight, and a generous enthusiasm to share it. Sarah, more practical, often got annoyed, scolding him for spending money when they had yet to start a college fund. But she was glad now that Eliza had these things.

There were some things he had decided not to give her, though. Todd had a vast collection of fairy tales from various cultures in his studio, and he was particularly fascinated by the Grimm renditions of his youth in Germany, the harsh dismemberments and deaths, the hopelessly lost and terrified children, the missing parents, the random cruelty visited on the most innocent, all told in a stark language that was absent from the children's books on Eliza's shelf. He had thought when she was an infant that he would introduce them to her, but as she grew into herself and her vulnerability became imprinted on his own skin, he decided otherwise. Instead, he gave her his memories of his early years in Dortmund. Eliza loved to hear about the way sacks of potatoes were delivered to his door along with milk, about the boat that brought him to America and his first sight of the Statue of Liberty on a gray, rainy dawn. These memories were rooted within her now and Sarah was thankful for that gift, too.

There was one memory of Germany that Todd told only to Sarah: his first dead person. When the woman who lived on the third floor of their small apartment building died, she lay in bed and all the neighbors went to visit her. He remembered her hard, pale skin, her carefully arranged thinning hair, her fingers with the blue veins rising up off the stiffened bones. "They hide death here," he remarked. Though when his own mother died, he refused to look in her open coffin, terrified of fainting in public, a habit he had acquired someplace along the road.

After Eliza fell asleep, Sarah sneaked back into her daughter's room and carefully took the pink plastic journal from her desk drawer. She tiptoed out and, sitting on her own bed, opened it to the latest entry, written the day before. Eliza, in a her large, childish hand, listed various theories of what might have happened to her father: a poisonous bird bit him, a car hit him and he was in gooey bits on the side of the road, he lay drowned in a swimming pool filled with blood.

"Daddy was my favorite family member," Eliza wrote in slanted block letters. "How could this happen???"

Sarah slept with her daughter's raw lament ricocheting through her skull, weaving around her organs, an unanswered cry in the night.

Seven

It was 5:00 p.m. the next day before Sarah heard from Karl Medford.

"How are you?" he asked.

She had no idea how to answer. How were you supposed to be doing in a situation like this? What was the bar? She was at work, her daughter was dressed, fed, at camp; she assumed these were signs that she was okay. Still, she feared that at any second she would collapse to the ground, a scream without end escaping.

"I don't know," Sarah admitted. "Did you see Linda?"

"Yes. I went to her house this morning."

"And?" Her voice was guarded, cautious. What she really wanted to ask was: Is she prettier than me, smarter than me, what was the spell she had on my husband?

"She's a cool customer, but she is not acting like a woman with something to hide. I pressed her pretty hard and she didn't waiver on her story. If she knows something she's not admitting, she's damn good at hiding it. I believe she is truly convinced Todd is alive. Whether that's due to some unconscious denial about playing a part in a potential suicide or because she has information she's not sharing remains to be seen."

"Did you see the garage where he left his things?"

"Yes. I spent a good deal of time poking around there. Everything looks as if he left abruptly with the idea of returning. His lighter was sitting on the desk, there was a sculpture he was designing laid out on the floor. His CDs, his tools, everything was all there. Whatever happened, it doesn't look to me like he planned it."

Sarah listening silently as Medford listed the accoutrements of Todd's life, all signs that he was putting down a stake there, with Linda, away from her.

"I didn't see any note, any statement of intent," Medford continued. His words, his modulated rhythm, remained those of a detective creating a cool distance between himself and the events he was describing.

"What about the drawings?"

"Well, like the police said, one seems to say *Lonely Head, Dead* and the other *Drowned,* but I'm not really sure. There appear to be other words scratched out, covered up. Maybe some numbers. It's hard to tell if they are actual words or just scrawls, some kind of design. I can't make them out. I don't know his previous work, so I don't have a context to put them in. Maybe you'll have better luck."

There were times when Sarah had felt Todd's work echoing within her. Just before Eliza was born, he had made a piece called *Sleep,* an oblong upside U with tendrils falling and curving down that perfectly captured those few moments of half-reality when thoughts dissipate into dreams. During the first months of Eliza's life, Sarah would rock her at three, four in the morning, exhausted beyond words, and picture that sculpture, concentrate on it, believing that if she could somehow impart the image into Eliza's brain, it would lull her into sleep.

There were other instances, though, when she did not comprehend what he was after, could not parse the oblique language of abstraction. Sometimes she admitted that to Todd, sometimes she merely nodded as if she understood.

"I'll FedEx the drawings to you," Medford said. "I also have his wallet and his address book. If it's all right with you, I'll make photocopies of the address book. I began to go through it and call some of the names, but I still have a way to go. By the way, are you familiar with a Dr. Carlin?"

"No. Who is he?"

"His name was in the address book, so I gave him a call. Turns out he's a psychiatrist in New York. Todd went to see him about six weeks ago."

"Todd went to a psychiatrist?" Sarah was shocked. He hated the idea of therapy, and all during the last year when she had been begging him to get help he had refused.

"Carlin said he only saw Todd once and that his presenting complaint was insomnia. He said Todd was blaming himself for the breakup of the marriage."

"How can he tell you all this? What about doctor-patient confidentiality?"

Medford paused. "Well, when there is the possibility of death . . ."

"Oh."

"Carlin did say that he thought Todd was a little manic, a bit of a whirlwind, but he made no mention of suicide. He didn't show up for his next appointment."

"Did he talk about Linda?"

"No."

There was no small satisfaction in this.

"I spoke to a few other people," Medford said, "just working through the alphabet, but so far no one has heard from him. One good thing came out of my visit with Linda, though."

"What's that?"

"I asked if she'd be willing to take a lie detector test and she said yes. Brook is going to give her a voice stress analyzer, which is basically the same thing."

"I'm surprised she agreed to that."

"She resents the innuendos. Like I said, she is convinced Todd will return."

Sarah, alone in her office a thousand miles away, said nothing.

"I don't know how much information Brook will share about the results," Medford added.

"Will you call me as soon as you hear?"

"Of course. It might not take place for a couple of days, though. In the meantime, I'll put all of Todd's things in the mail. There's a chance you'll see something in them that I wouldn't recognize as a clue."

When Sarah got home that night, Eliza stuck her head out of her bedroom, stared at her, and then promptly slammed the door shut with all her might. Whenever Sarah tried to touch her, to gently move a strand of hair off her face, to lean over and kiss the soft spot on her forearm just below her elbow, Eliza flinched as if in pain and pushed her mother forcefully away. She would not allow any form of comfort, and Sarah realized as she looked over at the anger contorting her daughter's face that they had entered a new stage. They did not talk of Medford that night. They lay side by side in the dark until Eliza's eyes finally fluttered shut. Only then did Sarah gently lean over to kiss her, deeply nostalgic for the little girl she used to be.

The phone rang an hour later, just as Sarah was climbing into bed herself. It was Harry DeVeres, an artist who had shown at the same SoHo gallery as Todd. The two men had been occasional drinking buddies in their heady early days, sharing the exhilaration as well as the discomfort of being the lucky ones who were getting solo shows, racking up important sales, when most of those they had started out with were still putting up Sheetrock and wondering if it would ever happen for them. Harry had married a woman with a sizable inheritance and ten acres of land in Rhinebeck, where they had moved three years ago. Sarah hadn't thought of him for years; he had only been resurrected by a call from Medford.

Harry was a large man, over six feet tall and stocky, given to great torrents of enthusiasm—for food, for wine, for art, for people. Sarah remembered a night early in her relationship with Todd when they all had dinner in her apartment and the two men argued about the recent Whitney Biennial for hours while Sarah listened, happy to have found the life she had wanted—passion and art and intellect all rolled into one.

"I told him to stop drinking," Harry said. "I told him ninety percent of all alcoholics die drunk."

There was frustration in his voice, and heartbreak, but it was laced with self-righteousness.

Harry's latest enthusiasm was for twelve-step programs; he had recently decided he had adult ADHD, along with incipient alcoholism, and he attended meetings six times a week, steeped in the language of confession and redemption.

"When was the last time you spoke to Todd?" Sarah asked.

"We talked on and off during the last year. I wish he had told me how bad off he really was," Harry said.

"Did he say anything at all?" she asked.

"He was mentioning this woman in Florida a lot. He seemed to feel a strong attraction to her. At one point, he talked about moving down there, starting over. The last time we spoke he said something about maybe driving cross-country with her."

Sarah's heart constricted. What world had she been living in? "What else did he say about her?"

"Just that they talked a lot. That they'd had a real connection when they were younger. He wondered what would have happened if they'd stayed together."

"Some fucking connection," Sarah muttered.

"What?"

"Never mind. Go on."

"He said that she was the only woman who'd ever truly accepted him as he was. I think they both had this romance with being outsiders."

"That's why he left Florida the first time. He wanted a different kind of life, a career, a family."

She was arguing a case, but not with Harry, not really.

"Look, Sarah, he knew that. He was just tired of what it took to keep it all going. With Linda, he didn't have to hold up any of those balls. She didn't expect as much from him. I figured it was just something he had to get out of his system, kind of like a vacation from the rest of his life. I wish I knew how bad off he was," Harry repeated. "I could have helped him."

Lurking beneath his conviction was an unspoken condemnation—you did not understand him, you did not help him, you did not save him.

Sarah got off the phone as quickly as possible, fury racing through her, crackling, electric, absolute, at Todd, at Harry, at Linda, at all the people who thought they could have helped Todd, changed him when she could not, at her own blindness. All the last year when she had wanted only to reach him, he had been confiding in everyone but her.

One night a few weeks before he moved out, she put Eliza to bed and went into the kitchen where Todd was cooking Caribbean chicken breasts.

"What do you want?" she asked quietly. It wasn't a demand, she was genuinely curious.

"For you to leave me alone," he replied, turning only partially to her.

It was the most honest answer he could give. She remembered that when they were first married, he would ring the intercom to her apartment, *their* apartment now, from downstairs rather than use his key, such a basic part of joining unnatural and fraught for him.

"How can I completely leave you alone? We're married," she said as he added more lime juice to the sauce.

"I don't ask anything of anyone," he answered. And he didn't. He seemed to live in an alternate universe, where the most basic obligations of relationships were alien. This is what his childhood had done to him.

"I ask for a damn lot less than any other woman would have," she replied angrily.

He turned to her with mocking disbelief. "You ask for so little? Are you out of your mind?"

"I got a job so we could survive," she hissed.

"Who asked you to?" he retorted.

No one, she thought. No one asked me to. And no one told me not to.

They stared at each other with mounting frustration, each feeling righteous, misunderstood, resentful.

Todd slammed the spoon he had been holding down. "I've had it," he said, and stormed out.

Sarah watched the boiling sauce furiously coat the edges of the pan.

"Mommy." She heard Eliza's voice calling from bed. "I need a snuggle."

She took a deep breath and went into Eliza's darkened room.

"I thought you were asleep." Sarah lay down beside her. "Did you hear Daddy and me arguing?"

"No."

The two lay in silence for a while. "Honey, I know it can be upsetting when Daddy and I fight. But you know we both love you."

"Why do you always have to tell me that?"

"Because it's true."

When she felt Eliza's breath begin to grow heavy and regular, she went back to the kitchen where the ingredients of the uneaten dinner lay about the counters and began wearily to clean up.

Two hours later Todd came home smelling of smoke and beer. His eyes had the glazed, slightly out-of-focus look they got when he was drunk. He found Sarah in bed. "I'm sorry," he said. "I overreacted." He sat down beside her. "I was out of line. I love you."

She nodded. "Do you know what I want?" she asked quietly.

"What?"

"For you to get help." She had never said it so simply, so directly before.

He moved out one month later.

Sarah got up suddenly and stormed down the hall to the front closet where so many of Todd's things remained, a suit jacket, a raincoat, some random CDs. She gathered them up in heaping armfuls and carried them out to the hallway, jamming them down the trash compactor and letting the metal door slam loudly shut.

She went through his closet, grabbing jeans, a khaki linen shirt he had worn to a dinner party just before they separated, stray papers, tax receipts. An old wool scarf fell from the pile and she tripped on it, landing hard on the parquet floor. Tears burned her eyes as she rose, picked up the pile, and carried it out to the compactor. After each trip she rushed back and searched for anything that he had worn, touched, anything that was his.

The living room was next. Todd had a great love of used book stores, spending hours in them looking for hidden treasures. Sarah tore his books off the shelves, tattered paperbacks of esoteric Greek poets, the collected works of Isaac Bashevis Singer, an oversize book on Louise Bourgeois, his large sampling of South African detective novels, and filled bag after bag.

By two in the morning she had slid eleven bags out to the hallway for dumping.

It was close to dawn when she finally fell into bed, spent.

But she did not feel purged. There were too many things she could not rid herself of: anger, hurt, doubt, love that had grown twisted like the metal pieces of Todd's sculpture.

Eight

Bleary-eyed, Sarah was stepping out of the elevator on the fourth floor of the CMH building the next morning, her head down, when she banged headlong into a man's chest. She looked up, startled.

"Did your husband make those?"

William Rowling looked down at her, his handsome face impassive, a strange mix of childlike curiosity and irony. He motioned to her bracelets.

"Yes."

William regarded them for another moment, then cocked his expensively tousled head.

"Talented." The single word was at once an observation and a benediction.

Sarah had no idea how he knew about Todd and whether this information stopped at his sculpture or encompassed the events of the last few weeks. William famously prided himself on learning everything that went on in the great glass building that he had championed, and he let just enough of a nugget out every now and then to let people know that he knew. This went a long way to enhancing the air of paranoia that filtered through the vents.

A movement caught Sarah's eye and she looked through the glass doors to see Pat watching them.

She looked back to William, but his soft gray eyes, distracted, searching, always searching, were already elsewhere as he stepped into the elevator that would carry him up to the ninth floor. He took his place diffidently among the most beautifully dressed women in the world, who were suddenly lashed with insecurity over their choice of designer, of shoes, of lipstick.

Pat said hello to Sarah as she came in and fell in step beside her. "How are you doing?"

"Fine."

"Good. Will you have that story on the food pyramid later today?" she asked.

"Definitely." Sarah knew this would be a stretch. She had taken a chance on a new writer who had turned in four thousand words of scientific gibberish. She had tried to make clear that his job was to sort through the research and tell women precisely what they needed to eat to lose weight and lower their risk of cancer—no one had ever lost money doing that—not give them a detailed explanation of the role of amino acids in digestion, but clearly he hadn't heard her. The worst mistakes often came from new writers trying to impress editors with their command of a topic.

They paused outside Pat's office. "Can I take you to lunch today?" she asked.

Sarah had no choice but to agree, though she hated going out to lunch in general, now more than ever, particularly with Pat.

Pat nodded, mission accomplished, and turned away from her.

Inside her own office Sarah put her bag down, checked her e-mail, and then walked over to Paige's. She moved aside a needlepoint pillow to sit in the pink director's chair facing her desk.

Sarah fiddled with the lid of an iridescent concealer while Paige finished up a phone call. "Pat wants to take me out to lunch," she said as soon as Paige hung up.

"Did she give you a reason?"

"No, but I'm sure she has one."

"I'm sure she has many," Paige replied dryly. "That woman doesn't pee without an ulterior motive. Well, look at it as dating."

"You look at everything as dating."

"Jobs, men, it's all courtship and rejection in the end," she remarked. "My point is that you should listen, gather information, and offer up as little as possible."

"Is that your dating technique?"

"Probably why I'm still single," Paige admitted, smiling. "Seriously, she's obviously threatened by you."

Sarah, wrung out, adrift, could not imagine anyone being threatened in any way by her. "That's pathetic."

"No, it's not. Among other things, Rena likes you."

"She wants Rena fired."

"Yes. But what if she fails? She's covering her bases. And you need to do the same."

"Do you think she knows that Rena asked us to work on *Splash*?"

"Well, Rena certainly wouldn't have told her. That doesn't mean she didn't find out some other way, though. Regardless, don't say anything about it."

Sarah got little work done for the rest of the morning. She moved around some papers, answered a few e-mails, and glanced at her watch every fifteen minutes. There was a good chance that what Pat wanted to talk to her about was the general realization that she was doing no work, that she was, in essence, faking it. Maybe she would be the body they offered up. Rena, who hated confrontation, was notorious for letting other people do the firing for her.

At twelve-thirty, Sarah met Pat at a discreet Japanese restaurant in midtown, a hushed place with taupe carpets and tables placed luxuriously far apart, frequented by Japanese businessmen on expense accounts. It was better than the Harvard Club, with its oversize portraits and dreadful food, where Pat took all new senior editors during their first week, unleashing a well-rehearsed speech as they walked past tables of middle-aged white men. "This is to remind you that, despite the preponderance of women in publishing, men still rule the world." Pat, who was political only about her own career and had gained access to the club through marriage, probably liked it more than she cared to show. If she resented the fact that men did still rule the world, she certainly wanted to be in the room with them. It was, to say the least, a mixed message.

After they ordered assorted seaweed salads and sashimi (Sarah suspected that Pat feared that the small amounts of rice in sushi contained too many carbohydrates), Pat leaned over and asked how Sarah's progress on the Body Issue was going.

"Fine. I handed the flat plan in to Rena. Both versions," Sarah added pointedly.

Pat did not acknowledge the barb. "Good. I told her I thought you were ready to handle it."

"Thank you."

Pat nodded. "So. How do you know William?" she asked, careful not to display an inordinate amount of curiosity.

"I don't."

"Really? I thought I saw you talking to him this morning."

"He was asking about my bracelets."

"Ah." Pat clearly did not believe anything could be as simple as that, but she let it go.

When their sashimi arrived, she picked up each piece of glistening yellowtail and examined it for hidden fat before placing it carefully in her mouth. When she finished chewing, she put her burnished chopsticks down. "You know that I think Rena is brilliant, but"—she paused and glanced over at Sarah—"I am beginning to wonder if this special issue will hurt us in the long run." She emphasized the word *us,* pulling Sarah into her orbit, colleagues, comrades.

"What do you mean?" Sarah asked carefully. Though she suspected the same thing, it made her uncomfortable to hear her own doubts coming out of Pat's mouth.

"Publishing is a business," Pat said. "People coming up today acknowledge that. In this age of consolidation, no one is as tolerant of titles that continue to lose money as they used to be. Yes, there is room for brilliant personalities, and every successful title has to some degree reflected the obsessions of its editor. But editors must also have commercial instincts. Maybe one story on the average woman would be commendable, but an entire issue . . ." She did not finish the sentence. "I've never been a big fan of themed issues, anyway. How many stories does anyone want to read on a single topic? Readers lose interest." Pat, who was a master at never going on record, had rarely been so open. She paused while the waiter cleared the plates, then leaned forward. "What do you think?" She seemed to expect some kind of commitment from Sarah, though commitment to what, for what, remained hazy. Regardless, this was obviously the moment when Sarah was expected to choose sides.

Sarah wanted only to run from the table. She knew that much of what Pat said was true, but it only made her dislike her more.

"I don't know," she said. "Maybe we can tweak it as we go to make it more viable."

Pat ignored this. "By the way, I've heard from good sources that Rena is in talks to become the creative director of a cosmetics firm."

Sarah looked at her quizzically. It was the only rumor she hadn't heard recently, and she did not believe Rena would willingly leave CMH. She used to joke that she would have to be carried out on her desk. Then again, many editors crossed over to fashion or cosmetics companies, tripling their income even as it lessened their prestige.

"You know, if Rena ever decided to move on and I . . . well, you would make a terrific executive editor," Pat said. She looked at Sarah with her piercing eyes for a beat too long. She was still waiting for something from Sarah, an acknowledgment, an affirmation, a pledge. Sarah nodded slightly but remained silent.

Pat paid the check with her corporate card and the two women walked out onto the midtown street, their eyes blinking in the bright sun. "I need to stop by Anna's office on my way in," Pat said. "Why don't you come with me?"

Anna Huffington, the publisher of *Flair,* had an enormous office three flights up from where *Flair*'s editorial side was housed. Though historically the lines between publishers, who sold the ads and oversaw the P&Ls, and editors, who created the content, were supposed to be those of church and state, they had grown ever more porous in recent years. The advent of shopping magazines, the increasing willingness of pharmaceutical, cosmetics, and fashion firms to yank ads out of an issue if they didn't like the edit, and their habit of counting up the number of times their products were mentioned in stories to determine how many pages of advertising they would buy had blurred the lines and led to the unstated—but undeniable—corporate mandate that publishers and editors cooperate more than ever. How deep that cooperation went was a closely held secret, especially among editors who had for years operated under the antiquated notion that there was a certain pride to be found in saying no to publishers' more odious commercial requests. Still, if an editor wanted to run an article on how eating too much meat was detrimental to your health, she would likely have to talk it over with the publisher to decide whether it was worth losing the tens of thousands of dollars' worth of ads from the Beef Council of America. (Editors did not like to 'fess up to this new twist in decision making, even among themselves on wine-soaked nights.) Nevertheless, CMH still housed their editors and publishers on separate floors, a message that, like so many things in the building, involved more show than substance. Then again, it was a company that had made billions on the conviction that show *was* substance.

Anna was on the phone when Pat and Sarah arrived, but she motioned for them to enter while she continued talking in her perfectly modulated prep-school voice. Anna hated one thing above all else—silence. When she developed bursitis in her left shoulder from too many hours spent cradling the phone receiver, she got a headset for both her office and cell phone and, like a secret service agent's, it was now permanently attached to her head. In her late thirties, given to dramatic silver jewelry and oversize cashmere shawls, she had preternaturally white skin, carefully tinted blond chin-length hair that grew lighter every year, a distinctly musky perfume that entered the room before she did, and a recent dose of Botox that had not relaxed enough yet and gave her a wide-eyed look that on a child might have appeared innocent but was merely disconcerting on her. Pat and Sarah waited while Anna fired off sentences into the phone.

"I'll get the recent MRIs," she promised. "You're going to be pleasantly surprised. Our age dropped point-five years and our household income rose two thousand dollars. I understand your reservations, but what's a few months of newsstand dips compared to that?" If editors tended to be grown-up versions of the kids in the back of the class who observed everything and offered up a running commentary, publishers were fast-talking masters of spin convinced above all of the power of their own likability. There were never problems, there were "challenges." There was never a slump in ad sales, just a "timing issue."

"All right, yes. Love you, too," Anna said.

She hung up the phone and focused her large blue eyes on Sarah. "I'm so sorry about your husband." There was an intensity to her concern that touched Sarah even as she distrusted it. "How is your daughter? Eliza is six?"

"Yes. She's all right."

Anna shook her head sympathetically. Like many of her colleagues, she was both sentimental and tough, and it was hard to tell which emotion was the most genuine at any given moment. Her eyes welled up at any story involving children, she gave lavish gifts to friends and employees, she prided herself on her ability to offer successful dating strategies to the more junior members of her staff. (Plotting a courtship with a man was really not that different from wrangling a commitment from an advertiser, which was surely why the young women in sales tended to marry earlier, and better, than those on the edit side.) Whether her acts of generosity were genuine or strategic was impossible to discern.

"So hard," she said, "so hard. You know if there's anything I can do . . ."

"Thank you."

Anna nodded, moving on. "I appreciate you coming by. I know this is the last thing on your mind, but you do seem to have Rena's ear."

Sarah was beginning to sense the setup. "I know she really respects you, too," she offered in return.

Anna shrugged this off. She and Rena had a polite if distant relationship that was getting more polite as it was getting more distant. "The Body Issue," she continued. "Let me be totally honest with you." She paused. "I can't fucking sell it."

Pat sat totally still, watching.

"Do you think any high-end cosmetics firm is going to want to be next to a naked woman with dimples in her butt?" Anna continued.

Sarah mentioned the notorious Dove campaign that had papered the city's bus stops with not-exactly model-slim women in white underwear.

"We're not soap," Anna retorted. "Our competition will trounce us. We have got to stop this."

If Pat had some motivation for letting the Body Issue go through, hoping she could pick up the pieces after its certain failure, Anna had none. When a magazine began slipping in newsstand and ad sales at the same time, one thing was certain: Someone was going to take the fall, it was just a matter of who went first, the editor or the publisher. As advertisers got wind of the Body Issue, they were nervously pulling out, bringing Anna's numbers down. She would miss projections for the issue by a landslide. Among other things, her rather substantial bonus was at stake.

"Is it set in stone?" Anna asked.

"I don't know," Sarah replied.

"It's not that I don't think it's an interesting idea, but maybe, just maybe, it isn't quite right for *Flair* at this time. Look," Anna lowered her voice confidentially, "we all love Rena and want to protect her. She's the most original editor in this building. But perhaps you can see if she'd at least scale it back?"

Sarah felt Pat and Anna boring in on her though they had not moved an inch. She nodded.

"They are good," Paige remarked an hour later as she sat in Sarah's office listening to her recount the conversation. "My God, they are good. They have successfully put you in a no-win situation. If you go to Rena, she'll think you betrayed her. If you don't, Pat and Anna will destroy you."

Sarah groaned, feeling it was all somehow her fault. "Let's get to work on *Splash,*" she said.

When the phone rang. Paige lingered to see if it was either Pat or Rena, but it was Karl Medford on the line. "I'm here if you need me," she whispered and closed the door behind her.

"Did Linda go in for the stress test?" Sarah asked.

"Not yet," Medford replied. "Hopefully tomorrow."

Deflated, Sarah listened while he filled her in on his activities of the day, poking into the corners of Loudon Beach that the police did not have the desire or the manpower to visit, from the aqua-and-white condos built for snowbirds to the smaller motels on the outskirts, from the large chain restaurants on I-95 to the tiny shacks a few miles away. He went to the car rentals, the bike shops; he left his card at dive bars.

"I'm covering all the bases," he assured Sarah. "The only potential lead was a woman at the ticket counter of the Greyhound station who swore she saw someone who looked just like Todd two days after he disappeared. She couldn't remember where he had bought a ticket to. Galveston, she thought, maybe Gainesville."

"Do you believe her?" Sarah asked.

"Hard to tell. But we need to follow every lead."

When Sarah got home that night, Pete, the doorman, handed Sarah two white FedEx packages from Medford. His fingers lingered on them, making sure they were firmly in her grasp before pulling slowly away. Though he did not know the details, whisperings of trouble in apartment 2B had spread through the building like mold.

Sarah waited until Eliza had gone to sleep and laid the boxes out on her bed. She cut off the wrapping tape from the ends of the canister and carefully slid out the two rolled-up drawings. They curled at the edges as she tried to unfurl them and she reached for some books from her night table to put on the corners before she truly looked at them.

The first one had a dense swirling aqua and sea-green background that had been scribbled over in torturous black lines. Murky and subterranean, it was a reverse doppelgänger of the cheery drawings Todd had shown her before he left. On the top left-hand corner, in slanted roman letters, *Lonely Head* was written in his clear, familiar hand. On the lower right quadrant, the word *dead* was thickly printed in black, strenuously underlined twice. It sank into her, the word, the vehemence of each stroke beneath it.

Falling in seemingly random patterns down the page, there were other lines, shapes that appeared to be letters that she could not quite make out. She traced them with her fingertips, held the paper sideways, upside down—but they hovered tauntingly on the brink of sense, stubbornly indecipherable. Every time she thought she had one figured out, it shape-shifted, its meaning eluding her, refusing her. Intensely frustrated, she tried to rub away some of the pastels to get at what was underneath—a hidden code, a signal?—but the paper had been sprayed with a fixative, the conscious act of an artist intent on preservation. Whatever the drawing signified, it was more than a fleeting impulse heedlessly dashed off.

She turned to the next drawing. In the upper right-hand corner, a red sun bled green streaks across a dreary gray sky marred by erasures. Thin black lines fell to the bottom of the page where a ball of marine-blue curlicues lay, watery sprays rising from its edges. On this drawing, too, there appeared to be almost-letters, almost-numbers floating through space, but their message, if there was one, remained veiled to Sarah as it had to the police and Medford. The only word Sarah could clearly make out was *Drowned.*

If Todd's sculptures had been compared to graceful lines in space, these drawings were outlines of an internal whirlpool, airless, claustrophobic, more despondent than anything she had ever seen him do.

But there was this, too: Each was not only sealed with a fixative but had a carefully delineated half-inch white border, evidence of Todd's conscious determination to shape, define, and control whatever emotional turmoil the drawings portrayed, to transform it into art. The borders gave her hope.

She removed the books and let the drawings slowly curl shut.

Sarah turned her attention to the oblong box, ripping it open with such force that the contents flew across the white summer quilt.

She picked up Todd's wallet first, its worn mahogany leather faded in the corners, and flipped it open. Inside she found his driver's license, his frequent flyer cards, his voter registration card, his American Express card, his cash card, his health insurance card—all the pieces of identification, the enablers of mobility, left behind. She opened the billfold. There was a crumpled Band-Aid, a taxi receipt from the Daytona airport, the baseball schedule of the Daytona Cubs, and a WNYC arts card. She emptied them all out and then peeled back the leather flaps of the wallet, hoping she would discover a note, a receipt, something that Medford had missed—a message, a clue, a piece of her husband that only she could understand—but there was nothing. She moved on to the cheap navy blue plastic billfold emblazoned with the logo of a travel agent on the Lower East Side not far from Todd's studio. Inside, she found his checkbook, the photocopies covered with handwriting familiar as a song. She went through each one, looking for information about the past few months of his life, but there was nothing out of the ordinary, just checks to Con Ed, his studio's landlord, UPS. Behind the checkbook was the unused e-ticket for his return flight from Florida and a neatly printed itinerary with the dates of his departure and return, a time frame clearly spelled out, as if the future could be predicted, reserved. Sarah studied the dates, times, flight numbers, as if they were a master code to what had happened.

Finally, there was his address book, the same black leather spiral that he had bought over fifteen years ago. Inside the flap were two flyers for Fiat parts, remnants of their pre-child years in Florida, the little red convertible he so adored driving on those winding back roads gone now, abandoned after he had replaced almost every part to no avail; it never went more than thirty miles without breaking down in some new esoteric manner. The rest of the pages were a lexicon of the past. Under "A" there was the acupuncturist Todd went to when he had thrown his back out years ago. Sarah had sat beside him holding his hand while the Chinese doctor twisted forty needles into his shoulders, his back, behind his ears. There was the metal dealer in Queens where he got great spools of shiny copper for his work, there were relatives in Germany and museum directors in LA, there were purveyors of used LPs and artists he had been in shows with, there were gallery owners he had promised to contact when the bottom began falling out, phone calls Sarah encouraged at first, then nagged about, and finally gave up on—a symbol of his potential and his paralysis; there were old girlfriends, including Linda.

Sarah came across a few entries in her own handwriting, written in fits of frustration with Todd's habit of jotting phone numbers on slips of paper and leaving them in jeans pockets along with piles of useless receipts, to be dumped out before the laundry was done and often not found for weeks. He was a mix of supreme organization—his neatly lined-up tools, his meticulous approach to art—and scattered pieces of anarchy, mail unopened, phone messages unchecked. Her own entries seemed so naïve to her now, evidence of a long-gone time when she still thought she could change him, help him.

And then, in Todd's hand, she found her own name written in, and the address of the apartment she'd had when they first started dating. Beside it, in black marker, he had drawn two interlocking hearts.

Nine

Linda finally went in for the voice stress analyzer two days later, but Medford had yet to learn the results. He called every afternoon as he had promised, but he had no hard news to report. Once he phoned midday to tell Sarah a body had washed up at Lake Kissemmee forty miles north of Loudon Beach. But by 4:00 p.m., it had been identified as someone else's body, someone else's story.

Each night, Eliza lay in bed, her legs twitching, and asked what Medford had discovered, but Sarah had little to tell her.

"But he's still looking?" Eliza asked, her back turned to her mother.

"Yes, he's still looking." She put her hands on Eliza's ankles to still them, but Eliza lurched from her touch.

"Wouldn't Daddy have known it was a red flag day?"

"Honey, I told you, the flags were down for the night."

"You need to take Eliza to someone," Lucy told her over the phone the next morning.

"I know, but who? A post-traumatic stress specialist? A grief counselor?" Even this decision was laced with uncertainty. How do you know how to treat a situation you cannot define—death, disappearance, a drunken accident, suicide?

"Doesn't Deirdre Gerard write a column for *Kinder*?" Lucy asked, mentioning one of the CMH magazines.

"Yes."

"I've heard she's great. Call her."

"She'll never be able to fit me in."

"Sarah, use some connections, call her editor. I'll do it for you if you want."

"No, it's all right. I'll do it." Sarah was not above using any weapon she had at the moment. Even for those in the building who had a circumspect personal code about how much and when to use the CMH clout, all bets were off when it came to your child.

When Dr. Gerard returned her phone call an hour later, Sarah outlined the circumstances as best she could. She liked Dr. Gerard immediately. Her soft voice was devoid of psycho jargon and she sounded calm, nonalarmist. "We will get your daughter through this together, you and I as a team," she promised. They made an appointment for Saturday morning, and Dr. Gerard gave Sarah precise sentences to prepare Eliza for her first visit. Sarah clung to them as if to a lifeboat, relieved that someone at last seemed to be in control.

On Friday night, Sarah looked up from the Junie B. Jones book she was reading to Eliza for the fifth time and slowly closed its tattered juice-stained covers. "Sweetie, there's something I want to talk to you about." Eliza inched away, but Sarah continued without a pause. "When people are going through something they have never experienced before, they get advice," she said, the exact opening that she had rehearsed all afternoon at work. She used the word *counselor* rather than *therapist* because Dr. Gerard had said it was familiar to children from camp and thus less threatening. Nevertheless, hot tears instantly welled in Eliza's suspicious eyes. "I don't want to go see someone," she protested. She knew instantly what Sarah was talking about. Even at six, she knew children who had been sent to therapists for biting, for being the wrecked bystanders of bad divorces, for punishment of crimes they had only the vaguest inkling of.

Sarah remained calm and, as instructed, moved on to the next line of attack. "It's my job as a mother to take care of you and this is part of it."

Dr. Gerard had explained to Sarah that children understood the concept of jobs, responsibilities; it had substance and boundaries. It was ironic to Sarah, who found motherhood, particularly lately, so overwhelming and so amorphous. She was not at all certain that she was doing her job well and deep in the night she worried about her fumbling, directionless parenting, the constant improvisation it had become.

The next morning Sarah and Eliza stood on the subway platform waiting for the E train to take them uptown. The underground air was hot and still, and seemed to be the same gray hue as the walls, the litter on the tracks. Eliza, whose life took place almost completely within walking distance, hadn't been on a subway in months. Usually, she liked to stand as close to the tracks as Sarah would allow, leaning over and peering into the white light snaking from the tunnel. She was thrilled when the air whipped her hair, and as the train approached, she would close her eyes and tip her head back, as if she were speeding in a convertible along the French Riviera.

Today, though, she perched sullenly on the chipped wooden bench, as far away from her mother as possible. She was furious about this outing.

Sarah glanced over at her daughter, pouting, resentful, nervous. Since the first moment she had told Eliza of her father's disappearance, she had felt as if she were speaking in a language she did not have a full command of. She did not have the grammar, the syntax to say what she needed to, and she was not certain what Eliza was taking away from her words. Sarah needed someone who could not only help her explain the circumstances to Eliza in a way that she could understand, but who could also explain Eliza to her, someone who could read her often inscrutable signals and decipher their meaning.

They got out of the subway on Eighty-sixth Street and walked toward Riverside Drive. The Upper West Side avenues had a breadth that was rare downtown, and Sarah was struck again by how many cities Manhattan really was, each with its own geometry, its loyalists, its dress code, even its own speech patterns. The women wore looser clothes here, their hair was longer, their shoes tended to be ballet slippers in a matte crackled gold that was enjoying a certain twenty-block vogue this summer. The wind from the Hudson River picked up as Sarah and Eliza walked past a group of formally dressed men and women gathering outside a synagogue. A few stopped to watch them, a scowling six-year-old walking five feet ahead of her mother, rushing stubbornly to a sentencing she did not deserve, before turning back to their own conversations.

Deirdre Gerard's office was on the tenth floor of a large prewar building on the corner of Eighty-eighth Street and Riverside Drive. Outside her door, there were two kids' bikes and it was clear that her office had been combined with her rambling apartment to take up the entire floor. The brightly colored helmets hastily slung on handlebars and the walls' slightly chipped paint, evidence of the natural dishevelment of family life, were reassuring to both Sarah and Eliza, whose facial muscles began to relax just a little.

They sat in the waiting room until Dr. Gerard came out to get them. In her midforties, she was delicate and thin, with Botticellian long curling red hair, a loose gray dress, the palest white translucent skin, no makeup, and a kind smile. A faint smell of vanilla enveloped her. "You must be Eliza," she said, reaching out her hand confidently, all but ignoring Sarah, as she should. "I'm Deirdre."

They followed her into a softly lit office filled with warm brown armchairs and couches, a Japanese Zen rock garden, walls of books, and a stack of colorful toys in the corner. A box of sixty-four crayons and fresh paper lay temptingly on a carved wooden coffee table. Eliza sat in a swivel chair, took it all in, and promptly began to turn in circles at warp speed, her body, her eyes, alighting nowhere, as if she would spin right out of the room if she could. Gradually, she slowed down enough to hear Deirdre and her mother speak. The two of them were sitting on the floor, looking at the photographs Sarah had brought in. Deirdre picked up a Polaroid of Todd, Sarah, and Eliza taken last Christmas.

"I like your dress," she remarked to Eliza.

Eliza looked down. She was balanced between her parents, her father's fingertips on her arm, lightly, protectively. All three were smiling tentatively at the camera, as if they were trying to make the best of it. Sarah noticed how gaunt she looked even then, her cheekbones prominent.

"Tell me about your father," Deirdre prompted.

"I think he drowned," Eliza answered. "I think the water was very rough and it swallowed him."

Deirdre nodded. "Can you draw me a picture of what happened?"

Eliza chose a deep blue crayon and drew giant swirls on the paper. She bit her lip, clutching the crayon so tightly her knuckles turned white. When she was done, Deirdre studied it for a long time while Eliza watched her intently. There was something in the way Deirdre considered the drawing, slowly, seriously, without automatically commenting on how good it was the way adults usually did, that won Eliza's trust.

Sarah studied it too, the blue swirls, their oceanic fury strikingly similar to Todd's last drawings.

When the hour was up, Sarah slipped Deirdre a check for $150 without Eliza seeing and made an appointment for the following Saturday.

Eliza was in a better mood as they walked toward the subway, and they spoke of silly things, a passing teenager's blue hair and ways to make temporary tattoos last longer.

Sarah looked down at her watch. It was eleven-thirty. The afternoon, the weekend, stretched out before them, an empty plain. She had not planned beyond the visit to Deirdre Gerard. Weekends were the hardest, without the distraction of work or camp, friends busy with their own families, the two of them, Sarah and Eliza, refugees in a sparsely populated land that they had not quite settled into yet.

Sarah could not face going home, the silence there, the shadows. They took the subway to Union Square and, weaving through the bustle of the farmers' market where couples linked arms as they picked redolent bushels of basil, rosemary, chives; children clutched paper cups of fresh cider; women balanced enormous bouquets of wildflowers for the evening's dinner parties, they made their way to Coffee Shop, a restaurant on the corner that had managed to stay cool for over ten years, an accomplishment that gave it an almost classic status in a city that deleted itself on a regular basis.

Inside, Sarah and Eliza were seated by a hostess in a Pucci miniskirt and fuchsia halter at a tiny table near the kitchen. All around them couples, mostly in their twenties, were having brunch, their skin bare, tanned, the smell of sex lingering just beneath the aroma of coffee. Every gradation of intimacy was displayed across the room—some read the paper together, some struggled with morning-after-first-night awkwardness. Sarah was attracted and saddened by their youth, by their Saturday morning haze, by their seeming freedom from responsibility, but most of all by their casual sexiness, all that awkwardness and intensity when romance is in its early stages. It suddenly all seemed over for her, that part of life, and she longed for it deeply, those sweet fumbling moments before the cost becomes known. Just weeks before she and Todd had separated she had walked by a diner on her way home from work and, looking in the window, spotted a woman eating alone with her nine-year-old son. She wondered if that was her future, joining the ranks of the city's single mothers too tired to cook, forcing snippets of conversation with children who had long ago lost the mildly illicit pleasure of eating out on school nights and longed only for a past they had never really had.

Eliza fiddled with the menu and decided on Belgian waffles without the whipped cream, strawberries on the side. There was a brief discussion with the waitress over whether it was more efficient to simply order plain waffles, but Eliza became upset with the idea and Sarah, exhausted, told the waitress to just bring what her daughter had requested, despite the extra cost.

"You should have called him," Eliza said as she played with the straw in her Shirley Temple, dripping its bright pink liquid onto the table.

"Called who?"

"You could have called Daddy and told him not to go swimming and you didn't."

Sarah took a deep breath. "We've been over this. I didn't know he was going swimming," she said. "He was in Florida. I was here in New York with you."

Eliza stared at her mother and scowled; clearly that was no excuse. She should have been able to do something, anything. Weren't mothers by their very nature, by the words and actions they committed every day—listen to me, follow me, do what I say—supposed to be omnipotent? And if not, then what? What control over the universe was there, what protection?

"Daddy made a bad decision," Sarah said. "He made a mistake."

But that was not what her daughter wanted to hear.

They sat there, Eliza betrayed, Sarah falsely accused, and ate their brunch largely in silence. While Sarah watched Eliza pushing pieces of her waffle around her plate, her cell phone rang. She dug into her bag to find it. It was Lucy.

"Can you talk?"

"No."

"Why don't you come over here when you're done eating?" Lucy suggested.

Sarah was devoid of energy, even motioning for a check would have taken an effort she could hardly muster. She did not have the will to speak anymore, to hold her head erect. She wanted only to be in bed, alone. But there was Eliza, a six-year-old who needed distraction, who deserved a life, Eliza who looked up at her now waiting for the day to be defined. "All right," she agreed.

They walked the eight blocks slowly, though the air was surprisingly clear, a rare summer day in New York when it seemed the sky itself had been freshly laundered to a sparklingly clear pale blue.

Mark was out when they arrived and Sarah wondered briefly if he had been banished—as if husbands as an entity might be deemed too much of a reminder—or if he had politely but firmly absented himself the way even the kindest men do when faced with the possibility of being asked to witness abject emotion.

Jane hovered behind the door for a moment, suddenly shy of Eliza. Surely it was hard for her, too, to suddenly live in a world where a parent, any parent, can simply vanish. Lucy touched her daughter's shoulder with her fingertips and prompted her over to Eliza. The girls scampered away to Jane's room, relieved to escape the watchfulness of grown-ups. In a minute, the sound of Jane's tinny radio seeped through the closed door playing the bubblegum pop the girls were newly mesmerized by without quite understanding the lyrics.

"So," Lucy asked while she opened a bottle of wine, despite Sarah's protestations that it was too early, "how did it go this morning?"

"Great. I'm sure she thinks Eliza is psychotic or has ADD. She couldn't stop spinning, it's the weirdest thing."

"Did you like her?"

Sarah considered for a moment. "Yes." She took a sip of the cold, slightly acrid Pouilly-Fuissé. "Most important, Eliza seemed to trust her in a way she doesn't trust me."

"You're doing the right thing," Lucy said.

"I know." Sarah stopped and ran her fingers through her hair. She was so very tired. "There are just so many strangers in my life suddenly." She took another sip of wine and looked away. "My daughter hates me."

"She doesn't hate you."

"She blames me."

"She has to have someone to blame. You're the safest one. She knows you'll love her no matter what."

Sarah nodded slowly. "I can't seem to help her."

"You are helping her."

"Todd was the fun one. He was the one she really loved."

"You are the one she needs."

"Well, she doesn't have much choice. I'm what she has."

This is what she wanted to say, that they had no relief from each other, she and Eliza, left behind, alone together. And this: that she hadn't been able to protect her daughter from the fallout of her own decisions, and it was breaking her heart.

"She'll understand one day," Lucy said.

"That's what I'm scared of. Because one of the things that she's going to have to understand is that her father walked into an ocean. What more rejection can there be?"

"He might have tried to swim back, you don't know. Maybe it will be better for her if you never know exactly what happened."

"Maybe."

They were interrupted by Sarah's cell phone. It was Medford.

"Sorry to bother you on a Saturday," he said.

"Don't be silly." How could anyone think there was anything but this?

"I finally talked to Brook's number two about Linda's stress test," he said.

"And?"

"Linda's response to one of the questions, 'Did you see Todd Larkin after he left your house that night?,' was off."

"What do you mean, off?" Sarah's voice rose enough to alarm Lucy, who leaned forward on the edge of the couch expectantly.

"She replied that she hadn't seen him again, but the test seemed to show she was lying. Still, it's not a clear indication of anything. She passed when asked if she had anything to do with his disappearance."

"Then what does it mean?"

"Maybe she followed him to the beach. Maybe he came back, they fought more, and he left again. She stuck to her story, so there's nothing else to go on. It could be an anomaly."

"But they're going to question her further?" Sarah pressed.

"Not necessarily. At this point the only charge they could use against Linda would be for filing a false police report based on the test results. But the state attorney general's office would drop the charge because, A, there is no body and therefore no evidence of a crime, and, B, she has nothing to gain by lying, no motive. She's not a beneficiary of a life insurance policy." Medford paused. "Brook still believes that Todd ran away to start a new life. Nothing has changed that, Sarah."

"What do you mean, nothing has changed? Linda is lying about something." Todd was alive to her again, walking through the dark Florida night, the fronds of the royal palms swaying in the air, but this time he was walking away from the ocean, away from the blackness, back to—what? "They have got to bring her back in," she insisted.

"I'll talk to Brook again," Medford said, "but as it stands now, that is not in their plans."

Sarah and Lucy spent the rest of the afternoon dissecting the conversation, pausing only to listen to their children's voices traveling like a rumor through the loft.

"I can't believe they are just going to ignore this," Sarah repeated, indignation coiling through her.

"It doesn't sound as if they have choice."

"How can you say that? I don't know what it is, but she clearly knows something she's not saying. I don't trust her for one fucking minute. If she's lying about this, who knows what else she's lying about?"

They heard the children go into the bathroom together, the water running, giggling.

"Maybe if I can go down there, I can convince Brook to change his mind," Sarah continued, gathering steam. "And Christ, if he's not going to talk to Linda again, I will. I want to go see the beach house, too. They didn't even go inside."

"What about Eliza?"

Sarah stopped short. How could she tell her daughter that she was going to Florida and expect her to have any faith she would return? "I can do everything I need in two days. She wouldn't have to know. I can take her to camp in the morning and tell her she's having a sleepover here. They always like that." She paused. "If that's okay with you?"

"Of course."

"Good. I can fly back the next day in time to pick her up at night."

Lucy agreed.

Before Sarah had a chance to change her mind, she called the airlines and made a reservation.

Ten

Sarah woke at dawn and packed Eliza's nightgown and spare toothbrush into her backpack. She tucked a Post-it with rows of *xxx*'s and *ooo*'s into the fold of the soft floral fabric and another in her lunch box. Like a wife about to cheat on her spouse, she tried to assuage her guilt about her impending trip with souvenirs of love, hoping they would not set off alarm bells. She put a few overnight things of her own in her work bag—anything more would raise suspicions—and waited until it was time to wake her daughter. When she had asked for a couple of personal days at work, Rena had instantly agreed.

Eliza had always been excited to sleep at Jane's, whispering in the dark, creeping through the house at midnight, gorging on Mark's homemade banana pancakes in the morning. She was more circumspect at the prospect this time, though she said little as they walked to camp. Sarah recalled Eliza's first day of preschool when other children had begun to wail as soon as their parents tried to leave, one setting off the next, dominos of three-year-old despair while Eliza sat stoically in the corner, watchful, silent, refusing to display her fear.

When they reached room 303, Sarah tried to kiss her good-bye, but Eliza slid away.

"She'll be fine," Lucy said, coming up behind her.

Sarah looked at her skeptically. "I've never lied to her this way before."

"Really? I consider it an indispensable parenting technique." Lucy touched Sarah's arm. "You're doing the right thing."

"Maybe." Sarah had called Deirdre Gerard the previous day, asking if she should tell Eliza about her trip. The answer was a resounding no. "The timing is not ideal," Gerard admitted, "but it's important for Eliza to learn that when you leave you will return. A sleepover is enough of a challenge without throwing Florida into it."

"What if something happens?" Sarah asked Lucy now. All night she had been haunted by images of her plane crashing, someone telling Eliza, Eliza betrayed, abandoned. The overwhelming weight of being her sole protector had expanded in the past few weeks, pressing down on Sarah's every breath.

"She'll be fine," Lucy repeated, misunderstanding the question, the fear. "Go. You don't want to miss your flight. I'll see you tomorrow night."

Sarah nodded, glanced through the glass door one last time, and headed out.

She got to LaGuardia just in time to make it through security and get to seat 18A. She and Todd had taken this flight so many times together during those early years when they had been able to devise their own schedules free from the constrictions that governed others and would later descend upon them, parenthood, jobs. How lucky, how oblivious they had been. Six months after they had started dating, Sarah flew down alone to meet Todd's family. He had gone a week early and met her at the airport. She could still see the khaki J.Crew shorts he had been wearing, the light auburn hairs on his long, muscled legs, his Ray-Ban aviators, Todd at home in Florida, at ease there, in the same way that she was at ease in New York. He took her to the beach house and they made love at one in the afternoon before driving over to his parents' motel. A week seemed an impossibly long time to be separated then.

A shock of humidity assaulted Sarah as she stepped out of the airport, the swollen thickness instantly forming a film on her skin, tangling her hair as she went to pick up her rental car. The insistent physicality of the air, the sharpness of the southern light came back to her—the relief it provided when they flew down in winter, but how relentless, inescapable it came to seem in summer when they configured their lives around it—biking, playing tennis early in the morning and not emerging again until dusk. She turned on the car's air-conditioning and headed down I-95 to Fort Pierce, watching the undulating heat waves ripple across the road, a dizzying illusion she had never quite gotten used to, as exotic as the rapid changeability of the tropical weather when a ferocious blackness could descend without warning, bringing torrential rains that never seemed to wash away the humidity, the heat.

Sarah's plan was to go to the beach house first. She was sure the electricity had been shut off, the house added to the list of deserted properties Todd's parents had stashed throughout Florida and Minnesota. She would need to be done there before dark. Forty minutes later she pulled off the highway and drove past the cluster of strip malls that led into the small town. She passed the enormous rotating clock above the Sun Bank that proclaimed, as it always had, the temperature to be 84 degrees, ludicrous in southern Florida in August. She and Todd used to speculate that this was due to a town edict designed to seduce visitors and brainwash the locals, one more absurdly optimistic illusion in a state historically rife with penny-ante schemes.

She turned left and drove over the intracoastal to the barrier island. They had always felt a surge of excitement going over this bridge, the house, the pocket of time they had carved out from their city lives for art, for each other, waiting just on the other side for them. She drove slowly by the motel the Larkins had once owned, the Dockside Inn, and stopped across the street, peering into the U-shaped courtyard dotted with palm trees that led past the small rectangular pool to the boat slips. Inga Larkin had bought huge freezers for the fish that guests gave her from the day's catch, enormous mounds of grouper that Todd would cook out on the long wooden docks. Often, the mosquitoes were so thick they'd have to take their food into one of the empty guest rooms. The apartment the Larkins lived in behind the check-in desk was too cluttered to maneuver through, chairs sitting on top of couches, boxes stuffed with years of old tabloids, dirty laundry, the entire place nauseating with the stench of grease. Each time, Todd would go in and wash all the dishes for them, weeks' worth, though he knew that they would begin to collect again within hours. Sarah, frustrated by his blind devotion to the Sisyphean task, begged him to stop, to leave, but he could not. His need to instill some semblance of normalcy, of order, combined with his guilt at abandoning his mother to this for seven years, overrode reason.

She turned the ignition key; it was six blocks to the house. She drove slowly down Dinmore Lane to the large corner lot bordered by a Circle K convenience store. His parents had bought the small yellow stucco house not because of its charms, a relic of Florida's more gracious past nestled amid the seventies ranch houses, but because it was zoned commercially and they had once had high hopes of making a profit from it.

Her pulse quickened as she pulled into the gravel driveway. The front yard was lush with banyan trees dripping their roots into the ground, yellow hibiscus in showy bloom flourishing despite neglect, the natural impulses of the land here constantly straining against efforts to tame it. She looked up at the kitchen window, half-expecting to see the cat they'd once had, Dusty, waiting for them, a feline sentinel who unerringly sensed their return. But the window was dark, empty; the house was silent.

Sarah walked slowly up the front porch with its dark red–painted stone floor where Todd used to sunbathe nude, protected from the street by the waist-high wall, seeing but not seen; still, he retained a permanent pink triangle at his neck from his polo shirts that refused to fade even after months, years in the city. She dug out the key she'd found buried in her desk drawer and turned the lock, pushing open the squeaking door. Inside, the air was hot, dank, mildewy. She stopped, listened, but there were no sounds, just a car going by outside. She peered into the dim light. In the living room she spotted piles of worn-out quilts from the motel in waist-high pyramids, a collage of old tools, a stack of grimy window screens. The house had clearly been used as a repository once the Dockside Inn had been sold just as it had been when it was still in operation. Every time she and Todd returned, they would be greeted by a fresh infusion crammed into every corner. Todd, outraged by the seepage of his parents' illogical hoarding, would begin to clean within minutes, moving, hauling, flinging it all to the far reaches of the second porch they had designated as storage, his desire to get it out of his visual ken so great that he threw his back out once within a half hour and had to take to bed for days. When Sarah saw the numerous piles now her heart sank. No matter what state Todd was in, she could not imagine him leaving the clutter untouched. So much of his life had been a reaction against his family's madness. He had gotten out, gotten away, gone to college, to New York, forged a career on his own terms—it seemed that he had won. She was just beginning to sense how hard he had been fighting the threat of chaos within his own mind as well. His art, with its element of control, of cool intellectual reasoning, and its adherence to strict methodology, had been his strongest weapon. Without it, he was defenseless.

She looked up, glancing at the long, gold, filmy curtains dappled with sunlight. One summer Todd had held his Polaroid camera an inch from the fabric and taken a picture. He brought it into Sarah and she studied the amber knotted pattern, unable to place it, name it. After that, they made a game of it, capturing the textures of their lives—the black beveled trash can top, the clay of the local tennis court, the red striped canvas umbrella—each microscopic detail a surprisingly beautiful abstraction, rendering the familiar unrecognizable. The following Christmas, Todd had them framed for her in a neat matte grid—an atlas of their lives in Florida—and signed it "Love, Always."

There was time, then, for that kind of thing. The days were so much longer here, alone together. They taught themselves backgammon and played for oysters at the bar up the street; they made love in the afternoon; they rented videos and experimented with exotic grilling recipes; they learned each other's deepest rhythms.

Sarah walked through the kitchen and pushed open the door that led to Todd's studio. The room bulged with drop cloths grown gray from years of dust. Even his stepfather stayed away from this room; Sarah suspected he was scared of it, the mysterious process that went on within so hard to quantify. Once, Todd had given his mother a three-foot-long horizontal sculpture of lines that rose and dipped in mathematical patterns, the ever-changing, ever-constant ocean. Inga put it above the check-in desk and bought a garish wooden neon fish to hang under it. Todd, seeing it, shrugged, said nothing, though if you looked carefully you could see him shake his head in despair every time he passed it.

The room was ghostly now, the covered tools in the center like a pile of snow that had stayed too long on city streets. She pulled off the cloths one by one, uncovering half-finished pieces, vivisections of later sculptures. She used to find Todd's willingness to leave mid-process pieces behind for months at a time surprising, but he was confident that when he returned he would be able to see them with a clearer eye. He did not need them in New York, there were so many pieces, so many ideas then, an endless stream in drawing books, on brown paper, the backs of envelopes, lurking in his mind, his dreams. Sarah ran her hands over a large wall piece that resembled a tangle of antlers. She saw Todd, felt him, in every swerve of copper, every line. She tried to recall if it was exactly how he had left it, or if there had been additions, alterations, but it had been so long ago. Perhaps she hadn't been paying close enough attention.

One morning when Todd had ridden his bike to the tennis courts ten minutes away to hit balls against the wall, the phone rang with a man from the Pollock-Krasner Foundation in New York, calling to say that they were awarding Todd the $20,000 grant he had applied for months earlier. "Your husband has a unique talent. His pieces have an elegance and sense of completion rare in someone so young. We believe he has a brilliant future ahead of him." Sarah tore off on her bike to tell Todd, thrilled for him, thrilled, too, about the official affirmation, reassured that she had made the right choice.

She pulled off another drop cloth.

Lying on the worktable was a three-foot oblong netted copper wire shell. One end was left open, as if waiting for something to be inserted.

Sarah's heart stopped.

Todd always sketched out each sculpture before fabricating it. She was certain that on her last visit to Todd's New York studio she had seen a recent charcoal drawing for that exact piece.

She touched the copper.

There was no dust on it.

She stared at it, trying to figure out a logical explanation, until she grew light-headed from the stultifying heat.

Dizzy, she went into the master bedroom and lay down on the bed, curling up on her left side and staring at the Edward Hopper print they had hung their first summer here. They had been dating for eight months and to Sarah, it felt like a trial run: If we get along playing house, surely we will decide to marry. To Todd, it was simply a summer vacation. While she waited night after night for him to propose, he talked of playing tennis in the morning, of what to cook for dinner. He spoke often of where they should go for vacation the following year, and the year after that; he told her he loved her repeatedly. But marriage was never mentioned.

Each night, Sarah remained silent. As the end of summer approached she grew increasingly restive, resentful. Finally, in the middle of an August night, she reached over and shook him awake. "Are you going to marry me or not?" she demanded. Todd sat bolt upright. "Where did that come from?" he asked, his ruddy, sunburned face at once opaque and stubborn, fearful and confused. She realized then that he hadn't been avoiding the topic—it had simply never occurred to him. The son of an unwed teenage mother, he had few preconceived notions of how a man and a woman should progress in a relationship. The daughter of a lengthy close-knit marriage, she probably had too many. They ended the night with their backs to each other, pretending to sleep, each terrified of the precipice they found themselves on.

The next morning, Todd traipsed about the house, picking up a book, putting it down, cooking food, ignoring it. Whenever Sarah walked into a room, he walked out of it. Finally, she slammed out the door and went for a drive. She parked their ten-year-old Volare by the ocean and wrapped her arms around the steering wheel, sobbing. She did not regret her words, their implied ultimatum, only that she had lost. There was no choice but to go back and pack. But when she returned to the house an hour later, Todd was waiting for her, smiling. "All right, if you want to do it, let's do it," he said. "Don't do me any favors," she replied. He touched her face gently. "Will you marry me?" he asked. And she said yes.

Three months later, they sat in the downtown Manhattan government building waiting to apply for their marriage license. The couple ahead of them were loudly tallying up their previous divorces, which made Todd and Sarah laugh—that would never happen to them. Afterward, they headed out into the wet, gray city streets, unclear as to what to do with the rest of the day. As they walked, Todd spotted a jeweler on the next block and, despite the fact that it wasn't the kind of place Sarah had envisioned (too many gold chains, pinkie rings), she was pleased when he suggested going in to look at rings—another step closer.

Inside the jewelry store, they stared down into the smudged case of gold bands. Todd pointed to a set of plain wide rings and asked to see them. She had pictured something thinner, subtler, but Todd, who had large hands, liked them. "I'll get this one and you get the one you want," he suggested. It never occurred to her that they wouldn't have matching bands. It seemed part of the point, a secret shared, a bond. "But why shouldn't we each get one we're comfortable with?" he replied rationally. They split the cost of the matching bands and left.

All that first year, whenever they fought, Todd insisted that they ritualistically clink rings as part of making up and dance to a Rodney Crowell song they had played at their wedding,

Five years later, Sarah got pregnant. It was a difficult, dangerous pregnancy and she had to have abdominal surgery at twelve weeks. As she lay on the gurney about to be wheeled to the operating room, the nurse told her she had to take off her wedding ring. This seemed like bad luck to Sarah. She begged to keep it, but the nurse insisted. She slipped it off her finger and gave it to Todd, who cupped it in his hands before leaning over to give her one last kiss. Six hours later, hazy from anesthesia, she saw him walk into her hospital room with tears in his eyes. The baby was alive, she would be all right. Todd leaned over her bed. "Here," he said, and slipped the ring back into her hand.

It was beginning to grow dark. Sarah sat on the front porch one last time, rummaging through the moments of her life with Todd, searching for an intersection where there might have been a word, a sentence, something she could have said that would have made a difference.

But there were too many—and there were none.

What is it that causes someone to wake up one day and not be able to keep up the façade another second? If Todd had committed suicide, she did not believe it had been planned but was instead a single act of desperation, a last-ditch attempt to escape the pain in his head, his heart. She remembered a morning in this house, one luminous instant that remained as sharply delineated and precious as a stage set viewed through the wrong end of a telescope. It was midsummer, the year after they had married. It was around eleven-thirty, maybe twelve. She and Todd had just made love and they sat on the front porch in white terry-cloth robes eating a late breakfast of thickly sliced sourdough toast, fresh tomatoes from the local stand still redolent of the earth. The southern light was so strong, so pure, it made the outlines of everything it fell on sparkle. She was deeply satisfied; they were young, tanned, healthy, in love, with the simplest pleasures to look forward to, working that afternoon, she on a story, he in his studio, a movie that evening, holding hands, eating popcorn, their bodies finding each other once more in the night. She looked over at him and had one piercing thought: This is happiness.

She would never forget not just that flash of unadulterated happiness, but of recognizing it. It is not something we do very often, after all.

Sarah stood up and locked the front door, leaving the best part of her past behind, and headed to Loudon Beach.

Eleven

It was early evening when Sarah drove through the outskirts of Loudon Beach. If Fort Pierce had a transient quality with its semivacant malls, its preponderance of drive-through liquor stores and used-car dealerships, Loudon Beach was more firmly entrenched. Decades before the state had been rediscovered by fashion magazines looking for warm places to shoot, by wealthy New Yorkers searching for an alternative to the Hamptons, by drug dealers flush with cash, and land developers with grandiose dreams for the few remaining stretches of unprotected swamp land, Loudon Beach had been a genteel destination for snowbirds who came down for two, three months in winter, men and women who had worked hard, raised their families, and wanted relief not just the from the biting cold but also from the increasingly random dangers of the northern cities they were leaving behind. Sarah drove past gated communities with names that sounded like outposts of heaven and broad streets with faux Mediterranean homes, their manicured lawns punctuated by imported cypress trees and swimming pools netted to protect against mosquitoes. She glanced down at her map and turned left onto Ocean Drive, where identical white hotels were stacked next to each other like Lego blocks. Five minutes later, she pulled into the Sea Breeze Hotel and Resort.

She had no need of the bellboy and, after three unsuccessful attempts, finally got the key card to work. The second-floor room had a king-sized bed, two laminated wicker chairs with vaguely floral cushions, and a decorative ceiling fan that was more Kmart than Key West. She and Todd had been in a hundred Florida hotel rooms just like this in St. Petersburg, Marathon, up and down the Gulf Coast. She sat down on the bed, dug out her cell phone, and called Eliza for the second time.

"They're in the bath," Lucy told her.

"How is she?"

"Fine. Maybe a little quieter than usual, but fine."

"Will you see if she'll talk to me?"

"Okay, hold on."

Sarah heard Lucy call out to Eliza and the muffled negotiation that ensued.

"She says she's too busy," Lucy reported. "They're making castles out of bubbles," she added in a futile attempt to soften the blow.

Sarah felt the kick of rejection land just beneath her solar plexus, just as Todd surely had the last night he called when Sarah, playing with the crumbs on the kitchen counter, had assured him Eliza's resentment would pass.

"Okay. Kiss her good night for me," Sarah said, trying to sound understanding, but it left its mark, that kick, it left a gaping hole.

She opened a half-bottle of California cabernet from the minibar and took it to the balcony, settling onto the white plastic lounge chair and staring out at the ocean below, the rhythmic sound of the waves an inescapable sound track. From her perch she could see scallops of white foam as they broke against the beach. She tried to calculate what a hundred yards from the shore would be, but it was all darkness without end. She could not see where the ocean stopped and the sky began. She had pictured it over and over again, but only now did that fathomless indigo night become brutally real to her, and it took her breath away. She did not understand how Todd, how anyone, could willfully walk into that blackness where all outlines, all sense of direction vanished so irrevocably and think there could be any way back.

The gash that had been gnawing at her chest all day spread, deepened as she finished the wine, more alone on that balcony than she had ever been, her husband gone, her child sulking a million miles away, until there was nothing left but a physical pain so fierce, absolute, and encompassing that she understood for the first time how you might do anything to stop it.

She stumbled inside, closed and locked the glass door to the balcony, pulled the curtains shut, but she could not keep out the incessant sound of the waves.

She thought of the vial of sleeping pills in her bag, how tempting, how easy it would be, the relief, the cessation they would bring.

But she thought, too, of Eliza.

And she knew she had no choice but to make it through.

The next morning, Sarah rose early, took a hot shower, and went down to the coffee shop for breakfast. Though she had wanted to go over to Linda's house first, Linda had steadfastly refused.

"I'd really like to see Todd's things, the garage," Sarah persisted.

"I gave everything to your detective," Linda replied. "I'll meet you at noon in my office on campus."

Sarah got in her car nevertheless and drove to Linda's house at 1178 Oleander Drive. She stopped in front of the contemporary white ranch with two American elms on either side of the front door, the lawn glistening with dew in the clear early-morning sun. There were no lights on, no car parked outside. It was a well-ordered house on a well-ordered street; its very ordinariness seemed to Sarah a carefully constructed deception, a scrim devised to cover up whatever had gone on within. She despised everything about it.

She drove to the corner and turned left, slowly making her way toward the ocean, the lush lawns growing sparser as she approached the shore, wondering if this was the route Todd had taken, angrily, drunkenly. The road stopped abruptly at the beach in front of a platform of gray wooden steps leading to an empty gazebo. Two couples were taking their morning constitutional in baggy shorts and sneakers, but other than that the beach was deserted, the ocean calm, almost placid, the salt air, the wide-open vistas, the scent of suntan oil that never quite dispersed a universe away from the black shadowless night before.

At nine o'clock, Sarah pulled up in front of the one-story beige brick building that housed the Loudon Beach Police Department. She parked between two empty patrol cars and asked at the front desk for Detective Brook. She had barely sat down on the cool edge of the metal chair in the corner when he came out to greet her. A compact man of five-eight in his midforties, Brook had close-cropped sandy hair shiny with pomade, rimless glasses, and densely freckled arms. His features were sharply defined; deep vertical creases cut his cheeks in two, his nose was short, thin, his eyes almost lidless. Everything about him seemed ironed, pressed, drip-dry.

"Mrs. Larkin," he said, a statement more than a greeting, as he shook her hand. His fingers were squat, slightly calloused. "Let's go inside." He led her past four other policemen who glanced up curiously from their work to his desk in the rear of the main room.

"I take it you had a good flight?" he asked, sitting down and motioning for her to do the same. He rested his hands on the spotless ink blotter, each fingertip aligning perfectly. The veneer of friendliness was wafer thin; she was on his turf now and everything in his manner let her know that.

"Yes, thank you."

"This time of year, the thunderstorms can be a problem." He leaned back, studied her. "On such a short trip the last thing you want is delays. Especially when you have a daughter to get home to." His voice was soft, southern, slow. Sarah had to lean forward to hear him.

"There were no problems," she replied tersely.

Brook nodded. "I'm forgetting, you used to spend quite a bit of time down here, didn't you?"

"Yes." Sarah, shivering from the air-conditioning, jiggled her legs, anxious to proceed.

"Well, it was good of you to come see me, though I'm not sure how much I can add since the last time we spoke."

"Karl Medford told me about Linda's voice stress test results."

"I see." Brook carefully moved a silver-framed photo of his wife and children an eighth of an inch to the left with his forefinger before glancing back at Sarah.

She waited for an acknowledgment that Linda's answers were at the very least suspicious, but Brook said nothing further.

"Well," Sarah pressed, "don't you consider it significant? It's obvious she's lying."

"Mrs. Larkin, Sarah, I'm sure Karl Medford also told you that Linda's replies showed no aberration when asked if she had anything to do with your husband's disappearance, which seems to me the crucial piece of information."

"But she was lying when she said she didn't see him after he left the house."

"I'd be careful with that word if I were you. That sole answer could be a statistical blip. There could be any number of explanations."

"Such as?"

"Linda has no motive to lie."

"That doesn't answer my question."

Brook remained motionless, his narrow eyes clear, steady. "It answers mine."

"You're going to question her further, aren't you?"

"As far as she's concerned, she's done."

"But it's not up to her." Sarah's voice rose and filled the otherwise silent room.

"As a matter of fact, it is." Brook, behind his armor of professional patience, regarded her as a parent would a child on the verge of an irrational tantrum. "At this point, it's all voluntary on her part. Frankly, she didn't have to do any of this. That tells you something right there."

Sarah exhaled in frustration. "Then what is your next step?"

"I'm not sure that I have one. I can't justify keeping my men on this if there are no new leads."

"Linda's test is a lead."

"We don't consider it one."

"That's crazy."

Their eyes met.

Brook remained calm, devoid of any evidence of emotion. "Mrs. Larkin, I would appreciate it if you did not try to tell me how to do my job. I've been doing it for over twenty years."

Sarah felt a knot of heat rise through her esophagus, burn her cheeks, her eyes. "What about the *Crime Stoppers* video?"

Brook began to fiddle with a pencil. "No one has called in. Not even the usual nut jobs. I've never seen that happen before," he admitted. "Whatever occurred, it's clear Todd vanished soon after he left the house."

"But Linda saw him again."

"Perhaps, perhaps not. The bottom line as far as I'm concerned is that your husband does not wish to be found."

"What you mean is that you can't find him."

Brook leaned forward, pausing before he spoke. "You seem to be having a hard time accepting what has happened. Maybe you should find a support group."

"It's your job to find out what happened," Sarah snapped.

Brook rose. Their meeting was over. "I'm truly sorry about your husband, Mrs. Larkin. You can be assured we'll be in touch if we learn anything more."

"If?"

Brook regarded her coolly and did not answer.

Sarah was shaking with anger as she walked back to her car and jabbed the key into the ignition.

Medford's office was located ten minutes away, just off A-1A in one of those nondescript buildings that spring up when Main Streets disappear to house dentists, lawyers, and accountants in inexpensive suites. She parked in the near-empty lot and went down three wrong corridors before finally coming upon his name discreetly written in thin gold lettering on a brown door. Unable to find a buzzer, Sarah knocked insistently, her outrage with Brook still roiling her.

The door opened slowly. "Sarah? I'm Karl Medford. I'm so glad to put a face to the name. Come in." His handshake was firm and cool, his fingers closing around hers with reassuring strength. Medford was close to six feet tall, all clean-cut eagerness in khaki pants and a spotless white short-sleeved button-down shirt. He had faded blond hair, unusually green eyes, and the taut body of someone who ran three miles every morning. Unlike Brook, he seemed genuinely pleased to see her.

He led her into his office and sat down behind a large antique oak desk, its age and solidity a bas relief against the harsh overhead lights, the industrial gray walls. "It was my grandfather's," Medford explained, seeing her notice it. "He was a lawyer in Biloxi, died a couple of years ago. It was a bitch to get this thing down here. Can I get you anything? Coffee? Soft drink?"

"No, thanks."

"So. How did it go with Brook?"

"He's an asshole."

Medford smiled slightly. "Well, he's set in his ways."

"He's an asshole," Sarah repeated vehemently. "What I can't figure out is why he's protecting Linda."

"This is a small town. Brook and Linda both grew up here. He tends to distrust outsiders. From my talks with him, I honestly don't think he believes she had anything to do with this. If anything, he's suffering from a dearth of imagination, but it's not devious."

Sarah frowned. "He's not going to question her again."

"No."

"Do you think you can get her to explain that answer?"

"I certainly have every intention of trying. Sometimes you can wear people down, sometimes it just makes them dig their heels in, hard to say with her. She strikes me as someone who has a cutoff point. Keep in mind that the results of the police test are supposedly confidential. If Linda finds out I know about them, she could decide to stop talking to me. And then we'd have nothing. It would be best if you didn't mention them to her either. What time are you meeting her?"

"Noon."

"Do me a favor, tread carefully. I know, I can imagine anyway, how you must feel about her." Medford's voice was low, thoughtful, the even features of his face marked by genuine concern. "I appreciate how difficult this is. But right now Linda is cooperating. We don't want to do anything that might change that."

Sarah nodded unconvincingly.

"The same goes for Brook," he continued. "Backing him into a corner isn't going to help us."

"I think it's a little late for that," she admitted.

"So I gathered. Did you go to the house in Fort Pierce?"

"Yes."

"And?"

"It's the weirdest thing. I found a piece Todd was working on there."

"Working on when?"

"I don't know, that's what's bothering me. I'm sure there's a recent drawing for the exact same piece in his studio in New York. He usually did a sketch just before he started constructing it out of copper."

"Don't artists often repeat similar motifs?"

"Yes, but not over a seven-year period. And this wasn't just a similar motif, they were virtually identical. Todd never made the same sculpture twice." She hesitated. "Maybe I'm wrong, but I don't think so. I'll go to his studio when I get back to New York."

"Were there any other signs that he had been there?"

The piles, the clutter, the accumulations that had gone untouched. "No."

"Did you see anything in those last drawings the police found, anything I overlooked?"

Sarah shook her head. Beyond the words *Lonely Head, Dead* and *Drowned,* she had remained unable to decipher the scrawls and symbols no matter how many times she stared at the drawings, determined to make sense of them. Her frustration with herself, with the drawings themselves, mounted inexorably; they were so close to language, to a meaning she could almost but never quite grasp. "I can't figure out any of the other words or letters," she said. "I can't even tell if they are actual words. There's a chance they're just random patterns. I just don't know."

Medford nodded. In the silence that followed, Sarah could hear the air-conditioning whirring.

He reached for a spiral steno pad and flipped it open, rifling through a few pages before speaking. "I had a friend at the phone company pull Linda's records. Keep in mind it's only her land line."

"Did you see anything?"

"Nothing that seemed unusual. There were a number of incoming and outgoing calls from Todd, as she had told us. There were a few to a plastic surgeon over in Miami. I thought," his eyes lit up a bit, "I don't know, it sounds crazy, but maybe she was going to change her face, something. But she only wanted her breasts done."

"What about the woman at the bus station who thought she might have seen Todd?"

"She was a lot less certain when I talked to her again. I don't think it's anything. I'm going to circle back to some of the other people I spoke with last week. Sometimes they're too defensive the first time you meet with them to think clearly. Memories can pop up once I'm gone. And there are a few more people in his address book I still haven't been able to get a hold of."

Medford put the notebook down. Sarah watched as he gently closed it, the palm of his hand resting on top of it. It did not seem a good sign.

"Have you ever heard of Rudy Burckhardt?" he asked her.

"No. Who is he?"

"A photographer. One of Todd's friends, Harry DeVeres, mentioned him. He committed suicide by walking into a lake. DeVeres said Todd mentioned this a number of times."

Sarah sat quietly as one more unknown piece of her husband's psyche pushed its way into the constantly shifting mosaic.

"Will you call me after you meet with Linda?" Medford asked as he walked her out.

"Of course."

They shook hands awkwardly, the formality of the ritual at odds with the intimacy of their conversation.

Loudon Beach Community College was made up of four identical buildings on a flat parcel of near-barren land dotted here and there with a few plantings, as if someone had started to design the landscape but had given up halfway through. Sarah parked and was directed to the art department on the second floor of the northwest building. The long white corridors were nearly deserted, though classes had already resumed. She found Linda's office just past the faculty lounge. The door was open, and peering in, she recognized Linda from the photo on Todd's refrigerator, a petite sinewy woman with alabaster, slightly shiny skin and dry shoulder-length brown hair loosely tucked behind her ears. She was wrapping a strand of it around her forefinger nervously as she stared at her computer. She looked up slowly, her face expressionless, and parted her thin lips.

"Sarah?"

"Yes."

Linda stood up, walked around to the front of her desk and embraced Sarah, the smell of cigarettes evident just beneath a breath mint and powdery perfume. Sarah could feel the narrowness of her back, the slight roughness of fabric against her fingertips. She pulled away quickly.

"Have a seat." Linda smoothed the front of her navy sheath dress. Her large almond-brown eyes were at once avid and guarded. "How are you holding up?"

"I'm fine." She had no intention of giving this woman any piece of her soul, any proof of her pain.

"And Eliza?"

Sarah bristled. "She's doing as well as can be expected."

"Todd loved her, *loves* her, more than anything. He always has."

Sarah clenched her fingers. She did not want to hear Linda's version of her past, her marriage, her child, did not want to acknowledge that she *had* a version, though that was of course why she was here.

"You got the drawings?" Linda asked.

"Yes."

"Todd was always the most talented of any of us," Linda observed. "Even in school, it was clear he was going to leave here, make something of himself. Nothing was going to stand in his way." There was admiration in her voice, but Sarah sensed resentment as well. He had left her behind, after all.

"I think Todd was on the verge of a breakthrough," Linda continued. "He always had such an intellectual approach to art, but his recent drawings show a new willingness to loosen up, break out of the constrictions he'd placed on himself." She spoke in an authoritative voice, reminding Sarah that she was, in fact, a teacher, albeit at a second-rate community college. "They were an arrow into the future."

"It's possible the looseness you're talking about was the first sign of a breakdown," Sarah replied tartly.

Linda leaned forward, her tone superior, condescending. "Collectors and dealers are always afraid when an artist enters a new stage, stops doing what was successful. They want everything to stay the same; it's so much easier to understand, so much safer."

"I am not a collector or a dealer," Sarah answered sharply.

Linda leaned back, satisfied with her case. Sarah noticed that her unvarnished fingernails were bitten to the quick.

"I wish you had let me see where he left his things," Sarah said.

"I cleaned everything up." Linda's eyes narrowed, her manner once more intimate, confidential. "I found beer bottles everyplace, in the closet, behind the desk. I knew he drank, but never like that."

"What about that piece he was working on, *Lightning Rod to Take to the Beach During a Thunderstorm*?"

"The elements were all loose. I stacked them in the corner. They're just lines of copper, that's all. They'll wait."

"Wait for what?"

The phone rang before Linda could answer. "Excuse me." She picked it up on the second ring.

While Linda spoke in a low voice, her hand cupped over the receiver, Sarah looked around the office. The walls were lined with books on art history, museum catalogs, cheap ceramic figurines of pugs, a Daytona Beach baseball cap. She glanced back at Linda, wondering what, precisely, Todd had found so hypnotic about her, this almost plain woman with wiry arms and excitable eyes. There was an air of defiance, an intense sexuality pushing against the veneer of conformity, as if the house, the job, the simple navy dress were merely a disguise. Sarah imagined him holding her, moving with her, both of them unleashed—and then she willed it from her mind.

Linda's tone assumed a firm, warning cadence. "I'll have to call you back, this isn't a good time." She hung up and looked at Sarah. "Bill," she explained, her voice tinged with the resignation women express when bonding over the obstinacy of men.

Sarah stared at her blankly.

"McCrory," Linda added, as if that explained everything.

Sarah recalled Linda's ex-boyfriend, his addiction to Internet porn.

"He's been bent out of shape since that weekend with Todd."

"What does Todd have to do with it?"

"Nothing, really. At least as far as I'm concerned. Bill came by to drop off some things of mine, a few CDs. Let's just say he wasn't overwhelmingly happy to find Todd there."

"What happened?"

"You know men. They growled at each other, but they didn't really say much. Bill had no reason to be so angry. It was none of his business. I told him Todd was just an old friend. Jesus, he gets pissed if I talk to the garbage collector." Linda was obviously taking some pride in the notion of the two men facing off over her affections. "It was crazy. He drove by the house three, four times that night."

Sarah's nerves spiked against the surface of her skin, but she attempted to sound casual. "Which night?"

"I don't remember, Saturday maybe." Linda stopped, changed tactics, changed tone. "Sarah, I know Todd. He was in bad shape, especially those last few days. But trust me, he'll come back."

"What makes you so sure?"

Linda shrugged. "Men usually do."

The two women looked at each other, then away. Sarah began to speak but, remembering Medford's warning, stopped. She stood up. "I have a plane to catch."

Linda made no move to embrace Sarah this time. She simply nodded.

Sarah walked quickly down the long corridor, her heels clicking on the linoleum. As soon as she got outside, she called Karl Medford. "I want you to check out Bill McCrory, Linda's ex-boyfriend."

And then she drove ten miles above the speed limit to the airport, longing only to be home with her daughter in a city she understood.

Twelve

Sarah awoke at three the next morning to find herself in Eliza's bed, her right arm numb from being pressed against the wall. They had gotten home late from Lucy's house and Eliza, already drained from the sleepover, didn't protest when Sarah lay down beside her. She did not ask what Sarah had done the night before, she did ask about Medford. She registered her relief at her mother's return silently. As they walked to camp a few hours later, she glanced over at Sarah repeatedly as if to verify her presence, but other than that, there were no obvious repercussions.

As soon as Sarah dropped Eliza off, she hurried to a cab. She had missed two days of work and she did not want to give Rena or Pat any further ammunition. She quickly went through her in-box, overflowing with unread manuscripts, useless PR pitches, and invitations to events she had no intention of attending, then walked over to Paige's office for a debriefing.

"Let's just say it hasn't gotten any better around here," Paige informed her after hearing about the trip to Florida. "*Flair*'s second-quarter newsstand numbers are due out next week and rumor has it they'll be down yet again. We've lost four points of market share this year. There's only so long Rena can last if this continues. If she goes, *Splash* doesn't stand a chance. We have to move quickly."

"Maybe we can work on it over lunch today," Sarah suggested.

Paige considered this. "Okay. It's a little risky, but Pat has never once set foot in here." The office, with its onslaught of ribbons and mini champagne bottles, dried floral arrangements and beauty products spilling over every surface was anathema to Pat; she did everything she could to avoid it.

At noon, Sarah carried over a pile of clips in an unmarked manila envelope and they worked behind closed doors, surrounded by tear sheets from English, Australian, and American fashion magazines.

"What do you think of this?" Sarah asked, holding up a collage of shoes from a Japanese shopping monthly.

"Hmm, anime meets Manolo. I've always thought the ultimate cover line would be 'Win a Month of Free Shoes.'"

"To wear while having mind-blowing sex that burns six hundred calories."

Paige smiled. "Put it in the 'yes' pile for now. We can always take it down later."

Now that they had a semi-green light and had to actually define the magazine—preferably in a single easily digestible sentence—it was not so simple. They hadn't quite decided if it was a life-stage magazine for those first years after college, a stars, style, shopping, sex magazine for all twentysomethings, married, single, urban, suburban, or if they could somehow combine the two.

Sarah had a legal pad on her lap with three headings: Identity, Differentiation, Direction. On another page, she had left spaces for a mission statement and a summary of financial risks and rewards—a task that left them both thoroughly bewildered.

"I think we need to play up the life-stage thing," Sarah said. "Advertisers will get that. The reader in her first job needs advice on how to furnish her first apartment, buy her first car. I don't know about you, but I was clueless."

When Sarah met Todd, one of the things she was most attracted to was how certain he was of his own taste, the artful way he arranged food on a plate, his studio with its intriguing little pictures scattered in unlikely places, the European music he played. It promised a more aesthetic, sensual appreciation of life that was deeply attractive to her. Unswayed by what was cool or expected, Todd trusted his own eye with objects as he did with people, while she remained diffident, uncertain.

"I was never clueless," Paige replied airily. "Often wrong, but never clueless."

They had lunch delivered and ate the thin-crust pizza on the floor while they continued to clip articles, take notes. "It's healthy," Paige remarked as she reached for a second slice, "all that lycopene in the tomatoes." Unlike so many of the women they knew who believed that all food was evil, Paige had a charming ability to convince herself that anything delicious was healthy if not downright dietetic, dark chocolate, red wine, ice cream, so rare in a world awash in food guilt. "Let's get some Tasti D-Lite," she suggested after they had finished the pizza.

"I don't have time to go out."

"They can deliver."

"They are not going to deliver two small cups of fake ice cream."

"Sure they will. I have them bring it to me all the time."

It was an unwritten competition among the editors of *Flair* to see who could have the most outrageous thing delivered. All of them had gotten good at calling stores to deliver a bag they had spotted on the way to work; they knew how to get stockings delivered if the pair they had on ripped and have their legs waxed at home at the last minute, but having someone bring a $2.75 dessert was impressive.

"So, I am swearing off Internet dating," Paige said, after placing their order for two small Snickers Bars cups, one with sprinkles.

"And the reason for that is?"

"I went out with this guy from Nerve last night. Let me just say, one thing the Internet has done is make lying about your age an equal opportunity. He was at least ten years older than he said. I don't know, maybe the picture was of his son, or a younger brother."

"Was he at least nice?"

"Once I got over the shock of the old? No, not particularly. He's really involved in this Slow Food movement. He kept lecturing me about the evils of modern life, e-mails, fast food, even cell phones. His rant about BlackBerrys alone took fifteen minutes. It made me want to chain-smoke in McDonald's. Did I mention he was still wearing a wedding ring?"

"He's married?"

"No. His wife died last year."

"That's horrible."

"Yes, but I would take the wedding ring as a sign he's not quite ready to be out there. There is, by the way, an entire subset of men online who have been recently widowed and have no idea how to date."

"Yikes, is this my future?"

Paige looked up. It was the first time Sarah had mentioned any future at all, much less one that might involve another man. "This guy is living too much in the past to be anyone's future."

Paige began to clean up a few stray snips of paper from the floor. The two women were standing up now, it was time to turn their attention back to *Flair*.

"Sarah?"

"Yes?"

"There's something I need to tell you."

"What?"

"I'm going out with Ethan tonight."

"Excuse me? How did that come about?"

"I e-mailed him and asked. Well, I've done that before. But this time he said yes."

"Paige, Ethan has managed to disappoint you every time you've gone near him. Christ, just last week you told me you had a dream that while you were kissing he kept his hand between your mouths. That seemed to totally nail it as far as I'm concerned."

"I knew you wouldn't approve."

"It's not that I don't approve. He's a nice guy. I don't think he means to do it, but he can't get out of his own way."

"Maybe he was telling the truth when he said it was bad timing. Maybe he just needed more time to get over his divorce."

Sarah looked at her skeptically. A man in love does not use the phrase "bad timing." But Paige knew that. Or at least she did when it came to other people.

"Look," Paige continued, "he's the only man I've met in years that I have felt any real desire for. I can't stand a repeat of last night."

"All right. I hope it goes well."

Paige frowned.

"I mean it."

"Thanks." She looked, for a moment, more vulnerable than Sarah had ever seen her.

Sarah took her notes back to her office, put them in the bottom of her file cabinet, and turned to the pile of manuscripts marked "Rush." The afternoon passed slowly as she waded through the increasingly nitpicky requests, comments, and criticisms Pat had written on each in spider-thin red ink.

It was close to five before Medford called.

"Did you check on McCrory?" Sarah asked.

"Yes. He's a real charmer. For starters, he has a previous arrest record for DWI. And he was in court-ordered anger management classes for another incident."

Sarah's pulse quickened. "What did he do?"

"A little episode of road rage."

"Did you tell Brook about his run-in with Todd the night before he disappeared and the way he kept driving by Linda's house?"

"I spoke with Brook."

"Are they going to question him?"

"Not at this point. They don't think there's enough to call him in."

"I don't believe this."

"It's all circumstantial."

"Everything in life is circumstantial, for God's sake. Can you at least talk to him?"

"I tried to reach him all day, but he didn't return any of my calls. Turns out he took the week off from work to visit his mother in New Orleans, so we'll have to wait until he comes back."

Sarah moaned audibly, the skeins of waiting never ending.

All evening, though, a theory grew, gaining momentum, gathering force, Linda with her penchant for drama purposefully getting McCrory riled up, his jealousy, his violent past, meeting up with Todd in the night.

Thirteen

On Sunday afternoon, Sarah took Eliza back to Todd's studio on Rivington Street. As they rode down Avenue A, Sarah remembered taking the same trip to her first date with Todd on a hot August evening. He boiled two enormous lobsters he had bought in Chinatown and she brought a bottle of Veuve Clicquot. They sat on stools at his worktable, covered for the occasion with brown paper that he had decorated with a paisley design and talked until two in the morning about the commonalities in various countries' fables, about the future of art, about Todd's burning ambition to have a seat at the table. When they reached that moment when an evening's outcome hangs in the air, he told her, "I just don't think I'm ready for a relationship." He was in the midst of breaking up with someone, a waiflike abstract painter who was pressuring him to have a baby. It took him another six weeks to tie that up, but when he called Sarah again, he was fully ready. They never went another day without talking. Years later, when Sarah found out that his ex-girlfriend had in fact gotten pregnant and miscarried, she could not help but wonder if her own marriage, her own child existed because of that loss.

They got off the bus and walked two blocks west to the studio. Sarah's legs felt weak as she climbed the three flights, Eliza dragging behind her.

Inside, Eliza looked around suspiciously. She had spent so many afternoons here, playing with wires and pastels while Todd worked, occasionally looking over from his own drawing pad and smiling at her.

"Why don't you take some things that will remind you of Daddy," Sarah suggested.

Eliza walked over to Todd's desk where the metal letter stamps Sarah had given him last Christmas sat in a neat stack. She had loved watching him hammer his initials into copper, the letters magically appearing in the soft metal. She touched them gently as if unwilling to disturb them.

"Here, sweetie." Sarah handed her a canvas bag and Eliza put the stamps carefully in. She slung the bag over her shoulder and walked away, scavenging for pieces of her father she could put inside, take away with her until he came back to claim them, a few small copper wires Todd had twisted like clauses to a sentence, two large jewel-toned glass marbles that he liked to roll in his hands while he stood in front of his work, contemplating his next move, a box of worn-down oil crayons, his fingerprints still visible on the paper wrappers.

Sarah watched her for a moment, then turned her attention to the far wall.

Rendered in charcoal on brown paper was an almost exact blueprint of the copper oblong sculpture she had seen in Fort Pierce. A variety of shapes had been drawn and erased inside the netted enclosure as if Todd hadn't quite decided on the most suitable form to insert. She stepped closer and touched the surface, smudging a line. It hadn't been sprayed with a fixative; it was recent, still in progress. The paper rustled and she noticed the edges of another sheet behind it.

She peeled off the top page and unearthed a finished drawing of a very similar sculpture, its title written on the bottom, *Between the Truth, 24 Times a Second.* Todd had sold that piece to a museum in Massachusetts years ago. The title referred to the speed at which film moves through a spool to create the illusion of movement, the mechanics of images, of memory itself. The drawing was dated seven years ago, the autumn after their last stay in Fort Pierce.

She let the more recent sketch fall on top of it, so similar to its predecessor, but she saw now how tentative the variations were in comparison. Todd, blocked, barren, tracing the lines of his past successes, as if he could relearn how to make art, the missteps, the erasures themselves desperate perhaps though there was something valiant about his refusal to give up. It was his determined spirit she had first loved.

Sarah left the drawings and sat down with a pile of his journals, his drawing pads, the scrapbooks he pasted Polaroids and snippets of ideas in. She opened a red leather journal he had begun in his early twenties to record the memories of his first eight years in Dortmund, Germany, he was worried he would forget. She put it down, opened another journal from college and found this: "I know drinking isn't a problem now, but I also know it could become one."

How many things they had never discussed, questions she had never asked. Was it because they hadn't occurred to her, had she been too busy, or were there patches in his mind that she did not want to touch on? She saw now how much closer they could have been. She knew, too, that there were things about herself she hadn't shared with Todd, tidbits of her own past, tics and fears, either because she deemed them irrelevant or because he did not want to know. He had never asked much about her previous relationships, only vaguely knew that she had never stayed with anyone longer than six months before him (rather than confront problems she had always found it easier to leave), she did not tell him how superstitious she was about anything happening to Eliza, that she knocked on wood in complicated sets of three, believed in psychics, had recurring nightmares of tsunamis, he did not know how uncertain she felt most of the time. Still she believed that he had known her better than anyone ever had.

"Who said it first?" Eliza asked, interrupting Sarah's thoughts.

"Who said what first?"

"For Daddy to move out."

"Sweetie, I've told you, we decided it together. Sometimes

grown-ups can love each other very much but just not be able to live together."

"But who said it first?" Eliza demanded.

She was rooting around for blame and Sarah never knew when a missile would be fired, landing in her flesh.

"It was your fault he moved out," Eliza proclaimed.

"We decided together," Sarah repeated.

"You could have stopped him from going swimming that night."

"Honey, I told you, I didn't know he was going swimming. He was in Florida and we were in New York."

Just as toddlers crave the repetition of favorite stories, finding order in the familiar, Eliza needed the repetition of her nightmare. Sarah looked over at her and it was all she could do to keep from screaming, "I'm not the one you should be angry at! He's the one who fucked up!"

But she and Todd had made a pact when they separated never to say a bad word about each other and she honored that now. Eliza lay down on Todd's narrow bed, the colorful woolen Mexican throw chafing her skin as she curled up and closed her eyes, absenting herself, while Sarah went over to his drawing desk and sat down on the high stool, resting her elbows on the slanted wooden surface. She looked up at the corkboard with its pictures of Eliza, the postcards of Nadelman, Yves Klein, photocopies of poems by John Ashbery. Half covered up, she saw a black-and-white photograph of the Flatiron Building, deeply shadowed in black, the city at its most romantic, ominous and melancholy. She took it down, turned it over. It was by Rudy Burckhardt, the photographer who had walked into the water. Sarah touched the heavy black skyline, the hulking buildings, then carefully pinned it back up.

She rose and went to the main worktable where a large black portfolio was resting. Inside, she found the drawings Todd had shown her the night before he left for Florida, each one carefully inserted into a plastic sleeve for protection. She flipped through them, the colorful scrawls, the simpler ones that were clearly sketches for potential pieces, their jagged shapes delineated as if waiting to be cut out. The drawings grew darker, less airy as she flipped the pages. She turned to the last one; within its borders the page was completely filled with agitated deep blues and greens circling over and over each other, the ocean viewed from beneath where there is no air, no light, no day, just an endless violent swirl of blues that almost swallowed up the single word written in black, *Drowning.*

It fell to her lap, her hands shaking.

If the drawing Medford had sent her, *Drowned,* had a certain stillness, a morbid peace, this one was all movement and churn. She tried to remember if Todd had shown it to her before he left, if she had noticed only the colors, the patterns without the single word, the signal—or if he had kept it hidden from her. She wondered, too, where in the weeks between the two drawings and their change in tenses there might have been a moment, an opening, to alter the progression, to stop the sequence from unfolding.

Woozy, the colors blurring before her, she zipped up the portfolio and went to get Eliza.

Just as they were about to leave, the phone rang, startling them both. Sarah ran to the desk to pick it up. "Hello?"

There was silence, the faint sound of breathing.

"Hello?" Sarah repeated.

No one answered.

The breathing continued for another minute and then whoever it was hung up.

Fourteen

The beginning of the school year loomed before Sarah like a photographic negative of its usual excitement. The shopping for new clothes and notebooks, the cheerful chaos of parents and children reconnecting after a summer apart, the effervescent promise of fresh starts all seemed a spectral taunt.

She pictured the scampering about in the school yard that first day, the mothers animatedly comparing notes on camp experiences and country houses, lamenting summer's end but pleased to be back, to be freed of their offspring full-time, gossiping about teachers and school supply lists while they watched their children out of the corner of their eyes finding their places anew. Sarah did not know how many of them had heard about Todd and she couldn't imagine how to impart the information standing in a school yard bustling with children. This was not, after all, a simple tragedy she could hand them—my husband died of a heart attack, my husband ran off with another woman—that, no matter how dreadful, was at least in the realm of the familiar. She would have to find a way to give enough of a shape to her situation without stripping herself bare.

She would also need words to hand Eliza, sentences she could utter when other kids asked how her summer had been and teachers put forth the standard beginning-of-the-year question: What did you do on your vacation?

Sarah wanted to run away, pull Eliza out of school, anything to spare her the queries, the eyes, the muted, confused responses that would surely follow.

The day before the beginning of school, she called Eliza's first-grade teacher, Alicia Harcourt, and told her in halting sentences what had happened. Once more, she found herself leaking out the inky mess of her personal life before a stranger. This time, though, the stakes—her daughter's well-being, the way she would be seen in the world from this moment on—were higher than ever. Sarah tried to appear as normal and matter-of-fact as possible as she outlined the last month, attempting to impart that Eliza was, despite everything, coping well, that she was fine. She hated that this would be Miss Harcourt's first impression of them—a woman who had literally lost her husband and a little girl with nothing but open-ended questions.

Miss Harcourt murmured her sympathy, promised to keep a special eye on Eliza and report anything that warranted comment or concern.

For the past two years Todd had photographed Eliza on the first day of school against the same white wall in the living room. Their plan had been to continue the tradition until she graduated from high school, a visual record of growth and expectation. Sarah picked up last year's photo from where it rested in an engraved silver frame on the bookcase—Eliza in a green-and-blue-striped knit dress, her hair in pigtails, clutching a stuffed pink flamingo, her face open and filled with anticipation as she headed off to kindergarten. She put the photo down and called out once more to Eliza, who was sulking in her bedroom, unused to the schedule, unhappy with her chosen outfit, dreading school for reasons she could not specify.

"Come, sweetie pie, breakfast is waiting."

"I'm not hungry."

"I have chocolate chip muffins." Sarah, who usually forbade sugary treats in the morning, would do anything to tempt her daughter, to offer what little pleasure she could.

"I'm not hungry," Eliza repeated churlishly.

Sarah took a deep breath, her anxiety about sending Eliza off on an empty stomach warring with her desire to avoid any further arguing.

"How about some juice?"

"I'm not thirsty."

Sarah ran her fingers through her hair. Despite her concern, her patience was wearing thin. Her own anger was pushing against the membranes of her skin, desperate to be let loose at the nearest object, the nearest person. The problem for both Sarah and Eliza was that the nearest person was the other.

She walked back to Eliza's room, knocked gently on her closed door—a formality more than an actual request—and entered. Eliza was curled up on her maroon fake fur beanbag chair, staring off into space. Sarah knelt down beside her.

"Are you okay, sweetie?"

"I'm fine," Eliza replied irritably, turning her back to her mother.

"Come then. You need to get your shoes on."

"I hate my shoes."

"But we just bought them. You chose them yourself. You loved them in the store."

"I changed my mind. I hate pink."

"Fine," Sarah said, rising, her patience exhausted, tears about to spill out. "Wear whatever you want. But you have got to get up and come out of your room." She softened, tried a new tactic. "Let's do your picture, okay?"

"No. I do not want my picture taken."

Love and exasperation knotted Sarah's brain until she could not think straight and she stood silently in the center of the room wondering what to do. Which traditions do you cling to, which do you alter, which do you let go? She went into the living room, grabbed the disposable camera she had bought for the occasion, flung it into the garbage, and slammed the cabinet door loud enough to scare both Eliza and herself.

A half hour later, they sat on the Third Avenue bus, barely talking to each other. Eliza pressed her forehead against the window and stared out at the morning traffic. When an elderly woman in a brightly flowered dress sitting across from them smiled and rolled her eyes in sympathy at the stubbornness of children, Sarah smiled wanly back, embarrassed. "First-day jitters," she remarked.

Sarah and Eliza walked the two blocks from the bus stop to the school yard, already filled with clusters of children running up to each other excitedly. The boys greeted each other with tackles, tussling on the ground, rolling over and over in clumps of skinned knees and elbows, the only way they could express their joy at being reunited. The girls ran up to each other, hugged, and then stood in tight groups, talking rapidly. Eliza walked slowly toward them without looking back at Sarah and hovered on the outskirts of her circle of friends. Slowly she inched in further, and further still, seduced by their laughter, until she had forged a place within. Sarah watched her begin to talk and finally exhaled, her shoulders relaxing.

She glanced back to the gate, planning her escape. She was tempted to dart out without speaking to anyone but she had felt the eyes on her already, noting, appraising, waiting. She steeled herself and walked purposefully over to a group of mothers from Eliza's class. She knew their conversations, she had been a part of them, been soothed and amused by them so many times, their complaints about their children's unpredictable sleeping patterns, the recalcitrance of husbands, their diet frustrations and impossible mothers-in-laws, the lack of heat in their sex lives. They helped each other out when one got sick or a babysitter quit, they made inordinate amounts of Duncan Hines cupcakes for bake sales, they passed along rumors about whose child had lice. And she knew the boundaries, the commiseration but deep-seated fear when a marriage broke up—they were aware of the odds and, like cancer, they hoped it would happen to someone else, sparing them. All of them had heard one way or another about Todd's moving out last year.

Sarah was cognizant of the impression she and Todd had initially made—living slightly to the left of the rules, the romance of an artist so much headier than that of their own lawyer and banker husbands—but she sensed now that they were relieved, vindicated, as if their more pragmatic choices inured them against anything similar happening to them. Perhaps they were right. Sarah had realized lately how little thought she had given to the future and its looming responsibilities when she married Todd. She had only wanted to be with him, nothing more. Love truly is the greatest act of naïveté.

"I heard what happened. I'm so sorry." Sarah looked up to see Tara Benson, Jackie's mother, talking to her. The other mothers stood a few inches back, looking on sympathetically, desperate to hear the conversation but wanting to at least appear to give her space.

"Thank you," Sarah said.

She did not know what they had heard, which version of events. She did not know what, precisely, the sympathy was for.

The mothers waited silently for details.

"He drowned," Sarah told them. "They haven't found the body, so we're not exactly sure how it happened."

Even as she said it, she wondered how she would explain it if he came back, or if it turned out he had died another way.

"If there's anything, anything at all I can do." The other mothers murmured in assent.

"Thank you." Sarah looked away, then back to them. "I should get to work," she said.

She walked quickly out of the school yard and then stood, her face pressed against the cool metal of the gate, watching her daughter until the class was led inside and Eliza's blond head disappeared behind the heavy red door, taking a piece of Sarah with her.

All day, she pictured Eliza silent, Eliza in a corner, Eliza hiding from questions; and she pictured her relenting, joining the games at recess, sitting on the rug at story time, leaning on her elbows, listening intently. We never truly know who our children are when they are away from us, their personalities alter outside the familiarity and proscribed roles of home, but Sarah knew less than ever now.

"How was your first day of school?" she asked over dinner that night. She had set the table, made the effort.

"Fine."

"What did you do?""

"Stuff."

There was little more information to garner, Eliza had shut the door.

Miss Harcourt called on the third night to say that Eliza was doing fine. "She's participating in class, though not as much as I'd like to see yet, but that's true of many children in the beginning of the school year. I didn't know her before, so I don't know what her 'normal' is."

Sarah wanted to say that she didn't either.

"Most important," Miss Harcourt continued, "she is engaging with other children. I haven't seen any outbursts or signs of withdrawal that would indicate a cause for concern. She seems to enjoy the class." Dora, also, reported no problems when she picked Eliza up from school each day. Sarah was both relieved and surprised—it certainly didn't mirror the silent fury Eliza was exhibiting with her. She realized then that Eliza would put on her best face in public, much as Sarah did. They shared a stubborn pride, an unwillingness to show fault lines, survivors both. But they would end the day worn out from the effort and in the safety of their own apartment collapse, no longer feeling the need or possessing the energy to pretend anymore. They saved the worst of themselves for each other.

Sarah was no longer allowed to kiss Eliza. In fact, she was not allowed to touch her. Whenever she approached her, Eliza made an angry groaning sound and pushed her away. It was as if she had decided that she could not risk needing anyone ever again.

Deep in the night, Sarah sneaked into Eliza's room and kissed her head, her neck, her arms, her touch illicit, unwanted, but not, she believed, unneeded. Their love had gone underground. She called Deirdre Gerard to describe this latest development.

"Was she a physically affectionate child before this happened?" Deirdre asked.

"Yes," Sarah replied. She remembered how Eliza used to crawl onto her lap every morning for what they called a "love fest," how when Sarah told her, "I love you this much," widening her arms, Eliza widened hers more and said, "I love you *this* much," each trying to outdo the other until Eliza finally proclaimed triumphantly, "I *infinity* love you." Was that child gone for good?

"Tell Eliza she has to let you kiss her," Deirdre recommended, "but let her decide when and for how long, five seconds, ten. Tell her you'll give her a gold star every time you kiss her and agree on a reward at the end of the week, a toy she wants, an ice cream sundae."

This is what it had come to, then, bribing her daughter, coercing her into accepting love again.

"If that doesn't work, we'll try something else," Deirdre assured her.

Sarah agreed to try it and report back.

The gold star system was not an overwhelming success, but she accidentally discovered another way to hold on to Eliza. Two nights later, they were watching a documentary on dinosaurs that turned suddenly scary, all gaping jaws and enormous teeth. Slowly, wordlessly, Eliza crept closer to Sarah, their thighs touching, a thin stream of warmth between them. As the dinosaurs grew more ominous, Eliza slid onto her mother's lap. Sarah carefully wrapped her arms around her, hoping that if neither of them acknowledged it, it could not be rejected.

Sarah rented scary movies every night for the rest of the week.

Fifteen

By Thursday, when Bill McCrory still hadn't returned to Loudon Beach, both Medford and Sarah were beginning to get edgy. Medford checked with the stereo supply store where he worked and was told he had decided to extend his trip by another few days.

"Something's not adding up," he told Sarah. "You know how he said he was visiting his mother in New Orleans?"

"Yes?"

"His mother died six years ago."

"Do you believe he's even in Louisiana?"

"I'm not sure. He's still not answering his cell phone."

"What if he doesn't come back?"

"I've checked his house. There's no sign of it being closed up for an extended period. Let's give it a little more time before we jump to any conclusions."

Suspended, with nothing but more waiting before her, Sarah decided to visit a psychic famous for working with the New York City Police Department. There were a handful of seers popular with editors in New York, and like surgeons, each had a specialty. There was one renowned for her acumen with real estate: If you were searching for an apartment, she was brilliant at telling you what streets to look on; sometimes she dreamed actual addresses and called her clients in the morning with the building numbers, 1045 Park or 310 East Fifty-seventh Street. Another psychic, whose duplex was filled with leopard skin throws and four Siamese cats that rubbed up against nervous clients' legs, was a specialist in romance. She used tarot to predict three, six, and eighteen months into the future and had all her clients tape-record the session, convinced, rightly, that there would be too much information for them to remember. Some, "the affair tapes," she stashed herself for clients who could not risk their spouses stumbling upon them. And there was Alexandra Fumillo, a squat woman in her sixties famous for helping the police find missing bodies and runaways. She had cemented her reputation by leading a New York City detective to the site where the dismembered parts of a Staten Island teenager were buried after months of investigative dead ends.

Though psychics were an acceptable excuse to be absent from work (along with emergency bikini waxes before last-minute dates and the annual Chanel sample sale in the Regency Hotel that only a very select few were invited to) Sarah left word with Maude that she would be at a meeting with a writer to discuss new statistical information on the leisure habits of American women that Roper was set to release next month, and headed to the Upper East Side.

She walked into the high-rise apartment in the East Sixties with mirrored walls and a sparkling view of the East River to be greeted by an assistant with a lacquered pitch-black beehive hairdo and heavy liquid eyeliner. As per instructions, Sarah had brought a photograph of Todd and an item of clothing. Rigaud candles dotted the room and the thick white flokati rugs were spotless. After ten minutes, Alexandra Fumillo emerged from the back, wearing a worn flowered housedress and terry-cloth slippers. Her short gray hair was not entirely clean-looking and she had a rough smoker's voice. "Come, baby," she said.

Sarah followed her into a bedroom where a rectangular glass table stood in the corner with gold tapestry chairs on either side. The two women sat opposite each other.

"I'm so sorry, baby," Fumillo said, taking Sarah's hands in hers.

Her nails had been freshly manicured, the petal-pink polish shining and bright against her otherwise drab appearance.

There were no tarot cards, no questions about birthdates, astrological signs, no crystal ball. Fumillo took the photograph of Todd smiling in the front seat of the red Fiat convertible and pressed it between her hands. She made soft grunting sounds of assent while Sarah sat on the edge of her chair, waiting. Fumillo reached for the scarf Sarah had brought and closed her eyes, rocking back and forth, back and forth. Sarah was at once cynical, wondering how much of this was show, and primed to believe anything the woman had to say.

Finally, Fumillo spoke. "There's been a blow to the head. And another woman. She's no good."

"Is he alive?" Sarah asked.

"I'm not sure. He was hit in the head or there's something wrong with his mind. His consciousness is not there."

"He was hit?"

"Tell the police to look for a blue car. A blue car," Fumillo repeated.

Sarah was ushered back into the living room where she paid the assistant $250 in cash. She called Medford from her cell phone on her way back to the office. "Listen, this might sound crazy," she began, "but I went to see a psychic."

"It's not crazy. The police here do it all the time."

Sarah told him what Fumillo had said, her voice faltering when she mentioned the "blow to the head."

"Well, when I see McCrory I'll check out his car," Medford assured her.

"So?" Paige asked when Sarah got back. She looked up from the sparkly yellow powder she was rubbing on the back of her hand. The product was supposed to refract light to disguise wrinkles without the usual cover-up, but Sarah thought it looked suspiciously like the glittery stage makeup little girls wore for their first ballet recital.

"I don't know. There was a lot of shtick. She kept calling me 'baby.' She didn't seem to know if he was alive or dead. Just that there was 'no consciousness.' "

"Did you believe her?"

"Who knows? I called Medford and he didn't discount what she said."

"Of course not. Cops are sentimental and superstitious."

"He's not a cop. He's a private eye."

"Same difference. Besides, he used to be a cop. Trust me, cops and psychics are always having affairs." Paige claimed to know the sexual proclivities of any given profession or ethnic group. More often than not, she was right. "I have to admit, the part about the woman who is no good is weird," she admitted.

"I keep thinking about the 'no consciousness' thing, the way Todd was muttering in German. What if he did have some kind of breakdown? He didn't have any ID, no one would know who he is."

"They've been checking all the hospitals, haven't they?"

"Yes," Sarah admitted. "But people get lost in the system all the time."

"It's possible." Paige leaned over. "Are you okay?"

Sarah nodded.

"Then we should get going," Paige said gently, wiping the last bit of powder from her hand and grabbing a pink silk notebook. "Rena's waiting for us."

Sarah nodded and picked up her notes on *Splash*.

As they walked down the hall, they could feel the air of mild agitation that had permeated the fourth floor for months escalating into barely concealed panic. As Paige had predicted, *Flair*'s second-quarter numbers for newsstand and advertising sales had taken a precipitous nosedive. Editors were staying late to polish up their résumés and e-mail them around town from personal AOL accounts they had downloaded onto their computers. (CMH was widely rumored to read its employees' e-mails at will. Some believed they had access to personal accounts as well, though most discounted this on technical rather than moral grounds.) Surreptitious phone calls were placed to friends at other magazines and the top headhunters who specialized in editorial talent. In a sure sign of perceived weakness, Hallmark had been calling around offering editors lucrative contracts to write greeting cards for them. There were no takers so far, but anything could happen.

Inside Rena's office there remained an aura of calm, carefully constructed optimism, though it was hard to tell whether this was evidence of her supreme talent for denial, a brilliant corporate strategy, or the outcome of her honest belief that all would be well. Sitting across from her, Sarah found her as inscrutable as ever.

Three days ago Sarah and Paige had given her a packet containing *Splash*'s mission statement, a list of adjectives that described the look and tone of the magazine (*cheeky, exuberant, in-the-know*), a sample TOC, and an analysis of the newsstand metrics pointing out the specific hole *Splash* would fill.

They looked on as Rena studied the packet in front of her, reading it one last time, her forefinger going down the lines as they tried to infer from her expression what she might be thinking. Every now and then they glanced down at their own copies, pretending to read along.

> Splash *is a celebration of the singular time in a young woman's life when anything is possible. Post-college, pre–settling down, the* Splash *Girl is in her first job, her first apartment, her first serious relationship. Adventurous, flexible, filled with energy, she's faced with more options than any other generation. She's still figuring out who she is (clothes, hair, makeup, her home, the music she listens to, even her job and the car she drives are all part of her search).*

Finally, Rena looked up and, patting the piece of paper as she would a well-behaved child, allowed a sly smile to spread across her face. "You've done a wonderful job," she said. Paige and Sarah exhaled in unison.

"It's focused and fresh. What I'd like for you to do is work up a few sample logos, three covers, and four or five spreads so that I can get a feel for the visual language you have in mind. I will give you a small budget, say twenty thousand dollars, to hire an outside designer. This must all be done off-premises, you understand, on your own time."

"Of course."

"And we will keep this strictly between us."

Paige and Sarah agreed.

As they headed down the hallway, Sarah asked, "Is she going to take credit for everything we did?"

"Well, if—and it's still a big if—it launches, she'd oversee it. And yeah, she'd get the top spot on the masthead. But we'd still get to work on it, and it's a helluva lot more fun than *Flair.* Do you know Tim Wakefield?"

"I know of him." Wakefield and Co. had designed the hottest fashion ads of the last ten years, images that not only sold the goods of almost every important European designer but helped to set the agenda for styles throughout America, from overt sexuality to prim Hitchcockian schoolmarms. They had created an oversize German magazine that did not sell more than five thousand copies but did more to influence the currents in art and fashion than any edition of *Vogue* and had such individual clients as the head of the AIDS America Foundation.

Tim Wakefield was something of a mystery in the world where fashion, design, art, and advertising intersect. Known for his high level of taste, his aversion to parties, and his soft-spoken manner, he preferred to let his front man, the chattily flamboyant Noah Jenson, do the talking. Though early on, people had assumed the two men were a couple, Tim was straight, recently divorced, and had a young son. Paige had done her research.

"I've always wanted to meet him," she said.

Sarah's eyebrows raised.

"No. I mean, professionally. He'd be better for you."

"Oh God, Paige, I am so not ready for that. Besides, men who care more about fashion than I do hold no appeal for me."

"I hear he's something of an intellectual."

Sarah glanced at her skeptically.

"Anyway, that isn't why I brought it up. He'd be the perfect designer for *Splash.* I put in a call this morning to set up an appointment."

"What if Rena hadn't liked it?"

"I would have canceled."

They looked up to see Pat walking toward them with a curious expression narrowing her eyes.

"You two look happy," she said suspiciously. It was not, after all, a common emotion at *Flair* these days despite Rena's edict that Happiness was the next big thing, attainable for the cover price of $3.50.

Paige and Sarah both assumed more neutral demeanors.

"Sarah, can I talk to you for a minute?" Pat asked. "In my office."

"Of course."

She peeled away from Paige and walked in silence to Pat's office, the click of her heels echoing down the long hallway. The lift had come off of her Sigerson pump and the lopsided rhythm added to her general sense of vulnerability, as if this evidenced yet again that she was too clumsy for this building, this project, this subterfuge.

Pat closed her door behind them and sat down briskly at her desk.

Her displeasure with Sarah had been growing since she had proved unwilling—unable, Sarah protested—to sway Rena from the Body Issue despite the meticulously argued case Pat and Anna had laid out for her.

In fact, the Body Issue was proceeding close to how it had been originally conceived—or ill-conceived, as many still insisted. The manuscripts were all in, though few had gotten final approval, the photography was complete, and initial layouts were making the rounds. Among other stories, they had found two women to switch lives, managed to invent 87 Ways Real Women Get What They Want Every Time, come up with 29 Tantric Sex Tricks to Try Tonight, and promised a Road Map to Lasting Body Confidence at Any Size. The only real adjustment had been the cancellation of the life-sized poster of a naked woman. Though Rena had fought hard for it, it was pulled for financial rather than aesthetic reasons—the extra paper and production costs were simply too prohibitive given the current state of affairs.

Pat, seeing that the issue was going ahead despite her objections, took on a calibrated stance of benign neglect. She no longer voiced her opinion, at least within earshot of Rena, nor did she make any pretense of enthusiasm. She was simply going to ride it out, leaving as few fingerprints as possible on either side of the deck.

Sarah settled into the chair opposite Pat and watched as she straightened her French cuffs, prolonging the moment.

Slowly, Pat opened a desk drawer and pulled out a single sheet of paper.

Sarah was shocked to see that it was the supposedly confidential mission statement for *Splash*.

"You did a good job," Pat said. "I took the liberty of showing it to my niece in Chicago. She's nineteen, a little younger than your demographic, but everyone knows teenagers buy up. Anyway, she liked it, though she thought that there should be a few more interactive elements. She asked about a Web site. Do you have a model for one?" Pat asked.

"Not yet."

"I'd work on that. And you might want to bring the target age from twenty-four down to twenty-two."

Sarah nodded.

"Anyway, I just wanted to let you know that I'm here if you need me. I do think this has a good chance of success if properly executed, and I will do everything I can to help ensure that. One last thing, Sarah."

"Yes?"

"Paige is a wonderful big-picture thinker. There's no doubt she has a certain . . . style. But as I'm sure you know, she's not exactly terrific on the follow-through."

Sarah looked at her without saying anything.

"I'm counting on you to make certain she's not distracted from her main duties here. Her job requires her to be out in the marketplace a lot. Beyond editing copy, she must be the face of *Flair* at cosmetics events. I wouldn't want to hear she had missed any."

There was an implicit threat—to Sarah, to Paige—though it was squirrelly and hard to pinpoint.

Sixteen

The next morning, Paige and Sarah met on a street corner in TriBeCa a block from the offices of Wakefield and Co. The winds from the Hudson River whipped through their hair, and trucks rattled noisily by as they headed for 215 Vandam Street. Thrown off by a sudden dip in temperature unusual for mid-September, they had taken different sartorial routes. Paige was wearing a sleeveless chiffon dress under a thin belted jacket with bare legs and open-toed Jimmy Choos. Sarah had on knee-high black Ralph Lauren boots that she had "invested" in one particularly gloomy afternoon in Barneys last year, a black wool pencil skirt, and a fitted blazer that didn't quite match but that she hoped she could get away with. Both, despite working in the most fashionable building in Manhattan, had tried on and discarded numerous outfits that morning. Not only would they be meeting the architect of some of the most iconic designer advertising campaigns of the past decade, but there hovered over Wakefield's reputation the insouciant taint of downtown cool that found only pale imitations above Fourteenth Street.

"You look great."

"So do you," they reassured each other.

Sarah was holding the packet that contained copies of everything they had put together on *Splash,* though they'd sent over the same material the night before. They had, since their meeting with Rena, decided on four stories to ask for layouts of: "The $250 Apartment Makeover," "I Was Addicted to Vicodin," "Win a Month's Worth of Shoes," and "Beauty Rehab, 27 Good Moves for Bad Girls." The stories had not in fact been written—nor would they be, there was no budget for that—the titles alone would have to give Tim Wakefield enough of an idea to design the layouts.

They entered the large eleven-story industrial building that had recently been taken over by numerous photography studios, design firms, and nascent modeling agencies and rode up in the oversize elevator.

Opening the brushed gray metal doors of Wakefield and Co. they found themselves in an enormous open space washed with sunlight pouring through an entire wall of floor-to-ceiling windows. The loft-like room was filled with at least twenty people seated in two rows of long, connected white desks, the latest large-screen Apple computers before them while Beck played softly in the background. The receptionist, who had a striking resemblance to Patti Smith in her earliest incarnation, offered them sparkling water, cappuccino, green tea, or vitamin water as she led them into a soundproofed conference room. Sarah and Paige looked up at the walls lined with blown-up ads for Gucci, Prada, Dior, YSL and shelves decorated with the innovative bottles Wakefield had designed for a new Italian perfume as well as an iced white tea that had become the latest obsession of models who swore it was the best way, at least of the legal options, to help in weight loss. (The fact that it contained extremely rare herbs that none of them could pronounce, said to be used by ancient Mayans before heading into battle, added to its allure.)

"Remember," Paige whispered, "we're the clients. It's their job to sell us."

"Funny, it feels like we're the ones trying to prove we're cool enough for them to take our job."

"Well, there's that, too," Paige said with a half laugh.

Noah Jenson, office manager, financial negotiator, public persona of Wakefield, strode in first, wearing jeans, a white Izod shirt, and battered Pumas, his hair ruffled and hinting at highlights just growing out, though of course they could have been put in last night with that very intention. He smiled openly at them. "Thanks for coming down. We would have come to you, but we understand the delicacy of the situation."

"No problem," Paige said.

"So," he began, setting down his iced latte. "CMH hasn't launched a magazine in, what, four years? Are they serious about this?"

"Totally," Sarah assured him.

"But don't they have their own in-house incubator system for this sort of project? I've heard rumors about a mysterious idea lab on the fifteenth floor."

Both women nodded. The room existed two doors down from Leon Compton's vast office, but no one they knew had ever been inside of it. Some suspected that is was actually used by married executives to meet their mistresses, but others swore they had seen layouts go in and out.

"This is more of a personal project for Rena Berman at the moment," Sarah replied.

"I haven't seen Rena in years. How is she?" All three turned around to see Tim Wakefield walking in. "Can she still sell you your own shoes?" He was smiling indulgently, as if a lovely memory had coursed through him. His warm brown eyes, flecked with gold, crinkled at the corners, casting an alluringly weathered look. His was a face of shadows and planes, exotic in its unabashed show of experience.

"Yes, as a matter of fact, she can," Sarah said, smiling.

If Sarah and Paige had been expecting a style icon decked out in Hedi Slimane, they were mistaken. Tim Wakefield was wearing nondescript jeans, a blazer, a white oxford shirt, and a light brown stubble that matched his attractively shaggy hair.

Sarah watched, curious, as he sat down opposite them and leafed through the packet on *Splash*.

"Have you thought about size?" he asked without looking up.

For a moment, they could not figure what he was referring to.

"For the magazine," he explained, his voice soft, unhurried. "In Europe, the exciting titles for younger women are pocket-sized. It's so much more modern to be able to throw it into your backpack, don't you think? And scale, of course, must help to dictate content. Simply doing the same thing but shrinking it down is the lazy way out."

"Yes," Paige replied enthusiastically. She was an enormous fan of British *Glamour,* which had enjoyed brilliant success with its digest size.

"The only problem is display space." Sarah didn't want to be seen as the prosaic naysayer standing in the way of creativity, but she did feel obligated to point out the biggest commercial drawback. "CMH's racks in stores are designed for standard-size books. If we can't get space at the newsstand or checkout counters, we won't have a shot."

Tim cocked his head slightly, studying her. His eyes were steady, inquisitive, absorbent. She looked down, feeling herself flush.

He smiled. "You're right. But I've been looking into creating plastic inserts for existing racks that wouldn't be prohibitively expensive. It might allow us to have the best of both worlds."

Sarah nodded, alert to the word *us*.

"Why don't we do up a few pages in both sizes," Tim suggested. "We have some outtakes from fashion shoots that might be perfect for a couple of these stories. Since it would not be for commercial use at this point, I'm sure if I make a few phone calls the photographers won't mind. Did you have any specific celebrity in mind for the cover?"

Names were thrown out, mainstream, edgy, classically beautiful, not.

"Well," Tim said. "In my experience, no one at CMH knows what they want until they see it. Why don't we do covers with four or five different faces? I see some handwriting for the cover lines, a mix of fonts and graffiti. Primary colors. Nothing too formal. Lots of layers, quick hits. That's how people get their information these days, in pop-ups. It should be quite multidimensional. We'll need to come up with a signature icon you can repeat throughout the pages as well as in marketing kits. I'm assuming you've done an analysis of the competitive set?"

"We can get it to you," Sarah assured him, impressed—and a

little surprised—by the pragmatism that lay beneath his creative instincts, though of course you did not build a company of this size or reputation by ignoring business realities.

"Good. Well, this is all very exciting. It has a lot of potential," Tim said. Again, that cipher of a half-smile, confident, interested, amused.

"We think so," Paige agreed.

They talked for a few more minutes about deadlines, how pages and images would be shown, approved, rejected, how copy would flow. Finally, an awkward silence ensued. The subject of money had not yet come up.

As if reading their minds, Noah piped in, "I'll e-mail you over some projected costs later today."

"Perfect," Sarah said, relieved.

Five minutes later, Paige and Sarah stood on the wide windy TriBeCa street, trying to get a cab.

"Okay, you have to admit he's hot," Paige said.

"Who?"

"Tim Wakefield."

"Yes."

"Well?" Paige prodded.

"Well what? It's business. Besides, I told you, I'm not ready."

Paige frowned. "He is single, successful, straight, handsome, and supposedly a good father. How long do you think he's going to last in this town? Five minutes, tops. Hell, it's probably already too late."

"So," Sarah said, anxious to change the subject, "dare I ask how it's going with Ethan?"

Paige smiled. "It's good. Really good, actually. We've been talking about everything, including our breakup. I told him I didn't understand how his feelings could change like that for no apparent reason and he said that they never really had."

"What does that mean? If his feelings didn't change, why did he break up with you?"

"He just got scared. It became too real."

"I thought that was generally the goal."

Paige ignored this. "It's so much easier talking to him this time. We're both much more honest."

"Did he give you any reason other than cowardice for his behavior?"

"He said I intimidated him."

"Do you really want to be with someone you intimidate?"

"The funny thing is, *I* was intimidated by *him*. I always felt that I was breaking some rule I didn't even know existed."

"Sounds like a great relationship."

"We're past all that," Paige protested. "I still get butterflies when I see him." She shook her head, laughed. "Get this, he started going to therapy and he's taken up kickboxing."

Sarah laughed. These were both things that Paige had been messianic about before she decided that the $150 an hour her therapist charged was better spent at Manolo Blahnik and Pilates was a more effective workout. "All right, maybe he has changed," Sarah conceded.

"His divorce becomes final next month."

"Do you want to marry him?"

"I don't know. It's funny, one of the things we've talked about is his paranoia that I was trying to rush him into a second marriage. It always pissed me off. It's so stereotypical, this belief that all women want to trap men. It's crazy. First, they convince themselves that you're trying to manipulate them into marriage, then they freak out about the commitment and run away. And none of it has anything to do with you. It's all in their heads. But he said that he realized now it was all coming from him, his need to re-create the life he had before."

"Remind me never to date."

"You can't just give up on that part of life."

"Spoken with the conviction of the newly reunited. Be careful, okay?"

Paige nodded, but caution was clearly the furthest thing from her mind. There was nothing left for Sarah to say. As the CMH building came into view, she turned to Paige. "Listen, don't give Pat any ammunition."

"What are you talking about?"

"Just be sure you show up at every meeting, get your copy in early, that kind of thing."

Paige's back arched. "What did she say to you?"

"She hates us both, Paige. You know that."

"She's such a bitch."

"Yes, but she's a very smart bitch."

"The best ones always are."

By the time they arrived at the office, rumors had grown that Paige and Sarah were working on a secret redesign of *Flair,* though opinion was split on whether this was at Rena's or Pat's behest. They were the anointed ones or the traitors, depending. Regardless, they were treated with a certain grudging respect. In a building that thrived on furtiveness, innuendo created power.

For the rest of day they buckled down to their separate duties, though Paige could not help but glare at Pat whenever she saw so much as her shadow in the hallway.

Sarah edited final copy for the Body Issue and read some proposals for future lineups, but she found it difficult to concentrate. For weeks now she had functioned with such deep exhaustion that at first she did not recognize the sensation that was rattling through her—anticipation. She only knew that she had enjoyed the way ideas had bounced around the table at Wakefield, the sense of open-ended exploration.

At 4:00 p.m. an e-mail arrived with Wakefield's proposal. When Sarah first saw who it was from, her pulse quickened. She was mildly let down when she discovered that the enclosed message was from Noah, containing a friendly if brief note that ended with the line, "We are all, particularly Tim, very excited at the prospect of working on this project with you."

Sarah read this last sentence far more times than its brevity and content would justify before turning her attention to the complicated fee structure.

Seventeen

Eight days later, Bill McCrory finally came back from New Orleans. Sarah, who had been profoundly suspicious of his ongoing absence, was surprised at his return; his disappearance had become a crucial factor in the increasingly baroque theories about Todd's disappearance that had been forming in her mind.

Medford met with him in the back of the stereo supply store as soon as he showed up for work.

"Linda had already spoken to him," he told Sarah, "and he definitely had an attitude. He made it clear he was only talking to me because she asked him to, but I get the feeling he doesn't want Brook on his back either."

"I thought Brook wasn't interested in McCrory," Sarah remarked, confused.

"He's not, but I implied otherwise. Look, the guy already has a record. He doesn't want any more trouble."

"And?"

"Well, McCrory's version of his relationship with Linda is slightly different than hers. According to him, they never really broke up. Seems they have been doing this on-again/off-again dance for a couple of years and he had no reason to think she wasn't going to get back together with him."

"That would make him even angrier to find Todd there."

"He did admit he was unhappy about that, but he denies driving by her house that night."

"Do you believe him?"

"Hard to say. He's not exactly a stand-up guy. He seemed a little fidgety, nervous, but that's not unusual, given the circumstances."

"Did you ask him what he was doing in New Orleans?"

"Yes. At first he told me the same story he told his boss, that he was visiting his mother. When I told him I knew his mother was dead, he got pissed and told me it was none of my business. I'll root around and see what I can learn."

"What about the night Todd disappeared?"

"He claims he was visiting a cousin over in Daytona. I'm going to drive up there tomorrow and check it out as soon as I can get a hold of him." He paused. "I might need to stay overnight."

Sarah didn't reply.

"Is that all right with you?" Medford asked carefully.

She had forgotten that her life was a job to him, and that she was paying him by the hour.

"Yes, of course. Whatever you need."

"Good. Oh, and one more thing."

"Yes?"

"McCrory's car is white, not blue."

Sarah hung up the phone slowly. Whatever answers she was hoping for were once again vaporous and impossible to clasp; she was no closer.

"You need a lawyer," Lucy told her later that afternoon.

"For what?"

"You're in a no-man's-land, Sarah. You have to get advice on how to proceed."

"What do you mean?" Sarah asked warily. The notion—how to proceed—was alien. One of the strangest by-products of what had happened was her complete inability to envision the future more than a week ahead. Every time she tried, her brain seemed to hit a brick wall that she could not get around. She was an emotional amputee, some crucial part of her consciousness cut off, and she had yet to learn to operate without it.

"It's been two months, Sarah. No matter what happened, I don't think Todd is coming back. There are legalities, life insurance, wills." Her voice was kind but firm.

"I know," Sarah said softly. "I do believe he died that night. But I still see him everywhere I go. I still expect to round a corner and find him there, or to come home and find a phone message from him, or news, any kind of news." She took a deep breath. "I just can't believe they won't find his body."

"I hope you find out what happened that night. But either way, you need to know what your options are."

Lucy gave her the name of her lawyer and Sarah dutifully wrote it down, but she did not make the call. Even that act, a single preliminary phone call, seemed a step in a direction she was not ready to take.

The next morning, she sat with her knees pressed up against the splintery underbelly of the small wooden desk in room 216, watching Eliza's class in their first play of the season, a reenactment of *Jack and the Beanstalk.* Eliza, one of the townspeople, walked out in a long printed skirt that Sarah had stapled the night before when, after turning the linen closet upside down, she could not find a single needle. Eliza seemed so much smaller and more vulnerable here than she did at home, where she expanded to fill the space. Her thin arms and legs, her eyes so heartbreakingly serious, lent her a defenselessness that cut through Sarah's being.

Sarah, sitting alone in the third row, could feel other parents glance over at her with a mixture of curiosity and sympathy, but they didn't take their gaze off their own children for long. They took videos with impossibly small, sleek new cameras and snapped pictures to e-mail to grandparents that very afternoon; they smiled and nudged each other with delight. Even the divorced couples who fought in lawyers' offices with a terrifying venom sat near each other and managed to make prideful, if fleeting, eye contact.

When Eliza came to the fore and recited her lines, tears formed in Sarah's eyes. She kept smiling and tried to wipe them away before anyone, particularly her daughter, spied them, though she could not stop the trembling of her lower lip.

This is what Todd was missing: his daughter growing up, the growing strength of her voice, the first time she poured her own milk into a cereal bowl, so solemn as she closed the carton and put it away, this first-grade play. Sarah could not understand, no matter how many books she read, no matter how many therapists she talked to, why the touch of his daughter's flesh on his didn't mean more than anything else, didn't mean everything, why these simple joys, this love, weren't enough.

And if not love, curiosity to see who his daughter grew up to be.

And if not curiosity, responsibility.

Unless, of course, that choice had been taken away from him.

Sarah stepped out of the room to keep Eliza, her teacher, the other parents from seeing the tears leaking down her face. She stood in the hallway, leaning up against a wall covered with self-portraits of second- and third-graders, aware of the curious looks from the librarian, the stray child or two on their way to the bathroom.

Finally, she composed herself and went back into the classroom, where the children were clustered around tables of cupcakes with orange icing, powder-sugared donut holes, and apple juice, greedily grabbing and jostling with each other. She was pleased to see that Eliza was right in there with them, a streak of icing on her chin. When it was time for the parents to leave, though, she sullenly turned her face away from Sarah's kiss. Separations, even if just for a day at work and school, remained loaded.

Outside the school building, Sarah waved frantically at every passing cab, empty or not, anxious about being so late, giving Pat an infringement to mark in the ledger she was surely keeping hidden somewhere in the reaches of her desk, her mind. School plays were not necessarily an acceptable excuse to the childless.

She worked straight through the afternoon and was surprised when Paige knocked on her door. "You ready?"

Sarah looked at her watch. It was already 7:00 p.m. She had reluctantly agreed to go out with Ethan and Paige for the first time since they'd started seeing each other again. Though Sarah was not particularly looking forward to it, Paige was anxious to prove Ethan's viability and get her approval. Dora was happy to stay late with Eliza, giving her no easy out.

"I made a reservation at Barona," Paige offered as further encouragement.

"How'd you manage that?" Barona, which had just opened after a month of carefully staged private parties for editors, models, and a few select trust fund babes, was already notoriously impossible to get a table at.

"I have a way with maître d's."

Sarah stared at her, waiting for details.

"Okay, I went to Brown with the owner's sister, who's working as the hostess," Paige admitted. "She was a notorious bulimic. Left hideous stains every time she borrowed my clothes."

"That's disgusting."

Paige shrugged. "Everyone thinks her raspy voice is so sexy, but the truth is she destroyed her throat with all the throwing up. Anyway, I sent her over a bag of product and voilà. Combine La Mer's latest serum with fear that I'll tell her stodgy new Wall Street fiancé about her college bathroom antics and basically, I have a table for life."

Sarah was not sure she was up to witnessing another couple's display of newfound happiness and she could not completely forgive Ethan for his previous behavior, but, because it was important to Paige, she nodded and shut off her computer.

Barona, with its subtly marked façade on the farthest reaches of the West Village, was, despite its vaguely provincial Italian–sounding name, a place of sharp edges, bad acoustics, and spectacularly overpriced food of indeterminate origin. Sarah and Paige squeezed past the scantily dressed women and coolly avid men clustered at the bar to where Ethan was sitting, a scotch-and-soda before him. In his slightly rumpled deep gray suit and Thomas Pink shirt, he looked exactly like what he was, a well-educated, tasteful man with the best of intentions. He had gone to the same schools as his father, and his father before him and there was, Sarah recalled, a football stadium, perhaps a library, carrying the family name on at least one of the campuses. He was one of those men, growing ever rarer in New York, with patriarchs they can never live up to and shrinking dynastic expectations, riddled with all the arrogance and insecurity that entails.

Sarah watched as he and Paige kissed hello, their lips lingering, and then she pecked him on the cheek herself. They had not seen each other in months.

"I'm so sorry about Todd," Ethan said, his light brown eyebrows knitted together in concern. "Is there any news?"

"Not really."

Sarah ordered a glass of Shiraz, Paige a martini while they waited for their table. Ethan, a lawyer who specialized in First Amendment causes, began to tell them about a case he had just taken on, representing a well-known journalist who refused to give over the name of her government source to a newly appointed special prosecutor. The story, which was just beginning to hover around the edges of the news, interested Sarah and for a little while she was content to listen. Ethan's passion for the case, his strong convictions of right and wrong, were contagious, and Sarah could see why Paige was so drawn to him. Paige downed her martini while they spoke—she had a tendency to drink quickly around Ethan and then be too rattled by desire and nerves to eat. She had lost five pounds since she started seeing him again. She also had a near-constant hangover.

When their table was finally ready, Sarah followed the two of them as they wove single file around animated groups seated calculatedly close together. She watched Paige's hand touch Ethan's back and stay there, slowly sliding down as they walked, a connection, a promise, and she felt an ache in her chest so powerful that it made her rock back on her heels.

A smile played across Ethan's lips as he watched Paige order, flirt with the waiter, cajoling him into special side dishes. His eyes lit up with delight and a certain wonderment—that Paige existed, this woman with her platinum hair and her frill-encased cleavage and her unabashed zest—but Sarah sensed, too, a detachment that she could not put her finger on. He seemed a man struggling to move beyond the limitations of his world. Whether he would succeed or not was anyone's guess.

Paige, halfway through her second martini, began telling a raucous story about a seventy-one-year-old friend of her mother's who had taken up Internet dating. "She went out with a forty-five-year-old man, but he got 'fresh' at the door," Paige reported. "Then he e-mailed her the next day, something 'gross,' as my mother so eloquently put it, about wanting to put her legs over his head."

Ethan rolled his eyes, amused, uncomfortable. For all of his liberal views and his sophistication, he was bound by a code of manners that was clear to him but often murky to others. Paige, heedless, continued at full-speed. "She was all ready to go out with him again until her daughters put a stop to it. Here's my favorite part: My mother's take-away from the whole thing was, 'He lives in Pittsburgh. Who on earth lives in Pittsburgh?'"

Paige's voice had crescendoed as she reached the punch line and her laughter filled the already noisy room.

"Lower your voice," Ethan told her.

"Why? Am I embarrassing you?"

"You're only embarrassing yourself."

Paige shrugged it off and the conversation moved on to *Splash,* their visit to Wakefield, their plans for the magazine, the moment seemingly forgotten, though it lingered in Sarah's consciousness.

It was close to ten when they stood on the street as Town Cars pulled up, expelling the next round of diners, who grew chicer as the hour grew later, and began the awkward parting of a threesome. Sarah, worn out from the effort required by the evening, was as anxious to be alone as they were to be together.

She kissed them both good night and got in a cab, slumping against the backseat as it drove up First Avenue, past the Christmas lights decorating the row of Indian restaurants on Sixth Street, past Beth Israel Hospital to home.

After Dora left, Sarah turned on the radio in the bathroom, listening to NPR as she washed her face, put on whatever esoteric lifting cream Paige had given her that week, took out her contact lenses.

Finished, she climbed into bed and pulled the quilt tight to her neck. The room seemed so large, so empty and silent after the bustle of the restaurant.

She turned over, rearranged the pillow, rearranged it again, as if finding the right position would provide her with a comfort she could not find elsewhere. Paige, Eliza, *Splash,* Medford, McCrory, Todd's drawings, all swirled in her mind, but there was this, too, emerging from the ether: Tim Wakefield, his lean stubbled face, his curious, warm brown eyes as he watched her so closely.

She dreamt that night of touch, of longing.

The man was faceless, but as their bodies, their lips came closer she could feel the heat intensifying between them.

Sarah awoke with a feeling of yearning so overpowering that for one moment there was no room for the past, for regret, for grief, for fear, a desire so palpable that it reverberated through every cell in her body.

Eighteen

Sarah no longer knew what she was hoping for, she no longer knew what good news would be. She was stumbling through the blackness, arms outstretched, still hoping her fingertips would brush up against a discovery when Medford called three days later to say that he had met with Bill McCrory's cousin in Daytona.

"McCrory's alibi seems to hold up," he told Sarah.

"Seems to?"

"It's actually pretty solid. The cousin is a little skanky, but he gave me the timeline of their night and it checked out. I paid a visit to the bar where he said they went and the bartender remembers seeing them, as do a number of the patrons. They were there past one a.m."

Sarah's arms pulled back, the blackness encroaching once again. "What was McCrory doing in New Orleans?"

"Visiting an old girlfriend. A little bit of revenge romance. That checked out, too."

"Now what?" she asked dully.

She listened quietly while Medford told her that there were no further leads. "Brook is not going to question Linda again," he continued. "He and Linda are both still convinced that Todd is alive someplace. It looks like the voice stress test results are going to remain just another unexplained part of that night."

There is an aperture of time after a death or disappearance when clues, evidence, tips are most likely to accumulate. If that doesn't happen, interest begins to wane as attention and curiosity are gradually subsumed by the next case, the next story. Sarah saw that prospect looming ever closer and it terrified her.

"I've been getting calls," she said.

"Calls?"

"There is someone on the other line, I can hear them breathing, but they never speak." After the first time at Todd's studio, there had been three similar hang-ups on her home phone. Sometimes she pictured Todd standing in a phone booth in another part of the country listening, breathing.

"I can check your phone records if you'd like."

"Okay." She clutched the receiver tightly. "Karl?"

"Yes?"

"You're not going to give up, are you?"

There was a long pause. "Not yet. But Sarah, at some point you'll have to decide whether this is worth it. There is a law of diminishing returns."

"What do you mean?"

"Not all bodies, dead or alive, are found. I'm sorry, I know that's not what you hired me to tell you, but I need to be honest. There are still some things I want to follow up on, but you have to consider that possible outcome. I don't want to waste your money."

Sarah hung up without saying another word.

This is the nature of nightmare: a downward spiral of hope, when the body of someone you love becomes your most fervent desire.

And what would happen if they did give up, what was the course of action then?

She dug out the phone number of the lawyer Lucy had given her and made an appointment.

The following morning, she sat alone in Barnett Thompson's large, hushed midtown waiting room, staring at the perfectly dusted ficus tree by the end of the leather couch. When the ash blond receptionist looked down to answer the silently ringing telephone, Sarah reached over and touched one of the leaves to see if it was real. Caught, she quickly withdrew her hand, repeating her opening salvo in her mind: I am married to someone who may or may not exist.

"You can go in." Her thoughts were interrupted by the receptionist staring intently at her. Sarah wondered if she had been talking out loud. Lately as she walked to work, random words would escape, causing passersby to glance over at her with curiosity and alarm.

Barnett Thompson was standing at his open door, his thick tanned hand outstretched to shake hers. He closed the door behind them and touched her back lightly as he guided her to the oversize wing chair across from his mahogany desk. Settling into his own chair he leaned forward on his elbows. He had the kind of skin that had been permanently stained a reddish brown from years of sailing and made it hard to guess his age, though Sarah took him to be in his late forties. She waited for him to speak first, blinking in the glare from the large window behind him. Mixed in with the Stanford and Harvard degrees were Chagall lithographs, a late-period Picasso drawing. Tom Paxton played softly on the stereo—a sign Thompson hadn't given up his ideals, that he was a good guy. Sarah wondered if the music changed depending on the client.

"Lucy tells me you work at *Flair,*" he began.

"Yes." Sarah was momentarily nonplussed. She couldn't tell if this was merely a polite opening gambit designed to put her at ease or evidence of the rampant—and often prurient—interest CMH tended to elicit.

"My ex-wife used to work at CMH. Julia Reardon? Do you know her?"

"No, sorry." Sarah refrained from saying that it seemed at times that half of Manhattan had worked at CMH and either moved on to other media companies or left so traumatized that they were convinced the only possibility for real happiness lay in owning a farm in Vermont. "I've heard the name," she added, lying out of politeness.

"Crazy place," Thompson remarked.

He seemed to be waiting for more, an anecdote, a glossily salacious tidbit that he could dine out on. CMH had that effect on even the most successful people, instilling a mixture of moral superiority and envy.

"So," he leaned back. "Tell me what I can do for you."

Sarah laid out the facts in a controlled monotone. She pulled the police report out of her bag and watched as Thompson read it. He grunted slightly as he turned the pages with his forefinger. Then she told him of Medford's work.

Finally, he looked over at her. "Well, Sarah, we need to discuss two options," he said. "Death and divorce."

Sarah felt a cool sweat form in the back of her neck and the breath sputtering in her windpipe. She wondered what would happen if she fainted in his beautifully appointed office.

"Our first choice would clearly be a death certificate," Thompson continued. "Was there life insurance?"

"A small amount." Sarah and Todd had talked about increasing the policy last year but had never quite gotten around to it. They thought they had all the time in the world.

Thompson nodded. "You are pretty much at the mercy of the Florida PD. They can sign one now or they can make you wait five years."

"Five years?"

"That's how long it takes before the state is forced to issue one automatically. What's this Detective Brook like?"

Sarah paused. "He doesn't believe Todd is dead," she admitted. She searched Thompson's face for signs of doubt—about her story, her credibility—but did not discern any.

"Let me see what I can do. The evidence does lead one to believe that Brook should sign the certificate, but if not, you are going to have to divorce your husband."

"Divorce him?"

"Without a body or a death certificate, your life could get very sticky very quickly."

"It already is," she said wryly.

Thompson's eyebrows raised at the tinge of sarcasm. Sarah sensed a certain professional curiosity mixed in with sympathy.

Though he had surely seen numerous permutations of tragedy, Sarah wondered if this was his first missing body. "You need to protect your daughter and yourself," he said patiently. "I'll call Brook today and see if I can get him to budge. But if not, divorce may be the only option open to you."

There was a paternal tone in Thompson's voice that made Sarah realize how deeply she felt the absence of a husband, a father, the subtle net of protection men provided, in feeling if not in fact. Perhaps it was as simple as a deeper voice, a larger body, a barrier, but there was an element of safety, of comfort that had been taken away. There was no one left to defend her, protect her. Guardianless, she had become the guardian.

"What do you mean?" she asked.

"I'll give you one example. In New York, you need your husband's signature if you'd like your life insurance to go to your daughter instead of him. Without a death certificate or a divorce, that's not possible. There are any number of forms you have to sign all the time that ask if you are married, divorced, widowed, or single. At the moment, it appears that you are almost all of them and none of them."

"How on earth can I sue my husband for divorce?"

"Abandonment," Thompson replied.

The conversation continued for another ten minutes before Thompson walked Sarah to the door and squeezed her shoulder reassuringly. She felt the imprint of his hand long after she had left.

"Well, you have to admit walking into an ocean certainly qualifies as abandonment," Sarah remarked dryly to Paige later that morning. "I actually began to hyperventilate."

"Death and divorce at the same time? That would make the Dalai Lama hyperventilate. Maybe he can talk some sense into the police."

"I doubt it."

Thompson called Sarah later that afternoon. "I spoke to Detective Brook," he told her.

"And?"

"You're right. He doesn't believe your husband is dead. He will not sign a death certificate."

Sarah waited, nervous that Brook had convinced him that Todd was alive and she was delusional.

That did not seem to have happened, though. "You have two options," Thompson continued. "You can go to Florida and sue for one. But I have to warn you, there's a good chance you'd lose. I gathered from Brook that this Linda Granger would back him up. Plus, it would be extremely time-consuming. Court dates are subject to last-minute changes. There's the chance that you'd have to stay there for weeks."

"I can't do that."

"I didn't think so. In that case you will in all likelihood have to wait the five years until a death certificate becomes automatic. Unfortunately, you won't be able to get the life insurance before then either. In the meantime, we should pursue a divorce."

Sarah said nothing.

"There are the legal reasons that I outlined for you earlier." Thompson paused. "Sarah, you may find this hard to believe now, but you will also at some point want to get on with your life."

Sarah reluctantly gave him the go-ahead to do whatever he needed.

Nineteen

The following Monday Sarah got a cab in front of Eliza's school and gave the driver Wakefield's address. The first round of layouts was ready for viewing. She pulled out a compact and put a touch more sheer highlighter on her cheekbones, hoping it would minimize the hollows in her eyes. Her hair, freshly washed, blown out, flat-ironed, had actually managed to stay in place, grazing her shoulders.

Paige was already waiting for her. "I'm a bit nervous," she admitted as they headed into the building. "Not bad nervous. Excited nervous. It's all so Pygmalion, seeing what's in your mind come to life."

Upstairs, the receptionist had abandoned her Patti Smith look and seemed to be working on an alternative country-meets-Vegas kind of thing, with a sequined denim mini, a wife beater, and a new tattoo, hopefully temporary, of a weeping rose on her extraordinarily thin upper arm. She smiled broadly with a friendliness that let them know she didn't take it all that seriously and led them into the conference room, where an assortment of layouts were pinned up on the long white wall. Paige and Sarah stared at them in silence, neither wanting to say anything first, neither, for that matter, sure what they thought. It was like seeing a movie of a beloved book. No matter how good the actors were, they would never match what you had imagined; there is a sense of vertigo while one image recedes and another arises to take its place.

Noah walked in and looked at them looking.

"Can I get you anything?" he asked.

"No, thanks," they both answered.

"Okay then, we might as well get started."

Sarah glanced at the door just as Noah was closing it behind him.

"I need to apologize," he said, taking a seat. "Tim wanted very much to be here, but there was an emergency on a shoot and the client was basically holding the entire set hostage. Seems the model quit smoking a week ago without telling anyone and packed on ten pounds." He rolled his eyes, though whether it was at the thoughtlessness of the model or the extreme reaction of the client was unclear. "It used to be that if you saw a girl in person within one week of a shoot you were reasonably safe," he continued. "Now they show up with a new set of tatas or balloon lips or some crazy-ass tattoo on their shoulders. Well, the tattoos you can airbrush out, but some of these boob jobs are so bad, it's unbelievable. They're not even symmetrical, for God's sake." He paused, collected himself. "Anyway, we didn't want to hold you up and since this is just the first go-round, I'll transmit the changes you want to Tim."

Sarah and Paige took this all in and finally turned their attention to the wall.

The Beauty Rehab story was first. Four different versions were displayed in a row. In the first, a wrecked-looking model with black eyeliner smudged about her vacant eyes stared down into an empty martini glass. The story's title was written in messy script across her chest. Sexy, alluring, dark, it was far too over-the-top for anything they could actually show to Rena.

"Well?" Noah asked excitedly.

Or were they wrong? Sarah and Paige both suddenly doubted their instincts, their eyes.

Wakefield had set the course of so many fashion trends in the last five years, after all.

"I love them," Paige said. "I love the snapshot feel, I love the type—"

"But?" Noah interrupted. He was a master at reading clients.

"It's a little too hard-edged for us," Sarah said. "This is going to be a mass magazine."

He studied them closely for a long beat before he spoke. "You're right. You're totally right. Tim always likes to push the envelope and then pull back step by step until we reach the right balance. We'll fix it."

Relieved not only by Noah's assurances but by the validity of their own initial reaction, Sarah and Paige spent the next hour going over the layouts one by one, pointing out details they liked, images they thought should be blown up, cropped differently, or removed. On the long table a stack of forty European and American magazines sat in all their glossy glory and Noah, who seemed to have memorized the contents of each and every one of them, pulled out a picture here, a paparazzi shot there, selecting fonts, graphics, charts, holding them up and asking, "Is this what you mean? Is this it?" And they excitedly answered "yes," as they began to discover—to create—the look that would be unique to *Splash.* All the while, Noah took detailed notes and stuck Post-its on layouts and magazine spreads. "We'll have revisions to you in a few days," he promised. Sarah was quiet in the cab ride uptown. If she was disappointed Tim wasn't there, she didn't acknowledge it to herself or to Paige. There was only the slightly deflated feeling you get on the way home from a party that hadn't quite panned out.

That evening, though, Sarah's BlackBerry pinged with an e-mail from Tim Wakefield. "Sarah, Sorry I couldn't be there today for the first round. Had a crazy client threatening to blow up a set—trust me, there's no bigger diva than an Italian auto magnate who suddenly wants to make a name for himself in luxury goods—and a model sobbing in the bathroom because he insulted her hip size in four different languages. Not that she spoke any of them. Funny how there's always someone willing to translate bad news. Anyway, working on the prototype with you would have been infinitely more rewarding. Noah filled me in, and your feedback seems right on target. Best, Tim."

Sarah reread the e-mail three times before going to bed.

Though she was sure no response was needed or expected, she lay in the dark composing possible replies. Finally, she flipped on the lights, reached for her BlackBerry and sent him the following: "Hi, Tim, You forget, I work in the building where diva-dom was created. One fashion director here actually did trash a set when her assistant brought the wrong Marc Jacobs bag. Can't wait to see more layouts. Best, Sarah." She pressed Send and was instantly filled with nervousness and regret.

She did not hear back from Tim the next day, or the next.

The unanswered e-mail hovered in the air like pollution.

When the revised layouts from Wakefield arrived via messenger on Friday afternoon, Sarah tore open the oblong package. Inside there was a thick, freshly printed stack of the new pages and a white envelope clipped to the top with her name written on it. She quickly pulled out the note. It was from Noah, detailing the changes they had made. Sarah pushed it aside, leafing through the rest of the package quickly to make sure there was nothing else.

She saw immediately that the layouts were fantastic. The garish colors had been toned down to just the right degree of vibrancy, exciting but not blinding, the graffiti scrawls were used judiciously to give a sense of informality rather than assault, and the photos were cropped in original and often unexpected ways; even the models were more appealing. They had nailed it. Sarah called Paige and told her to come into her office to see them.

Paige closed the door and they began to spread the layouts out on the floor, getting a feel for the pacing, the way the images and words built to a crescendo, then came slowly down. Wakefield had changed the font to one that managed to be friendly and authoritative at the same time, designed triangular section tabs for the corner of each page that were slightly off-kilter but helped the reader navigate, and created a *Splash* icon with quick hits of humorous information semirelated to whatever story it appeared on (for a photo spread of celebs smooching in public, there was: "Splash Point: Play lip hockey for 26 minutes and you've burned off one Hershey's kiss"). Even the models had the perfect degree of edginess without making you want to call social services.

"These pages look amazing," Paige said.

They made an appointment to show them to Rena the next day.

Sarah dressed carefully for the meeting in a tweed pencil skirt and a white Anne Fontaine shirt that she hoped would convey confidence and good sense—they planned to ask for the next round of financing. When she got into her office, she opened the box from Wakefield and went through the pages to make sure that her initial impressions had held up overnight. Once more, she was pleased with what she saw—the energy, the originality, the impact of the images excited her just as much as they had three days ago.

She noticed that the note from Noah that she thought she'd left on top was gone, and she rooted around the box, then searched the papers on her desk without finding it, but it didn't really matter. There was nothing important in it, and besides, she lost so many things these days—four bank cards in the past three months, her iPod, more pairs of sunglasses than she cared to count, an entire stack of bills she accidentally put out with the newspapers for recycling. She was so often lost in the caverns of her own imagination now that her actions, disconnected from her brain, were never imprinted and thus could not be recalled.

As she settled down to work, Sarah grew vaguely aware of the offices filling up around her. It was earlier than usual for such activity, but she ignored it as she went through her in-box. If she sensed a growing low-level hum spreading across the floor, the air itself vibrating with an unusual level of phone usage, e-mailing, she put it out of her mind.

Ten minutes later, though, Paige walked into her office and shut the door. "Have you seen this?" she asked, tossing the latest copy of *MediaWeek,* the weekly industry magazine, on her desk. Sarah picked it up.

"Page three," Paige instructed.

Sarah turned and immediately saw the picture of Rena that ran on *Flair*'s Editor's Letter page every month, a casual shot airbrushed to look like someone Rena might have been twenty years ago. She glanced up at Paige.

"Read," Paige demanded.

Under the headline "Can the Downslide Be Stopped?" the story went on to report *Flair*'s disastrous newsstand numbers, the precipitous dip in advertising paging and revenue. It recapped a number of the lowlights since Rena had taken over—the issue last year that had five entire stories devoted to various aspects of death, the cover shot of a minor celebrity that had been airbrushed so heavily that the actress's hand resembled a fingerless claw, the unusually high turnover in art directors. Worse, it compared the sales of other titles in the same category, which, unfortunately for *Flair,* were not down, removing any possible spin CMH and Rena could offer. If, in newsstand parlance, flat was the new up, being down more than anyone else in your given category was simply down.

"Good Lord, this is awful," Sarah exclaimed.

"It gets worse," Paige said, grimly. "Turn the page."

Sarah flipped—and came bang up against a sidebar with a quarter-page photo of one of the *Splash* layouts with a separate title: "Is This Rena Berman's Salvation or a Splash in the Bucket?"

"Oh my God, how the hell did they get this?" Sarah exclaimed.

"Good question. We left the layouts in your office. You did lock the door, didn't you?"

Paige looked at her fiercely.

"Yes." Sarah fidgeted. "I'm pretty sure I locked it."

"Excuse me?"

"It wouldn't matter," Sarah replied, trying to picture herself locking the door, but unsure if she had or not. "The cleaning crew comes in at night anyway. They could have left it open by mistake."

"Well, someone got in here," Paige said. "The only other possibility is that Wakefield leaked it."

"Why would they do that?"

"Ostensibly, they are the only people besides us who had access to the layouts. But you're right. I don't see what their motive would be. They certainly don't need the publicity. Keep reading," Paige instructed.

Sarah looked down and began to read the rest of the story, which recapped the *Splash* mission statement, offered an overview of its possible competitors, and critiqued the initial layouts.

"This is unbelievable," Sarah said, putting it down. "Do you think Rena is behind this?"

"Maybe. If she's come to the conclusion that there's no way to save her butt at *Flair*, it would help to start talking up *Splash*. It gives her an out. Even if *Splash* doesn't work, it makes it appear that she's still in the game."

"What about Pat? She could have done it to push Rena out. I can't imagine Rena would want these numbers in the press."

"They're readily available to anyone. If they're going to come out, you might as well spin them. But yes, Pat could very well have planted this. I have to admit, I find it easier to imagine her sneaking into your office than Rena."

"It's just so creepy."

"Sarah, do you realize how this is going to look? The layouts were in your office. Supposedly you and I were the only ones who had access to them. People are bound to think we leaked them."

"That's crazy. Our names don't even appear in the story in conjunction with *Splash*," Sarah protested. "What possible motive would we have?"

"Lots of people know we're working on it. If it gives Rena an out, it also gives us one. I'm sure the thinking in some camps is that we're so closely tied to her that if she goes, we go. Look, bottom line, no one is going to trust us right now."

"I don't believe this," Sarah said.

"Welcome to CMH."

"What do we do?"

"Nothing yet. No one's going to say a thing right now. Not Rena, not Pat—no matter which of them is behind this. They are going to wait to see what the reaction from upstairs is. Do you have the monthly management meeting this morning?"

"Yes."

"All right, well, keep your cool and call me as soon as it's over. I'm going to go back to my office. The two of us huddled behind closed doors isn't going to help."

"Clearly closed doors are just an invitation to enter in this building."

Twenty minutes later, Sarah summoned the courage to leave her office and headed quickly down the hall to conference room 4C.

Though the meeting usually started at least ten minutes late as people straggled reluctantly in—this was never anyone's favorite hour, all those numbers, all that bad news, all that accountability—the room was already near capacity. No one wanted to miss a minute of whatever might happen.

Seated about the long table were representatives from the circulation department, newsstand and subscriptions, consumer research, PR, finance, and marketing. Anna had already taken her customary place at the head—the publisher always sat at one end, the editor at the other, parents leading the troops. Pat planted herself precisely in the center. Only Rena's chair remained empty as people began to fidget with their papers, taking sips of their water or coffee as they looked nervously around, eager spectators waiting for the show to begin.

The room hushed for a moment when Sarah took her seat, then resumed its soft distracted chatter.

Finally, Rena walked in, and the pressing question of her demeanor was immediately answered. She had a huge smile on her face as she sat down and brightly said, "Good morning." She picked up a copy of the update report. "Shall we begin?"

Everyone turned to the first page, baffled. How could she not even mention the *MediaWeek* piece, if only to dismiss it? Was it possible that she hadn't seen it yet? Peeved, cheated, they had no choice but to begin. The research department gave an update on a study they were about to embark on that promised to yield interesting proprietary information on how active women's attitudes toward beauty were changing. The PR department gave a roundup of media hits, including stories that had been picked up by the wires (a grand total of two this month) and a list of editors they had gotten on national and regional television. Unfortunately, this number, too, had shrunk. Rena blamed this on the PR department's lack of dedication, they blamed it on her misguided story choices, all parties smiled wanly at each other and moved on. Anna was just about to go through the list of advertising accounts they'd won and lost when the conference room door opened and William Rowling walked in.

Though a representative of the ninth floor was supposed to attend every month, that rarely happened. Certainly no one could remember William himself ever appearing. Despite the fact that these meetings offered one of the most accurate overviews of a title's true status, they were simply too prosaic for him.

Anna stopped midsentence. "Hello, William."

"Hello." He glanced politely about the room, including everyone in his greeting. His pale English lips parted slightly. "Please continue."

Anna paused. "I was just going through the numbers."

William nodded and, after a moment's hesitation, she picked up where she had left off with auto accounts in Detroit. Her voice was quieter now, but she could not hide the fact that the numbers were abysmal. The issue would come in $475,000 under budget. There were certain magazines in the building known to be William's and Leon's pets. Despite losing substantial amounts of money month after month for years, they added luster, respect, a raison d'être to the company and thus were bestowed absolution from the necessity of showing a profit. *Flair,* which had none of those attributes, was granted no such forgiveness.

As people moved their fingers down the columns of numbers, pretending to concentrate, they stole surreptitious glances at William who, ever the Buddhist businessman, remained silent, impregnable.

The circulation department went last. *Flair*'s newsstand sales for the previous month were down 17 percent from last year. Regrettably, there had been no hurricane, strike, national or international disaster to blame this on.

Rena, still smiling, remarked dismissively, "*Flair* has historically gone through dips and rises. These numbers will turn around."

The head of circulation, a balding man never far from his Treo or his calculator, pursed his lips. "Perhaps."

There was nothing left to say.

It was usually up to Anna to end the meeting, but she looked up at William and paused.

He did not move, he did not even appear to be breathing. Finally, he began to speak in his carefully modulated tenor. "We are not a company that appreciates leaks."

Everyone nodded, their eyes downcast and solemn as children being scolded, though in fact they all knew it was a company shot full of leaks, a regular floodgate of rumor and misinformation. More than one editor had learned that her job was in jeopardy by reading about it in the *New York Post;* in one famous case an editor in chief found out she'd been fired when her son happened to hear it on the evening news. Her belongings had already been boxed up and were on their way over to her Park Avenue apartment.

"The story was deeply unfortunate." Sarah swiveled to see Pat speaking directly to William. "There's no question about that. But it did raise an issue that I believe, that *many* of us believe, needs to be addressed."

There was a disconcertingly rehearsed quality to Pat's words.

"The truth is," Pat continued, "there has been a level of, shall we say, distraction, going on here that may at least in part explain the numbers."

Anna leaned forward, nodding as Pat spoke.

"I'm glad *MediaWeek* seems to have liked the *Splash* layouts," Pat went on. "They certainly look, at least from what I can tell, interesting. But the question remains, has the project caused attention to be turned away from the main book? And can we afford that at this particular juncture?"

Rena's smile faltered, though she quickly regained control. "I believe this has always been a company dedicated to growth and creativity," she replied.

"Yes, of course," Pat retorted. "But not at the cost of existing products. This is a time for focus, not frivolity. *Flair* still has great potential. I would hate to see it brought down by a lack of attention."

"My attention has never once wavered from *Flair,*" Rena stated firmly. "Nor do I consider exploring new ventures a 'frivolity.' "

William, who let the moment play out, leaned forward. "The point is, *Flair*'s numbers have to improve." He rose and slowly walked out the door, having ascribed no blame, accused no one, taken no side.

No one moved until he was safely down the hall. Rena and Pat filed out without saying another word, and everyone else followed suit, rushing to their offices, their phones, their e-mails. The encounter, which grew to a screamfest as versions bounced around town, took on a life of its own. Arguments within CMH were always of interest; those that involved two powerful women were irresistible.

Sarah sat glumly in Paige's office. "Well, you were wrong about no one saying anything," she said.

"So I gather. Rena's assistant called to cancel our meeting to show her the *Splash* layouts," Paige informed her. "She wants you to send them over to her, though. She said she'd study them when she has time. Look, if the Body Issue somehow does well on the newsstand or creates enough of the right kind of buzz, all could still be forgiven."

Sarah nodded. The number of editors and publishers who had somehow managed to outlast bad numbers or egregious acts of personal behavior at CMH was legion; there was the marketing director who had, in the days when windows still opened, thrown a television off the eleventh floor to make a point that the medium was dead, just missing three tourists who sued for psychological distress; there was the married editor who had her driver fetch a single slice of her lover's favorite cheesecake from Brooklyn every day and bring it to his office wrapped with a fuchsia satin ribbon; there was the publisher who fired three assistants in a row because she didn't like the sound their shoes made clicking on the floor. All were, for various reasons, taken back into the fold, excused as big personalities who contributed to CMH's lore and ultimate success.

But there were just as many who'd been fired for far less cause, some for motives they would never truly understand, despite desperate calls to everyone they knew pleading for an explanation.

"It's a waiting game," Paige said.

"What do we do about *Splash*?"

"I have no idea."

That question was settled when Rena called them into her office later that afternoon. "Sit," she said, smiling as she pointed to the couch.

She dispensed with a sentence or two of pleasantries before getting to the point. "You know what a good idea I thought *Splash* was," she began.

Sarah and Paige nodded numbly, conscious of her use of the past tense.

"You are both so talented. I have never doubted that. But," Rena leaned forward, still smiling, "there is some corporate doubt. As much as they liked the idea, they have decided that the early-twenties market is not one we should be pursuing at this point. They have decided to beef up their men's division and put their financial and creative resources toward that."

"I don't understand," Paige said. "They knew who our target audience was all along."

"Yes," Rena agreed. "But after further study of advertiser patterns, they have concluded that a larger base of male readers will enhance the potential for auto and tech advertising and soften any blow during a potential recession in luxury goods."

Neither of them had ever heard Rena speak in quite this corporate a manner, though whether she was mimicking words she had been told or was making them up was unclear.

"Listen," she continued, leaning forward more intimately, "nothing you do in life is ever wasted. You will use what you learned on this project in the future. Trust me."

There was little left to say and certainly no room for argument.

Sarah and Paige assured Rena that they understood. All three wanted this meeting to end as quickly as possible and were relieved when Rena's phone rang.

"Have you heard anything about launches or acquisitions in the men's category?" Sarah asked Paige as they headed out.

"Nope."

"Then did she just let us in on insider info or totally snow us?"

"It's impossible to tell with Rena," Paige admitted. "Do you want to call Wakefield and tell them?"

"I can think of things I'd rather do," Sarah replied dryly.

They walked a few more feet in silence.

"That last round they sent us was so perfect," Sarah went on. "I can't believe all the work they put into it is useless."

"They're grown-ups," Paige said. "They know this kind of thing happens all the time. They're not going to blame us."

"I know." She slowed her pace. There would be no more e-mails from Tim, no more meetings; that was over, too. "Would you mind calling them, though? I just can't face it."

"You sure? Wouldn't you rather talk to Tim yourself?"

Sarah shook her head. "No."

Twenty

Deflated, with nothing but dead ends at work and no news from Florida, Sarah dragged through the hours as if sedated.

And then, four days later, she got the phone call that she had been most dreading.

Maude answered the phone and told her Karl Medford was on the line.

Sarah picked up anxiously.

"Hello, how are you, Sarah?"

"I'm all right. You?"

It was painful to get through the conversational pleasantries when all she really wanted was to pounce: Did you find anything, hear anything, do you know anything? Yet she sensed something different in his voice this time, a hesitancy that made her not want to hear what was coming.

"I checked the calls you told me about," Medford said. "They were from Linda. I don't think they mean anything."

"All right, thanks." Sarah had called Linda's house as well, for reasons she could not explain, listening to her voice, hanging up.

There was a long silence. Sarah could hear Medford breathing.

"I'm sorry," he said at last. "But I feel that I've exhausted every avenue. I don't want to waste your money any longer. I believe your husband died that night in August. August eighth. But at this point it's unlikely we'll ever find his body. The ocean has a mind of its own. I have called Detective Brook and told him of my conclusion."

"And?"

"He doesn't share this view. He is not a man to change his mind. He will in all likelihood leave the file open, but he is doing nothing further to investigate."

"I see."

"Sarah, there's nothing more I can do for you at this point. I'll send you my final report today. If anything changes, if you hear anything, find out anything . . ." He left his sentence, his promise, open-ended, but it was clear to Sarah that he did not think this would happen.

"Thank you." She hung up, a deep weightedness filling her lungs, her stomach, her very being until she could no longer hold her head up and had to rest it on her forearms.

She had never truly thought it would come to this.

The waiting had sunk down to the subterranean thrum of her blood, indistinguishable from her breath, the dull throb of a headache that would not go away, it had become who she was.

But there would be no more daily reports, no phone calls.

This was it.

Her worst fear, being left with no answers, no body, had come true.

Worse than death. That is what she thought. Worse than death is this nondeath, this emptiness.

Even now, after months, she could not believe they would not find him.

She had decided nothing, knew nothing.

Shipwrecked, she was left to draw her own conclusion, to make a decision, formulate a belief of what had happened that night. The narrative, the explanation was hers to choose, death or disappearance, intentional or not. But she found it impossible to settle firmly on a version, ruling out all other possibilities, when there was no hard proof.

She was waiting still.

She told no one of Medford's call.

When his report arrived by FedEx the following morning, it delineated each step of his investigation, from talking to workers at the local pizza parlor to interviewing Bill McCrory. On the last page, the conclusion read: "Based upon extensive investigations, it is believed that Target is not currently living in the Loudon Beach area. He is believed to either have died (with the body not found) or to have left this area. However, it does seem unlikely that he planned this event to 'get away from it all' because he: left without personal belongings; hasn't contacted his daughter who he cares for deeply; hasn't contacted any of his closest friends or family members. Target also had an extensive CD collection (10,000-plus titles) and his art studio, which were believed to be impossible for him to just 'give up.'

"We have closed our file until such time as new information comes to our attention. This includes leads obtained from Detective Brook, the Target's address book contacts, the *Crime Stoppers* show, or any new database information on Target. We appreciate your business. If you have any questions concerning this report, please do not hesitate to call."

Sarah put the report in her desk drawer and shut it tight.

Any vestiges of the past months' nervous energy were gone. It was all she could do the next day to get Eliza up, to school, fed, bathed, all she could do to put one foot in front of the other.

After dropping her off, Sarah walked the eighteen blocks to work. The first early nips of winter wove through the buildings; women were wearing their new boots and slim coats. She strode with her head down, her mind completely empty as she veered around pedestrians, crossed obliviously through blinking red lights.

When Eliza asked that night what Karl Medford had found out, she told her, "Nothing yet, sweetie." She did not tell her that he had given up, that this was it, what they were left with.

But as days, nights of nonanswers, evasions piled up, Eliza, sensing an ebbing, grew more and more angry.

On the last Saturday of November, Deirdre Gerard asked Eliza to take a picture book into the waiting room after their session so that she could talk to her mother. Reluctantly, turning back once, Eliza complied.

Deirdre waited until the door was closed before speaking. "I think it's time you told Eliza that her father is dead."

"But I still don't know what happened."

"She's a child. You need to give her something to hang on to. She'll never begin to get better until she has that. Tell her the police know for sure that he drowned. She is young enough to still believe they are omniscient. She won't question it." Sarah flinched, about to raise objections. "If you find out otherwise down the road, if he comes back, we'll deal with it then," Deirdre said gently. "But Eliza needs this. The mental agitation of all this uncertainty is too much for her."

Sarah nodded, but still she did nothing.

She could not speak those words, taking any last hope away from her daughter, when they rang so hollow to her, so false, premature.

And so she walked. And she waited. And she watched her daughter pull further away.

"Think of that night as a closed-off room," Deirdre suggested the following week when Sarah admitted she still had not told Eliza. "You will never be able to open the door, see inside. You just have to move away from it."

Sarah knew that Deirdre was right, but she knew, too, that she would be aware of that room, that locked door, forever. She felt herself dancing on the lip of a bottomless pit, teetering, every muscle, every fiber spent from the effort it took to keep from falling in, where there was only blackness, that night without end, a life without finality, without answers.

She knew in her heart that, if nothing else, she had to pull Eliza away from there, away from the abyss of haunting ambiguities.

But she could not bring herself to say the words.

Twenty-one

Sarah stopped opening the mail, wandered off in the middle of conversations, left water boiling until it scorched the bottom of the pot. There was only this: the growing realization that this was all there would be—and the words she could not say.

Eight days later, on an icy Friday night, she was walking home when she heard music wafting out of the open doors of a store, James Taylor's "Fire and Rain," his song about the suicide of a friend. She looked down; on the ground by her feet lay a crimson and gold pack of Dunhill cigarettes, the brand Todd had smoked when they first met.

She would never admit it to Lucy, to Paige, to anyone, that this was the tipping point, this sign.

She slept deeply that night for the first time in weeks. Perhaps it was because she had given up, given in; perhaps it was avoidance of what was to come, for in that moment on the street she had made a conscious decision to believe that Todd had died. It was not a conviction born of faith, but one formulated from the outside in, inorganic. It was a discipline she forced on herself, one that she vowed to adhere to despite her relentless imagination. She continued to waver about whether Todd swam purposefully out into the black water or tried to turn around. She did not know which was worse—picturing him trying to get back to shore, arms thrashing, water filling his mouth, his lungs—or seeing him continue to swim, farther and farther into the black horizon. But finally, she tried to steer her thoughts away even from it.

At six in the morning, Sarah lay in a hot bath trying to calm herself, rehearsing the words she would use with Eliza, tears rolling down her face. She climbed out of the water, sobbing, and curled onto the bathroom mat in a tight ball, naked, shaking, clawing at her own skin until bloody red streaks marred her arms, her thighs, pain on pain, knowing that she was about to rip her daughter's life in two, change it forever.

She stayed there until she was hollowed out and there was nothing left but the knowledge of what she had to do. She heard Eliza stir in her room, get out of bed.

The clear early-winter light filled the living room. Sarah looked over at Eliza, reading a Pony Pals book on the rug, her head propped in her hands, her hair falling down in the softest of tangles. She watched her back rise and fall with each breath, her weight shifting slightly as she turned the page.

Sarah began to speak but stopped, bit her lower lip so hard that later a deep purple bruise would form. She inhaled and squared her shoulders, shutting her eyes for a minute as she reminded herself that she was doing the right thing, that she *must* do this. She opened her eyes and began, her voice cracking despite her effort to sound calm.

"Honey, I have something to tell you."

Eliza was instantly alert. She said nothing, though; she simply froze in place, refusing to look up from her book.

Sarah knelt down beside her. "The police called. They know what happened for sure now. They know that Daddy drowned that night."

Eliza darted behind the coach, her hands covering her head just as she had when they told her five months ago that they were separating. Sarah crawled behind the couch and curled around her daughter, stroking her hair.

Just as Deirdre had predicted, Eliza did not ask how the police knew with such sudden certainty; she accepted it as fact.

Sarah knew that at some point—at fifteen, sixteen—Eliza would ask to see the police reports, Medford's statements, ask the questions she did not know existed yet, and then she would have to mourn anew, and question anew. Sarah was thankful that there was one out—Eliza could believe that he tried to swim back to shore, to her. She believed it herself. Some of the time.

That November morning, though, Eliza curled into her mother's arms and buried her head in the crook of her neck. Sarah began to rock gently back and forth, back and forth, the deep maternal rhythm of comfort and protection.

It was a long while before Eliza finally spoke. "What do you think Daddy's last thoughts were?"

"I think he thought of you, of how much he loved you. Don't ever forget, Daddy loved you more than anything in the universe."

There was an endless silence. Sarah could feel Eliza's lungs fill with air, exhale, slowly fill again.

"Do you think you can cry underwater?" she asked at last.

Three weeks later, on a blustery Sunday afternoon, Sarah and Eliza held a small memorial service in their apartment for Todd. Sixteen of his closest friends came and sat in a circle on the living room floor reading aloud letters they had written to Eliza about her father.

"Make sure they print them," Eliza instructed Sarah when they planned the afternoon. "I don't read script." She had a panicked look in her eyes.

"I'll tell them, honey. I promise."

His friends spoke of his love of good food and his passion for his art and his overriding intelligence; they spoke of his first year in graduate school when the world was just opening up to him and of his encyclopedic knowledge of music. There were stories Sarah had never heard before. "When he first lived in New York," Harry DeVeres read from his letter, "he walked by himself from the top to the bottom of Central Park in the middle of the night. He figured if he survived that, he would never have to fear New York again. It worked. He was courageous and strong-willed." There were stories of kindnesses she had not known about, friends he had given money to when they were down on their luck, and encouragement, and comfort.

Most of all, they spoke of his love of Eliza. “When he talked about you,” Max Henley, a painter he knew from the gallery, wrote, “he was different than when he talked about sculpture or books or music. When he talked about you, his face would become so happy that sometimes I thought his feet would leave the ground. You were more important than the sun and the moon to your dad. I think that he thought of you every minute and every hour of every day.”

When the last reader had finished, they each handed the letters to Sarah, who put them in a leather scrapbook for Eliza, her father lost and found.

Twenty-two

In many ways, Deirdre Gerard was right, Eliza began to get better after the memorial service. Her legs no longer gyrated wildly in the air when she and Sarah lay side by side in bed talking at night. The electrical currents that had been charged by rampant uncertainty were gone—*the police know what happened.* If there was a sadness when they spoke of Todd, it was finite. Eliza was a child to whom a terrible thing had happened, but it was a singular event, not the open-ended madness it had been and in many ways, despite herself, continued to be for Sarah.

There was at times, though, a faraway look in Eliza's eyes that had not been there before. While others told her they saw it as the manifestation of an ethereal nature, Sarah wondered if it was in those moments that Eliza was remembering. Perhaps this floating quality would have appeared anyway. Sarah didn't know what behavior, withdrawal or neediness, uncertainty or stubborn independence, was purely developmental, something all children went through in varying degrees, what was part of Eliza's inborn personality, and what was a reaction to what she had been through. There were an increasing number of instances, though, when she was simply happy, fully immersed in an activity, when the past few months disappeared and she was grounded in the present.

Sarah was allowed to kiss Eliza again, and slowly she began to respond, not always, not fully, but often enough to offer hope. Sarah remembered when Eliza was a toddler and hadn't learned quite how to pucker, how she would press her lips against Sarah's skin and just stay there, affection expressed but not fully clarified. That was how it was now: her love had returned, though there were still unpredictable flashes of anger and resentment; grief, healing, forgiveness are never a straight trajectory, after all.

At *Flair,* editors whispered and wondered and waited, stilled by a paralyzing inertia: The magazine's future was completely out of their hands now. The Body Issue was at press and they worked in a desultory manner on the next issue, apathetic, burned out; it was impossible for even the most enthusiastic of them to summon much energy.

The story of the dustup between Rena and Pat burned over the phone lines, on the Internet, and in the gossip pages for a few days, then faded away. Rena stayed in her office for longer stretches than usual, forgoing her visits to the art department, her proprietary walks about the floor. Pat showed absolutely no sign that anything had changed. Her clothes, her demeanor, her attitude were as razor-sharp and apparently imperturbable as ever. "I have never met a more wrinkle-free person in my life," Paige remarked, searching but never finding even the smallest sign of weakness. There was no further mention of *Splash,* and Rena never returned the layouts. Sarah passed by the same newsstand's window every morning on her way to work, reflexively turning her head to see which magazines had the best cover lines, the most diverting colors, the hottest models, the best placement. Though most racks in supermarkets and airports are paid for by publishers to guarantee visibility, the small mom-and-pop operations throughout the city are left to their own devices, making them a good gauge of a magazine's popularity. *Flair,* like many of the CMH titles, hit the stands on the second Tuesday of every month. That morning Sarah looked over hopefully, but it wasn't in the window.

She walked in and wriggled by the queue of people waiting to buy lotto tickets for that night's $17 million drawing. There, jammed between a muscle and fitness magazine and *Southern Living,* sat an untouched stack of the Body Issue. Out of a show of loyalty and a superstitious belief that if others saw her buying it they would follow suit, Sarah picked up a copy, paid for it, and walked the rest of the way to work carrying it so that *Flair*'s distinctive italic logo was clearly visible.

Over the next week, there were a few minor columns about it in trade journals and a brief editorial in *The New York Observer* on how refreshing it was to see women in the pages of a magazine that more closely resembled its actual readers rather than Brazilian Amazons, but the tepid controversy was not enough to make up for the lack of sales. Perhaps it was the wrong season—at the beginning of December women everywhere were snapping up magazines that promised to help them dazzle over the holidays. Perhaps it was an error of judgment and it never would have worked. Newsstand sales are far from an exact science, and no one would ever be able to pinpoint with certainty precisely what had gone wrong. The only incontrovertible fact was that the Body Issue was a resounding failure. The preliminary scans showed it to have the lowest sales of any issue in four years.

Like a spurned lover who believes she has been rejected solely because of "bad timing," Rena convinced herself that the idea itself was not flawed, only that women weren't ready for it yet. As she walked down the hallways, held art meetings for upcoming issues, went to lunch at the most visible media-heavy restaurants, her visage showed no change, no fear or vulnerability, despite whispering in the building that her days were numbered. Rena's line was simply that newsstand sales varied all the time and this was just another example—next month would be better, it was no big deal. With a surfeit of bravado, or last-ditch desperation, in the few interviews she gave she even acted as if it were a resounding victory—the appearance of success had always worked for her in the past, or at the very least had bought her time.

Two days later, though, at precisely 11:45 on Friday morning, William Rowling and Petra Landon-Kerr, senior vice president for human resources, pushed open the glass door to the *Flair* offices and walked side by side down the long hallway past editors who glanced up nervously and quickly looked away, as they made their way to Rena's office.

The door closed gently but definitively behind them.

Editors quickly darted in and out of each other's offices, peering down the hall every few seconds to make sure Rena's door was still shut, while assistants exchanged worried looks. In fact, though assistants were always the most anxious, they tended to be the least affected—they were simply not important enough to fire, at least not right away. Regardless, this was, as far as anyone knew—and within minutes everyone in the building did know—unprecedented. Petra Landon-Kerr had never been seen on the fourth floor in all of her years at the company and, to the best of anyone's recollection, William himself had never actually visited Rena's office. People went to them, not the other way around.

Paige hurried into Sarah's office.

"We're fucked."

Sarah stared at her. "I can't believe this is happening."

"Totally fucked," Paige reiterated.

CMH had honed the art of firing people into a fine science calibrated to the millisecond. At exactly 11:50, while Rena's door was still closed, an announcement went out to the press that Rena Berman had decided to leave CMH after a long and successful career with the company to pursue other interests. At the same time, a single cream sheet of heavy stock paper was distributed to every single person in the company by an army of office service workers announcing her departure. There was no mention of who was to replace her.

"I should have known. They always fire people on Fridays," Paige observed.

Sarah, who was still relatively new to this, looked at her quizzically. "Why?"

"They miss a news cycle that way. It won't appear in the papers until tomorrow and no one reads the *Post* or media sites on Saturday. Plus, it gives everyone who works here time to gossip about it over the weekend so they don't waste precious work hours."

When Rena's door finally opened, William and Petra Landon-Kerr (no one ever referred to her by anything but all three names at once) walked quickly with their heads down out of *Flair*'s offices and back to the insulated safety of the ninth floor. The halls were totally silent as they made their way out, though within minutes there were vociferous if mixed opinions about why they hadn't had Rena come to them. Was it a show of respect for all of the years she had put in at CMH—or were they making the most public example possible of the dangers of falling numbers and dubious judgment?

A staff meeting was announced for 3:00 p.m. in *Flair*'s large conference room. At lunch tables across midtown rumors flew about when a replacement would be named, who it might be, and where, if anywhere, Rena Berman would land, her wealth of experience and breadth of contacts leveraged against her age in the heated calculations.

At 2:59 the entire staff of *Flair* filed into conference room 4C with appropriately grave looks on their faces and found plastic flutes filled with champagne in perfect rows on the enormous table. Uncertain of what the proper mode of behavior was, they lined up against the walls, a semicircle of gorgeous young women in narrow skirts and bare legs despite the cold, anxiously awaiting whatever was to come. Sarah looked over to see Pat standing in the corner, placid, expressionless.

Finally, Rena entered with her famous broad smile glued across her face.

"You have to admire her pride," Sarah whispered to Paige.

"Unbelievable," Paige agreed.

Rena took a glass of champagne and raised it up.

"Well, as you've heard, the time has come for me to move on," she began. "I want you to know that I have loved every minute of working with each of you, and I truly believe *Flair* is an exceptional editorial product. I am proud of what we have accomplished together."

The staff grew misty-eyed. Even those who had thought Rena

was a misguided eccentric and had plotted against her seemed to have developed a sudden case of amnesia and were awash in nostalgia. Of course, their gloom was also caused in part by the overt reminder that no one was indispensable.

"To the future," Rena said, and took a sip of champagne.

The room burst into heartfelt, if rather self-conscious, applause.

There was an awkward moment when the glasses were lowered and Rena stood silent, the semicircle static around her. Finally, people began to go up to her one at a time to offer condolences, thanks, encouragement, or to simply feel a part of the moment. Rena stood accepting the words, biding her time until she could escape.

"I have to say," Paige remarked as she and Sarah waited their turn, "she's a class act."

Sarah agreed. There was something noble about Rena Berman in defeat, the proud shtetl girl who would never let them appear to have won.

The only weakness appeared when Sarah inched close and Rena clasped her hand.

"I don't know what to say," Sarah began. "I'm so sorry. I want you to know how much I appreciate everything you've done for me, personally and professionally. I can't imagine staying here without you."

Rena looked at her without expression, the smile gone. "The waters will close up over me in one day," she replied. For the briefest instant she looked totally drained.

Sarah offered a mild protest but she knew that it was the first authentic thing Rena had said.

Rena talked to one or two more people and then left the room, the building, the company, her head high.

As soon as she was gone, the staff filtered out as quickly as seemed appropriate and hurried to their computers where they fired off e-mails to friends at other companies, excited to be on the inside of a media story even as they wondered who among them would be swept out in the housecleaning that was sure to follow. For the rest of the afternoon, they gossiped, whispered, and took bets on who the next editor of *Flair* would be. The majority assumed it would be Pat, and each editor ransacked her memory, reliving every encounter they'd had, wondering if she had been nice enough, smart enough, distanced enough from Rena. Of course, there was another camp that insisted Pat was too tainted and that CMH needed to make a major statement to the ad community showing they understood the importance of real change at *Flair.* Names from the outside circulated like hula hoops.

"Well," Paige said, slumped in Sarah's office. "Basically we're out of here no matter who it is. We were Rena's girls, like it or not. Whether it's Pat or someone totally new, we're part of the old regime."

A thick knot of tension lodged in Sarah's chest. She suddenly hated Todd, hated him for leaving her with no body and no life insurance, hated that he wasn't there to comfort her, hated, too, her own earlier choices that had left her in this position, alone, with a scanty résumé and too much responsibility.

She didn't know if the choices themselves were bad or merely the outcome, she didn't know if there was a difference. She had followed her heart and it had landed her here. Deep down, she knew that she would make the same choices all over again, though instead of that appeasing her, it only made her feel irrevocably flawed.

She was snapped out of her thoughts by the phone. Paige rose to leave as Sarah picked it up.

"Sarah? It's Tim Wakefield. I just heard about Rena. I'm sorry," he said.

She was so surprised to hear from him that for a moment she had trouble placing his voice.

"Are you okay?" he asked.

"Yes," she answered automatically. "Well, no, actually. I'm sorry about *Splash,*" she apologized.

"Don't worry about that. It was fun to work on and, who knows, maybe down the road you can take it to someone else. You'll use it in some way."

"Rena said something similar. She said nothing is ever wasted."

"She's right."

There was a long pause.

"I'll make sure you get paid for the work you've done," Sarah said.

"I know. That's not why I was calling. I was concerned about you. And Paige, of course."

"Thanks. We'll be okay."

"Listen." Sarah could swear she heard a slight stutter in Tim's voice. "Would you like to have dinner with me?"

"Tonight?" Her mind raced—her hair was unwashed, she had no babysitter.

"Not tonight."

She bit her lip, feeling like an idiot. "Oh."

"I meant next week sometime."

"I'd like that."

"Okay, great. Are you free on Tuesday?"

"Sure." The minute the word slipped out, Sarah regretted it. Did it imply that of course she was free, she never had anything to do, she was pathetic? Shouldn't she have said, "Let me check?"

"Good," he said.

There was another awkward pause before they each managed to say good-bye.

Twenty-three

At 7:00 p.m. on Tuesday evening, Sarah stood in the bathroom at *Flair,* carefully applying a new beigey-pink Chanel lipstick that Paige swore looked good on everyone from albinos to Africans. She leaned close to the mirror and studied her face for hidden flaws that might somehow appear unbidden to ruin her night. She was wearing a new soft black wool wrap top with ruffles along the neckline and she retied it to show a bit more cleavage, trying to figure out the line between alluring and desperate. She suddenly panicked that, combined with her black knee-length skirt and high-heeled black boots, it was all somehow too hard-edged, that, aiming for chic, she had ended up with intimidating. She seemed to remember reading someplace—or perhaps she had written it, edited it—that men preferred color. She had tried on a red V-necked sweater that morning, but it seemed too obvious, too jarring. A jumpy anticipation, not entirely comfortable, coursed through her and she started when Caitlin walked in.

Caitlin looked at her suspiciously. "Going out?"

Sarah, unwilling to admit that she had a date, as if that would give it too much import, replied, "No, just meeting an old friend." There was, too, a certain self-consciousness about stepping out of the role of mourner, widow—it was so soon. She had mentioned her plans with Tim to no one but Lucy and Paige. She even made a point of telling Dora she had a business dinner when she asked her to stay late.

Caitlin watched as Sarah put the makeup away and zipped up her Louis Vuitton makeup case, a hand-me-down from Paige. The two women had always done a wary dance around each other, each aware of the vast differences in their lives, their choices—Caitlin, with her connections, her pedigreed education, and her unerring taste; Sarah with her artistic bona fides, her bylines, and her marital drama.

"Good night." Sarah slid into her coat.

"Have a good time," Caitlin called after her, not taking her eyes off of her own reflection.

Tim was already in the restaurant when Sarah arrived, seated at the long polished mahogany bar waiting for her. She saw him first, taking a sip of his martini while he scribbled in a little Moleskine notebook. She had forgotten how attractive he was, and it hit her full force now, his vaguely European aura of quiet mystery and experience, his slim but strong body. As she watched him sitting there in his indigo blazer and navy cashmere turtleneck, her first instinct was to turn around, run out before he noticed her. She had no idea how to do this, she *hadn't* done this, not in over a decade.

"Sarah." He had spotted her, his eyes lighting up; she had no choice but to walk over to him. They pecked clumsily on the cheek.

"How are you?" he asked.

"Fine. Good." She put her bag down. What now, what next?

He ordered her a drink and they fell into a default banter about the goings-on at *Flair,* suspense over the naming of a new editor, Rena's fate, both relieved for a conversational overlay to help them establish a rhythm and provide cover while they observed, absorbed each other's physical presence. Sarah noticed how his eyes pleated when he smiled, his cheekbones growing even more prominent. She was deeply aware of the space between them, an inch, two.

When their table was ready, the hostess, a six-foot-tall woman with long tangles of honey-blond bed hair and a totally naked dress led them to a corner table in the back.

They stumbled for a moment in the new setting, losing a little ground as they adjusted to the proximity of their seats, the softer lighting, the intimacy it engendered.

"You have a daughter?" Tim asked.

"Yes, Eliza. She's six. And you have a son?"

"Chris. I'm still getting the hang of this single-parent thing. I had him this weekend and didn't make any plans. It seems that doesn't work with young boys. He was bored out of his mind by noon."

"Plans will save you," Sarah agreed. "How long have you been divorced?"

"Almost a year."

"What happened?" she asked, instantly regretting it. "God, I'm sorry, it sounds as if I'm interviewing you. Old habit. Never mind."

"I believe that's what first dates are, interviews with table service," Tim replied, smiling.

She felt her face redden, his acknowledgment that this was a date eroticizing the air, though of course she had known it was a date, what else could it be? Still, the public use of the word brought with it an admission of hope and vulnerability.

He took a sip of his drink. "Actually, it's a good question." He looked at her. "My marriage progressed like a certain type of surreal horror story."

"That bad?"

"No," he smiled. "What I meant was, with good horror stories, each step you take seems logical at the time, or the strangeness is so minute you hardly notice it. I don't know, maybe you decide not to notice it. Anyway, you keep going step by step until suddenly you open your eyes to discover you are in a very scary land and you have no idea how you got there." He stopped short. "Am I making any sense?"

"Actually, yes."

"It was an incremental decline. Until it wasn't. Incremental, that is. The end was actually quite steep. We woke up one day in a totally different place than where we had started."

"Okay, now I have no idea what you're talking about." Sarah was intrigued by the loops of his mind, but she had learned the danger of making assumptions about someone based on verbal abstractions, no matter how erudite. She knew how mistaken she could be.

"Bottom line, I worked too hard, she felt neglected, she was angry with me by the time I came home and sulked, I felt neglected, she fucked our accountant."

"No one fucks accountants," Sarah said, laughing. "Accountants and dentists are the last of the great un-fuckables."

"Tell that to my wife. Ex-wife. What can I say? She prided herself on her counterintuitive nature. We tried," he continued. Sarah could see the film of scar tissue beneath the facile rendering of events, the pain still fresh enough to leave soft spots. "After that. We still tried. For all of it, we both love our son. Now I see him Wednesdays and every other weekend."

"That must be hard."

"Yes. Harder than I thought, actually. The whole idea of 'quality time' is complete bullshit."

Sarah leaned forward, pulled in by Tim's devotion to son. "How old is he?"

"Eight. But I think divorce screws up kids' chronology. Some seem so much older than they are, others, from what I've heard, regress."

"And Chris?"

"Older. Most of the time. He still thinks we'll get back together and comes up with impressively complicated plots along those lines."

"Will you?" Sarah asked.

"No." There was a calm certainty in Tim's voice that reassured her. "Too much wreckage. The accountant is still in the picture, by the way."

"What about you, were you faithful?"

He laughed. "Now I do feel like you're interviewing me." He paused. "Sort of."

"It's kind of a yes-or-no question," Sarah said, smiling.

"I was faithful until I learned about her affair. Then I engaged in some rather stupid and, as it turned out, joyless behavior a couple of times. But I realized it just made me angrier at her, and at myself. It wasn't how I wanted to live. God, I can't believe I'm telling you all this." He took a sip of his drink. "I don't usually."

"Don't what? Screw around or bare your soul on a first date?"

He laughed. "Either. What about you, your marriage?" he asked carefully.

Sarah played with the edges of her paper cocktail napkin, ripping them into shreds, ripping them again until the table was littered with white confetti. "My husband was an alcoholic." She did not look at him when she spoke. "It's funny, I never say that. I didn't say it to myself for a long time, and not to him for even longer. I think in some ways it's more embarrassing to admit than how he died." She did, finally, glance up at Tim and saw that he did not think less of her, her judgment, her worth. The only thing in his eyes was empathy.

"My brother was an alcoholic," he said.

"Was? Past tense?"

"Yes. But not until he caused an awful lot of damage."

"It's not the kind of thing that was supposed to happen in my family," Sarah said.

"'Supposed to' is a very dangerous way of thinking."

"My husband wasn't supposed to walk into an ocean. When someone dies, they are supposed to find a body. I don't know, I guess you're right. It's not always as simple as that, though."

"No, of course not. I'm sorry. We don't have to talk about it."

There was, Sarah knew, no good way into this conversation, no good way out. "It's okay," she said. "Would you like the short version, the medium version, or the long, complicated, murky version?"

"Are there really that many versions?"

"More."

"Whatever you're comfortable with."

Sarah began with the day she and Todd separated, for that had come to seem the starting point of an unstoppable trajectory that ended the night he died, and as she spoke, details, shards of the truth—at least the truth as she knew it—piled up. She spoke softly but matter-of-factly, leaving her own emotions largely out of the equation.

When she paused, he said, "I cannot believe how hard this must be for you."

She shrugged. She did not want his sympathy—or perhaps she did, she wasn't sure. She wanted him to comprehend how difficult it was, yes, but she did not find that an easy or comfortable thing to admit.

She was aware, too, of how bizarre her story was and how it scared some people off with its shadows and lack of tidy endings. What kind of person, woman, does this happen to, after all?

"You're different than I expected," she remarked as dinner was winding down.

"In what way?"

"Well, you have a job, not a job, more than that, you know what I mean, you are this brilliant master of exteriors . . ."

"And you thought I'd be more superficial?"

She smiled. "Yes."

"I don't know whether to be flattered that I'm not as superficial as you expected, or disturbed that you think what I do is."

"I didn't say that."

"I manipulate façades," Tim said. "But façades can affect thought patterns as much as they reflect them. They can offer a history of a culture. And, if it's any consolation, I do know the difference between façade and substance. I happen to find the interplay between the two interesting. At least professionally."

"And personally?"

He laughed. "I'm just trying to stay out of horror movies."

"You and me both."

"Well, at least we have a common goal," he said, smiling.

Tim paid the check and they walked out, standing in front of the restaurant in the cold November air. They shifted their feet, looked at and away from each other.

"Look, my loft is around the corner," he suggested. "Do you want to come over for coffee, a brandy?"

She nodded. “Sure.”

They walked along on the windy West Village street where a new crop of designer shops had recently opened, English society handbag designers, downtown outposts of uptown clothiers drawn to the Federal town houses, the high-income inhabitants of a neighborhood that, until recently, boasted a cupcake café as its most popular venue. Once, as they waited for a light to change, their arms brushed against each other but neither acknowledged it. Sarah spent the rest of the walk trying to avoid it from happening again and hoping that it would.

Tim’s loft was on the fifth floor of an old industrial building and they rode up in the tiny, rickety elevator in silence. He opened the door to a long rectangular open space that spanned the depth of the building with huge windows partially draped in brilliantly colored Indian silks on either end. He took her coat and hung it from the antique iron coat stand in the corner, his fingertips brushing against the back of her neck. Inside, soft light from the streets bounced off the polished white-painted wood floors, illuminating the open kitchen, the fireplace, the two beds at either end of the loft, one of which, she noticed, was unmade. Tim lit a fire and poured them both a glass of cabernet. They took their shoes off and rested their feet on an old Eames chair. As they spoke of their children’s personalities and schools, their own upbringings, their jobs, their legs found their way over to each other until that was all there was, this line of heat where their calves, now their thighs, met.

Sarah was midsentence when Tim reached over and slowly brought her face to his, finding her lips, kissing her gently, pulling away as if to reassess, finding her again, more surely this time. For a moment she was lost in the strangeness of it—it had been so long since she had been touched except by a child, so long since she had kissed anyone but Todd. As his tongue found hers, she leaned into him, almost moaning with an overwhelming desire to be held.

They were standing now, his arms around her, and she was giving herself to him, opening herself to him. Standing there, in the center of this white-floored loft, she was completely aware of what she was doing and thought for an instant of pulling away, knowing that was what she should do, leave now, say, "This is too fast for me," make a graceful exit.

But she didn't.

She didn't care that it went against every bit of dating wisdom known to womankind, she didn't care what happened tomorrow or that she had told Dora she would be home by ten. This was all she wanted: to lose the constant anxiety, to forfeit consciousness to the purely sensate. To be irresponsible, the one thing she was never allowed, never allowed herself to be, completely irresponsible. To shed the weight of single parenthood, the incessant questions about Todd's death, the workplace machinations, and fill the gaping hole within the depths of which she had not truly comprehended until this very second. She thought, It's my turn. I am going to give this to myself. Now. Here. She had no faith the chance would come again.

They were on his bed now, their clothes off, exploring the contours of each other's bodies.

She sighed deeply as he entered her, the feeling at once so familiar and so new, ah here, this is what it is to be joined. She arched up to him, wanting to meet him, to be taken. He moved her about with a powerful sexual confidence and lack of self-consciousness unusual in a first-time union. She did not know if there was something in him that made her feel secure or if she was simply too worn out by the past months, too desirous of comfort to be shy, but she matched him without embarrassment or inhibition.

Afterward she lay in his arms, the sheets bunched around their waists, his fingertips lightly tracing the curve of her upper arm.

"It's so nice," he said, and it did not sound trite but true, it was so nice, the streetlights coming in through the windows dappling their skin, the air cooling them, to be in a man's arms, to be not alone. To be with him.

"Yes."

It was just past midnight when she looked at the clock and bolted up suddenly. "I have to go. I told my babysitter I'd be home by ten."

She found her clothes where they lay tangled on the floor and began trying to figure them out, pull them on. "I've never been late before. Not in the six years she's worked for us." She was telling him something else—*I don't do this. I have never done this.* She wasn't apologizing, she wasn't sorry, not for a minute of it. She had known exactly what she was doing and thought, even now—if he doesn't call, it's still okay, I just wanted this. But she was suddenly self-conscious, anxious that he might think she did this kind of thing all the time, sleeping with a man on a first date.

"I feel like I'm in college," she said, her back to him as she fastened her lace bra.

"Why?" he asked, perplexed.

What she meant was that she had the illusion of freedom here in this open loft, with a man she hardly knew, the meticulous structure of her life vanishing to a distant point.

"My life just feels so regimented," she said.

He nodded. "Yes."

He walked her to the door, his muscular torso bare above the jeans he had hastily pulled on.

They kissed lightly, their lips moist, more familiar now, but the ease of just a few minutes ago gone, replaced by a wave of awkwardness.

She turned, pulled her coat on.

"I'll call," he said.

She nodded.

He leaned over and kissed her one last time before she slid out the door.

Sarah walked alone past the club on the corner where people were huddled out in the cold smoking cigarettes, their night just beginning, and got the first cab she saw, anxious suddenly to be home.

Twenty-four

Sarah awoke the next morning with a vague sense of dislocation—something was different, but in the initial haze of semiconsciousness, she could not quite remember what. It dawned on her first as a sense memory—her skin alive as it hadn't been for months, a porous sexual hangover lingering, pleasant but disturbing. The previous night came back in disjointed words, touches, his lips, his face so close to hers. She felt her arms, the curve of her hips, testing, probing, remembering, her nerve endings reawakened in a way that just weeks ago she hadn't believed would ever be possible again.

Suddenly she did care, cared deeply, what he thought, if he'd call. She climbed out of bed and dug her BlackBerry out of her bag. Her heart jumped when she saw that she had two new messages. Neither turned out to be from him and she felt a pang of rejection, despite telling herself that the fact that he did not text her in the middle of the night was meaningless. There were so many more ways to feel rejected, so many more ways for men not to contact you than there had been when she had first started dating.

By the time Sarah dropped Eliza at school and got to work, it seemed as if hours had passed, hours with no word, though it was only 9:00 a.m. She opened her office door hoping to see the red message light of her phone blinking but it was a matte gray. She checked her e-mail (maybe her BlackBerry wasn't working for some reason; it could happen) but there was nothing. What was the acceptable time frame for a morning-after call, 10:00 a.m., 2:00 p.m., had it changed? At what point did the absence of communication imply an absence of interest?

Paige had a breakfast with the PR people for a new organic beauty line at a vegan restaurant near Gramercy Park that served only locally grown produce cooked below a certain temperature and wouldn't be in for another hour. Lucy was at a PTA meeting planning the spring benefit, which she swore every year she would never do again, and yet always ended up running. There was no one for Sarah to call, nothing for her to do but try to work. She read the same first paragraph of a proposal for a story about the rise in type 2 diabetes in young women at least four times before giving up and moving on to the second paragraph.

At ten-fifteen, Sarah's e-mail pinged.

"Well????????" It was from Paige.

Sarah walked over to her office, sat down in the pink director's chair, and rested her elbows on Paige's desk.

"What does that look mean?" Paige asked, studying Sarah. "It was bad? How bad?"

Sarah remained silent.

"How bad could it be? I mean, really."

Sarah waited another moment. "I slept with him," she said, a mixture of giddiness and resignation in her voice.

"You what?" Paige got up instantly and shut her office door. "I don't believe it."

"What don't you believe?" Sarah asked. "That anyone would want to sleep with me? That mothers of young children have the same desires as everyone else?"

"Oh please, that has nothing to do with it. Who wouldn't want to sleep with you? Who wouldn't want to sleep with him, for that matter? It's just not what I expected, that's all."

"It's not what I expected, either."

"So? How was it?"

Sarah smiled. "Great."

"Okay, how did you leave it, what did he say, has he called yet?"

"It wasn't one of the most graceful exits of all time. I was two hours late for Dora and I freaked."

"Sounds romantic," Paige remarked.

Sarah frowned. "Look, I've never done this with a kid, okay? The last time I slept with anyone other than my husband was fifteen years ago. The last time I slept with a guy on a first date I was in college and there were one-dollar whiskey sours involved." She took a deep breath. "I don't know, we kissed good-bye at the door, he said he'd call."

"And?"

"It's early still," Sarah replied defensively.

Paige nodded ruefully.

"What? I don't like that look on your face."

"Okay, you made a rookie error," she said. Sarah detected a note of condescension in her voice.

"I'm sure there are plenty of couples who slept together on their first date."

Paige raised one eyebrow.

"Well some, anyway."

"Sarah, I'm not being judgmental. We've all made the same mistake."

"Why is it a mistake?" Sarah was in the unfortunate role of defending a position she was not thoroughly convinced of.

Paige shrugged. "I'm not talking good girl/bad girl here. Men like the hunt, you know that. You made it too easy. But aside from that, the real problem is that you know each other really well in one way and not at all in another. It's hard to back up. The progression gets all screwed up. Literally. There's nothing wrong with it. It just makes things more awkward."

"Good Lord, hasn't anything changed?"

"Not a whole lot," Paige remarked cynically.

"I don't care. It was worth it."

"I guess the concept of delayed gratification didn't quite occur to you?"

"At that particular moment? No."

"Right."

"Look," Sarah said, seriously, "it wasn't just wanting Tim, which I did. I mean, I was wildly attracted to him." She paused. "It was the first time since August that I've forgotten about what happened, about my life. Maybe that's wrong, but—"

"It's not wrong." Paige softened, leaned forward, gently moved a strand of hair from Sarah's face.

As the hours passed, Sarah began to suspect Paige was right, though she hated the old-fashioned code it implied. She called Lucy, relayed the details of her night, and asked if she knew of any couples who had begun their relationship in bed.

Lucy managed to offer up one, no wait, two. "If it was meant to be, it won't make any difference how it started," she reassured Sarah.

The afternoon was winding down slowly, depressingly, silently, when, at close to 5:00 p.m., Maude buzzed Sarah to tell her that Tim Wakefield was on the line.

Sarah picked up nervously. "Hi."

"Hi. Did you get home okay? I hope your babysitter wasn't too pissed off."

"She was fine. I apologized profusely, overpaid exorbitantly, and sent her home in a car service."

Tim laughed. "I use the same technique with my designers."

"I'll remember that when I get your final bill."

He ignored this. "So," he said, "I had a good time last night."

"Yes. Me, too."

She could hear numerous voices in the background and someone calling Tim's name.

"Sorry," he said. "I'm on a shoot. Listen, I have Chris again this weekend. I had thought his mother, never mind, anyway, he has a birthday party Sunday afternoon. I know this is short notice, but do you want to meet for a glass of wine? I only have a couple of hours, but . . ."

Sarah flashed immediately to the logistics—who would watch

Eliza, what would she tell her, how on earth did people with young children do this? Nevertheless, she wanted to appear as if spontaneity was at least a possibility in her life. "That would be great," she said. And what kind of second date was that anyway, a couple of hours in the middle of the day? Was he downgrading her?

"Great," he replied.

As soon as Sarah hung up, she e-mailed Paige, "He called, Smarty Pants!" There was vast relief and not a small amount of vindication in the words. She hit Send and called Lucy to ask if she could leave Eliza at her house for a few hours on Sunday.

The wardrobe choices for a Sunday afternoon, kids-at-birthday-party glass of wine were far from clear to Sarah, and she spent much of that morning trying on various incarnations of casual-but-sexy, trying-but-not-trying-too-hard. She finally settled on tight, low-slung jeans and a white scoop-neck sweater that showed off her newly prominent collarbone (this had required taking on and off six tops and three different bras).

"Why aren't you staying?" Eliza asked suspiciously as they headed into Lucy's building.

"I have some errands to do," Sarah replied, not looking her daughter in the eye.

Upstairs, Jane and Eliza hovered about the living room with the sixth sense children have for moments when grown-ups want to talk out of their hearing range.

"Why don't you show Eliza that new beading kit?" Lucy suggested.

Jane made no move.

"Go on," Lucy prompted.

The children turned around and headed down the hallway, registering their protest with every step.

"I've outlawed beading kits," Sarah remarked as they sat down on the couch. "I can't stand stepping on those things all the time."

Lucy shrugged. "I outlaw a lot of things until I need some time alone and then somehow they magically reappear. It's the no-backbone approach to motherhood." She smiled. "You look beautiful."

"Really? When I look in the mirror all I can see is how much my face has changed in the past few months."

Lucy studied her for a moment. "Are you okay?"

"Yes. A little nervous, but yes. I like him. I think I like him. I don't know." Sarah looked away. "I feel guilty," she said quietly.

"To be seeing someone?"

"Yes. It's just so . . . soon. I think about Todd every day. Every time the phone rings, I . . . I still think there were will be some news," she admitted.

"Sarah, you'll always miss Todd. But that doesn't mean you shouldn't get on with your life. Only you can know if it's too soon. And you may not know that right away. But you have nothing to feel guilty about. Todd is dead. And you were separated even before that."

Sarah looked at Lucy, so absolute, so certain, and knew that as much as she might pretend otherwise, it would never be that clear-cut to her. She was waiting still, perhaps she always would be. "It's just not . . . clean," she said. "The way it would be with a real death. Not real, but you know what I mean. I still see the ocean every time I close my eyes. Maybe it will always be that night for me and everything else is just living around it."

"Maybe. But it is still living, *you're* still living. You don't need permission to start dating again. It's okay."

"I know. I guess I just needed to hear it from someone else." Sarah looked at her watch. "On that cheerful note, I've got to go," she said, standing up and getting ready to leave.

"Have a good time," Lucy told her as she walked her to the door.

Sarah nodded and kissed her good-bye.

The small bistro in the meatpacking district was one block from the rattle and squalor of the West Side Highway, just beyond the ever-encroaching borders of gentrification. Run by a French couple known for their friendliness to those they liked and their distinct frostiness to those they didn't, it was dark, brick-walled, intimate, and virtually empty in this off-hour between late lunch and early Sunday dinners. Sarah was the first to arrive, and she took a table by the far wall. The sole waiter had just managed to pull himself away from his seat at the bar to bring her a glass of water and the wine list when Tim walked in.

"Sorry I'm late," he said. He leaned over to kiss her hello and she offered up her cheek, realizing too late that he was aiming for her lips. "The party was over at Chelsea Piers," he explained as he took off his jacket and sat down. "Fifteen eight-year-old boys hopped up on sugar and bad rock 'n' roll. I can't stand that place. I need a sensory deprivation tank after three minutes there."

Sarah agreed. "I always get stuck pouring more and more money into those damn game machines in the back. Eliza gets this crazed look in her eyes the minute the paper tickets start spitting out. I'm sure she'll be in Gamblers Anonymous by the time she's ten."

Tim laughed. "Did you tell her where you were going today?" he asked, motioning to the waiter, who miraculously came instantly, greeted Tim by name, and took their order.

"No," she admitted. "You?"

"Nope."

They both smiled.

"You know how I said I felt like I was in college the other night?" Sarah asked. "Well, I'm regressing. This afternoon I felt like a teenager lying to my parents, only this time I was lying to a six-year-old."

"Which is actually far worse. No one on earth is as judgmental as your own children."

Sarah nodded. When they had spoken about Eliza the other night, she had given Tim a sketchy sugarcoated version; she had not mentioned her refusal to be kissed, her slamming of doors, her anger, in part because it felt disloyal, but also because she did not want it to appear that she had a troubled child—surely a mark against her in this new world of dating.

"Actually, I've found it's easier to date women with kids," Tim said.

"Have you dated a lot since your divorce?" Sarah asked carefully.

He smiled. "That's a trick question, right up there with 'Do I look fat in these jeans?' "

"And that's not an answer."

"I've dated some. You?"

Sarah began ripping up her paper napkin again. "I haven't been out with anyone since Todd died," she said.

"What about when you were separated?"

She took a large sip of her kir. Drinking in the middle of the day, even the smallest amount, had always made her warm, woozy. She looked over at Tim, a stranger really, and yet not, and felt a stirring deep within. "No."

He reached over and put his hands on hers. "You've got to stop that," he said, taking the shredded napkin from her. But he was smiling, they were in on this together.

"I guess you make me nervous," she admitted.

"Well, you make me nervous, too."

"I do?"

"Why are you so surprised?"

"Because you've dated 'some,' " she teased him. "Because you spend half your time with models. Because you just don't seem the nervous type."

"Well, in that case it must be something about you." He looked at her seriously. "Sarah, I've never dated a client before."

"I'm not a client anymore, remember?"

"Yes, that's why I waited to call you."

She smiled, pleased that he had been thinking of her, waiting for her. "So what was the shoot you were on the other day?"

"Two gallery owners are renovating a condo building on lower Madison Avenue, extremely high end. They're going to market it to the same clientele and in the same way they sell paintings. They want us to design the advertising campaign."

"Art justifying overpriced Manhattan real estate—it's a brilliant strategy."

Tim studied her for a moment. "The other night, I told you I know the difference between façade and substance. The thing that makes me good at my job, that makes Wakefield successful, is that I know in the end I'm an interpreter, a designer. I'm okay with that."

There was a slightly defensive tone in his voice and Sarah realized that he was, in his own oblique way, referring to Todd, feeling competitive with him, the craftsman versus the artist.

"I didn't mean to be sarcastic," she said. "It actually sounds like an interesting project."

"Well, you do have a point. Art dealers and real estate agents both appeal to aesthetics and snobbery. But every now and then they actually believe in what they're selling. Besides, we balance the big lucrative projects with a few smaller ones we really care about."

"Like *Splash*?"

"Exactly."

"Well, that didn't get you very far. I hope you have better luck with those condos."

"I don't know, I think some good things came out of *Splash*." He smiled. "What about you? Do you want to stay at *Flair* now that Rena's gone?"

"I'm not sure I have a choice."

"You always have a choice. I've given this a lot of thought, particularly toward the end of my marriage when I was trying to decide whether to stay or go. You choose every day how you want your future to look, with even the smallest decision you make. Choice is ongoing. I think you can choose happiness."

"Rena wanted to do a whole issue on that."

"Don't write her off. A lot of people have made that mistake. But I'm not talking magazine-speak. Look, you may not achieve it, you may get totally slammed, but I honestly believe that you can choose to at least aim for it."

Sarah looked at Tim without answering. It sounded ridiculously, annoyingly simplistic to her. But she realized, too, that it took a certain bravery to be so nakedly uncynical, particularly in the strata of the city he lived in where cool was so often mistaken for intelligence, irony for insight. She was drawn to him more than ever—after the past few months, nothing could be more attractive than a man who envisioned a future and was confident of his own ability to shape it.

"Okay if I get back to you on that one?" she asked.

"I'm counting on it." He reached over to touch her face and she rested her cheek against the palm of his hand, a catlike sigh of contentedness escaping from her throat.

They ordered another round of drinks and as people began to wander in from the nearby galleries and shops, they felt cocooned in their corner, their legs touching now beneath the table, the wine, the closeness distracting them both, their desire enhanced by their inability to do anything about it.

Tim looked at his watch. "I've got to go pick up Chris."

He paid the check and they walked out, standing on the street corner in the deep glow of dusk. The wind from the Hudson River whipped around them and he pulled her into his embrace. She wrapped her arms about his neck as they kissed, unwilling to separate, the intensity magnified by the fact that it felt mildly illicit, children, obligations waiting for them. Their hands were wandering down each other's backs, their legs pressed against each other. "I used to wonder why people like this didn't just go home," Tim said, pulling back an inch, smiling at her. "Maybe they just didn't have a place to go to. We are homeless romantics."

She laughed, buried her face in the crook of his neck.

"I really do have to leave," he said, convincing himself, convincing her.

"Okay."

They kissed once more and he hailed a passing cab.

Sarah walked a block and then caught a cab of her own. She leaned back against the black vinyl seat and stared out of the filmy window, slightly drunk, disjointed, desirous, confused, as the streets grew more crowded with people, restaurants, Korean delis with their brilliantly dyed flowers behind sheets of plastic protecting them from the cold. She grew almost dizzy, flooded with the colors, the afternoon, the beginning with Tim overlapping with a past still nibbling at its edges.

She went over their conversation in her mind, searching for clues to him, but it was filtered through a film of insecurity. She realized that he had not said anything about calling her, about getting together again, and she felt a wave of uncertainty—it was all just empty space ahead. She remembered her early days with Todd; there were no fits and starts, no strategies, no doubts that they were from the very start, a couple. Perhaps it was Todd, his nature—the very idea of dating was anathema to him—but perhaps, too, that can only happen at an earlier stage of life, before the barnacles of past lives, current responsibilities, young children, ex-spouses, ghosts. She and Tim were not, would never be, just the two of them; it would never be simple in the way it had been when they were each starting out.

Or perhaps that is only how Sarah remembered it now—it had never really been that simple, after all.

Twenty-five

The chill of early winter deepened overnight. Women wrapped in layers of wool wove through the crowded streets with heads down, lost in thought about shopping lists, the frenzied round of upcoming parties, while men in mufflers tried to hide their growing panic about the mysteries of gift-giving and lovers' expectations. But just beneath the hectic glittery surface a slower rhythm had descended upon Manhattan; phone calls took longer to get returned, nonessential business was put off until January, traffic reached a standstill as tourists and nontourists alike stopped to admire the tree going up in Rockefeller Center, the windows along Fifth Avenue, the tiny white lights sprinkled like fairy dust through the leafless trees on Park Avenue.

At *Flair,* editors came to work carrying sequined tops they could slip into at the end of day, impossibly high open-toed sandals to wear to parties, despite the frigid air, showing off toes freshly manicured in deep, rich crimsons. Glossy shopping bags, intriguing velvet boxes, mini champagne bottles, intricately decorated chocolates perfect for regifting piled up on their desks along with the endless stack of invitations, some coveted, some obligatory, for events given by friends, by PR agencies, by cosmetics firms, by each other. Some were planning vacations in St. Barts or Aspen, others were headed home to the Midwest where they would find more relief than they cared to admit even as they grew frustrated that their newly acquired patina of style was not sufficiently appreciated. The few mothers on staff grew weary from baking cupcakes and sugar cookies for school fairs; a number of the single editors hoped for engagement rings proffered under the tree.

The first snow began to fall early on a Thursday morning and covered the streets like a handmade crocheted blanket. Sarah got out her sheepskin boots, took Eliza to school, and arrived to find *Flair*'s offices surprisingly full. Word had somehow filtered out the night before that a new editor was about to be named. At ten-thirty an e-mail went out "inviting" the entire edit and advertising staffs to the ninth-floor boardroom, where few had ever been. They filed into the wood-paneled room to find a spread of coffee, bagels, exotic fresh fruit, and glass pitchers of fresh-squeezed orange juice awaiting them. No one touched a thing.

Standing in the front of the room was William Rowling with Pat by his side, giving her most avid imitation of a smile. Anna stood just a few inches away like a proud parent at a bar mitzvah. Sarah's heart fell. She had come to the conclusion that her only chance of survival was someone from the outside. At least then she would have a chance to prove herself. Pat knew who she was, what she could do, what she had done—and what she hadn't.

As soon as William began to speak, the room fell preternaturally silent. Editors smiled at him, hoping to make eye contact, to be noticed, to be liked.

"Thank you for coming this morning," he began.

"He makes it sound like a goddamned garden party," Paige muttered. The sight of a victorious Pat made her ill.

"Sshhh," Sarah insisted. "I'd like to see if I can go at least twenty minutes without being fired."

"I'm happy to announce that Pat Nolan has agreed to be the new editor of *Flair.*" The room broke into applause of varying degrees of sincerity. Most enthusiastic were the ad sales people, who'd had little personal connection to Rena and were relieved that they would have a new story to go out and sell. Visions of commissions danced in their well-groomed heads.

"Pat has a clear vision for *Flair* that I believe will benefit the magazine, the company, and most importantly you," William concluded.

Pat began to speak. "I am thrilled to have the opportunity to lead this wonderful magazine. Rena Berman did an amazing job. Her unique creativity never ceased to amaze me. I am looking forward to building on her endeavors and strengthening *Flair* as a powerful brand not only on the newsstand but online, in books, DVDs, and other potential revenue streams." She smiled out at the room. "But I will need your help. I know how very talented you all are. This will be an exciting time for us all. Now let's get to work!" She meant it as a rallying cry, but it came out as more of a demand. Pat trying to be warm and friendly was not a convincing sight, even to her most ardent supporters.

While editors crowded around Pat to ingratiate themselves, William Rowling slipped out of the room without getting cornered or having to talk to a single person.

By the time the meeting was over, Pat's boxes were already unpacked in Rena's old office, her name was engraved on the door, and the walls had been repainted. Rena was right, the waters closed quickly in this business.

"Didn't she promise you the executive editor job at some point?" Paige asked Sarah hopefully as they passed by Pat's former office, now eerily deserted.

"She dangled it for a millisecond, but she had no intention of actually following through."

Sarah paused. She had never warned Paige of what Pat had said about her when they were in the thick of *Splash.* If she told her now, Paige would be furious that she hadn't informed her earlier. Nevertheless, she had to warn her somehow. "Listen, you know the game," Sarah said. "The only thing you can do is go up to Pat and ask her what you can do to help her realize her vision for the magazine."

"What two-bit management book did you get that out of?"

Sarah ignored this. "Then send her a thousand story ideas."

"Is that your plan?" Paige asked.

"Frankly, yes. Look, we both know that the worst thing you can do with a new editor is tell her how you used to do things."

"She was here," Paige reminded her. "She knows damn well how we used to do things. That's the problem."

"Paige, please. At least try."

Paige didn't answer. "You know what's really depressing?" she asked.

"I'd like to know what's not."

"What's depressing is that the suits won. Because that's what Pat is. A suit disguised as an editor. I know that Rena had the worst commercial sense of any editor on the planet. And I know she had some really bad ideas. But she also had some good ideas. *Original* ideas. At least she was willing to take risks."

Sarah agreed, but there was nothing she could do. "Just send Pat an ideas memo, okay?"

"I thought I was the one who was supposed to get the politics around here," Paige replied.

"I'm learning fast," Sarah said. "Trial by firing."

Sarah stayed late that night writing up a six-page memo of story ideas, each with a potential cover line attached to display her commercial instincts and prove that she was willing to play ball. She left it in Pat's in-box but heard nothing back.

Two days later, Caitlin was named executive editor of *Flair*.

Sarah watched her move effortlessly into Pat's office as if she had been born into the position, and she knew that her days at *Flair* were numbered. Pat was a lesson in barracuda corporate politics; she surrounded herself with people who could be useful to her whether she liked them or not. Caitlin, with her coterie of society friends and her powerful father, had a habit of cutting whomever she disliked. Sarah began making copies of her computer files and taking home personal possessions one at a time.

But nothing happened.

The following week, *Flair* had its annual Christmas party at Anna's sprawling Fifth Avenue apartment. Sarah and Paige arrived together, deposited their coats with a black-tied attendant, grabbed champagne from one of the many hired help for the night, each more stunning than the next, and stepped into the living room with its enormous windows overlooking Central Park. It was the kind of view that hopeful college grads moved to New York to acquire, only to discover that the closest most would ever come was in a movie theater. An apartment like Anna's could turn you into a revolutionary or a desperate climber willing to do anything to gain entry to that world.

In the deep emerald dining room a lavish buffet was set up, and women circled each other noting what each was or was not eating. Out of the corner of her eye Sarah watched Anna swan about the rooms, slightly tipsy, deeply satisfied, glowing with confidence.

"Have you seen Pat?" Sarah asked Paige as she took a bite of the largest shrimp she had ever seen.

"She's in the living room."

"Good. I'll stay in here then." Paige's dislike of Pat had grown so encompassing that she no longer tried to hide it from anyone. Sarah knew that being so vocal was recklessly dangerous and self-destructive, but Paige didn't seem to care. "How long do we have to stay?"

"We just got here."

"As far as I'm concerned, we've put in our appearance, been marked present, and are free to go. Where are you meeting Tim?"

"His loft. He's cooking."

"Please tell me he has some fatal flaw."

"I'm sure I'll discover it any minute," Sarah replied with a cynicism she did not feel. She had a hard time admitting to herself or others how good it felt to be with Tim; she wasn't sure she was supposed to be happy now even if only for brief moments, it was so at odds with memory and loss. "Are you still planning on going skiing with Ethan?"

"It appears not."

Sarah looked at her quizzically.

Paige frowned. "Let's keep in mind that the whole thing was his idea when we first got back together, a romantic holiday trip to Vail, blah blah blah. Well, he never brought it up again."

"You could ask him."

"I did. He muttered something about how he needs time to mend fences with his family."

"I wasn't aware his fences were damaged."

"Neither was I. It drives me crazy. Anything to do with getting together that's his idea is fine. But if I bring something up, he acts like it's too much pressure and starts trying to weasel out of it. I don't know what to do." She looked at Sarah, who was clearly biting her tongue. "I don't want to hear it. Not now. He just needs time." She finished her glass of champagne. "I guess I'll go to my parents' where my sister will manage to make me feel old, childless, and uniquely unmarriable within fifteen minutes. Good thing they're all alcoholics." She smiled wryly. "Not to change the subject, but have you noticed that we are total pariahs?"

Sarah glanced around the room at the clusters of editors huddled together. A few had made insincere small talk with Sarah and Paige, but most merely nodded from a safe distance.

"Let's go," she agreed.

The two women parted on Fifth Avenue and Sarah hopped into a cab for the frustratingly slow ride downtown. It was past eight by the time she pulled up at Tim's building and paid the driver. As she climbed out, she did the calculations in her head: She had promised Dora that she would be home by 11:30; that gave them three and a half hours.

The smell of roasting chicken wafted through the door when Tim, barefoot in jeans and a navy T-shirt, kissed Sarah hello, his face flushed from cooking, his smile welcoming, relaxed, happy. "So this is a big step, cooking for you for the first time," he said as they stood in the kitchen where an inordinate number of pots and pans were boiling away.

"Have you been known to poison your guests?"

"Not recently. I have a few dishes I do really well, so I just keep repeating them."

"I have a number that I do with great mediocrity."

While he stirred the orzo, she stood by his side, drinking a glass of merlot and watching him with a mixture of desire and self-consciousness. It was so intimate, this act of preparing a meal together. She wanted to reach over, run her hands down his back, touch his arms, smoothly muscled from his weekly tennis games, pull him to her, and yet for some reason she couldn't. They were on their second glass of wine when they sat down at the small round table in front of the fireplace, tea lights in crystal holders glowing softly, Gaetano Veloso playing in the background.

"This is unbelievable," Sarah remarked as she took her first bite of the chicken he had roasted with shiitake mushrooms.

The perfection of the food, his pleasure in cooking it, the seemingly offhand style that informed everything he did added to the sensuality and confidence that he naturally emanated.

"What are you doing with Chris over the holidays?" she asked as Tim spooned orzo onto her plate.

"I'm taking him to my parents' in Philadelphia and then to an annual family gathering in Maryland." He put the spoon down. "I won't be back until after New Year's."

Sarah absorbed this without comment.

"My ex-wife is tormenting me," he continued. "She's insisting that we give Chris the exact same number of gifts of exactly equal value. Among other things, this requires constant e-mailing back and forth. It's insane."

Sarah, who was not particularly pleased with that degree of contact between them either, leaned forward. "Would you mind if we don't exchange gifts?" she asked. She had spent more time than she cared to admit worrying about this: What if she got him something and he didn't have a gift for her? What if the opposite occurred? And then there were the fraught questions of how much to spend, how intimate the gift should be, a veritable mine field of potential disappointment and misinterpretation. "I don't think I can handle the stress," she added jokingly.

He smiled with relief. "God, I'm glad you said that. I had no idea what to do."

"Good." Though it had been her idea, she was nevertheless disappointed that he didn't have a gift for her.

He cleared the plates, brought out deep red strawberries, luscious and out of season.

The wine, the fire, the meal had warmed them both. He leaned over and kissed her gently before they gradually separated and turned their attention back to the strawberries. The kiss was just an interlude, a precursor. Sarah looked down, flushed, and played with a leafy green stem while he watched her intently, studying her, considering her.

"You're very private," he said.

"What do you mean?"

"It's not a criticism. I find it intriguing. But I get the feeling you're holding something back."

She smiled lightly, not quite getting where he was going. "Ask me anything."

He touched her bare foot with his. "I mean in bed."

She stopped smiling. "You mean you think I'm repressed?"

"No, not at all. But sometimes I feel your mind is elsewhere."

She crossed her arms in self-protection. "It's not conscious," she said.

"I know. It wasn't a judgment, just an observation." He was by nature interested in all quirks of personality, including hers, curious, perhaps even delighted by them. Sarah could not decide if this was evidence of open-mindedness or detachment.

"We've only been seeing each other for a few weeks," she said defensively. She drained her glass of wine; it felt as if he wanted pieces of her that she wasn't sure she was ready to give. Maybe it was too soon after all.

"How did I end up with the only man in New York who actually wants to have relationship talks?" she said, teasing, though there was an element of protest in her tone, her words.

He smiled, waited. He was a patient man.

She relented, but not completely. "Part of it is that I always feel I have to rush home," Sarah said. "I'm so conscious of the clock. It's hard to relax when you feel you have a deadline."

Tim nodded. "I know," he said. He touched her face tenderly. "We need to arrange a sleepover date."

"For our kids or us?"

"Both. We'll figure it out. We have time."

She looked at her watch. "An hour and a half, actually."

"I mean in general." He reached over and pulled her to him. "We'll figure it out," he whispered again, and his voice snaked down her spine, melting her as they sank to the polished floor in front of the fireplace, their clothes giving way to skin, to touch, to lips.

She was aware of herself, and aware that she was aware, trying to give herself, open herself, pry herself free of her own overlapping desire and doubts and prove that she was totally here, and she almost succeeded.

And then she stopped thinking completely, it felt so good.

Twenty-six

As the end of another month approached, the question of what to do with Todd's studio loomed in Sarah's mind. It wasn't just the financial consideration of the rent. The studio, preserved exactly as he had left it, had expanded to take up an enormous space in the city of her mind; it was its own neighborhood of memory and remorse, of early courtship and unfulfilled dreams, tipping Manhattan itself, weighing it down. It was always with her.

Todd was most himself in that studio, a place he and he alone defined, retreated to, and the thought of giving it up felt like the ultimate act of betrayal, more harsh in its finality than a death certificate. Despite the memorial service, Sarah was haunted by images of what would happen if Todd did come back, the abject fury he would level at her if his studio was gone. She went over and over the justifications in her mind: It was five months. I did not hear a word from you, what was I supposed to believe, what was I supposed to do?

Lucy, unwavering in her belief that Todd was dead, assured Sarah that it was the right thing to do and offered to help her clean it out. "Sarah, if he was alive he would have contacted Eliza," she said.

It was the only argument that reached Sarah, the only one that she could always return to, believe in—Todd's love for his daughter—when all else seemed, even now, open to interpretation. "I know."

y, Sarah called Princeton Records and arranged for up Todd's vast music collection. She put the six thou- they paid for it into Eliza's college fund. She called his nd told him she would be giving up the place. He was The neighborhood had changed so much that he could e rent. There was the skylight, the square footage, the restau- it was a street with a brilliant future.

Lucy and Mark rented a U-Haul and cleaned out the studio for rah on a Saturday morning, delivering most of the artwork to her partment and arranging to put the rest in storage. Sarah crammed long legs of copper pieces into Todd's empty closet, under her bed, random segments of art pulled from the walls that she would never be able to put back together quite the way he had intended.

Tim left New York the week before Christmas and took with him the distraction, the electrical filter of sex that kept everything else at arm's length, leaving Sarah with nothing but her own life. Without him and without the promise of *Splash,* the future itself, at least a future that would be noticeably different, better, seemed to disappear. All that was left was the emptiness of her first Christmas alone with Eliza.

How many little things, rituals that you don't even regard as such—the habits of families that grow around a couple cementing their bond, children's needs—go barely noticed until suddenly you find they are solidified into the very fabric of your life. The champagne and cheap caviar Sarah and Todd had shared their very first Christmas morning together on Rivington Street and then continued to enjoy every year, married, pregnant, watching Eliza greedily tear open gifts. The cloves Todd stuck into oranges and set about the house to replicate the scent of his early holidays in Germany. The decision they had made, though neither had the slightest religious bent, to celebrate Hanukkah and Christmas once they had a child. Sarah, though she was Jewish, had no idea what the real meaning of Hanukkah actually was; it was Todd who did the research, taught Eliza what to say as they lit the candles, his hand on hers, guiding her more steadily as she grew. Sarah's parents, when they still lived in New York, agreed to celebrate Hanukkah on Christmas Day, no matter when it actually fell; she and Todd would cart eight presents (one for each night) over to their apartment and hand them out at midday. They had never spent a Christmas in Florida, even when Todd's mother was alive, though there were always long, nostalgic phone calls to her and to Peter.

Sarah held up each of these rites that had evolved over a decade's marriage and questioned them anew. The thought of doing the exact same things without Todd seemed unbearably painful; the thought of not doing them was no better.

What came to concern her most was not tradition, but logistics. She and Todd had always chosen the largest Douglas fir that could fit into their apartment from the stand run by French Canadians five blocks away. He would take one end, Sarah the other, and with Eliza toddling excitedly behind them they managed to get it home, squabbling about how to steer it the entire way. The problem of how to get the tree home by herself seemed insurmountable.

There was a world of things that not just Todd but other men did that she had never conquered, never, to be honest, even tried to: hooking up stereos, putting up shelves, carving. Men knew what to do in an emergency, they would know what leaves were poisonous on a deserted island (granted, not a huge possibility in her life, but still), what to do in a fire. Men took care of the physicality of life even if the emotional subtext seemed at times beyond their ken.

Sarah's apartment was growing tatty around the edges without Todd to fix things, adding to her general sense of helplessness. The cabinet door in the living room that only he knew how to adjust had come unhinged, the DVD player blinked with the wrong time after a power outage, Eliza's antique dresser that Todd had bought and painstakingly refinished when Sarah was pregnant was missing a glass knob. The underlying sense of powerlessness that had been festering since he died culminated into this one insoluble problem: the Christmas tree. She lay awake at night pondering it, obsessed about it at work. Finally she called Lucy to ask her advice.

Lucy answered with ill-concealed surprise, as if she could not quite believe the question. "They deliver," she said simply, all midwestern practicality.

"What?"

"The Christmas tree people, they deliver."

"You're kidding me?"

"Didn't you think to ask them?"

"Actually, no," Sarah admitted. One of the residual psychological idiosyncrasies of the past few months had been a stultifying, almost infantilizing, tunnel vision. Sarah, who by nature and by journalistic training had previously been able to examine a problem from various angles, to try a new route if the first one failed, to push and to probe anyone that presented an obstacle, had lost the ability to see alternatives or the confidence to seek them out.

"Good Lord," Lucy replied, "you have had more things delivered than anyone I have ever met. You had fishnet stockings delivered when a pair ripped before a meeting."

"That was Paige, actually."

"I stand corrected." Lucy laughed. "Go pick out a tree and have it brought over. Let me know if you want help decorating."

Sarah was learning that so many of the things she used to think only Todd, only a husband, could accomplish she could pay someone to do. It did not seem an act of independence or empowerment, though, but one of resignation, highlighting the manlessness of her existence. And it certainly did not help when she lay in bed late at night, alone, scared of things she could not name—disasters, illness, thieves—that she could not pay someone to see her through. At least this one problem had a practical solution.

Sarah did not want to go through the exact same tree-buying ritual as before with a delivery man taking Todd's place, leaving Eliza to scamper behind a stranger. She arranged a play date and went alone to the double row of trees overseen by a handful of the young French Canadian men who, for these few weeks, had taken over the city with their craggy youth and good looks, wriggling into the dream life of the city's entire female population; they were so rugged, so alluringly transient, so not New York.

She stood alone in the cold, the rich scent of pine making her ache in unexpected places. In years past, the three of them had patiently had tree after tree shaken from its plastic netting as they searched for the perfect fir, meticulously examining each for bare spots, appraising for symmetry. This time she chose quickly and paid the fifteen-dollar delivery fee.

She went home and poured herself an enormous glass of cabernet, drinking it while she moved the coffee table and straw basket of magazines to make room for the tree in the left-hand corner of the living room. She found the dented red and green metal stand in the back of the linen closet and tried to figure out how to screw in the legs, a simple task that suddenly seemed an impossible engineering feat. Frustrated, on the verge of tears, she gave up and decided to pay the delivery man extra to do that, too.

An hour and two glasses of wine later, a ridiculously handsome six-foot-tall man appeared at her door with a deep French accent and dark, almost black, thick, wavy hair. In his midtwenties, he brought with him the scent of the outdoors, the magnetism of a man who knew how to survive in nature.

He smiled at Sarah as he entered; people were usually happy to see him, he was, after all, a harbinger of the season. "Where do you want this?" he asked.

She showed him the stand lying in pieces on the floor. "I couldn't figure out how to put it together," she admitted.

"No problem."

He rested the tree against the wall and knelt down, assembling it in two seconds like a child doing a puzzle he had outgrown. She watched him crouching, his broad back to her, his jeans tight across his thighs. Maybe it was the wine or the loneliness of the occasion, but suddenly the only thing in the world she wanted was for him to take her, here on the floor, wordlessly, completely, obliterating all else. She began to calculate when Eliza would return, the potential horror of her finding her mother fucking the Christmas tree man on the living room floor.

Is this what she had come to?

Sarah found that she was crying, softly enough that she could hide it at first, then not, tears pouring down her face as she gasped audibly for breath. The poor man politely tried to ignore it, this woman sobbing a few inches away. He rose, picked up the tree, still tightly encased in plastic netting, and put it into the stand while Sarah knelt below him, her hands shaking as she twisted the screws until they bit into the trunk, the sound of her crying filling the otherwise silent room.

"My husband died," she said at last. "This is our first Christmas without him." She felt compelled to offer an explanation, but more than that, she had a overriding need for him to see, really see, her.

"I'm so sorry," he said, shifting his weight from leg to leg, obviously wanting to get the tree in straight and get the hell out.

She nodded, fighting to gain control of her breathing, deeply embarrassed; it had just spilled out unbidden, spilled over, she hadn't been able to jam it back down.

The tree was finally in and he stepped back, his hands in his pockets, unable to make eye contact.

Sarah tipped him three times more than she had planned and let him go.

When Eliza came home that night she accepted Sarah's explanation that she had wanted to surprise her with the tree as a special treat with an air of skepticism—nothing was as it used to be—that was somewhat ameliorated by her mother's gift of an elaborate bird cage ornament. Seduced, Eliza got caught up in the excitement of unwrapping the box of ornaments and exclaiming over each as if rediscovering an old friend. Along with the ones she had chosen every year, there were all of the ornaments Sarah and Todd had bought together on their travels to New Orleans, Milan, Budapest, San Francisco, Charleston, a life together marked in painted eggs and miniature wooden cable cars. Eliza picked her favorites and hung them within her arm's reach creating a traffic jam of glass balls and candy canes on the bottom third of the tree, leaving the upper branches nearly barren. When they were done, Sarah stood on the couch and put the knobby starfish she and Todd had gotten on their very first trip to Florida on the top. She looked down at Eliza, entranced with the white lights, the ornaments, Eliza who wanted so to believe in Santa Claus despite her suspicions, Eliza who still wished on the first star every night for her father to come back even though she knew it couldn't happen, wouldn't happen, she *knew* that, but couldn't she wish it anyway?

Last Christmas Eve, Eliza had slept in the living room beside the tree, which she had roped off with yarn and lined with tinfoil, certain she would finally catch Santa when he stepped on its crinkly surface. Near midnight, Sarah and Todd had tiptoed barefoot around her, successfully placing the presents without waking her, and then they made love as if they still could make it all okay. Even if they knew that the chances were slim, that it was ending, they, too, hoped that night.

Sarah felt grief rising in fresh waves and she struggled to push it down as she and Eliza sat on the floor beneath the tree, drinking hot chocolate as they admired their handiwork. When it was time for Eliza to go to bed, Sarah curled around her and held her tight, though who was most in need of comfort was unclear.

She was half-asleep when the phone rang and she stumbled through the dark to get it.

"Did you hear from him?"

"Excuse me?"

"It's Linda." She paused. "I thought Todd might call for the holiday. You know, people get sentimental, they come back this time of year. My father came back on Christmas Eve."

"Don't you get it? He's not coming back," Sarah spit out angrily.

"Maybe."

"He's dead, Linda," she hissed, and hung up, sinking to the bedroom floor.

Two nights later, she got out the gold-plated menorah she had bought when Eliza was two and placed it on the bookcase.

"If Daddy was alive, he'd be standing by the tree and you'd be standing by the menorah," Eliza commented.

"No," Sarah explained, "we'd all be standing in the middle, together. That's what a family is."

Eliza considered this. "No," she pronounced firmly, "Daddy would be by the tree and you'd be by the menorah."

Eliza picked out blue and yellow candles for the first night and put them in their holders. Sarah was just about to light the center one when Eliza interrupted. "Wait a minute."

"What is it, honey?" The unlit match was still in her hand.

Eliza disappeared into her room without answering and grabbed the picture of Todd holding her after she was born. She came back out and placed it a half inch from the menorah. "Now Daddy is here," she said.

Sarah lit the candles and they watched them flicker, the light playing across the silver frame of the photo that stayed there for the next seven nights.

Three days before Christmas, Sarah's mother arrived with presents and her own grief wrapped about her like a shawl. Though both women were relieved not to be alone on the holidays, they were almost shy with each other at first. In recent years, their husbands had provided them with a buffer from each other, and they were scared what they might find now that they were forced to come face-to-face without it. They both still remembered earlier, more volatile times when Sarah fought against her mother's interference, or "advice," as Lani would have preferred it called. It had seemed so intense, so inescapable as an only child. Sarah wondered if her own daughter would feel the same clawing need to ward off intrusion, however well meant. Within hours, though, Sarah saw how much smaller, more fragile, her mother was now. Her voice was missing its previous sharp edges, replaced by a slower melancholy cadence. Lurking deep within, Sarah sensed something she had never heard before—traces of self-pity.

"At least you have Eliza," Lani remarked to Sarah the first night of her visit as they sat in the living room drinking brandy, as if loneliness were a contest. Sarah said nothing, just pulled her arms tighter around her. She didn't want to argue, certainly not over whose predicament was sadder.

Over the next few days, they baked sugar cookies, went to Serendipity for frozen hot chocolates, window-shopped along Fifth Avenue, grandmother, mother, daughter; they went to *The Nutcracker* and paid too much to have Eliza's picture taken with one of the ballerinas during intermission; they tried most of all to be gentle with each other. On Christmas morning, they both watched Eliza tear open her gifts, a child happily lost in the moment, and it brought joy, albeit one with serrated edges that tore at the flesh on its way in.

That night, Sarah climbed into bed with Eliza. "Did you find the holiday hard without Daddy?" she asked.

"It was okay," Eliza replied. "I get busy with everything and then I don't miss him so much." She thought for a minute. "I think holidays are easier."

Sarah leaned over and kissed her, reminded once more how differently children and adults experience grief.

Sarah's mother returned to Santa Fe two days later and they settled into that lull between Christmas and New Year's, the office closed, the city wet, gray, lethargic, caught between recuperation and anticipation of New Year's Eve. Sarah waited for the holidays to end, looking forward to the earliest acceptable morning that she could pay someone to take the tree away. Most of all, she waited for Tim to call. They had not spoken since he left a week ago. But he did not call.

One afternoon, when snow was falling in amorphous, sloppy drops, as if it could not make up its mind about its identity—rain, sleet, hail—Paige came over to visit. That in itself should have been a tip-off to Sarah. Women in New York without children did not visit each other's apartments when they could be out getting manicures, at the movies, shopping the sales. It was a social tic that had long ago been written off as a suburban aberration.

They kissed hello and Sarah hung up Paige's shearling coat speckled with whatever it was that was falling from the sky while Eliza, who regarded Paige as a goddess, with her white-blond hair and her girly clothes and her numerous gifts of glittery nail polishes and gooey fruit-flavored lip glosses, ran to greet her.

"You can be her Auntie Mame," Sarah remarked. "When she is no longer speaking to me, you can take her out for fancy lunches and get the dirt on her boyfriends, which you will, of course, immediately report back to me."

"Does that mean you think I'll never have children of my own?"

Sarah looked at Paige carefully. "No, don't be ridiculous. Tea or wine?"

"Wine. Definitely."

"All right then," Sarah said, getting with the program. "Eliza, why don't you go make a picture for Paige?"

Eliza looked at her mother as if she were crazy. She had no intention of being banished.

"Eliza, please," Sarah said sternly.

Eliza trotted off reluctantly and Sarah brought the wine into the living room. "What's up?"

Paige drank half a glass in one sip before speaking. "Ethan and I broke up."

"Oh, Paige, I'm so sorry."

"Don't say I told you so."

"Of course not. I was rooting for you."

Paige began to cry and Sarah reached over and rested her hand on her knee. "What did he say?" she asked gently.

"Well, nothing. Or not enough. Actually, I was the one who broke up with him."

Sarah made no effort to hide her surprise.

"Shocking, I know," Paige said.

"What happened?"

"The last few weeks have just been so awful. There's been this wall between us whenever we see each other. It's all very polite, but I could feel him pulling away. I don't know what changed, I don't know why. And he seemed incapable of explaining it to me. But it just became unbearable. We'd go out to dinner and barely talk to each other."

"It's him, his problem."

"That's what women always say when a man dumps them."

"I thought you said you dumped him?"

"Have you ever heard that country music line, 'The taxi took her to the airport, but I'm the one who drove her there'?"

Sarah smiled. "Go on."

"We went out last night and I guess I drank too much. Okay, I definitely drank too much. We were struggling to make conversation and after all we've been through it just seemed insane. He doesn't seem to want to be with me and he doesn't not want to be with me. With my great sense of timing I waited till we were outside and he was in the street, dodging moving traffic trying to get a cab. I don't know what happened, I reached a breaking point." She stopped, shook her head. "I just yelled at him, 'What the hell do you want?' "

"And his reply was?"

"He didn't have one. The poor guy looked like a deer in the headlights, which he basically was with all the cars coming at him. He turned around and asked, 'Do I have to answer that right here?' "

"Maybe that wasn't the best way to approach this," Sarah observed gingerly.

"I know," Paige said, pouring herself more wine, "but I couldn't help it. I was just so frustrated. I asked him if he could say one thing that would make me stay. And he actually began stuttering."

"Paige, it was one night. And not, from what you're telling me, a situation exactly conducive to communication."

"It was one night and a year of my life. He couldn't do it. He couldn't say one thing. Look, I know Ethan cares for me. He may even love me. But not enough. Sometimes I think he's just humored by me, but I don't want to exist for someone's amusement."

"I'm sure it was more than that," Sarah reassured her.

"Yes, but that's what makes it so hard. I don't think he's a bad person, he's just hobbled."

Paige stopped talking and gave way to real tears. "Some fucking holiday." She wiped her eyes, steeled herself. "So. Have you heard from Tim?"

"No," Sarah admitted reluctantly.

Paige's eyebrows raised and Sarah grew defensive, mildly annoyed. "He's with his son. He's not coming back till after New Year's. We agreed on that."

"But not a single phone call?"

"He's with his family. Look, Paige, this week has been hard enough. I don't need any help from you to feel depressed and insecure. I'm quite capable of managing that all on my own."

"Sorry. What does Lucy say?"

Lucy, who had the most successful relationship history of the three of them, was often the court of last appeal. Then again, both Paige and Sarah suspected that because her marriage was so storm-free she did not truly understand the vagaries of romantic confusion. There was, of course, the chance that she had such a storm-free marriage because she had made it quite clear from the beginning that she would have none of that vagary business.

"Well, she's not as pessimistic as you," Sarah said. "But she doesn't think it's a fabulous sign. Look, do you want to come over here New Year's Eve?" she asked, anxious to change the subject.

"No, thanks. I plan on binge-eating to the point of sickness in the privacy of my own bedroom."

"Sounds like a plan."

"What are you doing?"

Sarah shrugged. "I just want the holidays to end. I've always hated New Year's anyway. I'm going to take an Ambien as soon as Eliza goes to bed and pretend the whole thing isn't happening."

"Good to see we have both developed such healthy coping mechanisms," Paige remarked. "At least yours has fewer calories."

"I really am sorry," Sarah said.

"I know."

"You did the right thing. You were spending too much energy trying not to scare him or disturb him in any way. You're worth more than that."

"I know," Paige said. "So why don't I feel better?"

On the afternoon of New Year's Eve, Sarah and Eliza went out to rent a stack of DVDs and get ice cream for hot fudge sundaes. Sarah had, much to her chagrin, promised Eliza that she could stay up till midnight after being informed repeatedly that all of her friends had been granted that privilege. Her real objection had little to do with Eliza. It was merely that it would postpone her own preplanned sedation.

By 10:00 p.m., though, Eliza had fallen into a sugar- and video-induced stupor. Sarah had just carried her to bed, her body warm, heavy, draped like a rag doll, and had gotten out a sleeping pill when the phone rang.

She picked it up quickly, desperate not to wake Eliza. "Yes?"

"It's Tim."

She took a deep breath, the first one she had taken in over a week. "Hey there. How are you?" Her attempt at sounding casual rang false, unconvincing to her own ears and certainly to his.

"I'm fine. Actually, I'm outside your window," he said.

"What?"

"Look out."

Sarah went to the window and saw him standing seven stories below, his cell phone pressed to his ear, waving up at her.

"What on earth are you doing here?" There was spontaneous pleasure in her voice and relief, too; he hadn't lost interest, hadn't disappeared, he wasn't gone.

"I came back a day early. Chris decided to spend the night with his mom and some cousins."

There was a pause as a truck rattled noisily by the near empty street, groaning as it hit a pothole.

"Can I come up?" he asked.

"Oh God, I'm sorry. Of course."

Sarah raced to fix her hair, but the doorbell rang before she had time to change out of her stretched-out "Beauty Rules" T-shirt with its single comet of hot fudge splattered down the front.

A broad smile creased Tim's face as he took her in his arms to kiss her hello, the cold clinging to his jacket, his hair as he hugged her. He stepped back and ran his hand down her cheek relearning her as a blind man might. "I missed you."

"I missed you, too," she replied, happiness flooding her.

They were still in the doorway.

"Come in."

She closed the door behind him. How good that felt.

"I didn't know if you had, you know, plans," Tim said.

Sarah smiled, looking down at herself. "Yes, and as you can see I dressed for the occasion."

"You look adorable."

"Just what every woman is going for on New Year's Eve."

"You look gorgeous," he amended.

"Okay, now you're pushing it, buddy."

There was no champagne in the house, but Sarah got out a bottle of vodka from the freezer where it was buried behind bags of organic vegetables that Eliza refused to eat. Tim made them martinis in an etched glass shaker from the thirties that Sarah had gotten for a wedding present.

They took them to the living room and sat on the couch talking in soft voices, their knees touching, as they related their holidays to each other, both aware of the child sleeping in the next room. Tim told Sarah of his parents' ill-concealed anger and disappointment over his divorce, of Chris's alternate sulking and sweetness as he tried to hide his sense of dislocation in his newly fractured family. Sarah offered up an edited version of her week, leaving out the Christmas tree man, leaving out the pain.

"I have something for you," Tim told her when she was done. He pulled a heavy cream envelope from his pocket.

"I thought we said no presents," she protested, delighted nonetheless.

"This isn't a present."

"What is it?"

He smiled. "Something for both of us."

She opened it up. It was gift certificate for a night at the St. Regis.

She laughed, kissed him.

"I figured that at some point we are going to have to see if we can actually spend an entire night together," Tim said. "We might as well do it with room service."

"I love it," she exclaimed. She snuggled up against him, her head on his shoulder, fitting perfectly.

"I thought of you a lot while I was gone," he said quietly, kissing her. "I liked thinking of you when I was alone, the little sounds you make like a satisfied cat," he laughed affectionately, "the way you rip up napkins."

"How would I know?" she asked, gently but still.

"Know what?"

"That you were thinking of me. How would I know that it wasn't out of sight, out of mind?"

"Why would you think that?" he replied, genuinely surprised.

"Because I didn't hear from you."

"Okay," he said, smiling. "Point taken. It was hard, okay? My parents, Chris, I never had a minute of privacy."

She nodded, making a conscious decision to accept his explanation, though it remained a piece of information.

"Come here," he said, turning her face to his, kissing her. They fell back on the couch and his hand slid inside her shirt. She shivered as it moved across her bare skin, up the curve of her waist to her breasts, he was what she wanted most. "Forgive me?" he whispered.

"Come," she said. Their clothes were already half off, leaving behind a trail of impatience, as she led him down the hallway past Eliza's room, closing her bedroom door as they pulled off what was left, a bra, a sock, and fell onto the bed, fell onto and into each other.

Afterward, as they lay haphazardly touching in a milky postcoital haze, they heard the eruption of gongs and hoots and car horns announcing the New Year. Sarah remembered the German tradition Todd had told her about; at midnight everyone would throw pots and pans out of the window, making a terrible cacophonous din—out with the old, in with the new. She looked over at the man beside her. They both had so much history but not together. They were starting in the middle of the story.

"What are you thinking?" he asked.

"I didn't think I'd find someone so quickly," she said. The speed, the apparent ease with which she had found him made her doubt that it was real.

"We don't have to rush anything," he said. "It's not like when you're younger and want children." He looked at her questioningly and she smiled, shook her head; that was settled, then, out of the way.

"I know," she agreed.

They lay for a long while without talking.

"I'm happy you're here," she said quietly, though the words scared her. Hope—for herself, for him, for them—seemed the most hazardous emotion of all.

"Me too."

Tim fell asleep, snoring lightly and she lay listening to him, watching the clock, dozing sometimes but never deeply.

She nudged him awake at 5:00 a.m.—she did not want Eliza to find him there. He turned to her and they made love wordlessly in that slow syrupy morning way she loved so much, different than the night, gentler, more intimate somehow.

Afterward, Tim sat on the edge of the bed, pulling his clothes on as she watched, perched cross-legged behind him. When he was dressed, she walked him to the door and leaned up on bare tiptoes to kiss him good-bye.

Then she climbed back into bed and lay still, watching the New Year's silvery dawn light spread slowly across the sleeping city.

Twenty-seven

A dank slate pall settled over Manhattan and refused to dissipate. There were a few brief hours when the sun made a half-hearted attempt to break through the sludge of clouds before skulking away, defeated. Women went for spray tans to try to cheer themselves up, stocked up on cashmere sweaters at the January sales, dabbed on their summer perfumes, but nothing helped. Lethargy abounded: Even the sky could not summon up the energy for a good snowfall, which would at least have offered the temporary relief of whiteness before it, too, faded to gray.

It appeared, in those uncertain first few weeks of the new regime, that Pat had no intention of letting Sarah go. At least not immediately. For all of Caitlin's savvy, she had little patience for digging into the nuts and bolts of a story, moving paragraphs around, cutting rambling quotes from self-important experts. Pat needed Sarah to be the bulwark—at least until her replacement could be found. Either that or she simply wanted to torture her. Sarah now reported to Caitlin—a situation that at least one of them found untenable.

One afternoon Caitlin had her assistant call Sarah into her office.

Sarah settled uneasily onto one of the new quilted chairs that had appeared, wondering if Chanel had starting making furniture.

"I have the ideas memo you sent to Pat," Caitlin began. "You have a few that we liked," she said, smiling, the word *we* intentional, lethal. "I'd like you to get proposals on the ones we've starred. Of course, we need to move quickly. Pat would like to reintroduce the new *Flair* as soon as possible. Can you have them by the end of the week?"

Sarah stared at her and took a deep breath. "I'm glad you liked them," she said. "But it's Wednesday. I'm not sure I can get any writers, or at least not the writers we want," she, too, used the *we* word, though admittedly to less effect, "within that time frame."

Caitlin's smile never left her face. She had placed a perfumed candle on her desk and the thick overpowering scent of gardenia was making Sarah nauseous. "I understand," she said, leaning forward. She tried to raise her eyebrows in sympathy, but due to a fresh bout of Botox last week (she prided herself as being the youngest person on staff to get it) nothing actually moved. "Nevertheless, this is what we need."

The meeting was clearly over.

Sarah went back to her office, closed the door, and called Paige. "She's setting me up to fail," she vented.

"At least she's setting you up. I'm getting the total freeze-out. Not one of my manuscripts has come back. My lineup for the next issue seems to have fallen into a black hole. Even my request for a merch meeting has gone unanswered."

Sarah had to admit that the only thing worse than bad contact was no contact.

"I don't care if they fire me," Paige continued. "At least I'd get the severance. But this is persecution. If I quit, I walk away with nothing and they know that. I'm stuck."

"We both are."

Sarah spent the next thirty-six hours calling every freelance journalist she knew and begging them to do proposals. A few initially agreed though when they heard that the deadline was Friday they backed off. "Doesn't anyone need work anymore?" Sarah, exasperated, asked one writer famous for taking the assignments everyone else had turned down.

"Why don't you write it yourself?" he replied.

Sarah hung up without answering.

On Friday afternoon she turned in her memo with only one proposal attached—which she had in fact written herself.

An hour later, when her phone rang, she assumed it was going to be Caitlin voicing her disapproval.

"William Rowling wants to see you and Paige in his office," Maude told her.

Sarah swallowed hard. "When?"

"Now. I'll call Paige and tell her to meet you by the elevator."

Three minutes later, after they had both hastily applied a fresh coat of lip gloss—you needed to look your best to go to the ninth floor, even if it was only to go get fired—Paige and Sarah stood waiting for the elevator, both too nervous to look at each other.

"William doesn't usually fire people himself, does he?" Sarah asked. "Isn't that HR's job?"

"I'm not sure there is a 'usually' in this building. Despite everything, he liked Rena. Maybe he's doing it himself out of some weird loyalty or guilt."

"Do you really think he feels guilt over what happened with Rena?"

"Actually, no," Paige admitted. "I sincerely doubt that it's in his emotional makeup. That's assuming, of course, that he has emotions, which anecdotally, at least, remains up for serious debate."

They rode up the five floors in silence and got off on the ninth floor, passing by the conference room that had been the scene of Pat's victory. It was a different, quieter world here, removed from the pace of monthly magazines, shipping schedules, deadlines, removed, to a depressingly large degree, from women's voices altogether, for despite the fact that the vast majority of CMH's titles were aimed at women, there were only a few token females present in upper management. When they reached the elegant reception area outside of William's office, his assistant had them wait ten painful minutes before leading them inside to the large corner office.

The floor-to-ceiling glass windows were spotless, the couch, the rug, the chairs were all covered in subtle gradations of white. It was like stepping inside a Robert Ryman painting. Sarah had never been in an office with so few papers visible, so few personal effects at all.

William rose to greet them.

Sarah and Paige walked over to his desk, about to sit down, when Sarah's heart stopped.

There, hung just behind William, was a piece of Todd's. It literally took her breath away, this fragment of her past life, her other life, unearthed and so publicly displayed. It was like hearing a snippet of your native tongue in a foreign land—deeply familiar yet disconcertingly out of place. The three-foot sculpture was titled *Phaeton*—the god who flew his chariot too close to the sun and crashed; its patinated copper rose in a gorgeous arc and then dropped off dramatically into spindly fragments. She remembered when she had first seen it in Todd's studio, a few months after Eliza was born. Every swerve in the copper brought him back to her.

William regarded Sarah. "I liked your husband's work," he said simply.

Sarah nodded. She had known that Leon Compton had bought Todd's sculpture but had no idea that William even collected art.

"Thank you." She had always been clueless about what to reply when people said that; it wasn't her work after all. "I did, too."

"Sit down," William said.

Sarah and Paige perched carefully on the colorless chairs. All that white made them nervous, there was so much risk of leaving a visible mark, a mistake behind.

"I understand that you both worked on *Splash,*" William began. His tone was flat, affectless; they could not tell if they would be punished or rewarded, or if this was simply an opening gambit before he executed them.

"Yes." So Rena had given them credit after all. Or was it blame?

"There were some interesting elements," he said. "I liked the layering, the voice. The graphics need some toning down, but Wakefield always goes too far in his first round."

Again, Sarah's personal life came crashing into the room. Manhattan, despite its millions of inhabitants, was a mine field of overlapping entanglements. Sometimes they helped you advance, sometimes they choked you.

"The project was necessarily stalled," William continued, "but I would like you to finish a prototype. If I like it, we will focus-group it and do a test subscription mailing. We'll make a decision based on that."

"I thought it was off the table because of the men's launch," Paige blurted out.

William looked at her curiously, the briefest evidence of confusion playing across his placid face. "Where did you hear that?"

Paige, flummoxed, did not reply. Rena had obviously lied to save face. The building was made of mirrors. "I must have been mistaken," she said finally.

William nodded. "Time is of the essence. There are a few similar launches coming down the pike from our competitors. I will tell Pat you are working on this." He paused, taking his time. "But you are in no way to let this interfere with your work on *Flair*. We can reassess that situation depending on the success of the prototype."

"Pat is going to be furious," Sarah said as she and Paige rode back down in the elevator.

"Yes, but she can't do anything about it," Paige observed with a certain degree of satisfaction. "You realize he's setting us up against her on purpose?"

"Not very Zen-like."

They were so lost in the politics of it all that it was only when they got off on the fourth floor that they looked at each other with anything approaching excitement—they hadn't been fired. Better yet, *Splash* was back on the table.

Within minutes, panic replaced relief. William had given them precious little editorial direction and no specific time frame. They were operating in a cloud, victims of one of his more Machiavellian management techniques.

Sarah went into her office and shut the door.

The first person she called was Tim.

Twenty-eight

All the next month, Paige, Sarah, Noah, and Tim worked in stolen hours in the large white conference room at Wakefield, before work, during lunch when they should have been with clients or courting new writers, in quick snatches at the end of the day. The four shared a bunker mentality—exhausted, excited, essentially cut off from anyone outside their project. Tim and Noah stroked clients they feared might suspect anything was superseding their own needs, Paige and Sarah made sure everything Pat and Caitlin asked of them was done on time, spell-checked, complete. But the only place any of them truly wanted to be was here, cutting up layouts, reconstructing them in new ways, scribbling revised titles, trying humor, trying too hard, toning it down, layering on images until the pages were too crowded, taking them off until they were elegant but dull, using scissors, tape, index cards, and the most advanced computer programs available. Some days it felt as if they could only get scraps right, a page here, a sidebar there, fragments that had little to do with each other. Other times, they soared on a communal high, convinced that they were creating something truly unique.

Paige and Sarah called a couple of writers they knew and assigned them stories to flow into the images. Immediately rumors swirled around town culminating in a reference to "CMH's high hopes for its *Splash* project" in Keith Kelly's media column in the

New York Post that pissed Pat off so much—though of course she could not admit it—that she gave Paige and Sarah four extra stories to work on, including one that involved interviewing a former cover model in Tennessee who had been in a disfiguring car accident a day after leaving rehab. Pat halfheartedly suggested that Sarah fly down to do the interview in person.

Tim and Sarah made no public show of their relationship other than brushing against each other like teenagers as they moved about the studio, but it was impossible to hide the charged air between them. In Wakefield's spacious main room with the twenty talented people at their twenty mega-computers, women glanced up and smiled—or not. More than a few were disappointed even if they knew they had never really stood a chance with Tim.

Only their children remained isolated from their burgeoning relationship. One night, Tim and Sarah sat in a near-empty Italian restaurant on the edges of SoHo that had been popular two summers ago and that Tim remained loyal to, discussing how to introduce Chris and Eliza to each other. They went through every permutation of possible reaction, but the truth was that neither of them had done this before and children, even your own, could be deeply unpredictable.

"Chris might be harder," Sarah said carefully. Commenting in any way on a lover's offspring is extremely dangerous territory.

"Why do you think that?"

"He's older and more aware of things. Plus he's still hoping you'll get back together with his mom. Eliza has no one to hope I reunite with."

"What do you think Eliza's reaction will be?"

"I honestly have no idea," Sarah admitted. "Did you ever introduce Chris to any of the women you dated before?"

"No. I didn't want him to think my bedroom had a revolving door."

Sarah frowned at him.

"Well, you asked." He took her hand. "There was no point before," he said gently. "But they're going to have to know about us eventually. Besides, it just doesn't make sense that we continue to spend our weekends separately. It would be much more fun to do things together."

Sarah nodded. It was a step, another step, and she was equally drawn to it, this integration, this slide toward solidity, and anxious about of it.

"What if Chris hates me?" she asked.

"No one could hate you," Tim said.

She looked at him wryly.

"Okay," he admitted. "There's a slight chance he might not greet you with open arms. At first. But Sarah, I am not getting back together with his mother. And Todd isn't coming back. They are both going to have to accept that at some point."

By the end of the meal they had set up a carefully orchestrated battle plan: They would meet at the Museum of Natural History on the following Sunday at eleven-thirty. They would look at the dinosaurs, have lunch in the restaurant, and call it day. The whole thing would take two hours, tops. They would not kiss hello or touch in any way in front of their children.

"You realize they are never going to believe we're just friends," Tim said. "Kids are smarter than that."

"Just stick to the plan," Sarah warned him. "No hoochie coo."

On Sunday morning, Sarah said nothing as she watched Eliza choose her tackiest green sweater and a clashing pair of pants. Despite her strong desire to fix her, polish her, she did not want to start the morning with a spat. Sarah could not risk throwing off her performance.

She went into her own room and put on her favorite pair of James jeans and flats, changed to high-heeled suede boots, worried that it would look like she was trying too hard, but decided to leave them on anyway because they made her legs look longer and thinner, which trumped any other consideration. Finally, they headed uptown.

Tim and Chris were already waiting on the museum's steps when the cab pulled up. The adults greeted each other self-consciously and then turned to the children, smiling just a little too hard. Chris, two years older and far more solid than Eliza, towered over her.

Sarah saw elements of Tim in Chris's tousled chestnut hair, his deep brown eyes, but she was searching for something else, too—clues about his mother, what she might look like, be like. Chris looked down at the ground and shuffled his feet while Eliza stood by Sarah's side and barely said hello. She was at heart an observer; like Sarah, she tended to weigh a situation carefully before entering it, and even then, part of her remained removed, watchful. Sarah saw herself in Eliza and her heart went out to her. She had wished something different for her daughter, the ability to jump in, to participate without a constant running commentary in her head. It seemed somehow an easier approach to life.

"Shall we go in?" Tim asked.

"Yes," Sarah replied too brightly, her voice annoying even to herself.

Tim paid the admission for all four of them and they checked their coats before walking through the marble halls with their dusty timeless scent and their panoramas of predators that had lodged in the imaginations of generations of New York City children.

Sarah watched Tim and Chris jostling each other affectionately as they went ahead, their stride similar in its firm-footed pace, their jocularity straight from the playing fields. They seemed so essentially masculine to her, attractive but almost alien, overpowering. Eliza hung back, her eyes drawn to the vividly painted scenarios behind walls of glass, purposefully not looking ahead at them. They progressed through the galleries as if they had chosen teams, boys versus girls. Every now and then Tim and Sarah met each other's eyes through the physical and psychological distance, but their allegiances were crisscrossed and fluid—to each other, to their own children, back to each other.

Eliza and Chris did not say one word to each other until they were seated at a table downstairs for lunch. There were a few tense moments on line at the cafeteria-style restaurant when, faced with row upon row of fries, chicken fingers, gelatinous puddings, and icing-drenched three-layer cakes, both children chose the absolute worst assortment of starches and sugars. Tim and Sarah said nothing, concerned that the other would think they allowed such horrid nutrition on a regular basis but terrified of lodging a protest that might set off unattractive whining or tears.

Only when they began to eat—boys on one side of the booth, girls on the other—did they both look down at their children's plates and roll their eyes helplessly.

"Did you watch the ice show on television last night?" Sarah asked Chris. Someone had to say something, start something.

He looked at her skeptically. "The Rangers didn't play last night."

She realized her misstep but wasn't about to give up. "There was a special on ABC. The funniest thing happened. One of the skaters was dressed up as Tarzan. Eliza, tell Chris and Tim what happened."

"He crashed over the gate into the judges' laps," Eliza volunteered dutifully, her tone meant to signal to Chris that she was being coerced and didn't think the whole thing was actually all that cool.

"On purpose?" Chris asked, curious despite himself.

"I don't think so," Eliza answered.

There were a few more questions about the event before the parents started in on the pro-forma round of inquiries about favorite teachers and preferred desserts. There were no incidents, no histrionics, and no sense of ease. All four were glad when lunch was over, the half-eaten food smeared across the pebbled brown plastic trays.

"Can we go to the park?" Chris asked as they headed out of the museum, the adults depleted from the effort of it all, thankful for even the chilled damp air.

Tim glanced over his head to Sarah.

"Fine with me," she agreed, sorry now for her high heels with their wafer-thin soles.

"Boys are like dogs, you have to take them out and run them," Tim remarked as the children raced ahead, Eliza struggling to keep up with Chris as he darted into the little pocket playground just inside Central Park's gray stone walls.

Tim and Sarah settled on the furthest wooden bench and watched their children climb about the tire swings and begin to talk to each other tentatively, shyly.

"Well, it's not an unmitigated disaster, anyway," Tim observed.

"Not bad for a first outing," Sarah agreed.

They sat in silence for a little while, their fingertips grazing, exploring each other's palms. Sarah had never been so aware of that single inch of flesh before, of how erotic it could be, their touches secret, stealthy, prohibited. She felt a charge of desire shoot through her stomach, down her legs.

"Eliza is wonderful," Tim said.

"So is Chris."

Their legs were pressed against each other now, hidden by their coats from their children's suspicious glances.

"I want so much to kiss you," Tim said, soft, guttural. "This is torture."

Sarah didn't answer. She looked out at their children scampering on top of a low stone pyramid, Chris clearly the leader, more confident, more assertive, but Eliza gamely following. Seeing them together changed everything, made it all somehow more real, and she had a sudden urge to pull away—from Tim, from this knitting together, this desire, from anything coming too close ever again.

"What is it?" he asked.

Her legs twitched unconsciously.

"Aren't you scared?" she asked at last.

"Of what?"

"All of this. Us."

Tim looked at her intently, waiting.

"Of caring again."

"Sometimes," he admitted. "It's always going to be a risk, Sarah. But I'm not Todd," he said quietly. "I'm not going to disappear."

She nodded slightly, thinking that there were no guarantees, that everything was transient, despite intent, and it was so hard to gamble with your heart knowing that.

"I'm not going anyplace," Tim reiterated. "When you said you never thought you'd find anyone again so quickly, well, neither did I. I don't think you find that many people in a lifetime that you feel a real connection to, friends or lovers. I don't know what this is.

And I can't give you any guarantees about where it's going to end up. But I do know we have something. Maybe it would have been better if we met a year later, but we didn't." He paused. "Look, I'm not pretending it's going to be easy. It's complicated, I get that."

"I know." It was so much easier the first time, before she understood how much she could lose. "I'm sorry." She looked at him. "I do want this."

Tim kissed the top of her head just as both children turned to look at them. "Damn. Caught in the act," he said.

Sarah smiled as Eliza came up to her and complained, "I'm freezing."

"I know, sweetie." Sarah pulled her onto her lap and wrapped her in her arms, thankful for the warmth, for the familiarity, for the anchor of this child she loved more than anything.

Tim rose to collect Chris, who offered a mild protest but finally relented, and they headed out of the park.

"You okay?" Tim asked Sarah as they stood on Central Park West, waiting for separate taxis.

"Yes." She touched his arm gently as he held open the door of a cab. Sarah and Eliza climbed in and he shut it firmly behind them.

That night, when Sarah lay down beside Eliza in bed, Eliza turned to her. "How do you know him?" she asked.

"Tim?"

"Yes. You didn't tell me how you know him."

"He's helping me with *Splash.*"

Eliza considered this. "So you work together?"

"Sort of. He has his own company."

"Did he know Daddy?"

"No. But I've told him all about Daddy."

"Does he know Paige?"

"Yes," Sarah replied, unsure where this was headed.

"Maybe he could date her," Eliza suggested.

This was going to be a little tougher than Sarah thought. "What did you think of Chris?" she asked.

"He's all right."

"For a boy," Sarah teased.

"Whatever."

"Eliza, I loved Daddy."

Eliza curled up tighter beneath the sheets.

"Nothing will ever change that."

"Sometimes you slammed doors," Eliza reminded her, a scolding tone in her voice.

"Yes, sometimes we both slammed doors. But Eliza, I still loved your father. I always will. That won't change if I have other friends."

"Boyfriends," Eliza corrected her.

It was hard to know what Eliza did or did not understand. Sarah guessed wrong so many times, finding pockets of sophistication when she expected ignorance, hollows of unawareness when she presumed insight. "Would that bother you?" she asked carefully.

Eliza pulled Snowball tighter into her grasp. "Can we just read?" she asked, closing the subject, closing the door.

"Okay," Sarah agreed. "But one last thing. I want you to know that no one will ever take the place of your father." She was flying blind, with no instructions, no idea if she was helping or hurting. She made a mental note to call Deirdre Gerard the following day.

Eliza handed her the book. "Read," she said.

"How'd it go?" Sarah asked Tim on the phone after both children had fallen asleep.

"Fine," he replied unenthusiastically.

"That bad, huh?"

He laughed. "He said you were very nice. That was right before he developed a suspiciously violent stomachache and insisted I call his mother immediately."

"All right then. So much for Plan A."

"We'll keep chipping away at it," Tim said. There was a long pause. "Are we okay?" he asked.

Sarah shut her eyes, ran her fingers through her knotted hair. "Yes. We'll be okay."

Twenty-nine

At *Flair,* Pat worked at warp speed to put her own stamp on the magazine. If Rena allowed in any picture, story, or idea that caught her fancy, Pat had an extremely disciplined view of what did and did not belong in *Flair.* A magazine dedicated to helping women realize their fullest potential in health, style, fitness, and beauty should not be running stories on death, she reminded the staff repeatedly—citing Rena's most egregious error as often as possible, savoring it.

"This is editing by default," Paige muttered. "There's not a creative bone in that woman's very bony body."

Sarah's agreement was halfhearted. As she watched the redesign of *Flair* begin to take shape, she recognized that it was a more cohesive magazine than it had been before. Somewhere between Rena's lack of discipline and Pat's lack of imagination lay the middle ground she hoped they could achieve with *Splash.*

William Rowling left Sarah and Paige largely to their own devices, though whether he was giving them enough rope to hang themselves or the freedom to be creative was questionable. He requested that they update their budget every two weeks, but he did not ask to see layouts or story ideas. Sarah actually wished he were more hands-on. She wanted reassurance that they were headed in the right direction before they put everything into it. "You have to trust your instincts," Tim told her. "That's a large part of what he's going to judge you on."

She frowned.

"Trust my instincts, then," he said.

"Your instincts are about the only thing I do trust," she admitted. But in the end, it was not his job at stake. Tim could afford to take more risks, and if Sarah thought the way he continually pushed the design was valid and intriguing, she remained more circumspect. *Splash* would be a balance of her desire for relative safety and Tim's conviction that only magazines that broke the mold were worth launching.

In mid-February, Barnett Thompson called Sarah to update her on the progress of her divorce. "We have passed the initial stages," he told her. "The court has ruled that you have to post banns."

"Post banns? Isn't that something out of the Middle Ages?" Sarah had no idea what the term meant, though images of Martin Luther came to mind for some reason.

"In cases of abandonment, the court needs to give the missing person every opportunity to respond," Thompson explained. "They have ruled that we must post a notice in the *New York Law Journal,* the *Columbia Journalism Review,* and a newspaper in southern Florida."

"Are you kidding?"

"Far from it," Thompson replied.

"What happens after that?"

"Assuming your husband doesn't reply, we will get a court date for the divorce proceedings."

"This is absurd." There were instances when the circumstances of Sarah's life still felt totally unreal to her—but never more so than sitting in her office at that moment. She had disciplined herself to talk of Todd solely in the past tense; being told now that she must act, sign documents, speak as if he were alive sent her spinning.

"Yes," Thompson agreed. "Yes, it is crazy. But legally your husband is still alive and unless the police in Florida change their minds, which it doesn't appear that they will do, he will remain so for the foreseeable future. Despite what you and I believe to be true."

Sarah started at the word *believe,* it was a universe away from *know,* and yet it was the only word, the only description, she had a right to. "Go ahead," she replied finally. "Post the banns."

That night, she wept as she hadn't since she told Eliza her father was dead. She wept for the mess she and Todd had made of their lives and for how far they had come from the day they married, promising to protect each other for life, she wept for that time near the end when he had said to her, "I thought we would dance together at Eliza's wedding." She wept for their inability to stop what neither of them wanted from happening, and she wept because she was losing another piece of him now.

"You look like hell," Paige remarked the next morning as she barged into Sarah's office and sat down.

"Thanks."

"I'll send over some of that new Shiseido cover-up that got me through the first post-Ethan weeks."

"Does that mean you are post-post-Ethan?"

Since Christmas, Paige had alternated between regret-filled tears, a fierce determination to date every man in New York, and a stubborn insistence that she would find a way to get Ethan back.

"Actually I do have a date tonight."

"With?"

"His name is Jason. His profile on Nerve said he works for one of the cable networks in promotion."

Sarah raised an eyebrow. Promotion was the least interesting part of most media ventures, without the remuneration of sales or the creativity of content.

"He writes screenplays, too," Paige said defensively. "We're just meeting for a drink, but I liked his voice on the phone and he chose this great little place in NoLita, so that's a good sign. What do you think?" She held up a kelly green deep V-necked chiffon blouse and a more sedate pastel pink sweater. "Too mumsy?" she asked.

"Depends what you're going for."

"You know, I've been thinking, all these years I've opted for cleavage, but what if Donna Reed is the way to go? Maybe men date cleavage but marry Donna."

"I'd like to think there's a middle ground."

Sarah's e-mail pinged and she glanced over at it. "It's from William."

"Open it."

She clicked on it and read silently. "Jesus Christ."

"What?" Paige asked impatiently.

"He wants to see a full presentation of everything we've done on *Splash.*"

"All right," Paige said calmly. "When?"

"At five p.m. today."

"Are you fucking kidding me? That's insane. We're nowhere near done."

The two of them sat stunned, immobilized.

"Call Tim," Paige finally suggested.

Sarah nodded and dialed the Wakefield studio.

"We have to get down there now," she said hanging up. "We've got four, maybe five hours if we hustle. Meet me by the elevator."

Twenty minutes later, they raced into the studio where Tim and Noah were pinning the entire magazine to the wall.

"Welcome to the war room," Noah said.

"I still can't believe William is doing this," Sarah remarked.

"I can," Tim said. "He gets off on this. Plus, he likes to see how people operate under pressure. He probably planned this a month ago."

Sarah and Paige threw their coats on a chair and began to update Noah on which stories were done, which were almost done, and which were beyond hope. They agreed to concentrate on the first two groups—the prototype would be smaller than they had planned, but they had no choice. The cover remained one of the thorniest problems; they had not yet decided whether the image should be a close-up of a model's face, a celebrity, or a fashion shot. Eight variations were displayed, but nothing seemed quite right.

"The cover lines you gave us will never fit," Tim said. He had left half of them off and shortened the ones that remained until none was over six words. "We need phrases, not novels."

"And we need to prove we can sell magazines," Sarah replied. "People buy them because of the promise on the cover."

The argument was one that took place every month across the city between designers who wanted covers to be stylish showcases of their talent and editors who were judged on how many copies were sold at newsstands.

"We'll work up some new lines," Paige said, shooting Sarah a "behave yourself" look.

"Good," Noah interceded. "Let's go over the layouts first."

They fell into a rhythm dictated by the detailed checklist he had printed out and would continue to update every half-hour, crossing things off, circling others in red. Sarah began rewriting the line for the "27 Bad Girl Beauty Fixes" story, trying to decide whether 23, 25, or 27 sounded best—there was a theory that odd numbers were somehow more believable and thus sold better than even ones. She wrote until words made no sense, certain with each new version that *Splash* was doomed, while Tim threw whatever she gave him into layouts and printed them out.

Noah ordered in poached wild Alaskan salmon from the local pseudo-French bistro where Wakefield kept a running tab, but they barely picked at it as they continued to work, checking the clock overhead every fifteen minutes. By three-thirty, they were beginning to put pages into a presentation book that Noah had an assistant race out to buy.

"What if he's expecting PowerPoint?" Sarah worried.

"Magazines should be touched, felt," Tim replied. "PowerPoint is for salespeople. You need to go in with the attitude that you're not trying to sell him on this, you're giving him a gift. He's the lucky one." Tim and Noah had built their business on their presentation savvy—all the brilliant design ideas in the world were worth nothing if you couldn't sell a client on them—and had been giving Sarah and Paige tips throughout the afternoon: Speak slowly, don't be afraid to stand up for yourself but show your willingness to listen to his opinion, always agree to change one thing so the client feels smarter than you. It was annoyingly clear that they would have preferred to handle the meeting themselves.

At four o'clock they put the last of the layouts into the portfolio and flipped through the pages one last time. Energetic, multilayered, graphic, and aggressively Internet-friendly, it did not look like any magazine they had seen before.

Exactly one hour later, Paige and Sarah sat in the reception area outside of William Rowling's office, their skin tingling, their mood alternating between overriding confidence and abject dejection. The pages, printed on paper that no publishing company would ever be able to afford, sat neatly on Sarah's lap. Paige looked over at Sarah and smiled wanly. William was fifteen minutes late and they could not help but wonder if it was accidental or strategic. At this point, their biggest desire was to get the whole thing over with.

Finally, the receptionist rose and ushered them into his office. William stood to greet them with a courteous smile and led them to the spotless glass table by the far window.

"So," he said, folding his body gracefully into an oak chair, a gift from a designer recently featured in one of CMH's shelter magazines. "What do you have for me?"

There was no small talk designed to put them at ease, no false bonhomie. Sarah placed the portfolio on the table. William nodded and, without speaking, began to study the cover. After much last-minute debate, they had selected an eastern European model with doe eyes and a daringly asymmetrical face who was just on the brink of breaking out, knowing that if the choice was a total failure it would be hard to recover from. This particular model—rejected by every catwalk last season as too gawky but recently picked up by a designer known for discovering latent talent and turning them into zillion-dollar beauties—was definitely a risk. In the end Tim had convinced them that William would be aware of the girl's backstory and it would signal to him their insider savvy. Paige and Sarah had lobbied hard for a celebrity and now, as William studied the cover without expression, they were both sorry they had caved to Tim's predilection.

"We have other choices," Sarah said. They had prepared three alternative covers which she began to extract from her bag.

"This is fine," William replied dismissively.

She slipped the covers out of view.

He turned to the table of contents, designed to resemble an informal scrapbook of paparazzi shots, shoes, makeup smears, handwriting. SplashPoints—quick pop-ups of information—were scattered throughout, a layering of images and words designed for an impatient generation. William's face remained blank as he began to flip through layouts, pausing on some to study the photographs, the display copy, turning others over with alarming disinterest. He ran his fingertips along the paper as if he were reading Braille, but he did not look up once. Sarah and Paige had no choice but to assume that the cover had taken them out of the running. Each time he pushed a layout aside without consideration they sank further into despair.

"I see you've mixed beauty, fashion, and lifestyle service on the same layouts," he remarked. "That's unusual." They could not tell from his voice if he thought this was a good idea or not.

"That's how young women think now. They don't separate them the way traditional magazines do," Paige replied.

William looked up at her, studying her face, pausing there a bit too long, his gray eyes almost translucent. It occurred to Sarah that he was the brains behind a number of the "traditional" magazines Paige had just denigrated. And that most of them were phenomenally successful.

"Perhaps," he said. He continued to flip pages. "You have aimed at a rather narrow demographic," he observed. He was passing the well now, there was not that much more to go. "Don't you feel that might eliminate too many potential readers and advertisers?"

"No," Sarah answered. "It's a very specific life stage that is not being addressed. And it's an advertising sweet spot. These women are buying their first car, decorating their first apartment. Five or ten years later they have children, their lives and concerns are completely different. Readers need to feel this is a magazine just for them." She had rehearsed these exact words numerous times and if they sounded stilted, she nevertheless delivered them without stumbling.

William turned the last page in silence. He put it down and interlaced his thin, pale fingers. There was a long pause; he was taking his time, his eyes half closed.

"I would like a few longer stories that show more depth," he said at last, "and I think the pacing is off. I realize you want it to be fast, but you need to give readers something to dive into every now and then."

Even the slightest criticism scalded. Still, Sarah managed to agree with him. "Yes, that's a good point. We can do that."

"Nevertheless, I do think you're onto something," William continued. "It has a spark, and I like that you were willing to take a few risks. I happen to agree about going after a narrow demographic, but of course, the test will be consumer and advertiser response."

Sarah and Paige waited. If his words were not the pure approbation they had desired, neither were they an outright rejection.

William closed the portfolio. "You two can't remain at *Flair* any longer."

Their hearts fell. They had talked about the possibility of William hating *Splash*—and they realized that Pat would eventually fire them when they returned to *Flair,* for they would have lost the only protection—William, the prototype—they had. But they had not foreseen it happening so quickly.

"I don't think you can give your full attention to both projects," he continued. "The only possible result would be mediocrity." The very word was grit in his mouth. "I'd like you to hire a skeleton crew, two to three editors, an in-house designer, and work on a final prototype that we can focus-group. We will set up a temporary space for you on the seventh floor. I'll talk to Pat," he said.

Sarah was so relieved not to have lost her job that the actual go-ahead for *Splash* didn't quite register.

Paige, on the other hand, was exultant. "Thank you," she exclaimed.

William stood up, signaling the end to the meeting.

A million questions began to form in Sarah's and Paige's minds—timing, budget, staffing, procedure. William had sent them spinning into space with little specific direction. But it was clear that he was done with the topic for today.

Sarah and Paige rose. They were unsure whether they were to take the layouts with them or leave them behind. William solved the matter by placing them resolutely on his desk; they belonged to CMH now.

He looked up, glancing directly at Sarah. "Oh, and another thing."

She looked at him nervously.

"An acquaintance of mine was in the other day. Brendon Keering, do you know him?"

"He runs a gallery in Chelsea, doesn't he?" Sarah asked uncertainly. "I think my husband knew him, the name rings a bell."

"Yes. It seems he has always been a fan of your husband's work. He quite liked this piece." William nodded to the sculpture behind his desk. "He wanted to know if there were others still available."

Sarah thought of the twisted metal beneath her bed, crammed into the closet, the inexplicable mess she had made of it all, thinking no one would ever want Todd's sculpture again. Incapable of describing the shock she had been in at the time—her only possible excuse—she merely answered, "Yes."

"I'm sure he will be pleased to hear that. I gave him your phone number," William said. "I hope that is copacetic?"

Sarah nodded.

Sarah and Paige waited to speak until they were alone in the elevator.

"I can't wait to see Pat's face," Paige said jubilantly. "I think I'm more excited about that than anything else."

"You do realize that we don't have the vaguest idea how to actually create a magazine from scratch?"

"We'll fake it," she replied blithely. "Sarah, can't you stop worrying for one minute and just enjoy this?"

Sarah relented. "We did it, didn't we?" she said, smiling broadly.

"Yes, we did."

News had somehow made it to the fourth floor before Paige and Sarah arrived.

"Pat wants to see you two right away," Maude informed them as they headed into Sarah's office to savor their victory.

"Tell her we'll be right there."

"Congratulations," Maude whispered.

"How'd you know?" Sarah asked.

Maude simply shrugged. "Everyone knows."

"Well done," Pat said brittlely as they walked into her office. "I suppose William will be able to spare you for the next week or so while I find replacements?"

There was something mildly insulting about the way she spit out the word *replacements*.

"A week would be fine," Paige replied, "but we really can't stay longer than that. We're on a tight deadline."

"Yes, I'm sure you are. And I wish you the best of luck. I'm certain it will be wonderful. Though, of course, I've seen many things die in focus groups."

"That bitch," Paige muttered as they left.

"Yes, but she's right. Has it occurred to you that William could decide to kill this after one bad group? We're giving up a sure thing. We could be out of work in three months."

"This," Paige said, motioning around them at *Flair,* "is not a sure thing, not for us. Good Lord, Sarah, don't you understand how amazing this is? We have a chance, a real chance."

Sarah smiled. "I know." She felt a certain disconnected wonderment, as if the opportunity were unrelated to the work they had done. It was hard to reconcile how an idea formulated over cheap white wine in a now-shuttered Howard Johnson's had morphed into a million-dollar investment.

"We need to celebrate," Paige said.

Together they phoned Tim and Noah, who had been waiting impatiently, unused to being relegated to the sidelines.

"We did it," Sarah blurted out.

There were four-way rounds of congratulations, thanks, it was all because of you, no you, a chorus of relief and triumph that culminated in a plan to go out for a ridiculously expensive celebratory dinner the following night and charge it to CMH.

"I'll talk to you later," Sarah promised Tim before they all hung up.

The next call was to Rena Berman who had, after all, given them the initial opportunity to work on *Splash.* Rena had been hired two weeks after her "departure" from *Flair* by an international cosmetics firm where she had been given the rather ambiguous title of senior vice president/imagery with vague cross-platform responsibilities and an enormous salary. Even she wasn't quite clear what the job entailed—something to do with rebranding. Regardless, with little bottom-line accountability and ample permission to shoot ideas to virtually any department, it suited her perfectly.

Rena was genuinely glad for them. "I was certain you two would do it, that's why I chose you!" she remarked, and if there was a self-congratulatory note in her voice, Paige and Sarah were happy to ignore it.

They spent the following week cleaning up their desks at *Flair* and scouting out their new offices on the seventh floor. Sarah recalled the gallery dealer William had mentioned at odd moments, but she didn't place much stock in it. Art dealers said things all the time, especially to people like William Rowling. Nevertheless on Thursday afternoon, Brendon Keering called Sarah and introduced himself.

After a few brief pleasantries, his tone changed to one of velvety professionalism. "I have followed your husband's career with interest," he informed Sarah. "He had a unique talent for capturing the intricacies of negative space. I particularly appreciate his use of mythology. His pieces appear so whimsical, but there's a surprisingly tensile strength running through them. It's a combination I haven't seen before."

Sarah listened carefully, trying to parse his language.

"I believe he was mismanaged in the last few years," Keering continued. "I don't like to speak poorly of my colleagues, but your husband's career should have been built much more carefully. Sculpture is always harder to place than painting, but an artist's reputation must be constructed with a master plan in mind, not a collection of random sales. I would like the privilege of recontextualizing your husband's work. By putting it in the right company it will be seen for what it is—was—an important contribution to the dialog that started with Julio Gonzalez and has continued straight through to Richard Serra. Todd—may I call him that?—deserves a place in that company. With your permission, I would like to put one piece in a group show I have coming up this spring that, I might add, includes Calder and David Smith. This would be the first step to reintroducing him to critics and testing the market. Then, assuming there are other pieces available, we can talk about a solo show next year."

Sarah agreed to bring Keering slides of Todd's work, though she had no idea if they would be able to replicate the sculptures from the fragments she had so heedlessly stashed about her apartment.

She was light-headed when she got off the phone, listening to the very words Todd had so longed to hear during that last shattered year of his life, his complaints about his dealer echoed, his vision affirmed, his artistic dreams resurrected—all too late. Her heart ached with frustration for all that could have been, for him, for them, for the immense joy this would have brought him. She wondered, too, if it would have saved him.

That night, she got out slides of his work from over the years and as she sat looking at them, she thought about how hard he had fought to create meaning and beauty despite the odds he had faced, and how frequently he had succeeded. She looked at the drawings he did in the last months of his life, darker, incomplete, sometimes desperate, but searching still. There was something magnificent and brave about his continuing to struggle right up until the end, his faith in the redemptive power of art unaltered even as it eluded him, and she loved him for it.

Sarah was deeply thankful that Eliza would see the best of her father, his truest self, affirmed, and have the opportunity to watch his legacy assume its place in the world.

But the person it would have meant the most to was gone.

Epilogue

The first crisp, lucent breezes of September wafted through Manhattan, washing away the last remnants of late-summer lethargy. The city sparkled with the energy of a new season and all the hope that brings for fresh starts, for budding accomplishments, for new love. Invitations began to pile up in mailboxes, much anticipated restaurants opened, theaters debuted new plays, children filled the stores gleefully buying back-to-school supplies. The midtown buildings glistened like polished glass in the sharp early-fall sunlight, as if purposefully showing off the best of the city, a reminder of why people came, why people stayed, a crystalline siren song. Even the most jaded New Yorkers felt a surge of optimism, a lightness of step.

Sarah and Eliza had spent the first anniversary of Todd's death on August 8 quietly together. Without a body, a grave, without religious ceremony or even a clear demarcation of death, they were left to invent their own ritual. Sarah recalled how much Todd had loved the Cathedral of St. John the Divine for its artistic workmanship, its avant-garde concerts, its AIDS memorial and, unable to come up with anyplace that made more sense, she and Eliza went there on a sweltering afternoon and lit a votive in his honor. They knelt together and watched the small flame grow stronger, taking on a life of its own. Sarah rested her hand on Eliza's narrow shoulder. "Daddy loved you very much," she said.

Eliza nodded solemnly.

Sarah knelt down, shut her eyes. She did not know what she believed about spirits or souls or karma, she only knew that when she had pictured Todd over the last twelve months, it was as an emotional tornado, a vortex of pain. She wished him peace now, peace finally, that was all, that was everything. She knew that could only come—for both of them—with forgiveness and in that darkened church on that heat-infested day, she began the long journey of forgiving him, and forgiving herself. She prayed that the time would come when all three of them would be free from anger and blame, from grief and remorse.

Sarah felt Eliza grow restless beside her and she rose, turning back just once to look at the glowing flame. Then she and Eliza got in a cab and rode downtown, where they bought ice cream bars and watched a movie together in the cool of Sarah's bedroom. While they were out, Linda had left a message marking the day, wondering if there was any further news of Todd, but Sarah didn't return her call.

She had phoned Detective Brook earlier, reminding him of the anniversary and asking if he would, now that a year had passed, grant her a death certificate. He refused. He did not, would never, believe Todd had died that night. He reentered Todd's criteria into the FBI missing persons' data bank, keeping the case open, if admittedly cold.

When Eliza started second grade the following month, Sarah filled in the standard first-week parental assignment of "tell us anything you feel we should know about your child" as simply as she could, though it would never be simple. Still, Eliza was happy to see her friends again and adored her new teacher. For her, too, September was working its magic. She continued to see Deirdre Gerard every Saturday morning, though on the last visit Deirdre told Sarah privately that she thought it was time to think about stopping. "Healthy children don't belong in therapy," she said. "Eliza is a child who had a terrible thing happen to her. She may need to come back on and off for tune-ups as her understanding of what happened grows. But for now, I think it would be best for her to stop. I'll always be here if anything changes."

The focus groups for *Splash* had gone well. There was a rocky moment when one of the participants in Seattle remarked, "This looks like a flamingo threw up all over the page," but they toned the colors down just enough to satisfy everyone. *Splash* was given the green light to launch in January, a multimillion-dollar gamble rife with pressure and excitement for all concerned. Much to Paige's chagrin, *Flair* was prospering under Pat's firm hand, but that did not affect them anymore.

Tim and Sarah had discussed taking a summer vacation together with their kids but finally decided against it, unwilling to disturb the organic if fragile blending together that was taking place. Their children needed patience, time, and they gave them that. In the end they overlapped in Amagansett for a couple of days—in separate houses—and had nighttime barbecues together on the beach. The gift certificate for a night at the St. Regis still sat in Sarah's desk drawer, a luxurious promise.

"Are you nervous?"

Sarah looked up to find Lucy watching her intently.

"Not nervous exactly. Happy. Sad. It all just feels so surreal." Sarah finished putting in the long ivory Tibetan earrings she had chosen for the night. "How are you feeling?"

Lucy reflexively touched her stomach, the graceful arc of early pregnancy just beginning to show. "Great. I only threw up twice today."

Sarah smiled. "Thanks for coming early."

Lucy looked about the walls. "It's nice to be here alone with the work. I always did love it."

The reaction to Todd's piece in the gallery's group show had been so favorable that, knowing how ephemeral the attention of the art world can be, Keering had decided to move his solo exhibit up to capitalize on the moment.

Sarah nodded and looked about her. His work truly did resemble drawings in space, the multilayered shadows they cast as complex and varied as the sculptures themselves. Their delicacy and intellect reminded her of Todd's tenderness, the empathy she had been so attracted to. She admired more than ever the will it had taken to forge them. Every drawing, every sculpture was a small victory.

"I wish he was here," Sarah said softly. "I wish he could see this."

"I know."

"Part of me keeps thinking he'll walk in the door."

Lucy touched her gently, there was nothing she could say.

Sarah looked about the room as it began to fill up with old friends and potential clients, with other artists and the curious onlookers who made a point of turning up wherever something might be happening. Mark came over and put his arm around Lucy, Jane between them. The three walked over to the linen-draped table in the back and got soft drinks. Paige came up to kiss Sarah hello, holding on to her boyfriend's hand all the while. She smiled at them both. Jason was good for Paige, down-to-earth, unmoved by embellishment, solid. She looked over to see Victor and Peter talking in the corner and was happy that they had both flown up from Florida. They, too, needed this night, this affirmation of all that had been good in Todd, all that he had accomplished. William Rowling walked through like a ghost, nodding his approval and disappearing into his Town Car.

The only person not there was Tim.

Sensitive to the bittersweet tonalities of the occasion, he had told Sarah he would wait for her in that little French bistro on the far edges of the meatpacking district where the reticent owners had finally taken her into their fold. Eliza was happy at the prospect of sleeping at Jane's house.

Sarah stepped back from the room, filled with Todd's work, his friends, and for a moment she was back on Greene Street in SoHo so many years ago, and they were leaning against a car, kissing after his first show, young and brimming with hope and expectation for art, for each other, for a life they were just beginning to imagine. The city promised them everything that evening.

She would never know what happened on that August night in Florida.

But she would learn to live in a world without certainty, without answers to the one question she had once thought she needed most. She knew now that all we have are moments—two people newly in love sitting on a porch on the sunniest morning in Florida, a child's hand touching yours, a man waiting a few blocks away to take you in his arms—and those moments are to be treasured.

Sarah looked down to find Eliza standing beside her. She saw the curve of Todd's mouth in hers, saw his intelligence and curiosity in her amber eyes. She leaned over and pressed her lips to her daughter's head, shutting her eyes, love like a current between them.

ACKNOWLEDGMENTS

I would like to thank Suzanne Gluck for her faith, support, and unfailingly good advice; Shana Kelly for her early reading and invaluable insight; Greer Hendricks for her enthusiasm and sharp editorial eye. To the friends who sustain me and make me laugh every day: Eve Bercovici, Diane Burstein, Karen Fausch, Diane Gern, Judy Glantzman, Sally Koslow, Rebecca Sanhueza, Lynn Shnurnberger, thank you. My heartfelt thanks to Richard Dudding and Maryellen Everett and Charles Dudding for their loyalty, as well as to Helen Listfield and Andrew Listfield. I deeply appreciate Carol Martino and Stacy Merel for providing light at the most difficult times. I would like to thank The Writers Room for providing the space to work and think, and Joyce Jones for helping me get there. And most of all, to my daughter, Sasha, for her abiding spirit, her humor, and her understanding far beyond her years, an infinity of love.

ABOUT THE AUTHOR

Emily Listfield lives in New York City with her daughter.

Waiting to Surface

Emily Listfield

A Readers Club Guide

Summary

A senior editor at a top women's magazine, Sarah Larkin's life is turned upside down when one August morning the police call to tell her that her husband of ten years has vanished. A noted sculptor, Todd Larkin went swimming at midnight off the coast of Florida and was not seen again. Sarah is sent spinning into a world of uncertainty, hope, and fear. At first, it seems inconceivable that the police will not find him, dead or alive. She wonders what to tell her six-year-old daughter, Eliza. Theories abound: Was it accidental? Did he leave to start a new life someplace else? Was it suicide? Foul play? Sarah, with the help of the police, the coast guard, and a private eye, tries to discover what happened.

Set in the high-powered world of magazines, the novel is filled with details that only a true insider with access at a senior level could know. Sarah moves through that competitive, often outlandish landscape, trying to balance its demands with motherhood as she struggles with the mystery of her husband's disappearance.

In the end, *Waiting to Surface* is the story of coming to terms with loss, learning to live in a world without answers, and trying to treasure love once more.

Questions and Topics for Discussion

1. Although the story is based on real-life events, the author writes the book in the third person. Why do you think she chose to do this? What does this voice allow her to do as a storyteller?
2. Discuss how the author uses pacing throughout the story. When does she speed up her narrative and when does she slow down? What effect does this have on the plot and character development?
3. Shock, denial, bargaining, guilt, anger, depression, acceptance, and hope make up what many psychiatrists call the stages of grief. Discuss if and how Sarah goes through these stages. Which lasts the longest? How do the circumstances of her loss affect her expression of grief?
4. The author writes, "People offer up fragments of themselves to friends, spouses, lovers, leaving each person to create the remaining whole according to what they have in hand" (p. 37). Do you think this is true? Discuss the different pieces of Todd that Sarah discovers throughout the book. What can we piece together about Sarah?
5. At one point Sarah remembers an argument she once had with Todd (p. 48). "'This is who I am,' he lashed out. 'You knew that when you married me.' 'Things change,' Sarah said. 'We have a child.'" Is one of them right and one of them wrong? Talk about Sarah's and Todd's individual propensity toward change and how it affects them, as both people and parents, and their relationship.
6. Harry DeVeres, a friend of Todd's, calls Sarah and talks about how he tried to help Todd with his alcoholism (p. 107). How does Todd's death connect, reconnect, or disconnect the many people who are in his life? What is the most important connection that Sarah makes through Todd's death?
7. The author scatters many of Sarah's memories of Todd throughout the story, some good and some bad. Is there any pattern to the memories?

8. On page 124 a body washes to shore at Lake Kissemmee, forty miles north of Loudon Beach. What is Sarah's reaction? How might the book have been different if the body had indeed been Todd's?
9. Discuss Eliza's character. Does she go through the same stages of grief as her mother? How do her moods change as the story progresses? Is Dr. Gerard effective in helping her deal with the stress of losing her father?
10. Sarah is a senior editor for a prominent women's magazine. How does the shock of Todd's disappearance affect her professionally? Is work a solace for her or something that causes her more anguish and grief?
11. Discuss the politics at Sarah's office. How do they affect her developing career and how she copes with Todd's disappearance?
12. The police and coast guard both play integral roles in the investigation. Which policeman is more trustworthy, Karl Medford or Detective Brook? As a reader, does how you view each of them change as the story progresses?
13. "He drowned," Sarah says to a group of other mothers at school (p. 171). Is this the moment when Sarah first publicly acknowledges that Todd has truly died? When is the moment when she privately realizes that Todd is, for certain, not coming back?
14. "Sarah was allowed to kiss Eliza again, and slowly she began to respond, not always, not fully, but often enough to offer hope" (p. 224). Discuss the concept of love and the concept of anger as they appear in the book. Do they ever intersect? Did Eliza's young concept of love or of anger change?
15. What are the defining characteristics of Todd and of Tim? How are they alike? How are they different? Who is a better fit for Sarah? Why?
16. *Waiting to Surface* provides readers with a character who suffers extreme emotional turmoil over the course of the book. How does Sarah change from the beginning of the story to the end? Or doesn't she?

Enhance Your Reading Group

1. Visit the Museum of Modern Art (www.moma.org) or a Chelsea art gallery (http://chelseaartgalleries.com) to see sculpture like that Todd might have made, or go to http://websearch.about.com/od/dailywebsearchtips/qt/dnt0608.htm to find a listing of Web sites for museums nationwide.
2. To visit or learn more about the Florida coastline, visit www.visitflorida.com.
3. The National Center for Missing Adults (NCMA) is a division of Nation's Missing Children Organization, Inc. (NMCO), a nonprofit organization working in cooperation with the U.S. Department of Justice's Bureau of Justice Assistance, Office of Justice Programs. Information about the agency can be found online at www.theyaremissed.org/ncma/.

A Conversation with Emily Listfield

1. Why did you decide to publish this book as a novel rather than as a memoir? What advantages did that format offer you?

Fiction has always been my way to make sense of the world around me. This book is extremely autobiographical, but writing it as fiction gave me the freedom to get at the deeper emotional and dramatic truth of what happened without worrying about reproducing conversations and events verbatim. I was able to condense certain events and create composite characters that gave the book dramatic shape. Fiction was the most natural way to come to terms with my husband's disappearance as well as examine the universality of some of the issues involved.

2. Authors often remark that they put a little bit of themselves into their characters. How strongly do you identify with Sarah, particularly with all of your many similarities? How are you different?

I must admit, Sarah is extremely close to me. I gave her my insights, emotions, and insecurities, as well as my hopes and love for my daughter.

3. Memories and dreams are prominent features throughout your novel. Sarah even visits a psychic. Do you personally believe that someone's dreams are mystically revealing or that the future can be read?

I don't believe or disbelieve—I'm open. Like Sarah I did visit a psychic who works with the police after my husband's disappearance. Interestingly, when I told the detectives of this, they didn't discount it. Nothing came of it, though, and I didn't go back.

4. Your novel is tremendously engaging and can easily be read in one sitting. Sarah goes through enormous personal changes over the course of a year. Did you work on the book for a long time or finish it very quickly?

I thought about the book and made notes for a long time before I actually started writing it. I needed distance from the actual events before beginning it in earnest. Once I started, it took me close to two years to write, in part because I was not only a single parent but the editor in chief of a magazine. I wrote in the very early morning and on weekends.

5. Do you see your book as more of a mystery or a love story?

Both. In a way, it is a detective story on various levels: a search for the truth about a marriage as much as for the facts of what happened to Todd.

6. What similarities and differences are there between your daughter and the fictional daughter in the novel? Did you discuss your writing with her? Did you ever talk with her explicitly to help develop the character of Eliza?

Eliza is very closely modeled on my daughter. Everything Eliza says in the book my daughter said to me at the time, but I did not talk to her or ask her for specific input. I did tell her what the book was about as I was writing it, but I also stressed that it was fiction, with certain dramatic aspects played up to make it more suspenseful for the reader.

7. What do you think will be your daughter's reaction to your novel?

She was very supportive throughout the writing of it, but I'm sure her reaction will be mixed. I'm not sure under the best of circumstances anyone wants to see their parents' marriage so intimately portrayed. But I hope that she will also see it as a testimony of how much her father loved her as well as an appreciation of all that was good in him.

8. Did you discuss your writing with any friends of your husband? What was their reaction to your very personal novel? Is there

anyone in particular who knew your husband who you hope will read the book?

I did not discuss it with anyone while I was writing it. I think that to write fiction it is necessary to go to a deeply private place. Now that it is done, I hope that my husband's brothers appreciate it.

9. What aspect of this story are you most proud of?

I am most proud of what I hope is the emotional honesty in the book. I also hope that it will help others dealing with various forms of uncertainty in their lives.

10. Many authors speak about writing as a type of therapy. Do you see this book as that? Did you come up with the idea to write this story, or was this at someone else's suggestion?

If you are a novelist and something like this happens to you, it becomes the only story you can tell next. I did not consider it a form of therapy, but writing it did help me come to terms with what had happened as well as gain a new appreciation for my husband. In some ways it became an act of forgiveness.

11. Magazines and the magazine industry play a big role in the book. As you have had a great deal of experience in the industry, do you see yourself as primarily a magazine editor or a novelist? Why? Which role have you found more personally fulfilling?

I love that I can move back and forth between the two worlds. I have always found writing fiction to be the most deeply satisfying. It is something that you and you alone create, a way to get in touch with a deeper sense of yourself and the world. But I also love the collaborative nature of magazines and have met many smart, wonderful people in that world. They provide a good balance between the internal and the external.

12. Can you talk about your own experiences with office politics?

I'm sure there are office politics in all professions, but because the magazine world is so personality and image driven, it is particularly rife. I will never forget my first day at Condé Nast and how intimidating just the elevator ride was.

13. How was writing this very personal book a different experience from writing your other novels? What was harder about the process? What was easier?

This book was in some ways harder to write because it meant reliving that difficult first year after my husband's disappearance as well as delving into my memories, good and bad. It brought it all back to me on a visceral level. Structurally it was easier to write than other books because I knew the plot, the characters, and the ending all along.

14. Do you have plans for your next book?

Yes, I am immersed in writing a new novel. Centered around four friends from college now in their late thirties, my new book explores the dramatic consequences that occur when you presume to know what someone you love is thinking—and you are dead wrong.